ALONG CAME HOLLY

CODI HALL

D1468817

sourcebooks
casablanca

Originally published in 2022 as an audiobook by Audible Originals.

Published by Sourcebooks Casablanca, an imprint of Sourcebooks
P.O. Box 4410, Naperville, Illinois 60567-4410
(630) 961-3900
sourcebooks.com

Printed and bound in the United States of America.
VP 10 9 8 7 6 5 4 3 2 1

This book is for Erica.
Thanks for threatening to beat my ass.
I love you.

CHAPTER 1

HOLLY WINTERS OPENED ANOTHER BOX, staring at the contents in horror. "More freaking gnomes!" She pulled one of the lightweight figures from the box and glared into its creepy, eyeless face. "I'm being haunted by these things. First Halloween and Thanksgiving and now Christmas!"

"I've heard gnomes are hot this year," her sister Merry called from the far corner of the shop where she was hanging lengths of holly leaves along the top shelves of the displays.

"Hot with whom?" Holly asked.

"Everyone in my online craft group." Merry climbed down off the step stool and grabbed another garland, cocking her head to the side as she studied the gnome. Merry's blonde hair was pulled back in a loose ponytail, little strands hanging around her face. "I think he's cute. Look, he's holding a tiny holiday wreath."

Holly turned the statue in her hand to study his face again. "I'm not convinced."

"Why did you order them, then?"

"I didn't. I bought the inventory from a holiday store in Boise that closed and I hadn't been through everything yet. Now I get why it was all so cheap."

The back door opened and their brother Nick came into view carrying two boxes stacked on top of each other, his face only visible from the nose up. He dumped the boxes on the floor next to the checkout counter, revealing his deep frown. "Is there a reason we're doing all this on Black Friday?"

Normally Holly wouldn't be, but she wanted to shift the store decor to Christmas before she opened up for Small Business Saturday tomorrow. Having a holiday decor store called A Shop for All Seasons meant being prepared to change inventory to the next holiday even at the crack of dawn the day after Thanksgiving.

They'd spent the first few hours boxing up all the fall decor and discounting any trinkets left over from spooky season. She'd sent Merry's fiancé, Clark Griffin, and Nick over to pick up the holiday inventory from storage while she and Merry did the fun part. Redecorating the place.

"Because I don't want to be doing a floor set during business hours. And this way, I get help."

"You're lucky I love you, little sister," he grumbled, running a hand through his short brown hair. "Do you want us to bring all of it in or let you go through it box by box and find places for it?"

"You can hold off bringing anything else in until Pike and Anthony get here. They are coming, right?"

"Yes, they're coming, but Anthony is on his way back from Black Friday shopping in Twin Falls, and Pike...Pike needs to wake up."

Holly grinned. "Of course he does. Single Pike equals lots of late nights and mornings of regrets, even on Turkey Day."

"Be nice," Nick grunted.

"I'm always nice." Ignoring Merry and Nick's unanimous snorting, Holly put the creepy gnome back in the box, and then set the box up on the counter. "If you want, you can take this box and display these gnomes on that shelf," she said, pointing to the shelf closest to the counter. "I'll get you the price gun and you can just label them on the bottom as you go."

Nick picked up the box with a grunt. "What do you want them priced at?"

"Nine-ninety-nine."

"Thought you said they were ugly?" Merry asked from her perch on top of the step stool.

"And you said they were hot this year. I'm putting your prediction to the test."

"Babe?" Clark stepped through the back door with a drink carrier in one hand and a large tote under his other arm. "I got caffeine, but where do you want your creations?"

Merry climbed down and crossed the room to take the tote from him, setting it on the floor before leaning up to give him a lingering kiss. "I got it. Thanks for grabbing that. Jace didn't want to come?" Jace was Clark's eight-year-old son and usually went everywhere with his dad when he wasn't in school.

"He was still sleeping when I left for the storage unit." Clark set the coffees down on the counter and tucked his shoulder-length brown hair behind his ears before adding, "But I talked to my brother a few minutes ago, and he dropped Jace at the main house before he went to work. Jace is helping your dad at the farm. I told Chris not to carry any trees, but you know your dad—"

"Stubborn?" Merry cut in. "Thinks he's still thirty-something? Invincible?"

"That would be him." He kissed her again, giving Holly a little wave when he caught her gaze. "You going to kill me if I bail?"

Holly laughed. "No, I'll forgive you. Just make sure Dad doesn't throw out his back." Clark was the foreman of their family's Christmas tree farm and Merry helped their father Chris Winters run the day-to-day operations.

"Will do."

"I'll come help as soon as I'm done here," Merry said.

"Take your time." Clark cradled Merry's face in his hands, and this time Holly averted her gaze with a smile. She loved that her sister had found someone who adored her beyond measure, and Holly didn't mind their inability to go without touching each other for long. She'd helped Clark orchestrate the epic proposal back in June, convincing her sister to hike with Holly for one of her YouTube video stunts. When they reached the top of the bluff, they found Nick with his phone at the ready and Clark on one knee. Jace stood next to his dad with a sign grasped between his hands that read: WOULD YOU MARRY HIM AND BE MY MOM? Merry burst into tears and Nick caught it all on video for the rest of their family to watch.

Since it was the first wedding for any of the Winters children, their mother, Victoria, may have gone a little crazy the last five months planning with Merry and Holly. With the wedding less than five weeks away and the two of them leaving for a week-long honeymoon trip in Honolulu right after, there was still so much to do. Between the store, her family, and her social media channels,

Holly couldn't remember the last time she took a moment to relax, let alone have some fun.

Come on, the YouTube videos are fun.

Holly couldn't argue with herself on that account. Since she started her YouTube channel Holly the Adventure Elf seven years ago, she'd been able to buy her store and her home with the money her social media presence brought in. While her extreme videos had slowed down, people continued to tune in and watch her shoot a crossbow in the little green dress with bells on the skirt or ride a waterslide while holding onto her elf hat for dear life, but Holly was growing weary of planning stunts. After this holiday season, she planned to retire the Adventure Elf persona, but had no idea what to do in its stead that wouldn't lose followers.

"Whatcha got in the tote?" Holly asked.

Merry popped the top and revealed a beautiful knitted baby blanket with mistletoe and white buds decorating the four corners. She pulled back the blanket and retrieved a red-and-white stuffy, holding it out for Holly. "I made this to go with your elf peen."

Holly laughed, taking the plush penis from her sister and studying the jaunty red-and-white Santa hat and ivory beard, and little black eyes staring at her from between the two features. When Merry started her online craft store, *Jolly Johnsons by Merry: Adult-Themed Plushies and Crafts*, Holly was her biggest cheerleader. Some months were better than others, but her sister had been pulling in a solid income for the last year, enough to be able to quit her front office job at the local elementary school. Not everyone in town had been as supportive, but Holly was proud of her sister for going after what she wanted.

"This is going to go perfect with my elf peen. Thanks."

"You're welcome. I've been playing around with a few patterns I'd like to get your opinion on after we're done here."

"Absolutely. But first I think we need some mood music to make the work go faster." Holly juggled the plushy between her hands as she crossed to her stereo and pressed the power button. A jolly rendition of *Jingle Bells* burst from the speakers and Holly made the Santa peen dance on the counter.

Merry burst out laughing, while their brother looked up from his pricing, one eyebrow cocked. "Isn't it a little early for Christmas music?"

"Thanksgiving is over. Don't be a Scrooge. I've got Declan Gallagher for that and luckily he isn't here to give me any guff—"

As if on cue, the wall behind her thumped several times and a deep voice hollered through the thin barrier, "Turn that shit off!"

Holly glared at the wall. "What the hell? He's supposed to be closed."

"Maybe he came in for inventory," Merry said.

"I don't care why he's there. My only wish is that the killjoy go away!" He continued to abuse the wall until she pounded back, shouting, "It's eight in the morning! Why don't you go home, fall back asleep, and climb out on the happy side of the bed?"

No more pounding or cursing from the other side, and Holly smiled at her siblings. "See? That is how you take care of a stinky old Grinch—" Holly stopped talking when she heard the loud crash of a door.

"Uh oh," Merry sang. "You were saying?"

"Shut up."

Vigorous knocking shook her front door, and she dropped the Santa peen on the counter and stomped her way across the shop to confront her odious, grouchy, pain-in-the-butt neighbor.

Holly unlocked the door and yanked it open, glaring up into bright green eyes. "You're going to break it with those giant hammer claws!"

Declan's dark brows nearly met in the middle as he scowled down at her from over a foot taller. His wide shoulders took up the entire doorway as he loomed there like a storm cloud shrouding her from sunlight. If she didn't know he was all bark and bluster, Holly might have been intimidated; but in the four years since she bought the building next door to his family's hardware store, the most Declan or his father had done was call in a noise complaint with the sheriff.

"I thought we had a deal?" he growled, that rough rumble sending a white-hot bolt of triumph through her. Why she loved tweaking Declan's temper was a mystery to everyone, including her, but she lived for these brief, fiery exchanges. The man never said boo about blasting musicals in the spring or chipper summer jams from June to August, but the minute her Christmas playlist popped on, he threw a tantrum like a six-and-a-half-foot-tall toddler.

"Remind me what that deal was?"

"I bought one of those expensive Christmas trees last year and in exchange you don't play that ear-bleeding shit before noon or after four."

"Hey, that only applies during business hours."

"I never said any such thing!"

"Seems only logical, though, and besides, what have you done for me lately?"

"I told your sister I'd buy a tree this year, too."

"Yes, but that's Merry, and you told her I'd have to decorate it. Again, I was led to believe our deal was one season long, not indefinitely. You should get it in writing next time." Holly placed her hands on her hips, leaning up with a smirk. "Maybe you should stop fighting the natural, joyous feeling Christmas brings and let your heart grow this year."

Declan took a deep breath and his flannel-covered chest rose with the force of it, as if he was calling upon every deity in the universe to give him strength. "Hell no." His voice came out tight, straining through his teeth, and a flicker of guilt coursed through her before she beat it back. Holly liked to think of herself as a reasonable person who would have been more than happy to entertain his request had he approached her at any point in the last two years with a modicum of politeness. Instead, he was surly, insulting, and all around reminded her of the Beast when he invited Belle to dinner. If only there was a Cogsworth around to remind him to say please.

"Then I guess we're at a stalemate and you should scurry on back to your hole of despair."

"I don't understand why you can't be reasonable!"

"Because I find you rude, cantankerous, and overall unpleasant, and the last thing in the world I want is to give you any kind of satisfaction." Declan opened his mouth, but before he could respond, she continued, "It's not like I was blasting it."

"The fact that I could hear it through the wall means it was too loud."

"Is it the traditional Christmas carols you hate? Because I

could probably find some heavy metal covers if you prefer. A little 'Heavy Metal Christmas'?"

"Don't make me dismantle your sound system again, Elf."

Holly puffed up at his snide tone. Over the years there were plenty of people who mocked Holly for her online persona, but she let it roll off her back. But every time Declan snickered at her through that ridiculous soup catcher beard of his, she wanted to reach up and tug him by the hairs of his chinny-chin-chin until he begged for mercy.

"Go ahead, you petty, furry waste of oxygen, and I'll get you when you least expect it!"

Holly closed the door in his face and locked it with a guttural, "Ugh, I really hate that guy."

"Funny, I couldn't tell," Nick said, setting the price gun down on the shelf. "I'm going to get another box."

"If you don't like fighting with Declan, then why not do what he wants?" Merry asked.

Holly picked up the price gun and aggressively pressed the button. "Because it's the principle." She snatched a gnome off the shelf and swiped the price tag along the base, wishing the labels were just a little bigger. She'd use one to tape Declan's mouth shut.

"Didn't you tell me once fighting with Declan was like foreplay?"

Holly choked on a laugh. "While that sounds like me, I've changed my mind. Declan Gallagher makes me want to avoid the entire male species for as long as I live."

CHAPTER 2

DECLAN GALLAGHER'S TRUCK HUGGED THE last few twists in the road before the Winters Christmas Tree Farm came into view on the right. The rolling hills of evergreens backed up to taller pines in the distance, and his tires crunched over the driveway as he parked south of the main house. He spotted Clark and his son Jace in the front yard with Chris Winters, heading for the gate that opened out of the white-picket-fenced yard. Clark had asked Declan to come out and help secure some Christmas decorations to the roof that had come off during the last winter storm they had.

It had been years since he'd been out to see the place and it still looked the same, except for a fresh coat of paint. Declan had come with his folks to the farm when he was a kid to pick out their tree, and the place always seemed a little magical, especially after it snowed.

Of course, he no longer thought that way. He was an adult and there was no such thing as magic or miracles. Life was a host of hardships and misery with a few sprinkles of happiness mixed in, and he'd go through it without any more expectations than that.

Man, maybe Holly had a point about him. Even lost in his thoughts, he was morose.

His hand flexed on the door handle at the thought of the youngest Winters sibling. God, she could make him absolutely insane. With her cheerful, upbeat personality and obnoxious love of the holidays, she'd been a menace on his calm from November until January the last two years.

Maybe he hadn't handled things with any reasonable amount of charm, but Holly pushed all of his buttons, even the ones he didn't know he had. When he'd stepped in to take care of his dad's store, he hadn't been ready for the bubbly redhead to pop in with a plate of cookies and a mouth that never stopped.

Declan remembered that warm day in September well. He'd barely unlocked the door when she burst through it, carrying a plate stacked with an assortment of treats.

"Hi, I'm Holly Winters. You're Declan, right?" She didn't give him a chance to respond before she scoffed, "Of course you are. You graduated with my sister Merry and haven't changed much, except for the beard." She set the plastic wrap-covered cookies on the counter. "You probably don't remember me," she continued, hardly missing a beat. "I was a sophomore when you were a senior, but I used to watch all your football games with my friends."

He did remember Merry from high school, a bright, bubbly blond who seemed to get along with everyone. He'd played football because that's what you did in a small town when you were six foot five and two hundred pounds, and while they'd run in the same crowd, they'd never been more than friendly acquaintances.

He hadn't encountered the younger Winters daughter, though.

"Anyway, we're neighbors. I run the holiday shop next door and I heard you'd taken over the store now that your dad's retired. Thought I'd drop by and say hi."

He hadn't fully recovered from her rapid-fire introduction, but he managed a "Hello."

She grinned in return. If he was the type of guy to use the term dazzling, it would have fit perfectly to describe her smile. "We share a wall, so I apologize in advance if my music is too loud. Too many concerts in my teens may have ruined my ear drums, but don't tell my mother she was right or I'll never hear the end of it."

"As long as it's not cheesy Christmas music, we'll be good."

He'd meant it as a joke, but the instant her face fell, he knew he'd made a mistake.

"You don't like Christmas carols?"

"Not particularly."

She suddenly shrugged. "Then it's up to me to change your mind."

Declan frowned, irritation ripping through him like a scalpel blade. "Or you could find something more productive to occupy your time."

Startled brown eyes blinked twice before they narrowed, her thick lashes nearly obscuring the chocolate depths. "I was only teasing. You don't have to be rude."

He should have apologized right away, but the way she'd said it reminded him of his mother. How she'd been so confident in

getting her way, and how his dad bent over backwards to make
her happy. To give her everything she wanted and yet it was
never enough.

"Just keep the Merry Christmas crap to a minimum and we'll
get along fine."

Clark knocked on his truck window, pulling him out of his
thoughts, and Declan jerked the handle, opening the door to step
out. Chris and Jace stood off to the side behind Clark, smiling.

"Hey, you all right?" Clark asked.

"Yeah, just spaced out. Good morning, Chris. Jace."

"Hi," Jace said.

"How's it going, Declan?" Chris asked, the older man adjusting his ball cap.

"Can't complain. Let me grab my stuff from the backseat, and
we'll get this place in shape." He shut the driver's door with a snap
and opened the back door, Clark hovering behind him.

"Have you had a lot of handyman jobs in town?" Chris asked.

"Enough to keep me busy." Declan picked up his toolbox
from the backseat and a leather sack of materials. "It supplements
the slow months at the store."

"How's that working for you?" Chris asked.

"Not bad." Truth be told, he could have had plenty more jobs,
but there weren't enough hours in the day for the store, jobs, and
spending time with his dad. When Liam Gallagher took a fall two
years ago, Declan left behind everything he'd been working for to
run the store while his dad recovered. When the doctor mentioned

that Liam was showing early signs of Alzheimer's, Declan's whole world fell out from under him, and he'd decided to stay in Mistletoe. It had been a point of contention with his girlfriend at the time, who'd agreed to move in with him a few weeks before, and when he'd told her about his dad and that he'd have to stay in Idaho, she'd let him know within a day she'd found an apartment she could afford. Alone.

Not that being in a relationship had ever been high on his life-needs list, but it was what you did as an adult. He'd had a life planned including teaching art, finding someone he could stand to be with, and living out his life with few hiccups and heartaches.

Being back in Mistletoe wasn't the life Declan imagined for himself, but he'd do what he needed to make his dad comfortable. Liam was still himself, just had moments of forgetfulness, but he'd stopped coming in to work after he'd called a long-time customer by the wrong name. Declan had tried to get him in to the counselor his doctor recommended, but his dad wouldn't go. Declan wasn't sure if it was denial or pride, but Liam spent his days either out in his shop building things or in his recliner watching sports.

Declan hadn't had the heart to broach the subject of selling the hardware store. Even though Liam had supported Declan going away to art school, Declan knew deep down his dad wanted him here, keeping the Gallagher legacy going. Three generations had poured their blood, sweat, and tears into that store, and Declan wasn't sure he had it in him to break the cycle of tradition.

"How's your dad doing?" Chris asked.

Declan swallowed hard. Many people had been asking about his dad over the last few months since he'd stopped coming in to the store, but Declan couldn't answer truthfully. In the years following his parents' divorce, his dad had become an angry, bitter old man, and a lot of his former friends had stopped coming around. Telling them about his medical diagnosis would send his dad into a tirade about how it was none of their business and if they'd stayed in touch they'd know how he was doing. So it was easier to just say, "He's enjoying retirement, sir."

"Well, give him my best," Chris said, nodding toward the flocking tent. "I'll let you fellas get to it. Someone should be down at the tent running this place. Come on, Jace."

When Chris turned to leave, Clark leaned over, lowering his voice. "Seriously, I know Christmas isn't your bag, but I appreciate you coming out. I thought I was going to have to tackle Chris to keep him off that roof and I didn't want to pull one of the other guys out of the rows to help me."

"What are you fellas saying about me?" Chris called back to them. He'd only gone a few feet and must have heard Clark.

Clark's cheeks were bright red. "Nothing."

Declan jumped in to save his friend with a wave. "I was just saying that I don't mind securing your Santa to the roof so you don't have to."

"You're not insinuating I'm too old, are you, Declan?"

Declan bit back a smile. "No, sir. Just that you've paid your dues and should take advantage of the rest of us."

"Hmm, I'll accept that explanation because I do not want to shimmy up that ladder." He gave Declan a little salute. "Thanks for helping out my soon to be son-in-law."

"Anytime, sir."

They stood there silently, waiting until Jace and Chris reached the tent before Clark muttered, "That man hears everything."

"I can see that," Declan said, hiking up his tool bag over his shoulder. "Should we get started?"

"Sure. You're more taciturn than usual. Everything okay?"

Declan nodded, wishing he could get out of his own head. "Yeah, a lot on my mind is all."

"Well, if you ever need anyone to listen over a drink or two, I'm sure I could lend an ear."

"Thanks, man. It's nothing dire. I'll be fine." They headed up the path to the main house without further conversation and Declan wondered if he'd offended Clark by not spilling his guts, but he was like his dad in that way. He dealt with his issues alone and without a lot of fuss. Declan appreciated Clark as a friend, though. He was quiet and serious for the most part, but he'd noticed a lightness in Clark since getting involved with Merry Winters. He'd heard love could change a man, but bending who you were, especially when relationships could end at the drop of a hat, seemed foolish to Declan.

"Ready to get Santa's sleigh back on that roof?" Clark asked, pointing towards the red plastic sleigh and mechanical waving Santa Claus set against the side of the house.

"That's what I brought my tools for."

"Smart ass. I heard you managed to piss Holly off already," Clark said, his eyes twinkling.

Declan scowled at the mention of his miniature nemesis. "I simply requested she keep the Christmas music down."

"Nick said he was about to have to step in and save you from her wrath."

"Please, I can handle your pint-size sister-in-law." Declan held his hand up below his chest. "She comes up to here on me."

"Which makes her the perfect height to high-kick you into becoming a eunuch," Clark said, wincing as if it pained him to even mention the possibility. "Trust me, man, you do not want to keep at it with her. Nick told me he got into a prank war with his sisters that escalated into Holly glitter-bombing his entire room."

"Good thing she doesn't have access to any of my personal spaces."

"Holly is pretty determined." Clark chuckled. "It's funny. I learned after being around Holly for a month not to get on her bad side. Why are you so slow on the uptake?"

Declan opened his mouth to answer but a truck came tearing up the driveway and parked in front of the gate. Nick hopped out of the driver's seat and gave them a little salute.

"'Sup, guys?"

"What are you doing here?" Clark asked.

"Pike and Anthony won't be at the store until noon, so the boss lady sent me to get snacks, and since your son is the apple of my mother's eye, I figured she's got the good stuff hidden away."

Clark shook his head. "You drove here to raid your mother's pantry instead of just going to the store?"

"Free snacks here, man. What are you two doing?"

"We were discussing Declan's and Holly's complicated relationship and I told him to watch out."

"Did you tell him about the giant glitter bomb?"

"Briefly," Clark said.

"She made it look like a package I ordered, and when that thing erupted I was finding glitter everywhere for weeks."

"And this is why I stay in her good graces," Clark said.

"Tell the truth, were you more afraid of Holly or of me when you started dating Merry?" Nick asked Clark.

"Her, one hundred percent."

"If you weren't about to be my brother-in-law I'd up my game." Nick snapped his fingers. "Speaking of which, how is the bachelor party coming?"

"Sam says it's a surprise," Clark said, frowning. "I told him no strippers or tattoos, but I can't guarantee one or both won't be on the agenda."

"My sister's cool with that?" Nick asked.

"Merry told me to have fun and take the night to my grave, but even if he books it, I will not be partaking."

"Me neither," Nick said, a sheepish grin spreading across his lips. "Noel would beat my ass."

Declan didn't try to join in the conversation, mostly because hearing about possible wild antics at the bachelor party made him want to back out all the more.

"How about you, Declan?" Clark asked, bending over to pick up the large plastic Santa, finally drawing him back into the conversation. "You seeing anyone?"

"No. Not at the moment." Declan didn't elaborate because this wasn't a subject Clark usually broached with him. Love was just another thing in his life that hadn't gone as planned, and he didn't need to hash out his bachelorhood with the two of them. "Let's get this stuff nailed down before a storm rolls in."

Clark tilted his head up, and Declan appreciated him not commenting on the clear blue sky and let him have his subject change.

"I'll leave you guys to it and get back to ransacking my mother's kitchen." Nick shot Declan a serious look before adding, "I get that you aren't into Christmas, but if you're mean to my sister, I'm going to have to hurt you."

Declan looked down at Nick, trying not to smirk from his height advantage.

"And I'll have to help him," Clark added, shrugging when Declan raised his brow. "What, she's my family too, and for the record Holly is great unless you piss her off."

"What if she's mean to me first?"

"I'd say she brought it on herself, but same rules apply." Nick shrugged. "It's a brother thing."

"I'll try not to engage, then."

"Good man." Nick gave them a little wave before jogging up the steps and into the house.

"That guy is a character," Clark said, tossing the Santa over his shoulder and carrying it toward the ladder. "I'm surprised you agreed to this, considering you called the Parade of Lights a fire hazard."

"Hey, if it pays, I'll play, no matter how much I may hate the overkill of the season. Besides, if it keeps a guy Chris's age off his roof, then I feel like I'm doing a public service."

"For money," Clark quipped.

"Touche." Declan hiked up his bag over his shoulder and

switched his toolbox to the same arm, waving towards the ladder. "Lead the way."

When Clark was nearly at the top, Declan started up the ladder one-handed. He'd made it up three rungs before he heard a commotion above and looked up in time to see the plastic Santa careening towards him. He barely had time to drop his toolbox before the large decoration hit him in the face, knocking him off balance. His arms flailed helplessly through the air as he soared backwards, hitting the ground with a painful *whoosh* as his breath rushed out. He stared up at that mocking blue sky in a daze, the back of his head pounding. Declan blinked against the harsh sun above, a steady drumbeat under his eye and the bridge of his nose, the sensation of liquid running above his upper lip and down the side of his face, tickling his skin, and if he wasn't in such a daze he would have reached up to wipe it away.

The front door opened and shut with a slam and rushing footfalls on metal preceded several faces coming into view above him, including Clark who knelt down next to him. "Declan, you all right? I'm sorry, I lost my grip on it."

Declan tried to sit up and groaned when the world spun. He reached up and ran his hand over his nose, pulling back enough to stare down at the bright red streak of blood across it.

"He's probably got a concussion," Nick said, loud enough to make Declan wince. "Maybe a broken nose. Let's get him up and into my truck, and we'll call Doc on the way to town."

"All right, Big Guy," Clark said, grabbing his arm, but Declan couldn't seem to keep his eyes open.

Snuffed out by a Christmas decoration. What are the odds?

CHAPTER 3

"HE'S NOT MY FAVORITE BROTHER anymore," Holly griped again, picking up the leftover Christmas decorations and carrying them into the storage room. It had been hours since Nick had gone for snacks but never come back, and in the meantime they'd managed to get through all the freight Holly was going to put out for sale this year.

"He's your only brother," Noel teased, hanging Christmas ornaments on one of three trees Holly bought from her parents to keep in the shop. Noel had come in with Pike and Anthony and had jumped in where Holly needed her, while Pike and Anthony kept hauling in boxes of freight. The place was chock-full of Christmassy cheer and Holly couldn't be happier with the results, although her grumbling belly put a damper on their success.

"If he keeps being a flake, he's going to be the brother formerly known as Nick," Holly countered as she came out of the storage room, nearly colliding with Anthony.

"Whoa, yield for oncoming traffic."

"Only if the man with the right of way has good news."

"Then you'll be happy to know that this," Anthony grunted, setting a large box down on the floor, "is the last of it."

"Thank God," Pike groaned as he followed behind and set his box down next to Anthony's, leaning into his hands like he was stretching his back. "This is the final time I get roped into being a free pack mule. There better be pizza and beer in the future when we finish."

"You're mistaken about the mule part," Holly said sweetly. "You're more of an ass."

"Aren't they the same thing?" Anthony mused.

"Nope. A jackass is a male donkey. A mule is a cross between a horse and a donkey but can't reproduce."

"Whoa, now!" Pike yelped. "I am not a castrated donkey!"

"I didn't say cas—" Holly rolled her eyes. "Nevermind."

Anthony lowered his voice and joked, "I think you meant dumb ass."

"Merry!" Pike called out toward the back of the store, where Merry emerged from. "Your sister and Tony are being dicks!"

"Why are you hollering for me?" she asked.

"Because I'd think you'd have sympathy for the man with a broken heart."

"Why would she need to coddle you, Fish?" Noel asked, shooting Holly a wink, and Holly grinned in return. "Didn't Sally break things off six months ago?"

"I'm about to dump the lot of you," Pike muttered, stroking his perfectly groomed red beard.

Noel threw her arm around Pike's shoulders and rubbed her knuckles over his head. "You can't get rid of me, Fish. I ain't going nowhere."

"Call me Fish again and you'll go right over the edge of a cliff."

"Hey now, everyone play nice. No murdering each other," Anthony said, forming a time out sign. "Or if you must purge, don't tell witnesses the method you'd use. That's how you get caught."

"And don't search for odorless and tasteless poisons," Holly added. "Dead giveaway."

"Pun intended. Ayo!" Pike held out his fist, and she bumped it with a grin. While she liked to give Pike a bad time, Nick's best friends were surrogate older brothers, and she adored them both. She just didn't tell them that.

"If you're all done giving each other a rash of crap, I would love to get home to my family," Merry said, picking her coat up off the counter.

"We're your family too, sis," Holly said.

"Yes, but I've been around most of you all day and I am done with you," she said, shrugging into her jacket.

Holly placed her hand over her chest. "Rude."

"All right, we're going to get some pizza and raid Nick's fridge for beer," Pike said, tugging Holly's hair as he passed. "Always a pleasure, Holly."

"I'll have breakfast for you next time if you get here before noon," Holly called after him.

"Beer is the breakfast of champions. Just saying."

"Gross."

Pike winked at her. "Hair of the dog, baby! Works every time."

"Later, Hol. Merry," Anthony said, saluting with the brim of his blue ball cap before he followed Pike out the door.

"I better go with them or they'll drink all our beer," Noel said.

"Good point!" Merry laughed.

Noel hugged them both in turn and headed out the door. "See you later."

Holly looked around the shop, admiring the array of red, green, and white, enjoying the twinkling lights and hints of glitter on the garland.

"You ready to get out of here?" Merry asked.

"Yeah, I just need to lock up. You can go if you want. I'm sure Clark and everyone are done with the set up by now."

Merry shook her head. "I'll wait for you outside."

Holly laughed. "You afraid I'm going to get attacked on the way to my car?"

"No, but in case I'm wrong, I'll stick around."

"Why don't you wait in here with me? That way we can keep each other safe and see our next birthday."

Merry giggled. "Only have about two weeks. I think we can manage that, don't you?"

Holly waved her hand in a so-so motion. "Could be dicey." All the Winters siblings were born in December two years between each. Nick was the oldest and turning thirty this year. Merry would be twenty-eight, and Holly was about to be twenty-six.

"Pretty sure Nick and I are safe, so that makes you our wild card," Merry said, poking Holly in the ribs. "I just hope the Adventure Elf doesn't do something wacky like play chicken with a chainsaw wielding maniac."

"The stunts I pull are things ordinary people do every day."

"Ordinary people with a death wish." Merry waved her hands in a shooing motion. "Now, hurry up."

"I'll only be a minute."

Holly took care of the back door and then grabbed her purse and coat before heading back to the front. "Let's motor, baby."

"Vroom vroom!" Merry said, heading out the front door ahead of Holly.

"I was thinking about those peen designs you showed me earlier and I've decided my favorite is the mistletoe Johnson and the reindeer Johnson."

"Duly noted. I will work on the reindeer and debut it this week and mistletoe next week. I sold my last turkey yesterday, so I am officially out of fall Johnsons."

Holly and Merry fell into step together and walked along the sidewalk to where their cars were parked, passing by the front corner and display window of Mistletoe Hardware. Holly slowed down to study the window display, which had an open tool box and some power tools covered in dust, the same display the hardware store had had for over a year now.

She stopped, staring into the window, and an evil plan formed in her mind.

"What are you doing?" Merry asked.

"Hatching a diabolical prank," Holly responded.

Holly jogged back to the front door of her shop, ignoring her sister calling for her to stop. In the storage room was another full box of those Christmas gnomes, and Declan Gallagher was going to benefit from the leftover inventory. She couldn't wait for him to get in tomorrow and appreciate her generosity.

"Seriously, what are you doing?" Merry asked from the doorway.

"I think the window next door could use a makeover. Don't you?"

Merry's eyes widened. "Holly. Let's not do anything crazy. I wouldn't put it past Declan to press charges."

"Is it B and E if I have a key?" Holly grabbed the emergency key Mr. Gallagher had given her two years ago off the hook on the wall and lifted the box into her arms. "You coming or do you want plausible deniability?"

"I have a bad feeling about this," Merry said.

"Ignore your bad feeling and grab a box!"

Carrying the box outside, she waited for Merry to follow empty-handed or not, and was pleased to see her sister come from the back with a large box in her arms.

"Atta girl, Mer."

"If I go to jail before my wedding, you're fired as my maid of honor."

"Harsh, but fair," Holly joked, setting down the box to lock up her shop. It took a few minutes to unlock the door to the hardware store because it kept sticking, but when Holly twisted and pushed the door open, she smirked when no alarm went off. Even if someone saw them go inside, they'd just think the Winters sisters were doing a neighborly favor. No reason to be suspicious.

Once they made it inside, Holly lugged the box over to the window and set it down. "First we have to clean up this weak ass set-up."

She removed the open toolbox and other power tools that currently took up the space Holly wanted to fill. When she shut the lid of the toolbox, a cloud of dust rushed up and down her throat, making her cough. Merry pounded her back until Holly was able to wheeze, "You're going to break something, She-Hulk."

"Hey, if you're rude, I'll drop a dime on you right now," Merry said with a poke to Holly's ribs.

"Or you can go back to the shop and get those other two winter boxes we didn't use. I left them in the back room. Oh!" Holly snapped her fingers. "And my Santa Johnson."

"We're not putting *that* in the display window, are we?" Merry gasped.

"No, of course not. I have other plans for him."

To Holly's surprise, Merry didn't refuse or try to talk her out of what she planned to do. Either she figured it would be futile or maybe Merry thought deep down Declan deserved a little razzing. "Fine, but only because I need the cardio."

Holly chuckled as she opened up the box at her feet and pulled out a girl gnome with Christmas lights in her hair and a boy gnome dressed as a reindeer.

"Whatever you need to tell yourself, sister dear."

Merry rolled her eyes and left Holly humming Taylor Swift's "I Did Something Bad." Holly unpacked one of each variously dressed gnomes and set them on the counter, eight in total.

"You ready to party?" she said aloud, picking up the Santa gnome and answering in a deep voice, "We sure are, Merry. We're going to make that Declan rue the day he ever told you to turn your music down."

"It's official. I'm Thelma to your Louise," Merry said upon her return.

"Maybe find two female criminals who don't die at the end of the movie? Just a thought," Holly said, loving that her older sister tried to talk sense to her even as she was aiding and abetting in the prank. While her siblings could make her crazy and vice versa, if she ever needed anyone to have her back, Holly knew it would only take a phone call and her family would be there.

"Idgie and Ruth from *Fried Green Tomatoes*," Merry blurted, opening up her box. "They killed a man and lived...well, until Ruth got cancer. Damn. Nevermind."

"First of all, that is not how the movie went. Sipsey killed Frank." Holly waved an electric drill at Merry and added, "I'm going to tell Mom you couldn't remember the plot of her favorite movie."

"And I'll tell her that her little princess is a burglar."

"I'm rubber and you're glue, Mer." Holly blew her a kiss and went to put the last of the tools away.

"What is your vision for this display?"

Holly made it back up front and started searching through the drawers behind the counter, looking for scissors and tape. "Like a gnome Christmas party."

"I thought gnomes were pagans."

"That would be Druids. Or maybe elves."

"I'll go get that other box while you figure out which one," Merry said, walking out the front door and closing it behind her.

When Holly pulled out the bottom drawer, lying on top was an upside-down photo frame. Holly flipped it over and stared at a younger version of Declan Gallagher wrapped up in the arms of a smiling woman who shared his deep-green eyes. His father stood next to them stiffly, almost like he'd been photoshopped in because his somber expression didn't fit with the joy on the faces of mother and child.

The front door crashed open and Holly dropped the photo back into the drawer and pushed it closed. When she stood up, Holly laughed as her red-faced sister set the box she was carrying down with a heavy sigh.

"Whew, I'm going to sit a minute. That was a workout."

Holly finally found the scissors and tape in the left bottom drawer and set them down on the counter.

"You ready to get this prank underway?"

"As I'll ever be," Merry said.

Holly came around the desk and opened up the top of each box, studying the contents inside. A slow smile stretched across her face as she thought, *This is going to be good.*

CHAPTER 4

DECLAN LEANED HIS HEAD BACK against the headrest as Clark pulled into the driveway of his father's house, closing his eyes as the world swam. The doctor had checked him over and after letting him know his nose was only bruised, not broken, but that he had a mild concussion and one hell of a shiner, told him to go home and take it easy. Declan hated to cancel jobs, but his head still throbbed even after the dose of pain meds the doctor gave him, and he didn't want to get on any more ladders today.

"You going to be okay?" Clark asked, putting the truck in park.

"I'll live." Declan reached for the door handle and groaned as the sore muscles in his back protested the movement. "Just need to take it slow for a few days. I feel bad leaving you all in the lurch."

"Eh, the guys will get it done. As long as you're one-hundred percent by the bachelor party we're good. I need you to help me keep everyone from going off the rails."

Declan chuckled. "Why did I get roped into babysitting duty?"

"Because you're the responsible one in the group. The title usually falls on my shoulders, but I'm the groom." Clark gave his arm a light squeeze. "Don't worry. It will only be my brother and Pike we need to worry about."

"Why isn't Nick helping us keep a lid on things?"

"He's a jokester and I wouldn't put it past him to join forces with my brother to mess with me."

"Gotcha." Declan remembered Nick talking about the prank wars he used to get into with his sisters and wondered if Sam and Clark had a similar relationship growing up. As an only child, he hadn't gotten into crazy situations with siblings and sometimes wondered if he'd missed out.

Then again, if he'd told his brother no strippers or tats and he did it anyway? He wouldn't handle it in stride the way Clark was.

Why he'd agreed to be a groomsman for Clark was a mystery to him. They were friends, but he hated weddings, especially the events leading up to them. All the fake smiling and the big fuss. If two people actually wanted to spend their lives together, why wouldn't they just go down to the courthouse and skip the expense and drama?

Clark got out of the truck on the driver's side, waving at Nick who had trailed behind them in his vehicle. Declan opened the door and stepped out, squinting against the afternoon sun.

"You need help getting into the house?" Clark asked through the open doors of the truck.

"Seriously, I'm good. I'm going to head in and make some lunch."

"I'll call and check on you later, so you'd better answer."

Declan rolled his eyes. "I'll do my best."

"If you don't, I'll send my soon-to-be sister-in-law to check on you, since she lives right there," Clark said, pointing to the adjacent road that took eager light enthusiasts to Evergreen Circle, where Holly lived.

"No, not that," Declan said. "She'd come by to make sure I was dead."

"Probably." Clark laughed. "I'll leave you to it. Thanks for coming out, Declan. I know it didn't exactly go as planned, but I appreciate you showing up. You're a good friend."

"Thanks. We'll talk later."

"See ya, man."

Clark jogged down the driveway to his brother-in-law's truck and hopped in. Declan turned and headed up the walkway to the front door, his back and butt aching with every step. He trudged through the door and hung up his coat, calling out, "Dad! I'm home."

"I'm in here watching the tube."

Declan hobbled into the living room and found his dad reclined in his favorite chair, his food tray in his lap.

"Hey, where's Kim?" Kim was their neighbor, who worked from home as a call center operator. While Liam was still in the early stages of Alzheimer's, he'd forgotten his way home a time or two. Luckily, Kim spotted him and was able to get him home without anyone else in town questioning how Liam forgot where his house was. She kept an eye on Liam while Declan worked and it made him feel better about not being here.

"I sent her home. She kept showing me all the great Black Friday deals on her phone and I had a hard time keeping my mouth shut about how they jack up the prices right before to make it look like you're getting a deal."

"Kudos for not bursting her bubble."

"Only 'cause I was promised dessert. She's dropping an apple pie off for us tomorrow to try. Apparently, she's entering it in some holiday baking contest for the festival of trees."

"We have pie," Declan said.

"Pumpkin, not apple."

"You have a point there. What'd you eat for dinner?" Declan asked, taking the food tray with the empty plate.

"I made some mac and cheese and hot dogs. It's on the stove if you want to polish it off."

Declan didn't, but he just squeezed his dad's shoulder and carried the tray into the kitchen.

"What's wrong with you?" Liam called after him.

"I got knocked off a ladder by a falling Santa."

"What?"

Declan stopped in the doorway of the kitchen and turned around. Liam let out a whistle. "Damn, boy. You look like you went a few rounds and lost."

"I was helping out at the Winters Christmas Tree Farm today and while we were putting some decorations on the roof, I got hurt."

"I'll say you did, but that's why I said not to get caught up in all that crazy commercial stuff. Your mother always wanted to enter those stupid holiday decoration competitions and I told her it was ridiculous. That I wasn't going to break my neck for her bragging rights."

Declan paused. His mom's holiday expectations were one of his dad's favorite complaints since she left, but usually it was spoken of with a healthy dose of bitterness. The last few times he'd brought up his ex-wife, there was an edge of nostalgia and warmth.

"Are you all right?" Declan asked.

"Me? I'm good." His father's smile slipped as he looked Declan up and down. "Are you okay, though? 'Cause I gotta tell you, that nose and eye are pretty tore back."

"My head feels worse, but it's nothing an ice pack and sacking out on the couch won't fix."

His dad picked up the remote and started flipping through channels. "I'll see if I can find us something better to watch."

"Thanks," Declan said, twisting away to set the plate by the sink. Although he'd played football in high school as a way to connect with his dad, Liam had accepted the fact that sports weren't Declan's thing and tried to find common ground with him. It had taken his mom walking out and Declan coming back to Mistletoe for the two of them to get to know each other for the first time.

The scent of smoke burned Declan eyes, and he rushed to the stove, where the remaining mac and cheese had turned black. "Dad, you left the burner on!"

"Oh, damn it!" Declan heard the clunk of the recliner closing and the heavy stomp of footfalls as he came up behind Declan. "I'm sorry about that. Is it ruined?"

"No, it's fine." Declan hated seeing the frustration in his dad's expression and clapped him on the back. "How about I scoop us up some ice cream, and we'll turn on an action flick?"

"Sure, sure, I'll just work on these dishes."

"No, I got these."

"You're hurt," Liam said, reaching for the mac and cheese pot handle. "I can scrub a few pots and pans."

Declan grabbed the pot first and waved his hand. "You go put your feet up. The last thing we need is for you to slip in here and break another hip."

"I'm not an invalid," his dad grumbled, but shuffled out of the room, leaving Declan to roll up his sleeves and get to work on the stack of bowls and plates piled on the side. He might be a walking bruise, but there was no reason to sit on his ass while his nearly seventy-year-old father did the dishes.

A familiar meow sounded before he felt the weight of his cat, Leo, rub against his pant leg. He glanced down from the plate he was scrubbing to smile at the orange tabby.

"Well, hey, buddy. You missed me? Was Papa rude to you again?"

"I wasn't mean to your damn cat," Liam hollered from the living room.

"Is selective hearing something that comes with age? Or is it a personal choice?"

"Less talking, more scrubbing."

Declan chuckled, using a wooden spoon to scoop out the charred remains of mac and cheese from the pot and dumping them in the trash. While he filled the pot with water and soap to soak, he scrubbed the remaining dishes and placed them in the dish rack, staring out the window at the beautiful sunny day. He noticed movement through the trees and watched as a giant red hat grew, waving at him from a distance, and he frowned.

It's started already, he thought.

With a town called Mistletoe, it made sense that the holiday season would be a big deal, but the citizens and city council took it to the extreme. There were competitions for everything. Window displays. House displays. Parade floats. Besides the bragging rights of having the best in whatever category, the winners won a thousand-dollar cash prize. Declan thought they were all overindulgent cries of *"Look at me!"* Especially Evergreen Circle.

During the holidays, the displays at Evergreen Circle lit up the town for miles from the second weekend in December until New Year's Eve, a beacon of holiday cheer Declan wished some days he could shut down completely. He had managed to petition the city to shorten the length of time the circle could function from six weeks to three, citing the miles of cars lined up every evening, jamming up the road and keeping the nearby neighbors trapped in their homes until ten when the lights shut off as a nuisance. The city council agreed to the terms, so he had another two weeks of peace before chaos ensued.

Declan's phone rang, and he wiped off his wet hands on his pants legs to pull it out of his pocket. He stared at his mother's smiling face and stiffened. He hadn't spoken to her in weeks and the last text he got from her was a picture of Diana Gallagher on a beach with the caption *Wish you were here.*

He'd call her on his way to work tomorrow. Declan didn't want to hear the snarky comments from his dad if he talked to her now. While he might be angry with his mom for ditching them, he still loved her.

Sometimes he thought his dad still loved her too. His parents had been high school sweethearts who'd broken up and married other people in their twenties, and after those relationships failed, reconnected in their thirties. Neither of them had other children with their previous partners, and after six years together they didn't expect it to happen for them. He'd been a miracle baby, making an appearance a few months after his mother's fortieth birthday. His childhood had been filled with warm, fond memories of his mother, especially at this time of year. She'd bake for weeks, making tins of treats for all the neighbors and the Christmas events for the town. She loved the holidays with all her heart and was always singing those silly songs about Frosty and Rudolph.

While his father worked ten-hour days keeping the store open, Declan noticed the changes between them in his teen years. The silent dinners, unless they were speaking directly to him. After football practice when he'd catch his mother crying and she'd blame it on the onions she was cutting. He knew his parents were unhappy, but when he'd ask either one about it, his father would answer him brusquely and his mother would change the subject.

It wasn't until after his high school graduation, when he was getting ready to leave for college in Maryland, that they'd sat him down and told him they were divorcing. His mom did most of the talking, telling him that they wanted to wait until he had graduated before they separated, but it was a long time coming and it wasn't anything he did. Through it all his father sat there stoic and strong, except for his eyes. Declan had seen the sheen in his hazel eyes and knew his father didn't want this. It was all *her*.

While his mother had taken off to explore the world, his father had stayed to keep the store going, making sure Declan's tuition was paid, but he constantly complained about the overindulgence of the people of Mistletoe, the wasted time and money on the town events. The first year he'd come back to Mistletoe for his holiday break, his dad griped about everything, from the displays on Evergreen that jammed up traffic to the expense and commercialism. And people came up to Declan at every turn asking about his mom, telling him how much they missed her cookies or her voice in the local Christmas caroling group, and anger twisted in his gut like a serpent. His dad had served Mistletoe at the hardware store since he was younger than Declan, but they didn't care about him. Nobody did except Declan.

All they cared about was their cookies and their choir being off a soprano and their stupid, expensive holiday crap.

His mother continued her travels and sent him texts about her experiences. She sent an airline ticket to join her in Paris for Christmas his junior year, but he'd declined. She'd made the choice to split up their family and it wasn't fair that his dad was alone.

With only the pot left in the sink, Declan leaned over and picked up Leo, wincing at the pinch in his back at the movement. The big tabby kneaded his paws against his shoulder and butted his head against his chin as Declan carried him into the living room, easing down onto the couch with a groan.

His dad glanced over and snorted. "You and that damn cat."

Declan grinned, but the expression pulled at the skin of his eye. As if sensing his discomfort, Leo rolled across his chest, purring loudly as Declan rubbed the cat's ears. "Says the man who likes to toss him raw chicken when he's cooking."

"Giving it to him keeps the raccoons out of our trash cans. It's not because I like the scruffy critter."

Declan didn't believe that for a second, but didn't call Liam out on it. He'd spotted Leo two years ago while doing some odd jobs on a farm outside town. The scrawny tabby was caught in a live trap the owner had set out to get rid of his neighbor's overabundance of cats. Something about the skinny orange kitten tugged at Declan's conscience, and he offered to take the kitten off the man's hands. He said he didn't care, and Declan learned a valuable lesson that day: Don't ever drive around with a loose cat in the cab of your truck.

Declan rolled onto his side to avoid his bruised back and head, Leo curled up along his front as the movie's opening credits played. The next thing he knew, his dad was standing over him, shaking Declan's shoulder.

"What is it?" he asked groggily.

"You doing something at the store I should know about?"

Declan blinked up at his dad. "What are you talking about?"

"I just got a call from Barbara Weaver, head of the city council. She wanted to tell me how delighted she was with our holiday window display and to let us know we were one of the top contenders this year."

"Display? Dad," Declan paused, dragging himself into a sitting position and dislodging Leo from his place beside him. The tabby dropped to the floor with a disgruntled meow and Declan groaned as a wave of nausea assailed him. He was going to need to take more pain meds. "I don't know what she's talking about. I've had the same tools in the window since last fall."

"She sent me a picture." His dad turned the phone around to show a brightly lit display of gnomes standing outside little twig huts and frolicking in leaves. A sign traced with twinkling white lights read *Rolling with my Gnomies.*

Declan stared down at the picture, his eyes narrowing until his lashes blocked the view.

You've done it this time, Elf. Get ready for war.

CHAPTER 5

HOLLY FLIPPED OFF THE SMALL bedside lamp in her bedroom Monday morning before exiting the room. It might seem silly to some for a grown woman to sleep with a night light, but something about being alone at night in her big house brought back child-ish fears of the dark. She knew a night light wouldn't save her if someone broke in, but there was a comfort to the dim, warm glow.

She walked into her kitchen and popped a new pod into her single cup coffee maker. She watched snow flurries fall in a swirl-ing white cloud outside the window above the sink as she grabbed her *Jolly AF* mug and set it under the drip spout. A fine layer of snow covered her backyard already, and she checked the time on her oven.

Hopefully it stops before I have to open the shop or it will be a slow morning.

Although after the success of small business Saturday, she wasn't worried if it turned into an off day. The people of Mistletoe had kept her hopping and even some out-of-towners had dropped in to purchase cute novelty mugs and ornaments. To Holly's surprise, she sold quite a few of those hideous gnomes and was tickled pink when someone mentioned they were the same ones used by the hardware store.

She leaned against the counter and pulled her phone out of her pajama pants pocket, clicking on her email. Most of it was junk or social media notifications, except a new edition of *Mistletoe News*. She tapped on it and scrolled down, past the top story discussing the holiday festivities, until a picture of a familiar storefront caught her eye. She gasped aloud and slapped a hand over her mouth before remembering that she was alone.

The holiday display windows are coming out with a bang and a surprise contender this year is none other than Gallagher Hardware. While it's been years since the store participated, their window is colorful and eye-catching with a detailed gnome village and punny lighted sign. The rest of Main Street is definitely going to have to up their game this year to compete with this delightful scene that signifies togetherness.

Holly was a little insulted that her woodland creature scene got no mention, especially since she'd spent hours on that display. Still, Declan must be hating all the attention and there was some gratification in that.

Although she'd expected him to come banging on her door this weekend and confront her about using her emergency key, so maybe he didn't care anymore. He could have turned over a new leaf, where the spirit of the holidays moved him to join in on the fun and not be such a stick in the mud.

Then again, she highly doubted it.

When her coffee finished brewing, Holly grabbed her favorite creamer from the fridge and poured a healthy amount into the black liquid until it was a lovely almond color. Her mother teased her constantly about having coffee with her sugary creamer, but she liked what she liked and Holly wouldn't apologize for it. Life was too short, and she planned on enjoying every minute she had on this earth.

Maybe she could do a video this morning before work. Drinking coffee in the snow. Tie a sled to the back of her car and ask her neighbor to drag her around.

Ugh, it was like she had writer's block but for a media creator. She was content blocked.

Holly popped her coffee into the microwave to warm it up after the cold creamer addition, and while that was nuking she headed out to the entryway, where her jacket hung from one of four hooks by the front door. She slipped it on. It was a nice morning to sit on the back covered porch bundled up under a blanket and watch the snow fall.

When she'd bought the large four-bedroom house with a living room and family room, three bathrooms, and spacious kitchen with attached dining room, she knew it was too much for her at the moment, but once Holly saw the master bathroom and covered back porch and the spacious yard, she was done looking. This was her home and eventually Holly planned to have a couple kids and would fill up the empty bedrooms. Maybe even keep a husband, if she could stand anyone long enough to marry them.

While she wasn't against getting married, relationships were oddly elusive. She liked a guy and dated him long enough to discover something about him she couldn't live with and then dumped him. Holly had no excuse for running in the opposite direction when it came to falling in love. Her parents were a prime example of a solid marriage, and both her siblings had found loving, sound relationships.

Finding someone whose personal habits wouldn't drive her bonkers? Holly couldn't see it.

She heard the microwave beep, but before she made it four steps there was a sharp rap at the front door. There was only one person who popped over this early without a call or text, and Holly walked back to the entryway to open it.

"Good morning!" Delilah Gill said cheerfully, holding up a beautifully wrapped present. "I come bearing gifts!"

Holly stepped back to let her friend come inside. "Thanks, but what's the occasion?"

Delilah smiled sheepishly and handed her the box. "It's actually not from me, it was on the porch when I walked up. There's a note attached." Delilah hung up her coat on one of the hooks on the wall and yawned. "Ooof, you got any coffee? I got no sleep last night."

"In the kitchen. You know where everything is."

Holly was able to briefly read the front of Delilah's baggy black t-shirt—*I'm Sassy and I Know It*—before she spun away, doing circles into the kitchen. Holly laughed, lifting the tag on the package to read it.

You've been Jingled! Happy Holidays!

"Huh. They didn't put a name on it." Usually the neighborhood didn't start the annual jingling until after the displays went up because there were only a dozen houses on the circle, but someone must have gotten excited. It was a fun activity to get everyone in the spirit of the holiday by leaving gifts filled with candles and holiday knickknacks on someone's doorstep, then they get the next person, and so on until the whole neighborhood had been jingled. Sometimes there was even a bottle of holiday cheer inside, but this box felt rather light so Holly didn't get her hopes up for that.

She carried it into the kitchen and set it on the counter.

"Why do you have your jacket on?" Delilah asked from her perch beside the coffee maker.

"I was going to sit on the back porch and watch the snow fall until I need to get ready for work." Holly grabbed her steaming mug from the microwave and took a sip.

Delilah leaned over and looked out the window before shooting Holly a sardonic expression. "Are you serious? This is exactly the kind of day I stay indoors where it's warm."

"Then why did you leave the comfort of your house to drink my coffee?"

"Whoa, let's get something straight. Your café au lait is my café au lait. That's in the bestie handbook under *Must help hide a body and share a jail cell.*"

"But you braved snow, cold, and slick roads instead of staying home like you claimed to enjoy."

"Yeah, well, I needed a distraction," Delilah said, her blue eyes twinkling. "That's your cue to distract me."

"Unfortunately, I have nothing exciting to report. I am an incredibly boring single female who no one wants to emulate." Holly hummed as she took another sip of her coffee, adding as an after-thought, "I am having trouble coming up with an elf stunt this week."

"What haven't you done?"

"I don't know. Want to drag me behind your car on a sled?"

Delilah brushed a dark strand of hair out of her face, eyes wide behind her black glasses frames. "That sounds incredibly stupid and dangerous."

"That's kind of the point. I'm the Adventure Elf, remember?"

"Yes, but I thought you were going to hang up your pointy elf hat and go in a new direction."

"I am, but I feel like I need to send off the last seven years of my life with a bang."

"Well, I cannot help you there, my friend. The most excite-ment and on-the-edge living I do is wasting ten bucks a week playing the Idaho lottery."

"You're a wild child for sure," Holly teased. "I'm surprised you don't have a sub job today."

"No, I need to get this article done by Friday and I've been stuck on what to write. So I'm not taking any teaching jobs until this is finished."

"Which is why you are here stealing my coffee instead of working?"

"Hey, I came over for best friend time, not so you can bust my ovaries." She walked over to Holly's fridge and opened the door, grabbing the container of half-and-half Holly kept in there for Delilah.

"I'm not busting, I am simply holding you accountable."

"Well, stop it. I don't want to think about it for the twenty minutes it will take me to finish this coffee and visit with you." Delilah hopped up on one of the stools, her thick jean-clad legs dangling in the air. She barely crossed the five-foot mark and had suffered through bullying for being short and plus-size her entire childhood, but she'd never let it get to her, firing back until she stopped being a target. Delilah wore her individuality like an armor, sporting glasses with magnetic frames she could change out with her mood, and funny t-shirts with funky patterned leggings and skirts. Holly had told her about the Adventure Elf channel when they were both nineteen, and Delilah had been her biggest fan and bought her the silly costume in the first place. It was why she loved her dearly, and although Holly loved to give her a bad time, she didn't care a whit if Delilah dropped by to raid her coffee stores.

"Okay, we aren't talking about the article." Holly sat next to her at the breakfast bar, cradling her mug in her hands. "What should we discuss?"

"Don't you want to open your present first? Maybe it's chocolate."

"There's usually some candy and small things inside." Holly took a drink of her coffee and set it down. "Stop staring at me. I'll open it, okay?"

"Yay!"

Holly rolled her eyes and ripped off the bow, followed by the shiny paper, revealing the plain brown box beneath. She sliced the tape along the creases of the box with her fingernail and lifted the lid—

POP! She barely had time to shut her eyes before a cloud of something exploded in her face. Holly coughed and wiped at her eyes, blinking tiny flecks out of her lashes so she could look down at her sparkling hands.

Glitter. She'd been hit by a glitter bomb.

"What the heck?" Delilah hollered, taking the box from her. "There's a nail in the side and a busted balloon. Who would do this?"

"I don't know," Holly mumbled, jumping to her feet and rushing to the sink to wash the grainy bits out of her mouth.

"Wait, there's something else in here," Delilah called behind her. "'Stay out of my store, Elf.' It's just signed 'D.' Who's D?"

The mouthful of water she'd taken in rushed out from between her lips when she realized that Declan hadn't turned over a new leaf but had spent the weekend plotting revenge. She could almost appreciate the prank if she wasn't the one currently hacking up a glitter ball.

She splashed some water in her face, running her palms over her eyes and cheeks as she turned around. "Declan Gallagher."

"Why, though? What did you do to him besides play your Christmas music too loud?"

"I used the emergency key to create the display in their storefront window."

"Seriously?" Delilah set the box back on the counter, her mouth set in a grim line. "And for that you deserve glitter in your face?"

"Apparently, but have no fear. That man is going to pay."

"You should put some itching powder in his underwear. Or hair remover in his shampoo."

"That would involve me getting into his house, and while it's doable, something tells me the guy would look good with a bald head."

"Oh, really?"

Holly sent Delilah a withering look. "No, thank you. I'm not into angry giants with mile-long whiskers."

"Come on, his beard isn't long at all. It's about the same length as Pike's and I think his looks great."

"That is because you've been in love with Pike since you were twelve."

Delilah's cheeks flushed, but she didn't deny it. Holly didn't claim to be an expert on what other people found attractive, but Pike was loud, dramatic, and over the top confident. If Holly ever thought of him as anything more than her older brother's friend, he'd have driven her crazy within a week, but Delilah still carried a torch for him after all these years and the dork was too blind to notice.

His loss, in Holly's opinion.

"I'll make us some fresh coffee while you scheme," Delilah said, hopping off the stool and picking up both cups. "We've got floaties."

Holly let the topic of Pike rest, her irritation simmering once more. "Thank you. It's one thing to sparkle me up, but to ruin my coffee after I've put my creamer in? That stuff is expensive." Holly shook herself out, watching glitter fly around the room. "I'm going to have to shower forever to get all of it off."

"Plus sweep and mop. Maybe you should call a truce."

"No way. I never back down from a fight, and this," Holly said, waving her hand over her glittery self, "is war."

CHAPTER 6

DECLAN DOUBLE-CHECKED TO MAKE SURE the front door was locked and set the alarm, something he hadn't done in years. While they got some tourists in the summer months, they'd never had a break-in until Holly pulled her garbage on Sunday, and he wasn't taking any chances of her retaliating after the gift he'd left her this morning. He'd been ready and waiting for her to show up today and rip into him, but nothing. He hadn't even heard her music kick on next door.

Maybe Holly didn't bother to open her shop today. The snow hadn't let up until after one, dropping nearly five inches, and he'd only had a customer stop by for ice melt. The rest of the day had been quiet—just him and the gnomes.

Declan glanced over at the display window, his jaw tightening when he thought about all the attention he'd received from the citizens of Mistletoe. Praising him for joining in on the festivities and setting an example, when it wasn't even his doing. He felt like a fraud leaving it up, but the damage had been done and if he took it down now, it would only draw more attention. Better to just let things go and be proactive in keeping Holly from wreaking any more havoc on his life.

It was twisted to admit, even to himself, but he'd been looking forward to seeing Holly covered in glitter and spitting fire at him. While Declan thought she was a pill, at least Holly didn't just roll over and admit defeat. She was tough, and he could appreciate that.

Putting his ear buds in, Declan pulled his phone out of his pocket and pressed play on his music app, his playlist blasting in his ears as he headed to his studio located in the back of the store. He always kept the door locked unless he was in there, mostly because he didn't like to show anyone what he was working on, even his dad, until it was finished.

Unlocking the door, he stepped inside and stripped, hanging his clothes up in the small armoire he kept in the corner and sliding his shoes and socks in the bottom cubby. Tuesday nights he brought home tacos for dinner, which only gave him about a half hour to work. He pulled on a paint-splattered t-shirt and some scrub pants, and the minute he picked up his paints a calm rushed over him like a spring breeze, and he smiled.

Therapy had nothing on standing in a room alone, listening to his favorite tunes, and using brushes to turn nothing into something. His sure, swift strokes across the canvas in various shades of green outlined the rows of Christmas trees he'd seen over the weekend at the Winters farm. The image stayed with him, locked in his mind, and he couldn't resist the nagging urge to capture it on canvas.

Declan had always loved art, but it wasn't until he was in seventh grade that he discovered he had a real talent for it. Kids in his classes would pay him to draw their favorite superheroes, monsters, even sports stars. He'd used the money that he made to buy sketch books, pencils, and eventually an easel and canvases. Art became his constant, his passion, and even after coming back to Mistletoe he hadn't given it up.

When his alarm went off, Declan cleaned his brushes and stopped his playlist. He still had some details to add on the trees, but he should be able to start on the main house in the painting tomorrow.

His phone blared to life with his dad's ringtone and Declan answered it with a hurried "I'm leaving in a few to grab the food. Should be home in twenty minutes."

"No need to rush. I was just calling to tell you don't worry about me. I'm going out."

Declan paused, sure he'd heard his dad wrong. "Where are you going? And who are you going with?"

"Out to dinner with an old friend. Don't worry about it."

"Dad, how are you going to get there? You know you can't drive—"

"I'm not an idiot or a child, Declan. Enjoy your night off from babysitting me."

"I'm not baby—" Declan checked his phone, realizing his dad had hung up on him. He was used to his dad having mood swings and being irritable, especially when Liam felt Declan asked too many questions, but it was his job to make sure his dad was safe. Even though his diagnosis was early, Declan suspected the reality of his illness hadn't hit his dad until the doctor told Liam he shouldn't drive anymore. He didn't like to constantly remind

Liam of his limitations, but Declan wanted to make sure his dad was being safe too. When his dad returned tonight, Declan was going to need to sit down with him and clear the air.

Declan finished cleaning up and redressed, stuffing his t-shirt and scrubs into a plastic bag so he could take them home and wash them. He turned off the alarm briefly and went out the back, arming it again before he locked up. The motion light behind the store lit up the tiny back alley where he parked his truck, and when it illuminated his white F-250, Declan stopped and stared.

Someone had covered his entire truck in plastic wrap. No, not someone. Declan knew who'd done it before he got close enough to pull off the big red bow on the hood, noticing the white envelope dangling from the festive red decoration. He ripped it open violently and stared down at the curling script.

Have fun unwrapping my gift to you! Ready to cry Uncle?

Holly

Declan crushed the missive in his hand before shoving it into his pocket, grinding his teeth with rage. Pulling his phone out, Declan took a picture of his truck, texting it to Clark with the caption Your sister-in-law is in for it now.

Clark sent back a shocked emoji followed by three of the little round laughing faces. Declan glared and backed out of his messages to call his dad again. He pressed the speaker phone as he used both hands to start ripping at the clear, clinging plastic. It went to voicemail and Declan pressed end, his fingers numb with cold as he continued to free his door. He'd check his family GPS app once he got all this off.

It must have taken her a while and a lot of determination. He'd barely cleared the driver's door and window and he was already out of patience.

His phone rang and he picked it up, figuring it would be his dad, but Clark's name flashed across the screen. Declan accepted the call and set the phone down, hitting the speaker icon. "Need another laugh?"

"Are you offering?" Clark asked, his voice shaking with amusement.

"No, and I could have done without this tonight. I'm cold, my dad has gone off without telling me where, and I haven't even finished clearing a quarter of this mess."

"This would not be the time to tell you I warned you, right?"

"Warned me?"

"Not to mess with Holly."

"Hey, I'll admit, this was good. I can give her points for that, but you should be warning her because now I'm taking the gloves off."

There was a long pause before Clark asked, "Have you ever stopped to think about *why* you want to escalate this whole thing with Holly?"

"Because she is a spoiled"—Declan grunted as he ripped a large hunk of wrapping off his truck—"princess who thinks she can do whatever she wants because she's cute."

"Wait, you think Holly is cute?"

Declan growled. "I am a man with eyes. She is attractive, but that does not make up for the fact that she is an irritating pain in my ass."

"Fair enough. But going back to what you were saying before, why are you worried about where your dad is?"

He paused, his brain stumbling over what to say. "I mean...I live with the guy and it snowed half the day. I just think giving me a heads-up on which direction to send the rescue team isn't much to ask."

"I get that. When my brother would stay out all night, I was constantly checking my GPS app to see where he was. I know he's older, but I swear sometimes I feel like Sam's keeper."

"He moved out of your place, didn't he?" Declan asked between grunts of exertion as he cleared the hood.

"Back in June, but I still check up on him. He comes over a lot, and he's going to stay at our place with Jace and Daisy while we're on our honeymoon. Although if I know Chris and Victoria, they'll steal the both of them whenever Sam allows it." Clark cleared his throat. "Do you want me to come down there and help you uncover your truck?"

"No, I got it. I'm going to do enough to get me inside and finish the rest tomorrow, but I do have a favor to ask..."

"Shoot."

Declan picked up his phone with one hand and reached for his door with the other. "I want you to pick your fiancée's brain about her sister. Her dislikes and fears. I need an upper hand to win this—"

Sinister laughter erupted from inside his cab when he opened the door, and he stumbled back with a shout, falling on his butt on the snow-covered asphalt. A gnome fell out of his truck and shattered on the ground with a high-pitched crack. Clark hollered faintly from the face-down position of Declan's phone, and when he flipped it over Declan noticed a spiderweb cracking in the corner of the screen.

"Son of a bitch." Declan wiped the snow off the glass as gently as he could, silently cursing himself for not getting a new glass protector.

"What happened?" Clark called.

"I've got to go. I've got a huge crack in my screen and I don't want to make it worse."

"Why did you scream, though?"

"Because my truck laughed at me. I'll call you later."

Declan ended the call and got to his feet, wiping at the back of his wet jeans. He picked up as much of the broken gnome as he could see and tossed it into the back of his truck before going to look for the source of that horrifying laugh. Declan found the voice box speaker taped to the back of his headrest and flipped the switch on the side before throwing that in the back with the broken gnome.

His body shaking with anger, he shoved the remaining statues to the other side of the cab. Declan estimated about thirty of the hideous ceramics were inside and clenched his jaw as he stuck his key into the ignition. Whatever started this feud, he was about to finish it.

Revving his truck to life, he backed out of his space and headed for Evergreen Circle. He was afraid to check his dad's location and make the screen crack worse, so until he got it in writing that

Holly Winters would be replacing his phone, Declan wasn't going to mess with it.

He took the right of way from his darkened home and hit a hard left into the holiday neighborhood. The houses were large, with well-manicured lawns and immaculate landscaping. He'd heard through several people that Holly made a hundred thousand or more a year with her online elf videos and it amazed him that her silly YouTube channel paid for all of this. People were easily entertained, it seemed.

Declan whipped into her driveway and grabbed a gnome, exiting his vehicle to march up her walkway while pulling his broken phone out of his pocket. The porch light was on, and he stepped directly below it to bang on her front door, waiting impatiently for her to answer. Finally, Declan heard the lock turn and Holly peered out at him with a dark glower.

"What are you doing here?"

Declan held up his phone, screen towards Holly, in his right hand and the gnome in the other. "Because of what you did, I dropped my phone and it shattered. You need to fix this."

Holly pulled the door all the way open and stepped into the doorway wearing a simple red sweater and buffalo plaid pajama pants. "You going to pay to deep clean all the glitter out of my house?"

"Are you serious? Glitter is harmless. This is a thousand-dollar phone and I can't even make a call out with it like this."

"Ever think its karma for being a bitter, angry human being?"

"No, although I sometimes wonder what I ever did to deserve you moving into the space next door."

Holly stepped all the way out, coming close enough to go toe to toe with him, although she was too short for nose to nose. "I'll have you know that most people consider me a delightful person."

"Your family doesn't count, Elf. They have to love you."

Holly gasped and a twinge of guilt squeezed his chest. Before he had a chance to back track and apologize, she leaned over and grabbed a fistful of snow from her porch chair, slamming the cold lump into his chest with the flat of her hand. All apologies went out the window and Declan slipped his phone into his pocket.

"You really shouldn't have done that."

Her eyes widened, but before she could run back inside, Declan tossed the gnome onto her lawn and wrapped his arms around her waist, hefting her up over his shoulder kicking and screaming.

"Declan Gallagher, don't you even think about it," she hollered two seconds before he dumped her, gentler than she deserved, onto her back in snow covering her lawn. Holly gasped, staring up at him with her mouth hanging open. "You cretin!"

Placing one hand into the frigid snow next to her head, he leaned over her until their faces were only a few inches apart. "Don't start a snowball fight you can't win, Elf."

When she tried to throw another fistful at him, Declan caught her wrist. "You really don't know when to give up, do you?"

Holly glared at him. "By the time I'm done with you, Declan, you'll be begging for mercy."

He chuckled. "That's not going to happen."

Declan didn't have time to stop her other hand from shoving a ball of snow under the back of his shirt, and he lost his balance, falling on top of her with a grunt. His knees hit the ground on either side of her legs, pinning her down.

"Ooof," she squeaked, her hand flying to his chest.

Icy wetness ran down into his jeans and along the sides of his waist, the skin of his butt stinging with cold, but Declan was frozen in place, distracted by the warmth of her outer thighs against his inner. He tried to hold himself off her with his hands lost in the frigid snow, but the angle only pressed his unmistakable hard-on into her.

It's been a while and you're lying on top of her. It's a natural reaction.

Declan's gaze met hers in the porch light, and he couldn't stop staring at her flushed cheeks, her full lips parted, and the arch of her neck. He knew she was gorgeous, he'd have to be blind not to, but this was the first time he'd taken the time to appreciate it.

Neither of them moved a muscle for several moments, until a flashlight beam honed in on them. Declan rolled off Holly, shielding his eyes from the blinding light.

"What's going on out here? I heard shouting."

Holly climbed to her feet with jerky motions and gave a little wave. "I'm fine, Mr. James. Declan was just returning my gnome to me, and we both slipped."

The man lowered the flashlight and it took a second for Declan to recognize his high school PE teacher but there was no mistaking the familiar disapproval in the older man's gaze. He'd tormented Declan relentlessly. Mr. James had told Declan on more than one occasion that he lacked discipline and drive, and when Declan finally lost his cool and told the older man off, he'd been on the verge of a three-day suspension. If his mom hadn't smoothed things over for him, Declan had a feeling Mr. James would have booted him.

"Is that right?" Mr. James asked. "You getting clumsy, Gallagher?"

Declan nodded before getting up and retrieving the tossed gnome, holding it out to Holly. When she wrapped her hand around it, he pulled her towards him and lowered his voice. "Be ready, Elf. You're going to be the one begging."

"In your dreams," Holly snapped. She took her gnome from his grasp and called cheerfully, "Goodnight, Mr. James," before she disappeared inside her house.

Declan turned around to face Mr. James, slipping his hands into his pockets. "Goodnight, Mr. James."

The older man walked away without a word, only to pause when he reached the front of Declan's truck. He didn't speak as he seemed to study the strips of plastic hanging off the side, then simply shook his head as he disappeared into the dark.

Declan shot one more glance at Holly's house and caught her standing in the corner of the window watching him, the light behind her outlining her curves dramatically, and he jerked his head around. He'd gone this long seeing Holly for what she was; no way was he going to let a tussle in the snow change his mind.

Holly Winters was the enemy, and he refused to forget it.

CHAPTER 7

WEDNESDAY MORNING, HOLLY WALKED OUT of her house with her eyes at half-mast under her sunglasses and took another large drink of her coffee. After she'd tossed and turned the last two nights, plotting another diabolical prank that would bring Declan Gallagher to his knees, she'd managed to squeeze in an hour and a half of shut-eye until her alarm went off. At least her employee, Erica Jackson, would be there today to help out.

Holly grabbed the snow shovel from the side of her porch steps and set her coffee on the railing. She needed to get the walkway cleared off and de-iced before the snow melted this afternoon and refroze, turning the cement into a skating rink. The scrape of the plastic snow shovel made her wince, but she kept on, tossing the scoops of ivory fluff onto her snow-covered lawn. Normally the boy across the street would shovel her walkway for ten bucks, but the family had put their house up for sale last spring and moved.

The shimmer of something sparkling caught her eye on the sleeve of her jacket. She brushed off the specks of glitter, something she'd gotten used to finding over the last few days, and her mind wandered to Declan.

They hated each other with every fiber of their being, but the other night when he'd been on top of her, staring down at her mouth, she thought...

Well, for a moment she'd expected him to kiss her.

Which was crazy, of course. Especially because they'd been at each other's throats moments before he'd dumped her in the snow. She didn't like to think about how good he'd felt or how tempted she'd been to reach up and run her hands along his arms and shoulders. He'd picked Holly up like she weighed nothing, so he had to have some pretty good muscles under that button-up flannel shirt, and that speculation had contributed to a moment or two of her sleepless nights.

Holly waved her hands in front of her and shook her head, as if the motion would ward off the spark of curiosity that had been burning ever since he'd fallen on top of her, his body pressed into hers. Maybe it had been too long since she'd been with someone and that's what had her hormones going bonkers, but Holly knew, logically, deep down, that she did not want to bang Declan Gallagher. That would be a monumental mistake.

A date. That's what you need. Another plan of attack on Declan and a handsome man to buy you sweets and call you pretty afterward.

"Good morning, Holly," Theodore James called as he rounded the corner of her garage, leaving footprints in his wake. In his early sixties, he seemed to spend his retirement using passive aggressiveness on his neighbors and rubbing his hand over his shiny bald head like he was trying to make a wish. "Glad you're getting around to this."

Getting around to it? It's barely eight in the morning and I just shoveled it yesterday, she thought grumpily. Mr. James had his good points, which was why they'd elected him as head of the HOA for Evergreen Circle, but he could be a pain in the butt and condescending to boot.

He stepped off the walkway onto her lawn and folded his arms over his chest. "Do I need to come over with my snow plow and do your driveway, or are you going to get to that before you leave, too?"

"I've got a plow on my four-wheeler." Which he knew full well. "I'll do it, don't you worry."

"Thanks, I appreciate it. We just want the neighborhood to be uniform and well-maintained so when the displays go up, people are discussing how amazing they are and not how unkempt the Evergreen looks. Like those people who bought the house across from you? I have to go have a talk with them about their cat."

"They have a cat?" Holly fought the urge to roll her eyes. Theodore had a thing about animals and took an immediate dislike of anyone in the neighborhood who had them, even if they kept them indoors.

"Yes, a long-haired black thing. You haven't seen it?"

"I haven't."

"Well, I've noticed it running around the neighborhood and I started finding poop on my lawn. If they can't keep it under control, I'm going to have to enforce Clause Nineteen Section B of the Homeowner's Agreement."

Holly didn't know for sure what he was talking about but the year Holly moved in, Theodore put a live trap out. He said it was to catch a rabbit who had been eating his garden, but after the third feline pet went missing, the neighbors had banded together against him and he'd put it away.

"I don't think you want to put out the live trap again. I'm sure you going over there and making them aware of the situation will be enough."

"I'll try that first, but they are from California," he said, his voice thick with disdain.

Holly didn't bother arguing because she knew it wouldn't make a bit of difference, and she didn't have the energy to go a round of "why Californians aren't to blame for everything going wrong in Idaho."

"Well, I'd better get back to it, or I won't have time to finish before I leave."

"Yes, of course, there was just one more thing. It's about the displays."

"Okay," she said, drawing out the word.

"Last year, your house got a little gaudy and out of control and I want to make sure that we keep the playing field level for everyone else."

Holly lifted her sunglasses and stared at him. She'd done a winter wonderland with a magnetic pond, ice skaters, and a snow machine, along with an entire miniature town to model Mistletoe. She'd won best display, beating Theodore out, something her neighbors said hadn't happened in years. He'd been snarky about it then and apparently time hadn't made him less salty.

"Since the judges didn't seem to find my display gaudy, I guess I'll do what I think is best with my house."

The fake smile on his face slipped a moment and his dark eyes narrowed. "I suppose when you come by money so young, it's easy to fritter it away." Holly's jaw dropped at his audacity, and before he turned, he pointed to the end of her driveway. "Don't just dump your snow pile for someone else to have to climb over."

"Of course not," she snapped, reining in her temper as he walked back around the corner and disappeared. Holly hated the closed-mindedness of some people who didn't think she worked for her money. While she might not have spent twenty years punching a clock from nine to five, she'd put in many hours coming up with content, reinvesting her money into her stunts, into her fans, and into her channel and it paid off.

Great, now she was tired *and* cranky.

It took her almost forty-five minutes to clear her walkway and plow the driveway. Holly pulled out of Evergreen Circle just fifteen minutes before she had to open the shop, leaving her with no time to pick up what she needed to break Declan. Although after her encounter with Theodore, her irritation with Declan had lessened considerably. That or the older man surpassed Declan's abilities to piss her off.

Holly pulled into a spot in front of the shop and realized she'd forgotten her travel mug of coffee on her railing. Leaning her head against the steering wheel, she took a deep breath.

It's okay. I'll send Erica to grab us a couple of coffees and get my head on straight with some cheerful Christmas tunes. Volume turned up.

The thought made her smile and Holly climbed out of the SUV, rummaging through her purse as she walked toward the front.

Holly retrieved her keys from the bottomless pit and stepped up onto the mat. A burst of static and then the sound of a rattle echoed in the alcove before something fell from above, raining long, twisting bodies down on her and dropping around her feet in a sea of—

Snakes.

Holly screamed and stumbled back, tearing up the pavement to put distance between her and the danger noodles until two things stopped her.

Holly realized the snakes weren't moving, and she heard the unmistakable sound of crackling male laughter explode from her doorway.

Her gaze zeroed in on a black walkie-talkie she'd missed tucked into the corner, and she stepped over and around the fake snakes to pick it up, pressing the button to talk.

"Declan...I'm going to wring your flipping neck."

She released the button, and he responded, "Are you sure you can reach that high, Elf?"

"Harmless pranks are one thing, but using my worst fear— wait, how did you know I'm afraid of snakes?"

"I cannot reveal my sources," he said smartly. "You got the money for my new phone?"

One of her siblings must have given her up and when she found out who, they would be in for a world of pain.

"You got me here, Gallagher, but you crossed a line. I hope you're prepared for the aftermath."

"You keep threatening to bring the heat, Elf, but everything you're hitting me with is tepid at best."

"I'm underwhelming you before I blow your mind," she

clapped back, turning when she heard the thud of boots behind her. Holly turned around to find Declan standing behind her, smirking.

"Talk is cheap. Put your money where your mouth is."

"I've never understood that expression, but I'm more than happy to show you what a swift kick in the ass feels like."

Holly lunged at Declan, lifting her leg in the air as she gave chase, but the infuriating man easily sidestepped her at every turn, that smug smirk curling his lips.

"Come on, Elf. My legs are twice as long and I can do this all day with no effort, while you're breathing awfully hard."

"Only because the hideous smell of your aftershave is turning my stomach and I'm trying not to breathe through my nose."

They went full circle before Declan finally stopped and put his hand out against her forehead, much like Nick used to do to her when they were kids. She glared at him all the while his green eyes twinkled like he was having the best time.

"First of all, I smell amazing and you know it. Second of all, are you aware you inadvertently called yourself a mouth breather?"

Holly grabbed his arm with a high-pitched huff of frustration and pushed it off her forehead. "I'll buy you a new flipping phone, but you'd better spring for the extra tough case because if you break it again when I take you down, it's on you, not me."

Holly unlocked her door, ignoring the snakes and Declan, who followed her inside. She set her purse behind the counter and pulled out her checkbook. "You said a thousand?"

Declan shook his head. "I was kidding. Justin at Ubreak gave me a new screen for three hundred and it's already fixed."

Holly filled in the amount and signed it, ripping it out of the book with a *rffft*. She held it out to him, waving the check up and down. "My goal wasn't to damage your personal property, so this makes us even on the phone."

Declan seemed to hesitate and Holly huffed. "What's the issue? I pay for your cracked screen, and we're square. We can go back to being mortal enemies hellbent on destroying each other."

"Destroying each other seems a little extreme," he replied.

"Not after you just took ten years off my life with those snakes. It was crafty, but I'm going to have to do some recon in order to tip the scales."

Declan took the check slowly, folding it in half and then slipping it into his jeans pocket. "I'll be watching my back, then."

"You better keep track of all sides because you never know which way I'm going to spring at you." Holly dropped her checkbook back into her purse with a grin. "Oh, and Declan?"

"What?"

Holly pressed the button on her stereo and turned up the volume on "Here Comes Santa Claus." "Have an awesome day."

Declan's eyes narrowed, but she could have sworn he was fighting a smile before he started to come around the back of the counter. Holly jumped into his path. "Hey now! No one but employees behind this line."

Suddenly, he lifted her off her feet and set her on the counter, turning the volume down to a hum without looking away from her face. "If that music goes above twenty today, I'll be back with my toolbox and this thing will end up in pieces."

Holly stuck her chin out. "I've told you once and I'll tell you again. You dismantle my stereo, and it will come back bigger, stronger, and with subs. You think my music is bad now? I'll make the walls shake so hard, you'll imagine—" Holly's mouth snapped closed as she realized where that sentence was heading and who with. After the other night with Declan on top of her, and hard, and that kissable mouth...

Kissable?

Was it hot in the shop, or was it him leaning in, a gleam in his green eyes she didn't like at all.

"What was that, Elf? I'll imagine...what?"

His face was inches from hers, which meant his lips hovered within kissing distance, and her traitorous body swayed towards him, her eyes glued on that lush mouth. Declan's beard looked soft, strokable, and her hand came up as if she actually meant to run her fingers through the dark strands.

Holly's heart hammered in her chest, words failing her. She searched his face, holding his gaze, and for a second she could have sworn she saw hunger in those mossy depths. A hunger for her or simply for sex, but she squeezed her legs together as a drum of desire throbbed to life between her thighs.

No. No no no no, I do not want Declan Gallagher in any way, shape, or form.

Holly put her hands on his shoulders and pushed him back far enough for her to jump down from the counter, but that had their bodies pressed flush against each other.

"Nothing. I lost my train of thought."

Declan took a strand of her hair and rolled it around his finger, giving it a gentle tug. "If you ever get it back, you know where to find me."

"I have so many questions," a teasing voice called from the front door, breaking Declan's spell. Holly turned around to find Erica in the entryway, watching them curiously with dark brown eyes, one ample hip cocked to the side. "Also, did you know there's a whole mess of snakes on the stoop?"

Declan leaned over her back and whispered against the shell of her ear, "See you later, Elf."

It took her a moment to find her voice and just as he hit the door, she called out, "You better take those snakes with you!"

Declan held the door open, peeking back in to wink at her. "Consider them a gift."

"Worst gift ever," Holly called out, trying to suppress a smile. The snakes were a nice touch, and she could appreciate his espionage and underhanded tactics. She'd have done the same if there was anyone in town she could get information about Declan Gallagher from.

Declan shut the door without responding and Holly's gaze followed him as he passed in front of the display window. The shop was silent for several beats before Erica said, "I don't want to pry, boss, but was I interrupting something?"

Holly ignored the question, the warm lull of Declan's proximity still wrapped around her like a fleece blanket and the scent of his cologne lingering. She lied about his cologne stinking. She actually loved the sharp, spicy scent of it and had been in the process of breathing it in before Erica showed up.

Still, this newfound pseudo respect for Declan—and fine, Holly could admit a slight attraction for the man—had thrown her for a loop. If Erica hadn't walked through the door and interrupted them, would they have ended up making out on top of the counter?

A little tingle of excitement tickled the small of her back at the thought, but she shut it down. She wasn't actually interested in Declan, was she? They didn't even like each other.

Right?

Turning the volume back up to forty, she waited a few moments before she heard Declan call out through the wall, "Don't make me come back over there, Elf!"

Holly grinned. *Oh, I wish you would.*

"Okay," Erica said, drawling the word, "we're not going to talk about all that chemistry with the handyman, but the snakes?"

"I'll take care of it," Holly said, adjusting the volume down slightly. She needed time to think about what she wanted to do next. "And then I have to deal with a dirty, betraying rat."

"Um, I still have so many questions, but I'll start with— who's a rat?"

"My sister or my brother. One or both are in for it." An idea popped into her head and Holly grinned, thinking she had something that would really get Declan's attention. "Would you open the doors for me? I gotta step back and make a TikTok real quick."

"No worries, I got this handled." Erica hung her coat up behind the counter, watching her with amusement. "Not gonna lie, boss, that smile is a little scary."

"Don't worry, it's not for you," Holly said, snagging her phone from her purse and heading for her storage room. She'd set up the space to make videos and posts complete with back drops, lighting, and a few different costumes. She picked up her green velvet elf hat and covered her ears with her hair so the attached ears of the hat would sit nicely. When she had her phone in the holder and everything ready, she pressed the red record button.

"Hello, fellow adventurers! Have I got a mission for you!"

CHAPTER 8

"MISTLETOE HARDWARE, DECLAN SPEAKING."

"Why do reindeer like Beyoncé so much?" a woman asked.

"What?"

"Because she sleighs! Remember that, okay?"

"Remember—"

The line went dead and Declan hung up the store phone with a frown. He'd been getting calls like that all morning, but that was the ninth person in less than twenty minutes, and he had a niggling feeling Holly was behind it.

The phone rang again and Declan picked it up with a brusque "Mistletoe Hardware."

"Bad day, sunshine?"

Declan recognized the cheerful voice and found himself smiling in spite of himself. "I'm guessing I have you to thank for all the festive jokesters?"

"You'd be correct, and it's just getting started. Do you have a favorite so far?"

"No, they're all horrible," he said.

"Then why are you smiling?" she asked.

Declan looked up and spotted Holly outside the window, smirking at him with her cell phone to her ear.

"Maybe because I think you're going soft on me."

"Soft? Asking my TikTok followers to entertain you with holiday comedy is soft when I know how much you hate Christmas?"

"Little bit. Now, why don't you come in here and harass me instead of tying up my line and disappointing all your fans."

He watched her walk through the door and Declan hung up the phone as she approached, grimacing when it immediately blared to life.

"Mistletoe Hardware, Declan speaking."

"How does a gingerbread man make his bed?" a child's voice asked with a slight lisp.

Declan met Holly's gaze. "I don't know. How does a gingerbread man make his bed?"

"With a cookie sheet!"

Declan chuckled. "That's a good one, kid."

"Thank you. Tell Holly Gunner says hi!"

"Would you like to tell her yourself? She's right here."

"Really?"

"Hang on." Declan held out the cordless phone. "Gunner would like to say hi."

"Ummm…"

Declan mouthed "Kid," and Holly took the phone without any more explanation needed. Declan studied her as she cheerfully said, "Hey, Gunner!" She paused briefly, that sweet, sunny smile stretching across her face. "I would love to hear it."

Something inside Declan's chest unfurled and warmth spread through him like a shot of whiskey. He'd felt it before, in smaller doses, around Holly but today, listening to her patient one-sided conversation with the kid was different. More intense.

Declan had thought Holly was self-centered and maybe a little fake after their first meeting, but the way people in town spoke about her had slowly changed his mind. Perhaps he'd wanted her to be too flawed to make him feel anything and that's why he'd constantly put her on the defensive.

She ended the call and held the phone out to him. "Such a sweetheart. He definitely needs to win."

"Win?" Declan asked.

"Yep. I posted a contest video this morning and I need to pick five winners," she said, leaning across the counter. "Any jokesters that stood out to you today?"

"Not that I can recall."

Holly propped her elbow on the counter and rested her chin on her palm. "Not a single one got even a chuckle out of you?"

"Only Gunner so far."

"Welp, I guess I'll check back then."

Before she could retreat, Declan reached out and wrapped his hand gently around her wrist. "If I'm part of the deciding team on who wins, shouldn't I know the details?"

"Who said team? I set this out to be a prank to drive you crazy."

"I'll admit the phone ringing off the hook doesn't make for a tranquil environment, but it's better than unwrapping my truck in freezing temperatures."

Holly bit her lip. "I'm sorry. I didn't think about you doing all that in the cold snow while I was setting it up. I guess I was too fired up at you to feel the cold myself. And it was earlier in the day."

His thumb rubbed across the inner side of her wrist, and he thought Holly shivered but couldn't tell for sure.

"It's fine. It was funny after the fact. Clark got a kick out of it when he called while I was trying to free my cab."

"Aha! It was Clark who said something about the snakes, which means Merry gave me up!"

The phone rang, and he picked up with his free hand, afraid she'd try to escape while he was distracted. "I had two full days to plot. I could have easily talked to Nick."

"Did you?" she prodded, but he hit the talk button.

"Mistletoe Hardware, Declan speaking."

"What do snowmen use to make snow babies?" a man's voice asked.

Most of the jokes had been family friendly, but Declan already knew where this one was going. "What?"

"Snowballs!"

"Sorry, bud. Not even a chuckle. Have a good day."

"Hey, wait! Are you Holly's boyfriend?"

Declan froze. "What?"

"Is she single? Can you tell her Wyatt from Utah would love to take her out and I'm not that far—"

Declan hung up the phone, his heart hammering in his chest.

Holly frowned. "What's wrong? What did they say?"

"Don't you think it's dangerous to let strangers on the internet know where you live?"

Holly's eyes widened. "My followers have known since the beginning I live in Mistletoe. It goes along with the elf persona. What's gotten into you?"

"That guy on the phone just now? Somebody named Wyatt in Utah, not too far away."

"Was he threatening to hurt me?"

"No," Declan grunted. "He wants to take you out."

Holly released a breathless laugh. "Well, that's a relief."

"Really? I think it's disturbing."

"Declan, I'm on several social media sites. Even if I didn't put it out there where I live, people could easily find out. They have found out. Most of them are harmless."

Jealousy and worry warred within him like a vortex, a part of him arguing Holly was a grown woman who'd been doing this a long time, and the rest of him knowing it only took one loon to tip the deck.

"What about the ones who aren't?" Declan asked quietly, realizing his fingers still circled her wrist a little tighter now. The thought of Holly in that big house alone when some obsessed fan showed up at her place bottomed out his stomach.

Holly didn't shake him off or get angry, but came around the counter next to him without breaking contact. "Are you worried about me, Declan?"

Why was she looking at him like that with those soft brown eyes sucking him in?

"I just think it's reckless to put everything out there on social media."

"Because I'm a woman?"

Her sweet perfume surrounded him, and he released her wrist, his fingers brushing back a strand of hair that had fallen into her face. "No. No one should share too much online, man or woman."

"At least if someone abducted me, you wouldn't have to listen to my music anymore."

"That's not funny, Elf."

Holly took a step closer. "Declan Gallagher, I think you'd miss me."

"Maybe I would."

The front door opened, shattering the moment, and Declan took the escape like a coward. Stepping away from Holly, he cleared his throat and greeted Maureen Johnson.

"What can I do for you?"

"Hi, Declan. I just bought this new entertainment center and it's missing a bolt like this," she said, holding up some small metal hardware. "I was hoping you might have something that would work. Hi, Holly!"

"Hi, Maureen." Holly backtracked from behind the counter. "I'd better pick up lunch and get back to my shop. Good to see you."

"You too."

Declan's gaze followed Holly to the door, where she stopped and smiled at him. "See you later."

No snark or sass-laced tone, just a cheerful goodbye before Holly disappeared outside. Something had shifted between them and while he couldn't exactly pinpoint what, his head was screaming to be afraid.

Every other part of him couldn't wait to see her again.

CHAPTER 9

AFTER SHE LOCKED THE DOORS, Holly headed down the sidewalk towards her car, which was parked in the opposite direction of the hardware store. She was tempted to backtrack and say good night to Declan, but the super-charged moment between them combined with his concerns left an anxious flutter in her stomach for hours. She'd ended up removing Declan's prank call video, although she still found little Gunner's mom in the comments and sent them a gift card, along with four others who were longtime followers. Holly posted a video announcing the winners and left it at that.

It wasn't that Holly didn't consider possible dangers of living in the spotlight. She'd blocked numerous creeps over the years, but never had anyone shown up here looking for her. She wanted to think Declan was paranoid, but his concerns got her thinking and she couldn't seem to stop.

Holly opened up her car door and as she climbed in noticed a baseball bat lying on the passenger seat with several loops of barbed wire wrapped around the head. She picked up the white sheet of paper next to the bat and read the short note.

Made for your protection. —D

Holly punched the number he'd written at the bottom of the paper into her phone and sent a text.

> **Is there a zombie horde in Mistletoe I don't know about?**

Several seconds passed before her phone beeped.

> **Huh? Who is this?**

She tapped out another message, smiling as she responded. It's Holly. Unless you go around leaving Negan's bat on other people's seats.

> **What's a Negan?**

Holly sighed in disbelief and texted: Are you for real? The Walking Dead's Negan? Anti-hero who wields a barbed wire-wrapped bat named Lucille?

> **Never seen it. I don't like horror. I just made it with some extra stuff I had lying around to inflict maximum damage.**

Holly laughed aloud. She could just see herself walking out every night with that bat in hand, waving to people as she passed. They'd think she lost her mind.

She texted: As far as pranks go, breaking into my car for this is a weird one.

> **It's not a prank. It's a gift.**
> Future reference, I prefer chocolate and caffeine to weapons of arm-length destruction.
> **Noted. Next time I'll make you a crossbow out of coffee beans.**
> That sounds cool, but you might want to include a coffee grinder. I buy k-cups.
> **You're missing out. Fresh coffee beats everything.**

Holly picked up the bat, spinning it in her hand. If anything, she could always dress up as Negan for Halloween next year.

She responded: I don't have the patience in the morning for that. I'm barely functioning before my first cup.

> I'll have to bring you over some.

Holly's stomach fluttered as she typed: I never turn down free coffee.

Delivering gourmet coffee sounded suspiciously like a date, unless...

> You're not going to put something funky in it, are you?

She put her car into gear and backed out of her parking space, but instead of heading directly home Holly drove towards Nick's apartment. Despite the shifting direction of her interest in Declan, that didn't change the fact that someone in her family had betrayed her. If it wasn't her big brother, she'd be hitting her sister's place next.

Holly parked along the street and before climbing out she grabbed the bat off the seat. She held her phone up and snapped a selfie of her and the bat and sent it to Delilah.

> Say hello to my wooden friend.

Holly backed out of her inbox and saw Declan had shot her another message while she was driving.

> LOL I promise the first cup is funk free. How do you take it?

It took a moment for Holly to realize what he was talking about and laughed. She responded: A little coffee and a lot of cream.

> Any particular kind of cream? I have special stuff if you want to leave room.

Holly climbed the stairs to the second-floor apartment with the bat over her shoulder, stopping a few doors down. She knocked on the door and when Nick answered, Holly said loudly, "Nicky, yous got some 'splaining to do!"

"What are you doing? Is that—"

Holly pointed the bat at him, cutting off his question. "Did you or did you not tell Declan Gallagher I am afraid of snakes?"

"I did not. Why?"

She squinted one eye at him. "Are you lying?"

"Why would I lie?"

"What's going on out here?" Noel asked, coming up alongside Nick.

"Just my sister threatening me."

Noel smacked his arm. "What did you do?"

"Nothing, she thinks I told Declan Gallagher she's scared of snakes but I didn't."

Noel stepped back, waving her hand. "He doesn't have that high, squeaky thing in his voice when he lies, so he's not your culprit. And in case I'm on your suspect list, I swear I'm innocent."

Holly sighed. "I was pretty sure it was Merry with Clark as her mouthpiece, but I had to be sure."

"Now that we've got that cleared up, you want to come in? We ordered a large pack of tacos and there's plenty."

"I love tacos," Holly said, stepping inside.

"Hey, we are not feeding her," Nick protested as the two of them walked farther into the apartment. "She just threatened me!"

Noel rolled her eyes. "But did she follow through? No. Stop being so dramatic."

"Yeah, Nick. Why you gotta make a big deal about everything?"

Nick shut the door with a grumble.

Holly took a seat at the counter in their kitchen, grinning when her phone vibrated. Delilah responded with three heart-eyed emojis.

OMG love it!

Holly clicked out of the message without responding and saw Declan had shot her a sendoff of: See you in the A.M.

"What's that smile for?" Noel asked.

"Delilah was responding to my bat pic." Although it wasn't the only reason, Holly wasn't willing to talk to anyone about Declan until she figured out what she was feeling.

"Speaking of, where did you get it?" Nick asked as he joined them in the kitchen.

"Believe it or not, Declan."

"I thought he hated you?" Nick asked.

"We've been developing a mutual respect for each other during this prank war. It's funny, I played another prank on him by asking my followers to call the store and tell him holiday jokes, but it made him paranoid."

"What do you mean?" Noel asked, placing two wrapped tacos on a plate and passing it to Holly.

"One of the callers said he is single, lives nearby in Utah, and wants to take me out. Declan thought it was strange that my followers know where I'm from."

"It's not strange, it's fucking creepy," Nick said.

Holly shrugged. "Maybe, but it's part of the glamorous life of an influencer."

"Is pranking going to be your new thing?" Noel asked, taking a bite of her taco.

"Who told you I was looking for a new thing?"

Noel pointed to Nick with a cough, and he paused mid-chew, his gaze shifting between them. "What? I didn't know it was a secret you were tired of dressing up like an elf."

"It's not, but I don't understand why my business seems to be everyone in this family's business."

"Because you are a part of this family," Nick said.

"To answer your question," Holly addressed Noel, ignoring Nick's sarcasm, "no, pranking isn't going to be my new thing. I want to find something not so intricate that I can just take a fun video and upload it."

"What about a cooking channel? I love BDylanHollis because he's funny and dramatic, just like you."

Nick snorted. "Except Holly can't cook."

Holly simultaneously finished her second taco and flipped her brother off.

"Am I wrong?" he asked.

Holly swallowed and hopped up from the stool, going to their fridge for a drink. "While I hate to admit it, no, you are not wrong."

Noel snapped her fingers. "You could play the drums."

"Meh," Holly said.

"Cosplay?" Nick offered.

"I said easy, not spending hours on make-up and costuming! I'm trying to get away from that."

"I'm tapped, then. I sing for a small audience and that's enough for me. I'd shit myself singing for hundreds of thousands of fans on social media. Hand me a cola too, please."

Holly went ahead and got one for Nick too, setting the cans in front of them. "It's okay, I'll figure it out, but I want to have Adventure Elf retired by the new year."

"You could take that dude from Utah up on his offer and do

a series about a perpetually single woman dating men from the internet," Nick said.

"And give Mom and Dad a coronary? No thanks."

"Well, if you ever get worried about shifty fans showing up, we've got a really comfy couch," Noel said.

"Or you could get a roommate or two," Nick blurted out, glaring at Noel.

"I've thought about roommates, but I like my space. Unless it was a fantastic friend or someone I trusted who was in a hard place, I couldn't imagine living with anyone."

Noel nodded. "I thought the same thing until I moved in with this guy. Now I couldn't imagine sleeping without his snoring."

"Aww, babe." Nick leaned over and kissed Noel, who turned a deep shade of red.

"Grossly romantic," Holly deadpanned.

Noel laughed. "Despite your brother's lack of enthusiasm, the door is always open to you, Hol."

"Thanks, but I've got Kringle now to protect me."

Noel cocked her head. "Kringle?"

Holly waved to the bat propped against the wall and Noel and Nick laughed.

"Great name. Declan's going to hate it though."

She grinned. "I know. It's going to be great!"

CHAPTER 10

SATURDAY MORNING, DECLAN SAT AT the kitchen table drinking his morning coffee and waiting for his dad to get up. Declan had been letting Liam do his thing all week without prying, but he felt like a parent worrying about a rebellious teenager. He wouldn't tell his dad that, but when Liam strolled in after midnight last night Declan had been ready to rip into Liam for worrying him. But his dad had a pretty good buzz on, smiling and singing his way down the hall. Whoever this mystery friend was, they weren't good for his dad and Declan planned on telling him so.

With as much finesse as possible.

His phone vibrated beside him several times and when he checked his phone, Holly had sent him a dozen Christmas GIFs via text message, the last of a young Grinch lifting a Christmas tree with the caption I HATE CHRISTMAS!

The final message was a picture of Holly standing in front of a tree holding a hammer ornament with a bow on it.

You could come help, you know.

Declan grinned and sent her a picture of him with his coffee. *Some of us have to work today.*

Liam's door opened and closed, and Declan heard the familiar sound of shuffling feet before Liam crossed the threshold into the kitchen, squinting at Declan. "You're up early."

Declan set his phone off to the side, ignoring the vibration. "It's after nine, Dad."

"Is it? Huh. Shouldn't you be opening the store?"

"I'm opening it late today. Got to get my tux for Clark's wedding."

"Clark who?"

Declan didn't get upset that his dad didn't remember him talking about Clark. The two of them had never met. "Just a friend. He's engaged to Merry Winters."

"Is that Chris and Victoria's girl? The redhead?"

"No, that's Holly. Merry is blonde."

"Ah, I like that Holly. Doesn't take any guff and isn't afraid to speak her mind."

Declan almost laughed. "You called her an annoying carrot top before."

"When?"

"Several times, but most recently last year during the holidays."

"Well, I've changed my mind." His dad hummed his way over to the coffee pot and poured himself a mug.

"What's wrong with you?" Declan asked bluntly.

So much for finesse.

"Pardon?"

"What's with the humming and the fluttering about and

coming and going all day and night? Who is this friend who's suddenly taking you out drinking and bringing you home stumbling to your room?"

Liam turned around to face Declan and crossed his arms over his chest. "Now wait a second. Last time I checked, I was the father in this duo."

Declan lost the threadbare rein on his temper and hit the table with his palm. "But you're sick, Dad! Like it or not, you have Alzheimer's and even though it's early, I worry. I want to make sure whoever you're with knows what to do if you have a moment and will take care of you, not feed you alcohol—"

"We shared a bottle of wine, Declan. I wasn't drunk, I was happy. For the first time in almost fifteen years. Like you said, I have a disease and my mind is going, but before it's gone I finally want to live my life." His dad sat down across from him, leaning back in his chair. "Which is why I'm thinking of selling the store."

Declan stared at him, his mind spinning like a fun tube. "You are?"

"Yes. I know running the hardware store was never something you wanted, and while I appreciate you stepping up, you should be living your own life. Besides, with the way things are going in the world, Mistletoe Hardware will be obsolete in a few years. Maybe sooner. At least if I sell everything, it's all profit and I can use the money to enjoy my remaining time on this earth."

Declan couldn't believe it. The man across from him looked like Liam Gallagher, and even sounded like him, but every word coming out of his mouth was foreign. No grumpy snark or pessimistic rants. He sounded happy, hopeful, and Declan had no idea how to respond to it except—

"Blink once if you need help."

"What?" Liam picked up his coffee with a huff. "Look, since my diagnosis, I've been evaluating my priorities. Really assessed my life choices." He took a sip of his coffee and set it down. "Maybe that's why I was so angry at your mother for leaving. She chose herself, the right way."

"The right—what are you talking about, the right way? She waited until I was leaving for college, packed up her stuff, and went jaunting around the world without a second glance."

"Marriage is complicated, son. I was furious for a long time. At her and...myself. It takes two to tango."

"What does that mean?" Declan asked.

Liam stood up with his coffee and patted Declan on the back with his free hand as he passed. "It means stop treating me like a child and get a damn life."

Declan turned in his chair, hollering, "Kim's supposed to come over and stay with you."

"I already told her not to."

He got up from his chair and followed his dad down the hallway. "Why the hell not?"

"Because I'm going out of town overnight, so there will be no one for her to keep an eye on."

"Where are you going?"

"Declan?" Liam said, stepping into the bathroom.

"What?"

"Mind your own damn business, kid."

His father slammed the door in his face and Declan shook his head, stomping back into the kitchen to pour his coffee into a travel mug. Get a life? His dad had the nerve to say that to him, after everything Declan had sacrificed? He'd had a life, a good life, and he'd given it up to come back here…and now his dad was telling him Liam didn't need him?

Declan sat back down with his coffee for a moment, going over the conversation in his head. If his dad sold the store, what would he do here in Mistletoe? He loved working in his studio, but his paintings were tucked away collecting dust. Before he'd left everything behind back in Maryland, he'd been working at a gallery, hoping to go back for his masters and run it someday, or become a professor if a position opened up teaching art. If his dad didn't need him, what was he going to do next?

Right, you give up everything and he dismisses you like you're a pest?

Declan gulped down the rest of his coffee angrily, wincing as the warm brew burned its way down his throat. He set his travel mug in the sink without rinsing it, something he never did, and stormed out of the house, tempted to not even open the store today. He'd stay in the studio and finish his landscape and forget about everything else. His dad's strange behavior. The holidays. The girl next door slowly driving him crazy.

As he backed out of the driveway, his thoughts drifted to Wednesday when he'd had her up on that counter. She'd almost come to his chin, and the scent of her surrounded him, putting him under a spell. At least that was the only way to describe his sudden need to tease her, taste her. If her employee hadn't walked in, he'd have taken that step forward and kissed her. It didn't make any sense, but it was the second time he'd been in Holly Winters' proximity that he'd been overwhelmed with the need to kiss her.

She'd probably have slapped him for trying, anyway, since she'd suggested they go back to hating each other as soon as her check was cashed.

Hate wasn't the right word for what he felt, especially the last few days. Something had changed between them since the prank calls, a shift of playfulness he found himself anticipating. When he'd brought her coffee on Thursday, she'd laughed at the snakes he'd drawn all over the white travel cup, then studied them with admiration he couldn't help being affected by. He knew that his work was good, maybe not great, but her reaction made him excited, especially when she started asking him how he'd done it and he'd spent almost a half hour talking about the different shading techniques, until he realized he'd been gone too long and had to get back to the store. As Declan was leaving, she'd taken a sip of the coffee and called out to him. "Declan?"

He'd stopped in the doorway and turned.

"You're right. This is amazing," she said, holding up the cup.

"I'm sorry, could you say those words again?"

Holly laughed. "Never. And if you tell anyone I said it—"

"Yeah, yeah, you'll come for me." He had no idea what possessed him, but he'd winked. "I'll be next door waiting."

Even when he'd found gel window clings on every window of his truck that night, it hadn't bothered him the way it used to. In fact it had the opposite effect, and that disturbed him, especially now with the possibility of getting his life back. He could have a playful acquaintance now, maybe even a friendship, but there were too many complications in play for romance.

As if he even knew how to be romantic.

Even when Holly exasperated him on the daily, there were other times she got fired up about something and he couldn't help watching her. The way her brown eyes darkened to near-black or that smile that seemed to light up every space she inhabited. The way she stood up to him, arms crossed over generous breasts or those soft hands planted on her curvy hips. Over the years he'd had a few dreams about Holly Winters he'd never tell anyone about, especially not her, but they'd seemed to increase with frequency the last few weeks. He thought about the night in the snow, and now anytime she was near he found himself watching that Cupid's bow mouth as she talked and Declan knew something had to be done.

Maybe instead of cutting himself off from the world, he should see if Clark and the other guys in the bridal party wanted to meet up for a drink at Brews and Chews tonight. Check out the single life of Mistletoe and stop thinking about Holly as anything other than his neighbor. If his dad wanted him to find something to occupy his time and keep Declan from worrying about him, he could do that.

But someone to occupy his time would be better.

His hand came up to stroke his face, considering his beard. He'd let it grow out before he'd moved back to Mistletoe because his ex liked facial hair, and he hadn't really settled on a reason to shave it. In the past, Holly had called it his soup catcher, but was an aversion to beards just *her* preference? Or did other women feel the same way?

Declan took a parking spot near the bridal shop and checked his phone.

Work my bahookie! I know you're getting your tux
on. Have fun. It's probably better you aren't here,
anyway. You'd probably put more than one ornament
on a limb and make my OCD spike.

Declan laughed aloud as he typed back: How did you know?

He got out, ambling toward the front door, and when he
stepped inside Nick and the other guys were standing off to the
side of the counter, watching Clark in a black tux getting pins and
needles stuck in him.

Clark pointed a finger at Declan when he spotted him. "You!
Your snake prank got me in hot water."

Declan smirked. "Why is that?"

"Because Holly called Merry, ripping into her for telling you
about her biggest fear, and when Merry said she hadn't talked to
you, my fiancée's gaze turned to me. Now both my soon-to-be-
sister-in-law and Merry are mad at me because of you."

"Don't feign innocence, man. You knew I'd use the information for evil."

"At the very least I thought you'd throw Nick under the bus,"
Clark grumbled.

"Hey, she came by my apartment and threatened me with a
baseball bat Declan made for her. I feared for my very life," Nick said,
rubbing his trigger finger over the other. "Shame on the both of you."

"Whatever, old man," Clark said, shrugging out of the tuxedo
jacket and handing it to the seamstress.

"Eat me, Clark," Nick muttered.

"That reminds me," Pike said, rubbing his hands together.

"We didn't give Nick his birthday spanking. Anthony, Sam, hold him for me."

Sam leaned against the wall, his plastic-covered tuxedo draped over his arm. "I'm not getting involved in your kinks, Pike."

"I second that," Anthony said.

"Is it your birthday?" Declan asked Nick.

"It was Wednesday, but we're having a joint birthday party tonight after the Festival of Trees. Since all the Winters kids were born in December, and with the wedding, it's a lot to do four separate birthday parties. Plus Noel's birthday is Christmas Eve and she always seems to get the short end. You should come."

"Nah, man, it sounds like a family thing and I don't want to crash it."

"We're not family, and we crash it every year," Pike said.

Anthony adjusted his ball cap. "I'm invited. He tags along."

"Dick."

"I'm technically not family either, but they let me come over and drink their beer because Victoria loves me," Sam said.

"Dude, I've told you. Don't say my mom's name like that," Nick growled.

Clark stepped down off the square platform he'd been standing on. "I'm going to get changed out of this monkey suit, but seriously, Declan, you should come. The Winters family is the definition of the more the merrier."

Nick clapped him on the back. "Besides, now it's a matter of principle, because if I tell my mom you're coming and you don't show up, you'll hurt her feelings."

"And we don't tolerate anyone hurting his mom's feelings," Pike said, cracking his knuckles.

Declan looked around the room at the expectant male faces, thinking that his plan to get away from Holly Winters just blew up in his face.

CHAPTER 11

"YOU INVITED DECLAN GALLAGHER TO my birthday party?" Holly said, punching Nick on the arm. They were standing in the Winters' living room next to the Christmas tree Chris and Victoria bid on at the festival of trees today. They'd decided not to go with their traditional ornaments and try something new. The kids had taken all the trimmings off, hauled it into their living room, and barely finished putting the star on the top before Nick dropped the bomb about Declan.

"Ow. Technically, it's my party too. But don't blame me! It was Clark!"

Holly drew back her fist to punch Clark's arm too, but Merry caught it, preventing her fiancé from being pummeled. "No more breaking my things, Holly. You aren't six."

"Should I be offended you're comparing me to a toy?" Clark asked.

"No, because I'm protecting you from her, even after you used me to help your friend seek revenge on Holly."

Holly pointed her finger at him, a mock scowl on her face. "Yeah, you failed as my future brother-in-law."

If Holly were being honest with herself, it wasn't anger at seeing Declan tonight that kicked up her heart rate, but excitement. Sometime today he'd swung by the Festival of Trees and wrapped her SUV in Christmas paper. Inside was an ice chest with a holiday chocolate box inside.

You said coffee or chocolates. You need to lock your car—D

"Come on, Declan's a good guy. I think if the two of you just stopped this dumb prank war, you might actually find some common ground."

"Or maybe that's what you should do for your new channel," Merry said, picking up an empty ornament box. "Pranking people."

Nick shook his head. "Noel and I suggested it, and Holly said it would be too much work. She wants something easy, with no elaborate costume changes, make-up, or props."

"That is correct. Although I could do a holiday series where I prank my siblings and in-laws until they beg for forgiveness."

"Hey, why am I lumped in with those two?" Nick asked.

"I'm sure you'll commit a future transgression against me. It's only a matter of time."

Nick turned to Merry and Clark with one eyebrow raised. "Will Mom miss her if we tie her up and throw her in the closet?"

"As the baby of the family, I think yes," Merry said grimly.

"Funny, I'm the baby of my family and my parents didn't care where I was," Clark mused.

"You're all hilarious, except Clark who's kind of sad," Holly said. "And by the way, Clark, your buddy wrapped my car like a

Christmas present today, so don't try to play like he's the innocent victim in this prank war. He's having as much fun as I am. In fact, since he's coming, I've got an idea."

Clark pointed at Holly. "This is why I'm scared of her and not you. That look on her face is pure diabolical evil."

"When Declan leaves, I'm going to sit in the back seat and let off one of those poppers Mom bought for New Year's Eve and scare the heck out of him. Merry, you want to record? I probably won't post it, but I want to relive the laugh when he jumps two feet in the air."

"Kids, get in here and help me set out the food. It's not fair that Noel, Jace, and I are the only ones doing any work," Victoria called, carrying a large salad bowl to the table.

"Hey, we decorated the tree," Merry said.

Noel arched an eyebrow as she carried several bottles of various salad dressings to the table. "Funny how it took four of you for that, meanwhile your mom and I have been running around like chickens with their heads cut off."

"Wah, wah, wah," Holly sang, and Noel reached out to yank a strand of her hair. "Oh, you want to hair pull now? Let's take this outside, sis."

Nick put his arm around Noel, steering her toward the living room. "Come away from the crazy sister, babe. She bites."

"I'm in charge of the pizzas," Jace said, carrying a lidless box with a browned pepperoni pizza inside. "This one's mine."

Clark chuckled, ruffling his son's hair. "I don't think so, little man."

"Where is everyone?" Victoria asked.

Merry looked over at the clock and shared a bewildered look with Holly. "You told people to be here at seven and it is six-forty-five."

"I'm wrong for thinking that people should be early?"

"Yes, because no one wants to be the nerd who is first to a party," Holly said.

The doorbell rang, and Butch, the Winters' elderly bloodhound, howled from the back room. A second round of deep, booming barks joined the mournful sound and Jace took a step down the hall. "Can I let the dogs out, please?"

"After we're done eating," Victoria said. "Daisy has a bad habit of stealing food when my back is turned. Holly, can you grab that?"

Holly went to answer the door, calling over her shoulder, "Speaking of nerds, this is probably Pike and Anthony with a thirty-pack for Nick and a couple of cases of fruity drinks for Merry and me. At least we won't run out of alcohol."

Holly pulled the door open mid-laugh and froze that way with her mouth hanging open and all sound died. Declan stood on her parents' front step in a pressed button-down shirt and jeans with four packages in hand, but that wasn't the startling part.

"You shaved your beard," Holly said softly, her gaze following the lines of his jaw to the adorable butt chin. It drew attention to the angle of his cheekbones, and the fading bruise under his eye from the incident with the rooftop Santa was more noticeable, but it made his green eyes pop brighter. With the soup catcher he was hot in a man-who-lives-in-the-woods kind of way, but with his full lips on display and no mustache to hide them?

The man was freaking gorgeous.

"Yeah, I thought it was time for a change," he said, holding the packages out to her. "I wasn't sure what to bring."

It was hard to believe this was the same man who dropped snakes on her a few days ago. He seemed almost shy, like all the confidence and anger came with the beard, and without it he was a completely different person.

"Are you going to let me in or did I drive fifteen minutes out here to get the door slammed in my face?"

Holly stepped back, giving him room to pass. "Sorry, I'm used to you looking like Gollum from *The Lord of the Rings* instead of an elf."

"I'm too tall to be Gollum," he said, leaning closer to whisper, "Elf."

The affectionate way he spoke that single word rippled down her spine like a shiver.

"Declan!" Holly's dad called, getting up from his recliner and extending his hand to the newcomer. "How are you doing? How's the head?"

"Hard as ever, sir."

"Call me Chris. We're all adults here." Chris waved to the gifts Declan was carrying and added, "Holly, why don't you grab those and put them somewhere. Come on in, son. Take a load off."

Holly held her arms out for the packages and Declan set them in her arms, his full lips smirking. "The pink one is for you."

"Is it a stink bomb this time? Or a real rattlesnake?"

"You'll have to open it to find out."

Holly didn't really think Declan would booby trap a gift for her to open in front of her family, but she could be wrong.

"By the way, thanks for the chocolates. They were worth unwrapping."

Declan grinned. "You're welcome."

Her dad called out to him again, and he walked away, leaving her still befuddled by the new Declan. She set the four gifts on the kitchen island, and her sister came up next to her, whispering, "Well, Declan sure cleans up nice, don't you think?"

"I know what you're doing and you need to stop," Holly grumbled.

"What am I doing?"

"You think there is some undercurrent of attraction and you're trying to make me realize it with your gentle prodding, but here is the issue, Mer. I'm a relationship no-go even with people I actually get along with and have things in common with. You really think anything is going to happen with a guy I'm constantly fighting with? I'm more likely to go out with Sam than Declan."

"Heard my name," Sam said, coming up alongside Holly and grabbing a beer from the large round cooler at the edge of the island. "Good things I hope?"

"Just that you're in my top five dateable men in Mistletoe," Holly said, slipping an arm around Sam's waist because she knew it would chase her sister off. Merry thought Sam would try to take advantage of Holly or something, but Sam was a friend, someone she never even considered crossing the line with.

She just hadn't told her sister that yet.

Merry shot Sam a death stare, and he threw up his hands. "I'm not touching her, she's touching me."

"Keep it that way," Merry warned, leaving them alone to go talk to Clark and Declan, who were hanging with Chris in the living room.

Holly's gaze met Declan's briefly before he turned his attention to whatever Clark was saying, and Holly extracted her arm from around Sam's waist.

"So, what did your sister do this time?" Sam asked, opening his beer bottle on the side of the ice chest.

"Trying to set me up with my mortal enemy, Declan Gallagher."

Are you really feeling that way, or putting on a show because you're afraid your family might pick up on your attraction to him?

She angled her head toward the living room and Sam followed her gesture, his expression considering.

"I didn't recognize him without the beard. I mean, not many guys are that tall, but he looks like an accountant all cleaned up like that."

"Well, he's not. He's a giant pain in my ass."

"Really? Then why do you keep sneaking glances at him?" Sam teased.

"I'm not!" she whispered harshly. Leave it to Sam to notice something like that!

"You sure? Cause he's doing the same thing to you. Of course, who could blame him. You in that dress?" Sam whistled. "We could make your sister's worst fears a reality."

Holly rolled her eyes, but appreciated the compliment. The knee-length black bodycon had been hanging in the back of her closet for far too long, and since she hadn't had a date in six months, by choice, she thought it was about time to bust it out.

"No thanks. I'm trying to avoid drama."

"Since when?" he asked.

"Since always!"

"Sorry," a deep voice said, drawing Holly's attention to Declan's moss-green eyes. "I want to grab a beer."

"Sure thing." Sam stepped out of the way, stroking the five-o'clock shadow on his own chin. "You look good, Declan. Did you do something different?"

Declan gave Sam a strained smile. "Funny, man." He popped the top off the beer and after a few seconds of awkward silence, he said, "I'll let you guys get back to it. Sorry to interrupt."

As Declan walked away, Holly's gaze drifted over the wide expanse of his shoulders until Sam cleared his throat.

"Maybe your sister has a point."

It took Holly a second to catch on before she scoffed. "Maybe you should climb a cactus."

Sam slapped a hand over his chest. "So aggressive."

Holly gave him a sharp nudge with her shoulder before she grabbed her coat off the hook and slipped outside to the front porch, drawing in a deep, crisp breath. The whole grade school analogy that if a boy likes you they're mean to you was so nineteenth century. Declan Gallagher did not have feelings for her.

And Holly definitely wasn't pining after him.

CHAPTER 12

AFTER ROUGHLY TEN MINUTES OF glancing toward the door, Declan excused himself from the conversation and headed outside. If Holly wondered why he was going to his car, he'd tell her it was to get his coat, when in reality he wanted to make sure she was all right. Watching her laughing with Sam before she stormed outside made him think there might be something going on, and for whatever reason, the thought of Sam and Holly didn't sit well with him. She was young, too young for Sam who was closer to forty than thirty.

Is it really the age difference that bothers you? Or was it seeing Holly's arm wrapped around Sam's waist?

When he stepped out onto the porch, Declan immediately caught sight of Holly leaning against the railing with her back to him, the multi-colored Christmas lights above her head turning her hair green, red, and blue. When she looked over her shoulder and saw him, Holly raised one of her brows in a high arch.

"What are you doing out here?" she said.

"Going to get my coat from the car."

"Why? It's warm inside and it's only a few hundred feet to your car."

He slowed on the top step. "You've got me there."

"Let me guess," she said, taking a few steps closer. "Not big on social gatherings?"

"What gave it away?"

Holly shrugged. "I never see you out at Brews or anywhere really. Just the store, and I assume you go home afterwards because your truck is always in the driveway."

Declan ignored the little leap of his heart that she'd checked on her way home.

"What is it?"

"What is what?" he asked.

"Is it the loud music at the bar? The conversation inside? Why do you want to be alone?"

"I don't. I just—" Declan struggled for an answer. "Why are *you* out here? You're Miss Social Butterfly. You do the plays down at the local theater, involved in all the town events. So why is Holly Winters outside during her birthday party?"

"Sometimes my family is too much and I need a break. My parents are amazing, loving, kind, but I'm still their baby. While Nick acts like a big brother when he wants, he's pretty laid back, but Merry always seems worried about me. I've been out on my own since I was eighteen, but they all check on me and worry—" Holly shook her head, a light chuckle escaping her lips. "Way to deflect the subject off you and onto me."

"It's a gift," he said with a small smile.

"I guess I don't have that barrier. I like talking about myself."

"I've noticed."

Holly stuck her tongue out at him. "Hey, you are more than welcome to keep moving if it bothers you so much."

"Did I say that?" he asked, her teasing like a warm glow drawing him in. "I was simply agreeing with you."

"Well, forgive me if I can't tell when you're criticizing me or not."

"I don't like the holidays. I'm not going to apologize for it. It doesn't make me a bad guy."

"Doesn't make you a good one either," she muttered.

"Fair enough."

Holly hopped onto the railing, putting her back to the front yard. "Can you at least tell me why you hate Christmas?"

Declan stiffened, hating the earnestness he saw in her eyes. She was genuinely trying to get to know him, and he couldn't bring himself to be honest. Not about his past, certainly not about his family.

"Santa didn't bring you what you really wanted and you swore revenge against the jolly fat man?" Holly asked.

"Is that the plot of a movie?"

"Probably, but now I'm just throwing out guesses."

"Why does it bother you so much?"

"Because I love it. I mean, I run a holiday shop and live on a street known for its Christmas lights display. My family owns a Christmas tree farm, we all were born in December, and all have Christmas-themed names. It's ingrained."

"Nick is supposed to be for?"

"Saint Nicholas, of course," she said.

"Gotcha. But that explains why *you* love Christmas. Why do *I* need to like it?"

Holly didn't answer for several seconds and finally shrugged. "That first day in the store, I thought you were cute. There was no point in making a move on you if you were a rotten Scrooge though."

Declan reeled back in surprise. "You thought I was cute?"

"Until you opened your mouth and were a giant turd, yes."

"I can see why you might have thought that. To be fair, your confidence about converting me rubbed me wrong."

"Oh, so not only are you a Christmas-hating jerk, you're against confident women?"

Declan spluttered. "That is not what I meant! I just don't feel like Christmas is all it's cracked up to be. The suicides skyrocket this time of year, power bills surge, people overspend and get themselves into debt."

"And that's why you hate it? Because of what other people do?" Holly grabbed his hand out of the blue and dragged him out onto the lawn.

"What are you doing? It's snowing."

"Barely, but hang with me for a minute. Look at my parents' place and tell me what you see."

Declan studied the dark roof lit up by flashing lights, the glowing wreath on the front door, and open windows where he could see the people inside talking and laughing.

"I see a house. Christmas lights. Snow-covered grass—"

"All right, Mr. Literal. Let me tell you what I see." She pointed to the Santa on the roof that had almost killed Declan, and the eight reindeer arranged to appear as if they were about to take flight. "The bright lights make me smile, which creates this warm glow in my chest and that heat spreads throughout my entire body. The music you detest so much brings back memories of my mother baking cookies, my siblings and I hanging too many ornaments on a branch and my mom sneaking behind us to fix them. I see my family inside, and even though I know we don't always get along there is so much love when we're together. That is what the holidays are to me."

Declan didn't know how to respond, so he said nothing. He hated Christmas carols because they reminded him of when his family used to be happy together. He despised the smell of holiday baking because it brought back memories of his mom, which took him back to anger because she got out and didn't come back. Christmas lights reminded him of traffic jams and his parents fighting about money—

"Declan?" Holly placed a hand on his arm and the warmth of her palm made him realize he was freezing.

"Yeah, sorry, was trying to relate and failed. I think I'm going to get my coat after all."

"All right, I guess I'll see you in there."

Declan made it onto the sidewalk before he turned and blurted out her name. "Holly?"

"Yeah?" she asked, turning on the top step.

"I wish I could see this time of year through your eyes. Maybe...maybe we'd be in a different place."

"You mean where I'm not spraying you with confetti and recording it for social media?"

"What?"

She came back down the stairs, shaking her head. "When I found out you were coming, I wanted to get you back for the snakes. I was going to pop confetti onto you as soon as you got into the car and scare you. I was going to have Merry record it—"

He stiffened. "And post it online? Without asking me?"

Holly's eyes widened. "No! I just wanted to see you jump." She took a step toward him. "It was only going to be a prank, Declan. Like we've been doing all week."

"It is one thing to stuff my car with gnomes or spray me with streamers, but you were going to put my business out there on the internet."

"I wasn't!"

"How do I really know that?" he said harshly. "You know I'm a private person, and just because you don't mind making an idiot out of yourself doesn't mean—" Declan caught the flash of hurt and cursed. "I didn't mean...I just don't want to make a spectacle of myself."

"Unlike me, right?" Holly stomped down the steps until she was less than a foot away from him and poked him in the chest so hard he took a step back. "You know, I'm not ashamed of what I've accomplished. I'm debt-free. I've had money put away and incurring interest since I was twenty, so retirement isn't an issue. If I have to put up with some judgmental assholes making asinine comments or calling me *elf*, I'll take it...all the way to the bank.

"And for the record, I would have asked your permission if I wanted to put your video up, but you assume the worst of me.

Why? I swear, every time I think there's more to you than being an angry, temperamental miser, you prove me wrong."

Holly spun away from him, and he chased her, taking hold of her arm. "Holly! Holly, stop. Please."

"Why?"

"I—" A lump lodged in his throat, blocking the words. He struggled to open up to Clark. To his dad. But for some reason, he wanted to explain why he was this way to this short, feisty redhead.

He dropped his hand from her and backed up a step. "You're out here trying to avoid your family because they love you too much. You have nothing but fond memories for this time of year, but not all of us get to have that. I may be a judgmental jerk, but you're not perfect."

"I never said I was perfect!"

"But you believe that anyone who doesn't think like you needs to be fixed or changed."

Holly stood there, mouth agape, and Declan couldn't stay. Why did everything with them go so terribly wrong just when he thought they were heading towards something more?

"Please convey my apologies to your parents, but I need to go."

Declan didn't wait to see if she'd try to stop him, not that he thought she would. Maybe if things had gone differently that first day they wouldn't be here now, but it was too late to change things now.

Two years too late.

CHAPTER 13

HOLLY FINISHED MAKING HER LAST pre-recorded TikTok and took off the elf hat, tossing it onto the side table. She'd set up this room in the back of the store to record content during her downtime and it had definitely come in handy, but lip-sync videos wouldn't satisfy her audience. Holly needed to figure out what was in store for her YouTube channel and how to transition her audience away from Adventure Elf.

She'd had some interesting requests, from climbing a pine tree and zip lining down, to the more scandalous suggestion that she wrestle another girl in a pool of eggnog. She hated to disappoint her fans, who were the reason Holly was able to buy A Shop for All Seasons to begin with, but she was running out of steam for adventurous content. Her current audience didn't appreciate her recent videos quite like watching her paraglide through the sky.

Holly shrugged out of the elf costume and hung it up on the metal clothing pole with a few other outfits she kept back there. Declan's reaction about taking a video of him had been eating at her. She'd managed to avoid him so far, but she still had four days of work left this week.

It didn't help that Declan's accusations made her wonder if she really was partly to blame for the breakdown between them. She knew nothing about Declan, and Holly could recall several times being so presumptuous she winced in response to the memories. She'd thought they'd been having fun, but maybe she misread the prank war.

Holly dragged a hand over her face. There was no maybe about it. He'd wrapped her car like a present and left her chocolates, and she'd tried to scare him. She was an idiot.

While he absolutely had a temper and a habit of saying whatever popped into his head without thinking about who it might hurt, Holly had heard the upset in his voice. The sliver of guilt that tone created only deepened when she opened his gift and pulled out a beautiful painting of the Winters family farm. She'd noticed the signature right away and yet another puzzle piece of Declan Gallagher she couldn't quite fit fell into her lap.

Once she'd righted her clothes, Holly turned off the light and headed out front. Tuesdays were usually slow, especially in the middle of the day, and she'd hired Erica, who was taking college courses online, to help out a couple times a week during the holidays.

Erica sat behind the counter, bent over an open textbook. She lifted her head when Holly stopped on the other side, her curly hair pulled back in a ponytail, drawing attention to her dark skin and high cheekbones. She smiled and rubbed her eyes as she leaned away from her book. "How did it go?"

"Got 'em done. Anyone come in?"

"Nope, it was quiet until Wes from Speedy Installations

called," Erica said, handing her a yellow sticky note, her red sparkly nails glittering in the overhead light. "He wants you to get back to him ASAP."

Holly frowned. Speedy set up her home display every year for the holiday season, and they were supposed to be over at her place tomorrow to work on her house.

"Thanks," Holly said, grabbing her jacket off the hook behind the counter. "I'll step out back to call them."

"No worries, I'm going to finish this chapter and then dust some shelves."

"I appreciate you." Holly went through the store and pushed out the back exit, sticking her little door prop in the gap to keep it open. The chilly air circled her immediately, stealing her breath and stinging the end of her nose as she pulled her cell out of her pocket. She couldn't help smiling when she didn't see Declan's truck. He'd parked out front the last few days, probably because there were more witnesses in case she tried anything, but Holly didn't have the stomach to prank Declan, not with the way they'd left things.

Holly tapped in Wes's number and hit the call button. He picked up on the second ring with a raspy "Hello?"

"Hi, Wes, it's Holly Winters. Everything okay?"

"Hey, Holly, it's actually not. Me and most of my crew are down with a nasty flu, and I'm not sure when we're going to be back to one hundred percent. I have to cancel some jobs and unfortunately your display is one of them."

Holly closed her eyes, panic settling into her stomach. "Please don't cancel. Maybe you'll feel better tomorrow. Perhaps you could do it in the morning and afternoon between other jobs?"

"I really can't. We were booked solid through the holidays before and this shi—" He caught himself, clearing his throat. "*Garbage* hit us all hard. I would squeeze you in if I could, but with most of my guys out, I'm stretched thin." Explosive coughing burst through the phone and Holly grimaced.

"It's okay, Wes. I get it. I hope you feel better."

"I can give you some other company recommendations, if you want."

"Sure, that would be great," Holly said.

He rattled off a few names, and she put him on speaker to type them into her notes app. After she told him goodbye, Holly leaned her head back against the building, thinking about her full story display featuring *How the Grinch Stole Christmas* she'd bought after the holidays last year. Some pieces were two-hundred pounds, much too heavy to carry by herself, and with her sister's bachelorette party next weekend and the wedding after Christmas, there was no way she could ask her family for help.

She dialed the first guy and got a similar story as Wes. Short-handed and overbooked. After fifteen minutes of phone calls, she'd deleted all the names and numbers he'd recommended and mentally crossed off the several she'd called after a Google search. If she didn't get that display up this weekend, not only would she get a fine from Theodore and the HOA but she'd be ineligible to enter the display contest. Every other house on the block already had theirs up, but Speedy couldn't get her in until now because everyone on the circle used Wes.

Holly went back inside the shop, running a hand over her face before remembering she'd put on make-up this morning. She stopped off in the bathroom to clean the smudges and headed up front, frustrated and defeated.

Erica was dusting the shelf of reindeer and glanced over her shoulder as Holly approached. "Hey, everything okay?"

"No, it's really not, but I'm going to keep smiling until it is," Holly said, pasting a painful smile on her face.

Eric turned away from the frolicking fawns with a frown. "What's wrong?"

"The guys who put up my Christmas lights display cancelled on me and it has to be up by Friday. People go to the Parade of Lights downtown, and after they leave they drive over to us, so it has to be finished by then. He gave me a bunch of names, but they're all booked."

"Oh, man. I'd offer to help but I'd probably fall off a ladder or electrocute myself."

Holly chuckled. "This is a huge job. Much bigger than one or two people could finish in a day."

"Are you sure? Because I think the guy next door does stuff like that. The one who dropped the snakes on you?"

"Declan!" Holly groaned.

"Yeah...why do you say it like that?"

"Because he's the devil." Did she mean it? No, but how could she walk next door and ask for his help after Saturday?

"That's an extreme accusation. Do you have any proof? Horns? A tail?" Erica teased.

"When did you switch your major to professional heckler?"

"Sorry, boss. I'm just saying you might want to ask him if you're in a pinch. I bet he'd be more than happy to help."

When hell freezes over.

"I don't think so."

"But why?"

"I thought calling him Satan covered it?"

"I think my lit professor is evil but I still go to class because I need him. Sometimes we have to suck it up to get what we want."

Holly mulled that over, thinking back to the day she'd walked into the hardware store with a plate of cookies for Mr. Gallagher because she'd hoped something sweet would warm the old grouch up a little. She'd been pleasantly surprised to find Declan instead, his beard neatly trimmed although she wasn't a big fan of facial hair, but his eyes were absolutely dreamy. While relationships had never been her strong suit, a little neighborly fun might have been in order.

If he hadn't turned out to be grumpier than his dad, their relationship might have gone in an entirely different direction, and last week she'd had hope that maybe they were almost becoming friends.

But she'd sunk that ship with a cannonball.

"You've been here when he stomps over like a giant man-baby about the music."

Erica shrugged. "Some people don't like Christmas music."

"People who hate joy and warm snugly feelings hate Christmas music." God, even Holly heard the judgy tone and grimaced. "I shouldn't say that."

Her employee laughed. "I mean, it's not my favorite but I'll listen to it."

"So I'm the bad guy because I like it?"

"I'm not saying you're the bad guy at all. He's definitely come in here hot and over the top, but I get the feeling *that's* about more than Christmas music."

"What do you mean?"

"The sexual tension between the two of you."

Holly sputtered. "There is *nothing* sexual between us. Period." Declan's face leaning into hers flashed through her mind, and she beat it back with a mental baseball bat.

Erica grinned slyly. "You may not want there to be any, but it's thick and juicy like an apple waiting to be sliced open."

"You're wrong."

"Then why don't you hire him?" Erica asked.

"Because I don't like him enough to give him my money."

"Looks like you've got more reasons than choices."

"Don't try to manipulate me with logic," Holly grumbled. There was no way Declan would take the job, not without extorting something from her. An apology? Another restriction on her music?

But Erica had a point. She was out of options.

"I'll be back."

"Where are you going?"

"To kill a piece of my soul."

Erica giggled. "Good luck. At least he's pretty to look at."

Holly couldn't disagree, but she didn't respond before pushing out the door and trekking down the sidewalk to the front of Mistletoe Hardware. Their very first conversation two years ago had ended on a sour note and their interactions had only gone downhill from there. She'd thought maybe last year he'd softened a bit when he'd agreed to buy a tree for the Festival of Trees, Mistletoe's biggest holiday fundraiser, but then he hadn't done anything with it. Just left it in the back of his store without even a bucket of water. When she'd confronted him about it, Declan told her he bought the tree, fulfilling his social obligation, but if she wanted it decorated to do it herself, same as this year. Here she was feeling guilty about one little mistake on her part, but he'd made a series of jerk moves.

The difference is you two weren't getting along when he hurt your feelings.

That little voice in her head was really starting to get annoying.

Now here she was, about to walk into the Grinch's lair and hire him to decorate her house for Christmas. How could she even be sure he wouldn't break her display or stall on purpose?

You're paying him, not asking a favor. Stop being paranoid.

Holly opened the door and stepped through. There were only a couple of people milling around the store that she could see, while Declan sat behind the counter with a pencil in hand, leaning over something intently. When he finally glanced up and noticed her, he took whatever he was working on and slid it into a drawer.

"What do you need?" he asked coolly.

"I—" She cleared her throat. "Thank you for the painting. It was lovely. I thought I might have to fight my mother for it."

Declan stood up straight, studying her with an inscrutable expression, the teasing, playful man from the week before gone. "You're welcome. Was there something else?"

Why was this so painful to get out? "You may have had a point about me being a judgy jackhole. There's no reason why you should have to love Christmas just because I do. I mean, you were more wrong, but…" Holly released a tense laugh. "Not the point."

"Anything else?"

Anger lit through her and Holly almost stormed out, but Erica's truth that she had more reasons than choices kept rolling through her mind like a mantra and Holly crossed the room to stand in front of the counter. "I know we've had our differences"—he snorted, and she pushed on without acknowledging it—"but I need to hire you."

His eyebrows shot up comically. "For what?"

"To put together my holiday home display."

Declan scoffed. "Yeah, right. Don't you have a company who does that?"

"They cancelled on me and everyone else is booked up. You're my last resort."

"What makes you think I'm not overwhelmed with jobs?"

"Faith, hope, and pixie dust?" she quipped.

"Huh?"

Holly rolled her eyes. "I was paraphrasing *Peter Pan*. You really were deprived as a kid."

"Judging again, Holly?"

Crap, get it together, Hol.

"No, of course not. Maybe you didn't own a TV."

"Just because I didn't sit around watching movies my whole childhood doesn't mean I was deprived," he growled, and Holly threw her hands up.

"I didn't come here to fight or insult you, honestly. Can we call a truce until our business is concluded?"

Declan leaned over the counter on his forearms and the sharp scent of cologne wrapped around her, spicy and delightful, and if he'd been anyone else she might have commented on it, but he'd probably think she was mocking him at this point. Her cheeks warmed thinking about how she'd mentioned how cute she thought he was.

Thought, past tense.

"I'll bite," he said, rubbing the side of his clean-shaven jaw. "How much are we talking?"

"I've paid twenty-five hundred in the past, but I'll give you three."

Declan whistled. "What kind of display? How big?"

"I mean…it's a five-man job."

"Are you sure? Or is that just what your former installer told you?"

"It's a huge undertaking. Everything has to go in a certain order and be specifically placed—"

"You're not going to be hovering over my shoulder the whole time, are you?"

Holly gritted her teeth. "Not if you're doing it right."

He crossed his arms over his chest with a sigh. "Before I agree, I'd like to take a look at it. Make sure I'm not getting in over my head because it is just me. How long do I have to finish this important undertaking?"

"Friday."

"Next Friday?"

"No, like, three days from now. Friday."

"You're killing me, Winters." Holly ignored the regretful

twinge that he hadn't called her Elf. Even though she'd brought it up when Holly was angry at him, the way he said it sometimes, almost tenderly, hadn't been horrible. In fact, it made her secretly smile.

"I'll come over tomorrow morning at eight."

"Great. Don't be late."

"I'll be punctual, but there's one more thing."

"What?"

"Should you really be so hostile when I'm your last hope?"

Holly was ready to tear her hair out. Or his. "I'm sorry, your other thing?"

"If I take the job, no more pranks. Ever."

Holly hated the triumphant gleam in his eyes but Erica had a point. She needed Declan. Painful to admit, but she did.

"If you fulfill your end, I'll never pull another prank on you."

"Magnanimous of you," he said.

"Oh, bite me!" Holly spun away from him, ignoring several gasps as she stomped out of the store and back to her shop. When she walked through the door, the alarm above let out a loud *ho ho ho* and for the first time she agreed with her sister Merry. That was annoying.

Erica looked up from dusting. "How did it go?"

"Like I need to bathe in holy water."

"But did he say yes?"

"He did."

Erica did a little hip dance. "Sexual tension for the win."

"Don't make me fire you."

CHAPTER 14

DECLAN CAME OUT OF HIS room Wednesday morning with Leo hot on his heels crying for his breakfast. It was half past seven and Declan glanced at the silent TV as he passed. Normally his dad was up at six tinkering around and then parked in front of the tube with a breakfast sandwich for a few hours to watch the morning news, but ever since he started hanging with this new friend, his father had completely abandoned his routine. And while Declan was glad his dad seemed happy, he still didn't like all the secrecy.

He poured a cup of dry food into Leo's dish and released a painful laugh when Leo used him as a climbing tree before launching himself onto the side counter where Declan put his bowl.

"You know, you're a little too big to be doing that."

Leo released an argumentative meow before diving face-first into his bowl.

Declan grabbed a protein bar from the cupboard, heading back down the hallway to knock on his dad's door.

"Dad? You up? I have to leave early for a job and wanted to say good-bye. I've got Kim coming over at eight, unless you've cancelled her again, so you might want to get moving."

The sound of muffled footfalls on the hardwood floors echoed behind the door for several seconds before it swung open. Instead of his dad standing in the doorway, his mom stepped out into the hall to face him, closing the door shut with a soft *snick* behind her. Her dark hair hung around her shoulders in disarray, silver threaded around her temples, and when she smiled at him the laugh lines around her eyes and mouth were deeper than they'd been the last time he'd seen her.

"Shhhh, your dad's still sleeping."

Declan's mouth hung open as he stared at her, processing what he was seeing at a snail's pace. It had been ten years since she'd left, and he'd visited with her a couple of times a year since but he always traveled to see her. His mother being back in Mistletoe was something he'd never thought would happen, but here she was coming out of the bedroom in his dad's robe and looking like they'd just—

Nope. No, not getting that image in my head today.

"What are you doing here?" he whispered.

"I called your dad when you didn't answer your phone last week or return my phone call—" She gave him a pointed look before continuing, "to let him know I was coming to town. He invited me to have dinner with him and we talked, a lot. He said I could stay with the two of you and one thing led to another."

All he could do was blink and stutter, "But why—you—there!" Damn, he wasn't making any sense, but his mind was completely blown. For years his dad wouldn't talk about her, but here she was coming out of his room after they'd obviously done more than sleep.

"I understand this might seem strange, but we were married for twenty-four years, Declan." She patted his arm as if he was seven again, upset about dropping his ice cream on the sidewalk. "Why don't we go out for breakfast and talk? Just the two of us?"

"I can't. I have a job this morning before I open the store."

"Okay, then how about I bring you lunch at the store early this afternoon? It's been a long time since I've seen it, and your father told me about all the updates and improvements you're making. What do you say?"

What he wanted to say, loudly, was that none of this made any sense, but all he managed was to nod.

"Great." She threw her arms around him and gave him a long, tight hug. "I've missed you, sweetheart."

Anger seethed through him as her words brought back memories of a million hugs just like this one, before she'd left them. Declan had been about to leave for college, but what about his dad? He'd worked his butt off for years to financially provide for them, and she'd dumped him the minute Declan was gone, as if all of her obligations were fulfilled because her child had grown up.

How could his dad let her walk back into their lives now and forgive her without even telling Declan what he was up to?

Declan extracted himself from her embrace and took several steps back. "I've got to get going."

"I'll see you later," she called after him when he turned and bolted for the door. Declan exited the house with a hefty slam, shaking his head as he made his way down the walkway to his truck. He looked up and down the street to spot what his mother might be driving, but he recognized all the cars on the block.

They'd still been out when he got home the night before, and he hadn't heard them come in. Had his dad driven without a license? Did she know her ex-husband was sick?

While he backed out of the driveway and cranked the wheel around to make the right onto Evergreen Circle, Declan went back and forth in his mind about what he would say to his mother later. *What are you doing back here? Did you run out of money or something? After ten years, what could you possibly want here that you didn't have before?*

If Declan really wanted to save himself a headache, he'd stay out of their business. But there were too many variables to ignore, and the most important of all: Was she back to take advantage of his dad's failing health?

The Diana Gallagher who'd tucked him in every night and been at every parent teacher meeting was nothing like the woman who'd practically disappeared when he turned eighteen. That woman was a stranger he didn't trust as far as he could throw her.

He didn't remember the drive or the walk up to Holly's door, he was so distracted by his convoluted thoughts. Holly swung the door open before he had a chance to knock, wearing a long cream tunic sweater and dark blue jeans, her long red hair up on top of her head, and a mulish expression on her heart-shaped face. "I wasn't sure you'd show."

"I keep my word," he said, spoiling for an argument. "Unless you want to fire me now?"

"No, we can see if you're up for the task." She looked behind him, clucking her tongue. "You really are a one-man band, huh?"

"What?"

"No help at all?"

"Just me." He waved his hand across the lawn coated with patches of snow. "You want to show me what I'll be doing?"

"Yeah, I do, but I need my wake-up juice first. I was just heating it up when I heard your truck." She hesitated a fraction of a second before she added, "Are you okay? You seem— out of it."

"Just a weird morning."

"I see," she said. "Would you like a cup of coffee?"

Declan was surprised by the offer, but nodded. "Thanks, I'd love some."

"It's not fresh ground and fancy," she warned.

"I don't care."

Holly stepped back, allowing him to pass into the house, and he was thrown once again. He'd assumed Holly's home would look a lot like her shop, with clutter everywhere for all the holidays, but the front entryway had four hooks on the wall and a light gray bench seat with cubbies for shoes, but nothing else on the walls.

"This isn't what I was expecting," he said out loud as she shut the door behind him.

"What do you mean?"

He followed her past a family room with a cream loveseat under the window and a large bookcase against the adjacent wall. No knickknacks or gnomes to be seen, just one layer of neatly placed books on each shelf.

And Declan's painting on the wall.

A flash of pride rushed through him that after everything

they'd done and said to each other, his gift was worthy of hanging on her wall.

Then he noticed the Christmas tree and stepped into the room to get a closer look.

"This was not what I was expecting your tree to look like," he said, fingering the tool ornament on one of the branches.

"Yeah, well, no one else bid on it this year, so I got it for a steal."

Declan's gaze swept over the various ornaments and the star of lighted wrenches on the top, shaking his head. "I guess I assumed you'd have decorations everywhere, with a tree that had bright, glittery ornaments."

"I don't usually have time for a tree," she said, leaving the living room with him trailing behind, several questions rattling around in his mind. They passed through the doorway into a kitchen and dining room area, but there was no kitchen table, just a couple of stools under the bar. Several ring lights of various sizes were standing next to the far wall, ready for Holly to make her next video, and a rush of regret flooded him. Although he'd given a halfhearted apology the night of her party, he'd followed it up with throwing all the blame on her.

"I do have some garland up on the ledge," she said, pointing above their heads.

"Wow," he commented, deadpan.

Declan caught her eye roll before Holly turned her back to him and stood up on her tiptoes, retrieving a mug from the cupboard. He watched her set up the single cup coffee maker, afraid she might have taken offense to what he said and throw the hot brew at him when it finished dripping.

"I didn't mean to offend you. I have this habit of saying exactly what I'm thinking and sometimes it doesn't work out for me," he said.

"Only sometimes?" Her light, teasing tone made him relax as she leaned against the counter, continuing, "I don't decorate much because I spend my holidays with my family at my parents' house, where we deck the Christmas tree and open presents. It doesn't make sense to decorate this big house for just me. I put all my energy into my outside display. Maybe after I get married and have kids I'll do something in here, but I'm so busy, thinking about setting up and taking down a bunch of décor in here every couple of months doesn't sound like fun."

"Considering you do it for your shop, it's strange to hear you say that."

"The shop is the reason I feel that way. I already do it there and it's hard enough to get help. I'm the youngest child and my family is busy with their own lives—" Holly stopped herself, as if she realized who she was confiding in, and handed him his coffee. "It's just not a priority at the moment."

Declan took a drink of his coffee, contemplating her reasoning. His family's holiday celebrations consisted of his mom begging him to visit her wherever she was at the time and his dad ordering a ready-made dinner from the grocery store and sitting around watching TV.

How would that change now that they were back together? Or were they just casually hooking up?

Declan gagged on his coffee at the horrifying thought.

"Oh no, did you get some grounds?"

"No, I'm good," he said and coughed. "You're going to live here after you have kids?"

"This street? Or Mistletoe?"

"Both."

"Yes to both. I always assumed I'd spend the rest of my life in this town. My family and business are here and I love everything about it. The people. The events. The lifestyle and pace. As for this house, why not? It's plenty big for a family, and being a part of something that brings so much joy to others makes me feel good."

Declan shrugged. "Not sure why you'd want the responsibility or the expense if you're going to have a bunch of kids. Seems like your attention should be on them and not this over the top display of commercialism."

"First of all, my future children will get plenty of attention. I'm an excellent multitasker," she said, brushing a loose strand of hair off her forehead. "Second of all, I like commercialism. When I have kids, I'm going to go nuts with all the traditions. Letters to Santa. Baking. Making footprints coming out of the fireplace or stomping on the roof on Christmas Eve."

"Why would you perpetuate a lie about a jolly fat man who brings gifts?"

"Because it's fun! It gives Christmas an air of magic!"

"Normal people consider it breaking and entering."

"What is normal? Being a Scroogey killjoy who thinks the parade of lights is a fire hazard?"

"Call me what you want, but if people really cared about the holidays, they'd keep it simple. Quality time, one handmade gift from the heart. You shouldn't have to go into debt to show others how much you care, or try to prove your holiday spirit by outdoing your neighbor's decorations." He took a sip from a mug that read *Let's Get Lit* in Christmas lights and caught her watching him. "What?"

"I'm just surprised you drank it, considering I made it. Not afraid I might poison you?"

Declan chuckled. "Maybe if I hadn't watched you prepare it, but there's also the matter of me being your last hope to have thousand-dollar power bills next month, so I figured I was safe regardless."

"For now," she declared.

Declan bit back a smile, taking a drink from his coffee mug as he watched her throw away the used pods and wipe down the drip tray. Somehow, he'd pictured her home chaotic, with piles of dishes in the sink. Definitely not spick-and-span.

"I do have one question," she said, turning to face him.

"I don't remember being interrogated as part of the job description."

"You need to look up the definition of interrogated. It's a simple curiosity, not me torturing you with a barrage of questions and possible waterboarding. Not that I haven't thought about drowning you a few times."

"Has anyone told you violence isn't the answer?" he said.

"Many, but I don't listen. Can I ask or what?"

"I doubt I could stop you."

"Why are you even here if you really hate Christmas so much?"

Declan shrugged. "You had me at three grand. I've got to feed Leo's catnip addiction."

Holly set her coffee down with a thud. "Wait, you have a cat named Leo?"

"Why do you sound so surprised?"

"You don't come off like a cat person at all."

"What are the typical personality traits of a cat person?" he asked.

"I don't know, but not...you. Most of the guys I know who own a cat are introverted, creative types who like to sit around talking about Dostoevsky with their slouch hipster beanies and iconic Buddy Holly glasses. You're a flannel-wearing mountain man who runs a hardware store and an after-hours side hustle as a handyman. I mean, you're a wonderful artist, but for some reason you keep that on the down low."

"That's what I do for work and to relax, not who I am."

"So, who are you?" she asked.

Declan hesitated. "Didn't we go through this the other night? I'm a judgmental jerk who can't go five minutes without pissing off Holly Winters."

"That's true, but I don't think that's all you are." Holly wagged her finger at him playfully. "I'm onto you, Declan. You don't open up to people, not even to Clark who seems to be your only close friend. Your dad's retired and even though you live with him you don't talk about him either." She carried her coffee mug in one hand and opened the sliding glass door in the dining room. "From what I gather, your mom's not in the picture—"

"I really don't want to talk about this," he said softly, keeping his urge to snap at bay.

Holly studied his face and sighed, her shoulders deflating. "I guess we won't talk, then."

Declan rushed ahead of her, putting his arm across the door

frame, blocking her exit. "I want to talk. To move away from this animosity and dislike of the other. I'd like..." Declan swallowed, hating how raw and open he felt just asking. "Could we start slow? Something simple like 'Holly, are you a cat or a dog person?"

Her lips twitched in the corners. "Well, Declan, I'm actually a cat person."

"That's so interesting. Please, tell me more as you lead the way to your display items."

"More about being a cat person? That's the gist of it. I want to get one, but it never feels like a good time. This year it's been crazy with Merry and Clark's wedding and figuring out something new to do with my YouTube channel."

"No more Adventure Elf?" he asked, surprised. Holly seemed to have so much fun in her videos...

Not that he'd seen very many.

"I've been wanting to retire her for months but wasn't sure how to do it. I've had so many ideas get thrown my way, but nothing feels right."

She opened the door to a large shed and held it for him so he could peer inside. "In the filing cabinet to your right, you'll find a schematic of the set-up and a list of the pieces. They have to go in order or the story will be out of sequence and won't make any sense."

Declan stepped into the small space at the front of the storage cube, his gaze passing over the floor-to-ceiling stacks of bubble-wrapped figures and boxes.

"All of this fits on that tiny lawn of yours?"

"Nope," she said cheerfully, a wide grin on her face. "Some of it has to go on the roof too."

His head hurt at the mention of roofs, and he turned back to the stacks of decorations. He could turn down the job, but three grand in the bank would be a nice bump in his slow-growing savings. Especially if he wanted to open his own studio one day, which had been the direction he'd been heading before he'd uprooted his life to come back to Mistletoe.

"Of course, if you don't think you can handle this by yourself, I'll keep trying to find someone else."

"No, I've got this, not to worry, but I need to make one more condition."

Holly released a breathless laugh. "Of course you do."

"I'd like you to find somewhere else to be for the next few days while I work on this."

"Excuse me?" she said, crossing her arms over her chest.

"I don't want you hanging over my shoulder distracting me or getting in the way. I'll use your schematic and get it done before the deadline, as long as you aren't around."

Holly stood silently for several moments before she finally grumbled, "You're making a lot of demands for a job I'm paying you to do."

"I'm just trying to make sure the two of us get through these two days without losing ground towards a positive, more copacetic co-existence."

"I can't decide if you're sincere or drunk."

"Was that a yes?" Declan laughed.

"Do I have a choice?"

CHAPTER 15

HOLLY SCROLLED THROUGH THE COMMENTS on her latest video, her stomach knotting with every snarky one-liner. Maybe the Adventure Elf doing the spicy jelly bean challenge wasn't mind-blowing, but she'd thought her reactions were at least funny.

According to the largely negative feedback, she was the only one who thought so.

It shouldn't have surprised her, after the content block she'd been having, but now being exiled from her place for two days while Declan handled the set-up? The man was pushing all her buttons, treating her like an obsessive control freak. If she peeked out to see how he was doing, it would only be because he'd never done it before and she was trying to help.

The door opened and Santa's jolly voice greeted Merry as she stepped inside, flipping off the alarm as she passed.

"Now, that isna verra nice," Holly said in an awful Scottish accent. "It's just a little ho ho ho."

"Santa must die. Can't you have a chime like a normal shopkeeper?"

"I thought about it, but your reaction amuses me and I needed a laugh this morning."

Her sister's frown deepened. "What's wrong?"

"I don't want to get into it."

"Why not?"

"Because you're getting married and have enough on your plate without listening to my first-world problems."

Merry set her purse on the counter and leaned across it on her elbows, cradling her chin with her hands. "Listen, solving your problems is exactly what I need right now. Hit me, sister." Merry held a hand over her face with a laugh. "Not actually, though, because this face needs to stay picture-ready through the honeymoon."

"You're a dork," Holly said, smiling.

"I know but that's beside the point. Come on, tell me all your troubles and maybe I can help you resolve them. Unless you want me to just listen and not try to fix, in which case I have enthusiastic responses at the ready."

"Enthusiastic responses?"

"You know, like—" Merry gasped dramatically before reciting, "No! You don't say. What a jerk! How dare they! I'll cream her corn!"

"Fine, I'll tell you, but don't use any of those, especially the corn one. Gross." Holly sat down on the stool behind the counter and continued, "I hired Declan Gallagher to set up my Christmas display and he keeps making stipulations. He's pretty much the last person available so I don't have a choice, but his attitude irks me."

"I thought everything about Declan irked you?"

"I'm serious."

"Maybe if you try not to needle him, the two of you can find common ground."

"Believe me, I have nothing in common with that man. He also called a cease fire to our prank war in exchange for doing the job, and then he said that while he's working on the house, I can't be there."

"Why not?"

"Something about me hovering and annoying him, but I wish I could tell him to shove it up his rear, you know? I don't understand him at all. He's all, like—" she deepened her voice to do a proper imitation of Declan—"Woman, you don't know me. Don't try to act like you do because I'm super mysterious and surly."

"He seriously called you woman?"

"No, but it fit with the tone I was going for. Plus there've been several moments the last few weeks that have seriously thrown me for a loop."

"What kind of moments?"

"The kind I can't stop thinking about."

"Intriguing. Tell me more."

"Fine, but don't get weird."

"Me, weird? Pshaw."

Holly didn't believe her, but she was also dying to talk to someone, and Delilah was deep in deadline still. "So last week when he was on top of me—"

"Whoa, time out, back up and repeat! On top of you?"

Holly rolled her eyes. "Not like that. He dumped me in the snow, then lost his balance and fell on me."

"You do realize how you made it sound, right?"

"It was all to keep you spellbound and riveted by what I'm saying."

"Then please continue, because I'm hanging on your every word."

"When he was on top of me, he kind of stopped and stared at me for a few seconds. I thought he might kiss me."

"Why would you think that?"

"Because he was hard."

Merry burst out laughing. "Or his body had a natural reaction to being up close and personal with your body."

"Fine, but the way he just stopped moving was weird."

"He was probably embarrassed. Getting a hard-on while trying to thwart your mortal enemy? Brutal."

"I'm being serious and you're laughing at me."

"Come one, sis, you are focusing on something that shouldn't even matter. You're not interested in Declan, are you?"

"No, I'm not."

"Then you shouldn't be obsessing about this."

Holly sighed. "You're right."

"Why do you say that with so much disappointment?"

Because, Holly thought with a burst of clarity, *I think I'm lying about not being interested.*

Which was so incredibly twisted. They'd done nothing but bicker and tear into each other, but then there were the moments when Declan smiled, usually involuntarily, or looked at her with those deep-green eyes and her stomach dropped out.

She should either get on that dating thing or convince Declan they needed to bang each other out of their systems.

"Holly?" Merry prodded. "What else is on your mind?"

Holly groaned, dropping her forehead to the counter. "I have to rebrand my social media presence and I don't think it's going to go the way I hope."

"I know I haven't always been the most supportive of the Adventure Elf stuff, but it's only because I don't want you to get hurt. You've done some crazy things in the past and I don't know how you've made it through without a scratch."

"I just don't know where to go from here without losing all my followers. I need a funny gimmick that is so good people won't even care that I'm not doing stunts anymore."

"The prank thing won't work out?" Merry asked.

"No, I'd have to get everyone's permission and some people don't appreciate being the butt of other people's jokes."

"It's too bad you couldn't cook. You could be the baking elf."

"Except I burn water."

"What if you tried different recipes and had a taste tester eat them on camera? Get their reactions. Good or bad."

"It's not a bad idea. I don't know who I'd get for that job, though."

"Definitely not me, because like you said I'm busy getting married." Merry danced in a circle with her hand in the air and was in mid-turn when the door opened again and Sam came in.

"Hey, I don't appreciate Santa calling me a ho. That guy really does see everything, huh?" He grinned, doing a little turn. "And how come no one texted me we were sexy dancing? Get in here, Merry, and let's get freaky."

While Holly laughed, Merry rushed her future brother-in-law and punched him on the shoulder. "I'm telling your brother."

"Hey, I no longer live with him, so he can't kick me out. Do your worst." Sam flashed Holly that straight white smile that had all the women in Mistletoe falling all over themselves. "How's my favorite redhead?"

"If you have more than one, we're through."

Sam crossed the room and gave her a lingering kiss on her cheek. "Please, threaten all you want but you can't quit me."

"All right, stop messing with me!" Merry grumbled, pushing her way between them.

Holly laughed. "Come on, Merry. If we married brothers, we could get on the cover of a magazine."

"Whoa, hold up, I'll be your sugar baby, but this guy doesn't do matrimony."

Holly grabbed her purse and jacket from behind the back of the counter before coming around to join them. "Except you're the elder, so wouldn't I be the baby?"

Sam slung an arm around her shoulders. "But you make more money than me."

"Would you two get out of here before I change my mind about holding down the fort? I only agreed because this meeting is for wedding stuff, but I do not want any close proximity romances blossoming."

"You hear that, Sam? We'll have to settle for forbidden love."

"Sneaking around could be fun," he responded, waggling his brows.

"I hate you both."

Holly reached out to pat Merry's cheek. "It's so sweet how you try to protect me from the big bad wolf. I love you."

Merry rolled her eyes. "I love you too."

"No love for me, Mer?" Sam pouted.

"I love you, too, but if you defile my little sister, you're a dead man. And your brother and Nick will help me hide your body."

Sam and Holly laughed as they walked out the door, arms still wrapped around each other. It didn't matter how many times Holly told her that Sam was just a friend, Merry wouldn't be convinced.

Holly glanced up at Sam, conceding that his sun-streaked blond hair and chiseled jaw were lovely to look at, but she'd never had that spark with Sam. They'd had an immediate connection and friendly, flirty banter, but that's where they left it.

"You angling for a kiss?" he joked, and she laughed, her face burning.

"Please, you couldn't handle this fire."

"You're probably right. A pretty young thing like you would kill an old man like me."

"You're not that old."

Sam stopped suddenly, right outside of the Mistletoe Hardware window display. "You hinting at something, Holly?"

Holly started, facing Sam, fully aware how they must look to the people inside. Like a couple having an intense conversation.

"No, I was just pointing out facts. Besides, I don't think of you that way."

Sam staggered back with his hands over his chest. "I've never heard those words from any woman before. I don't think I will ever recover."

"I bet if you pulled out your phone and scrolled, there's someone waiting on there to make it all better."

"You think? Should we give it a go?"

Holly pushed him lightly, grinning. "Will you stop flaunting your virility and focus? I only have an hour for lunch and we have a lot left to do."

"All right, boss, let's get some grub and iron out the details." Sam fell into step beside her, glancing back at the store.

"What's wrong?"

"Nothing, I was just wondering why Declan looked ready to fly through the window and throw a punch."

Holly's head whipped around, but the angle wasn't right to see inside. "It's me he wants to strangle, not you."

"'Cause he wants you and you rejected him?"

"What? No!"

"Don't tell me he said no to *you*?"

Holly loved the disbelief in that one sentence. "While I'm flattered that I shocked you, I have been turned down by men before."

"Idiots, you mean."

"See, this is why we're friends and not lovers. You'd never have my back like this if I let you take me for a ride."

"I hate to break it to you, but I'd never take you for a ride because Merry wouldn't forgive me."

"My sister, the cock blocker of the century. But back to Declan, no, I didn't come on to him. We just hate each other and yet he's setting up my Christmas display. Things probably aren't going well, and he was trying to make my head explode from a distance."

"You know what the other side to hate is?" he asked.

Holly groaned. "Do not say love."

"Nope, it's lust. I bet if the two of you worked out all that 'hate'"—Sam emphasized the word with air quotes—"you'd get along a whole lot better."

"How about I don't take lust advice from a man who needed to be rescued when one of his hate sex partners handcuffed him to the bed and left him there?"

"Probably wise."

CHAPTER 16

WHEN HOLLY AND SAM DISAPPEARED out of sight, Declan turned his head to crack his neck, but nothing seemed to ease the tension that had laced through his body watching the two of them cuddle and play. He hadn't meant to stare, but seeing that bright, easy smile on Holly's face come into view as they passed struck him like a shock of cold wind, freezing him in place. They'd stopped in front of his store, with Holly's back to him, but by the look on Sam's face, they were having an intense conversation.

When Sam caught him watching, Declan practically scrambled out from behind the counter and down an aisle. From that position in the store he could still see them, even as he tried not to look.

How did he not know that Holly and Sam were dating? Complaining about his brother's promiscuity was a favorite pastime of Clark's, and he couldn't imagine Clark was happy about his brother going out with his soon-to-be sister-in-law. Or maybe he didn't know?

It's none of your business who Holly dates, so why are you standing there like a dope obsessing about it?

Declan didn't have a rational answer. He'd wanted Holly to

stay away while he worked so he could surprise her, but after getting a look at the display, he might be in over his head and didn't want to admit it.

"Declan, I'm ready to check out now," Mrs. Paulsen called from the counter.

"On my way." Declan crossed the wood floor and stepped behind the counter, giving the older woman a forced smile. "Is this everything?"

"Yes, I ordered most of what I needed online but forgot these. I wish you would offer delivery, especially for us older folks."

Declan didn't get into the logistics of hiring someone to deliver when the store was barely making enough to keep them in the black, because it wasn't her fault times were changing. With the convenience of online shopping, most of the store's customers were like Mrs. Paulsen: popping in to grab an item they forgot or a small order they didn't want to go to Twin Falls or Mountain Home for.

"I'll pass the suggestion along to my dad," he said, slipping the package of screws into a bag. "Have a good day, Mrs. Paulsen."

"You too, Declan."

His mother passed by the window with a drink carrier and a take-out bag as Mrs. Paulsen exited and the two of them greeted each other like old friends did, hugging carefully and speaking for several moments outside. His mother had always been well liked and missed when she moved away, and the fact that Mrs. Paulsen hadn't asked about his dad while fawning over his mom set his teeth on edge.

When they finally said their goodbyes, his mother walked in and set her stuff on the counter.

"Hello, son." She flipped over the open sign and locked the door, then turned around with a wide smile on her face. "Ready for lunch?"

"It's a good thing there's no one else in here or you would have made them feel very uncomfortable locking them in."

"I checked first, unless there's someone in the bathroom?"

"No, there's not."

"Then stop looking for an issue when there isn't one," she said cheerfully, picking up the bag of food. "I dropped your father's lunch off first and then ordered ours, so hopefully it's at least warm."

"You know I don't usually close for lunch."

"Honey, come on, how much business are you going to get in the half hour it takes for us to eat our food and visit?" She waved the bag in the air. "Should we take this to the backroom?"

"No, it's full of stock," he lied. The last thing he wanted was his mother wandering around his art studio, lamenting on how he should be doing something with his talent. "We can eat in the office."

Declan picked up the drinks and took the bag from her, leading the way to the small room that his dad used for many years to balance the books and interview new employees. When Declan was growing up, he used to come into the busy store and pretend to help customers, anything to spend time with his dad, but he'd spent a lot of hours coloring at the large desk in his dad's office. An office chair, a couple of metal folding chairs against the wall, and a metal filing cabinet in the corner took up most of the small space now, but he hadn't done a thing to change it.

"Wow, this room hasn't changed at all," his mom said, following him into the musty office.

"I don't use it." Declan flipped on the light and it flickered a few times before it settled to life. He opened one of the chairs and sat down in it, waving his hand to the office chair. "You can take that one."

"Your father mentioned he hadn't been coming into work. How are you doing running it? I know that you had other plans after college."

"It's fine. When Dad busted his hip, he needed me." Declan opened up one of the containers and finding a green salad inside passed it over to her. "Being there for your family trumps everything."

"What about the times I invited you to come see me? Or asked to visit you? Aren't I your family?"

"You didn't need me. You were living your own life, the one we were holding you back from."

"I suppose I deserve that." She took the container and set it on the desk. "I wasn't abandoning my family, Declan. I was choosing happiness. I thought I explained that."

"Whatever you need to tell yourself, Mom."

"Now, wait a second," she said sharply. "We had this discussion years ago and you've punished me ever since, pushing me out of your life, and I let you. I thought eventually you'd understand, but I spent eighteen years caring for you, being on your side when you needed me. I am a good mother. How does all of that get erased because your father and I divorced?"

"That wasn't all you did. You made him pay you for your

half in the store and the house and you took off. He spent years providing for us and you just left, happy to abandon him and travel the world."

"Is that what he said happened?" she asked softly.

"I mean…I know he had to pay you a divorce settlement and then you were gone. He doesn't talk about it at all, but if it looks and quacks like a duck—"

"Have you ever asked him? Or was it easier to paint me as the bad guy?" She stood up suddenly, staring down at him with tired green eyes. "You were an adult, Declan. We decided to wait to divorce until you were out of the house and away at college, but you were still our *child* and we didn't want to drag you into our mess. If either your father or I choose not to discuss why we split, you shouldn't have taken it upon yourself to decide who was to blame and instead minded your own business."

"If things were so bad, then why are you here? Having sleepovers and pretending like the last ten years didn't happen?" Declan stood up, anger radiating through him. "He has no one. He was hurt and scared and I was there. Not you."

"It's because of the last ten years I can be here now. I needed time away from your father and this place. When I called Liam a year ago, I was out of options with how to reach you. I've tried to figure out what I can say to you that will stop this childishness, but I give up."

"Do you know what's going on with him?"

"Yes, he told me a few months ago. I couldn't figure out why you were still here." She laughed softly, adding, "You used to tell me every day that you couldn't wait to put this town in your rear view."

"Unfortunately, I guess I didn't inherit your selfishness. Are you here hoping to get in on whatever he's got left before his mind goes?"

His mom's lips thinned. "No. I'm here because your father and I reconnected and I thought if I came back you and I might be able to overcome this wall between us. That if things work out you can get back to living your life on your terms."

"Life isn't always apple pie and ice cream. Sometimes the pie is cold or the ice cream melts, but you make do with what you're served."

"That's a beautiful metaphor, sweetheart, but you only get one life to live. Relationships are complicated, honey, and sometimes when they fail, it's not about figuring out who is to blame but moving on and forgiving the past." His mom dropped her food into the bin without taking a bite. "I'll let you finish your lunch. Think about what I've said, because no matter how many times you ignore my calls or reject my overtures I love you unconditionally and will be waiting when you're ready to move on."

She walked out of the room, leaving him staring at the empty doorway. He heard the front door jingle as she opened and closed it with a snap and the quiet of the store surrounded him, suffocating him, and he needed to get out of there.

Declan wrote a sign for the door and left his food practically untouched to tape the note on the door. Once the till was in the safe and the back door was locked up, he set the alarm and went out the front, his keys jangling in his hand as he twisted the deadbolt into place.

"Declan?" Holly called behind him, and he turned to find her standing on the sidewalk alone, watching him.

"Yeah?"

"Is everything all right?"

He followed her gaze to his hand-written "family emergency" sign and shrugged. "It's fine. I was just going to get a jump on your display today."

"You're closing your store for that?"

He couldn't tell for sure if that was disapproval in her tone, but it rubbed his already raw nerves like sandpaper and he snapped, "Why not? I'll make more money doing that than standing in there all day waiting for someone to purchase a package of something they forgot to order online. Is your back gate unlocked?"

"Yes, but are you sure you're okay?"

Declan touched his chest. "It's sweet of you to pretend to care, but I'm good."

She reeled back like he'd slapped her with his sarcasm, and she held up a hand. "So much for taking things slow and changing our ways, huh? You know what? Forget it. I'll do the display myself. You're fired."

It was only for a split-second but he saw the sheen of tears in her eyes as she moved to walk past him and a knot twisted in Declan's chest. Holly relentlessly took his snark, his bad temper, and his cutting remarks in stride, but he'd gone too far once again.

He couldn't let her walk away not knowing it was him, not her.

Declan took Holly by the arm, maneuvering her into the alley between the hardware store and the vacant space next door. A flood of emotions slammed through him like waves, crashing against his insides, forging together until he couldn't decipher exactly what was propelling his actions, rage, frustration, or plain old unhappiness.

"Declan, let go of me," she snapped, jerking her hand out of his grasp, and he released her, hands in the air.

"I'm an asshole, all right? I've been one for years, and sometimes I even recognize it and think *why did I say that? I should apologize.* But I don't because it's easier to just move on and pretend like I don't care about anyone in this place. But that isn't true."

He ran a hand through his hair and gave a bitter laugh. "This was supposed to be temporary, you know. Come back to help my dad and then go back to my real life. I wasn't supposed to be here this long." He met her wide-eyed gaze and stepped out of her way, adding, "I don't know why I'm saying all of this to you, but I want to apologize. For the other day and a few minutes ago and, hell, probably a lot of other things the last few years. I thought you should know that."

Holly's expression softened slightly and the corners of her mouth curled up. "Go ahead then."

"What?"

"Saying you want to apologize isn't the same as actually doing it."

Declan groaned, dragging his hands over his face. "It's like you can't help yourself."

"What's that?"

"It's got to be involuntary, this constant need to get under my skin."

"So what? You've been getting under mine for two years. It seems only fair."

Declan shook his head. "I don't know why this keeps happening."

"What? Because I'm pretty sure this is the first time you've dragged me into an alley."

"Things between us getting blown out of proportion. Me lashing out. You calling me on my bullshit. It's become a pattern with you and only you."

"Or maybe it's that no one else cares enough to call you on your bullshit. Maybe I actually think that under the asshole there might be someone redeemable."

"I'm sorry to disappoint you, but I'm not an onion. There aren't any layers to peel back."

"Then why didn't you walk away? Why pull me aside and tell me you want to apologize if there's nothing more to you?"

Because I can't stand to see you cry, he thought.

"It felt like the right thing to do."

"Well, you know where I'm at if you want to actually follow through with that apology."

She started to brush past him, but he pressed her back against the wall of the building, hovering over her. "I'm sorry."

Holly paused, flashing him a brilliant smile. "Was that so hard?"

"Excruciating."

"Good." Holly lifted her chin, her dark eyes meeting his. "People keep thinking we're attracted to each other and that's why we fight. Because we don't want to give in and get it out of our system."

The way she said it, matter-of-fact with a touch of husky, lit his cock on fire. "Is that right? What about you?"

"I don't know, but it's something worth considering, don't you think?"

Before Declan could ask her to elaborate or, at the very least, how Sam fit into all this, she slipped out from under his arm, backing out of the alley.

"We'll talk later. You have a display scene to set up." She clapped her hands. "Better get a move on. I hear the boss is a real hard-ass."

CHAPTER 17

HOLLY PULLED INTO HER DRIVEWAY at a quarter to six and choked mid-sip of her soda when she saw Declan stomping and kicking around her yard in an obvious fit of temper. She rolled down the window while she waited for her garage door to open, calling out to him, "Everything all right?"

He turned her way, pointing at the stacks of totes and bubble-wrapped cutouts. "Whoever shipped this labeled everything wrong. I found what I think is part of number one marked as number three and number ten marked as number seven. It's a mess!"

Holly's brow furrowed. "Let me park and I'll come help."

She didn't wait for him to respond before she pulled forward, rolling the window up. There was no way that anything should be out of place because she'd ordered each item separately and her family had helped her pack them away scene by scene.

Holly got out of the SUV and carried her drink and bag of tacos into the house. She checked her teeth in the guest bathroom since she'd devoured a taco on the way home then set all of her stuff on the counter before she walked out the front door, closing it with a snap behind her.

"I'm surprised you're still here. I thought coming home this late I wouldn't violate your 'find somewhere else to be' rule, but now I'm glad I did." Holly came up alongside him, aware of his size, strength, scent, and cleared her throat, ordering her traitorous body to stay on task. "This is really weird."

"How do you mean?" he asked.

"When I ordered this last year, I grouped everything together and packed it up for safe keeping by scene and I know I did it right. Unless someone got into my shed and messed things up, it should have been good to go."

"I'm telling you, if that's the case, someone was in that shed," Declan said. "If you weren't meticulous about including pictures with your schematic, I would have been up shit creek trying to figure this out, but I think I have it now."

Holly scanned the assorted piles of what she could only assume were the designated parts to each scene and nodded. "I don't want to look over your work, so if you think you got it, I trust you."

"Really?" he said, one eyebrow cocked. "You trust me?"

"To not screw this up, yes. You've got three grand on the line."

Declan chuckled. "That I do. I've still got a little light left. If it's all right with you, I'm going to keep working."

Holly looked up at the dark purple sky. "Pretty sure the light has said good night. If you aren't ready to go home, wanna come in and have some tacos?"

"It's fine, I can eat at home."

"They're just tacos, prepared by La Fiesta, so you don't have to worry about laxatives or poison."

He laughed, an exhausted, breathless burst that made her feel sorry for him. Holly wasn't sure what was going on in Declan's life, but it was obvious he was unhappy and for whatever reason it made Holly want to work harder to change that. It made no sense, especially considering their history, but she'd opened the door to exploring this complicated attraction between them. Whether or not he wanted to broach the subject, the ball was in his court now.

"If you've got extra, I'll take them," he murmured, grabbing his sweatshirt from on top of a tote. "I may have skipped lunch."

"I don't know about extra, but my mother taught me to share."

"Funny, my mom taught me to do what makes me happy, no matter who it may hurt."

Holly wasn't sure how to respond to that, especially the anger in his voice, and headed back inside. She held the door for him as he followed her, and shut it while he hung his sweatshirt up on one of the hooks.

"The tacos are on the counter in the kitchen," she said.

"I'll wait for you. Can I wash my hands in your kitchen sink?"

Holly nodded. "Be my guest."

He waved her ahead, and she was keenly aware of the size and strength of him in a simple gray t-shirt stretched over sculpted chest muscles. Earlier when he'd grabbed her, towering over her with that almost desperate expression, all her anger and hurt melted away when she looked deep into his green eyes. She'd seen the pain and frustration and wondered why Declan Gallagher lashed out at people.

It was a mystery that she'd love to solve, especially if it helped her understand him better.

Holly could blame wanting to figure out Declan on being a psychology major when she'd first started college. Learning why and how people's experiences shaped them was fascinating, but if she were being honest, what she learned about Declan over the years didn't make a lot of sense.

Merry told her that while he'd played football and been an excellent offensive lineman, he'd been quiet and never went to places with the team. Clark let slip that he'd been studying at a fine arts college in Maryland and came back when his dad broke a hip and had to have surgery. Clark wasn't sure why he'd stayed after, but that he was glad because they had a lot in common. Both quiet outsiders in a small town who struggled to connect with people. Even her brother Nick had good things to say about Declan.

Holly split up the tacos, giving him six and setting three onto her plate. When he finished wiping his hands on her kitchen towel, Holly held out the dish to him.

"The portions look a little uneven."

"What do you mean?"

"You gave me twice as many tacos, but you paid for them. That doesn't seem fair."

"Will you eat six tacos?" she asked.

"Easily."

"Then seems fair to me. Besides, I ate one in the car, so that means I'll have four tacos."

"In that case, thanks." He pulled up a seat at her counter, and she went to the fridge to grab two sodas and held them up for his inspection.

"This okay with you?"

Declan nodded, his mouth full, and she laughed, setting the soda down next to his plate. "You were hungry."

"I didn't realize it until I smelled these things."

"Same, which is why I had to dig in before I got home."

They ate in silence for a few minutes, her arm grazing his every time either of them moved, and goose bumps traveled across her skin like a wave. Holly never had a problem sitting here next to anyone else without being in their space, but Declan was a big guy and his shoulders alone needed extra room.

"Are you sure you want me to take off tomorrow? I can hang around and help you finish. That scene is a lot of work and those cut-outs are heavy."

"Nah, I've got it. I might close down the store and just head over."

"Are you sure about closing the store?" she asked.

"I think my five customers will forgive me. Besides, my Dad's thinking about selling it. Says he wants to live for himself. Whatever that means."

Holly laughed. "I get that. He wants to spend his golden years relaxing and enjoying life. He's worked hard most of his life. I'd say he's earned it."

"He has, but it's strange. That store has been everything to him, and the last few months he's been...different."

"Good or bad different? Because at one point your dad was grumpier than you and that's saying something."

"Ouch, I'll tell him you said so." Declan grinned. "He told me he likes you."

"No, he doesn't."

"I'm just reporting the news," he said.

"He was always stomping or snapping whenever I came around."

"Gallagher men? That's kind of our thing. Take away our bad attitudes and what do we have? Nothing." He snapped his fingers. "Except Clark designated me as the responsible one for the bachelor party. Apparently he's worried about his brother getting crazy."

Holly laughed. "That sounds about right. You'd never guess Clark was the younger brother of the two."

"I guess that will make him fun into his seventies. Young at heart."

"Unlike you," she said, then regretted saying it aloud. The last thing she wanted was to offend him and ruin what was probably the easiest conversation they'd ever had.

Declan swung the stool her way, putting his knee between hers. "What was that?"

Holly relaxed when she saw the playful gleam in his eyes and continued, "You're more of an old soul. Like you've lived a thousand lives and all of them filled with tragedy. I think that's what makes you such a talented artist. All the great ones have a tortured past."

Declan's lips curved into a small smile. "Unfortunately, that isn't true. I've lived a rather charmed life. Two parents who divorced after I graduated high school. I attended my dream college, graduated, and got a job at a little art studio down the street from my apartment. Until my dad got hurt and I came back to help him, but all in all, nothing too terrible."

"Then why do you sound so sad?"

He seemed startled by her question. "I don't think of myself as sad. Frustrated. Mad at the world. Bitter." Declan took a drink from his soda and set it on the counter. "I guess I'm just like Ebeneezer Scrooge. A miserable old miser. Pretty sure you've called me that a time or two."

"Among other things," she said softly. "What will you do if your dad closes the store? Will you stay? Or go back to what you were doing before?"

"I left everything behind two years ago, and while I could find something else, I wouldn't want to be far from my dad."

"Is he all right? No one sees him around town much. I know he broke a hip and that's why you came home, but I always wondered why you stayed."

Declan didn't answer right away and Holly was afraid maybe she'd pushed him too far. He finished off his last taco and grabbed a napkin from her holder on the counter, wiping his fingers and mouth.

"My dad's okay now, but he's getting older, so if I did move I wouldn't want to go farther than Sun Valley or Boise."

"Oh." Disappointment flooded her, but she silently scolded herself. Everyone and their mother was right about her lusting after Declan Gallagher. But him leaving town made anything that happened between them the perfect affair, so why did she feel disappointment at the thought of him leaving town? They could hook up, burn a few weeks of energy, and go their separate ways. She wouldn't have to bump into him afterwards and make things awkward.

That is, if Declan even wanted to. He'd been pleasant, easy-going, and slightly flirty tonight, but he hadn't said a word about her earlier proposal.

And while she'd gotten more out of him in ten minutes than in the two years prior, she still wanted more.

"Sun Valley and Boise would be good choices for an artist. I doubt you'd be satisfied with displaying your paintings in the grocery store."

"It's more that I wanted to give back to the arts. Educate people. I thought about getting my master's and applying to be an art professor somewhere."

"So, college? Not high school?"

Declan shrugged. "I'd be all right with high school, but the people of this town care more about sports than the arts."

"If you really feel that way, change their minds, but I think you're wrong. We have crafters, and Clark's wood working business is doing well. It might not be highbrow impressionistic works, but I believe art is in the eye of the beholder."

"That's true. I've seen some of your sister's blankets. They're intricate and gorgeous."

"Which reminds me...you haven't found Santa Johnson yet, have you?"

Declan stared at her. "What is that?"

Holly grinned, pulling out her phone to show him a picture. "I've hidden this guy in your store somewhere."

"Where?"

Holly put her phone away with a shrug. "I guess you'd better keep looking."

"It's not anywhere a customer will find him?" Declan asked.

"No, just you."

"Thank God. I could just imagine that conversation."

Holly cleared her throat. "Speaking of conversations, that thing you said about your mom earlier teaching you to go after your happiness? Do you talk to her often?"

"I've talked to her recently, but my relationship with my mom is complicated and not something I want to get into." Declan leaned closer to her, his forearms resting on top of his thighs. "But we can talk about other things, if you really want to get to know me better. Do you, Holly?"

Her breath caught when he said her name in that deep, husky tone.

"I—sure."

"The first thing you need to know about me is I really—" he got closer, his mouth nearly brushing her ear—"really love tacos."

Quick as The Flash, he snatched one of her tacos off her plate.

"Hey! Thief!" she squealed, climbing onto the rung of his stool and leaning against him for leverage as she tried to retrieve her taco from him.

He held it above his head out of reach, shaking with laughter. "What? You didn't know this but I can eat seven tacos."

"And I can eat four." She made a wild grab for the taco and it cracked, spilling its contents all over the two of them. Holly got an onion in her eye and cried out, swiping at her face.

"You okay?" Declan asked, his voice trembling with presumed laughter.

"No! Not only did you waste a taco, but I think you blinded me with a hunk of onion. It freaking burns."

"Come on." Firm hands gripped her waist, helping her off the stool. Holly opened her good eye as Declan led her by the hand to the sink. He flipped the faucet on and while he adjusted the temperature, said, "Go ahead and wash your hands to get all the juices off, and then we'll rinse your eye."

"Ugh, just don't look at me while I do this. It's going to be a mess."

"What do you mean?"

"I put on makeup today. Once I start washing it off, I'm going to look like an angry raccoon."

"I'll watch for claws and teeth."

"You're a funny guy," Holly grumbled, cupping her hands under the warm water and attempting to keep her eye open so she could splash it. "This is why I could never wear contacts or do eye drops. I hate things going in my eyes."

"Like onions?"

"Hey, you might think this is hilarious, but you owe me a taco. With an additional plate of nachos for pain and suffering."

"You can deduct the cost of said pain and suffering from my wages."

"Don't think I won't." Holly splashed a few more times and blinked, clearing away the water. "Okay, I think I'm good."

"Ah, I see what you meant about angry raccoon."

Holly narrowed her eyes and grabbed the sink hose, flipping the switch. "Jerk!"

Before Declan could react, she got him right in the face,

spraying the front of his shirt until he reached out and wrestled the hose from her. She screamed as he doused her over the head, weak with laughter as Holly wiped the wet strands from her face.

Someone pounded on the front door, but when Holly tried to take a step to answer it, she slipped on the wet floor. Declan caught her with his arms under her pits, and she looked up at him, her feet sliding across the slick floor.

"Going down," she giggled. When her butt hit the floor softly, Declan grinned at her.

"You look like a drowned raccoon."

More pounding, and Declan got a better grip before hauling Holly to her feet.

"You go answer and I'll clean this up. Towels?"

"Hall closet. That way—" She pointed, shuffling across the floor. By the time she opened her front door, Holly found Theodore James on the other side poised to knock again.

"Hi," she puffed, out of breath from laughing.

"Are you all right?" Mr. James glanced over her shoulder into the house. "I was on my back porch and I heard screaming."

"Yes, I'm fine. I just got some onion juice in my eye and was trying to wash it out. Then I slipped on water in the kitchen and I'm just a hot mess tonight. But I appreciate the concern."

"Violent crime doesn't often happen in Mistletoe, but we should be ready for everything. You're sure you're all right?"

"Yes, just a little wet."

The older man turned as if he was going to leave then paused. "I noticed Declan Gallagher over here earlier messing with your display."

"Yes, I hired him to put it up for me."

"Why?"

"Because the company who usually does it cancelled and everyone else was booked."

"I'm sorry to hear that, but as head of the HOA, I don't want you to get stuck with sub-par work."

Holly cocked her head to the side. "I don't know why you'd think Declan wouldn't do his very best, but I assure you I trust him to set up my display better than it's been done in years."

"You've always taken a lot of pride in your home, Holly. I just don't want you to regret it."

"I think we'll be okay, even after someone got into my shed and messed up how I'd packed away my display. You haven't seen anyone skulking around my house, have you?"

Something flickered across Theodore's face before his brow snapped into a scowl. "With the exception of Declan Gallagher, I can't say that I have."

"Well, I guess the new cameras I installed will tell me if anyone is messing with my cut-outs and I'll let the police know."

"Cameras? I didn't see you put in a security system."

"It's very discreet. I'm thinking of putting in one of those camera doorbells too. Have more electronic surveillance than the CIA," she said with a chuckle. "Thank you for checking in on me. Have a good night."

"You do the same."

Holly closed the door, and when she turned around, Declan was coming down the hall.

"Hey, I don't know if you heard that, but I think Theodore James is the one—"

Before she could finish her sentence, Declan towered over her, his warm palm cupping her cheek. "Why did you do that?"

"What?"

"Defend me?"

"Because it's true. I do think you'll do a great job. I have three grand riding on it."

Declan's thumb ran along her bottom lip and her body jerked with awareness as a shock of desire followed the length of his touch.

"Where did you come from?"

Holly didn't have a chance to respond before Declan's head dipped down and his mouth brushed hers in a soft, slow kiss. Before she could even register the kiss, he pulled away, retrieving his sweatshirt from the hook with one hand.

"Good night."

CHAPTER 18

DECLAN KNEW WHAT HE'D BEEN thinking when he kissed Holly. He'd been standing in the kitchen listening to her defend his work ethic after having one of the best nights he'd experienced in years, and that was it. He couldn't *not* kiss her.

Well, if she'd put up her hands and said no, he would have stopped, but for the several seconds that his mouth met hers, she'd leaned into him. He hadn't imagined it, either, because when he pulled away, Holly hadn't appeared disgusted. Instead, she blinked, her brown eyes dazed, and the moment had been too perfect to mess up. Instead of staying and having her tell him they shouldn't have, he'd bolted out the door.

Which led to a whole internal conversation that boiled down to *what the heck had he been thinking?* Yes, she'd brought up the two of them exploring whatever was going on between them, but the way Holly talked about Sam with so much warmth and affection in her voice told Declan she cared deeply for him. Maybe the suggestion earlier was a moment; she had been walking back alone. Maybe she had a fight with Sam and impulsively propositioned Declan.

And what did he do? Took full advantage of it, sweeping in like a vulture and throwing her off balance with a kiss she hadn't even asked for.

Damn it, he was going to have to apologize again.

For a while there, sitting with Holly had been unexpectedly wonderful and he'd relaxed, something he struggled to do with most people. Yet this woman he avoided crossing paths with had made him laugh. Forgot about his usual dark and gloomy mindset and engaged him to tease and play. He had no idea what came over him, but Declan wanted to experience it again.

Declan got out of his truck and headed into the house, preparing himself for whatever waited inside. He hadn't heard from his dad, or mom, but Declan expected the man inside wasn't going to be thrilled with him about upsetting his mom.

He unlocked the door and walked inside, barely getting the door closed before Leo greeted him with a happy meow. Declan picked up the cat, tossing him over his shoulder like a sack of potatoes as he made his way into the kitchen, patting the cat's back gently.

"At least you're always happy I'm home, huh?"

While Declan poured dry food into Leo's dish, he heard a door down the hallway open and close and the steady tread of his father's gait.

"Your mother told me what happened today," Liam said from behind him.

Leo jumped off his shoulder onto the counter and Declan put the cat food scoop away before turning to face his dad, who stood in the doorway in a button-down shirt and khakis.

"Well, don't you look spiffy."

"Cut the crap, Declan. What happened between your mother and me is about us, not you. I'll admit I was angry for many years and I—I didn't discourage you from being angry too, but your mother is a good woman. She was, *is*, a great mother to you and a better wife than I deserved. If you want to blame someone for the divorce, you should point the finger at me."

"What are you talking about? *She* left."

"No, son, she stayed." His dad took a breath, as if mentally preparing himself to continue. "Even after she discovered my affair, she stayed. It was me. I left our marriage first."

"Your..." Declan's stomach bottomed out, and he gripped the kitchen counter behind him. "When?"

"It was a long time ago—"

"When did you screw around on Mom?"

His dad winced, but the rage coursing through Declan's veins was too hot to control. Liam had always told him to be a man, to respect women, and to treat every promise with honor. The man before him wasn't honorable, he wasn't a victim, and the reality of it was a slap in the face.

"It happened when you were thirteen. I met someone and we were involved for four months. When your mom found out, I broke things off and the gravity of what I'd done, what my choice could cost me, finally sank in. She wanted a divorce, but I begged her to wait until you were older. I thought I could make her forgive me, but she never did. She agreed to stay until you graduated from high school. It didn't help."

Declan swallowed. Guilt and resentment, mostly at himself,

sliced through him like a knife. He'd treated his mother like a criminal, and she hadn't deserved any of his animosity. She'd said as much, and he hadn't listened. He was no better than his dad.

"Why didn't she tell me? I thought she was selfish."

"No, Declan. That was me. I took her for granted and when we drifted apart, I didn't see her anymore. I didn't appreciate what she did for us. I broke my wedding vows and then instead of being a man and owning up to what I did I let you think she was the one at fault. I punished her with my resentment because she wouldn't forgive me and move on." His father took a deep, shaky breath. "The worst of it was she never threw me under the bus because she didn't want you to hate me."

Liam's eyes were shiny with tears as he continued. "These last few years I've come to realize I did both of you a disservice, not just after the divorce but before. I wasn't a good father to you, and I was an absent husband to your mother. The only thing I ever did right was keep that store going, and instead of selling it when I got diagnosed, I let you handle it for me. You had your own dreams and I took them away because I was scared to let go of the only thing I had left. And maybe I was afraid if I told you, you'd never come back. Your mother always understood you much better than I did, and I realize that was my fault too. I didn't see you either. Not until you came home."

Declan remembered years spent trying to show his dad one of his art projects or paintings, but he'd absently tell him "*Great,*" while never taking his eyes off the TV screen. How many times he'd spent trying to engage his dad in conversation only to have him brush him off to go out to the garage or plop down to watch TV.

"You're right," Declan said softly. "Growing up, you were always working or exhausted from being at the store, so I didn't push. I knew how much you loved football, and I went out for the team thinking it would give us something in common. I hated every second of it, but for the first time, you looked at me. When you had surgery and got diagnosed, I didn't leave because you needed me and I thought we'd finally get the chance to know each other. But the thing is...you still don't understand who I am. If you did, you'd have told me the truth a long time ago. Because if you had, I may have forgiven you for what you did to her, but how—" Declan's voice broke, and he straightened up, swallowing past the lump lodged there. "How do I forgive you for what you did to me? I punished her because of how I thought she treated you and you let me... I can't even look at you."

Declan moved to storm past Liam, but the older man grabbed his arm. "Please, son, your mother has forgiven me for everything. Can't you see that I was angry and hurting and I behaved poorly? I'm human."

"Being angry doesn't give you the right to say and do whatever you want, especially if it hurts others," Declan said, realizing that was almost exactly what Holly said to him. "This is no longer about you, Dad. I have to forgive myself first for the things I've said and done, and until I do that I can't be here with you." Declan scrubbed a hand over his face. "Is Mom picking you up?"

"Yes, she should be here soon. I was going to ask you to join us for dinner."

"I've already had dinner. What I need is space. I'll find somewhere else to sleep tonight and I'm closing the store tomorrow. I've got a job that pays well and I have to finish it before Friday."

"I understand." Liam dropped his hand from Declan's arm and stepped back. "I want you to know that I am proud of you. You're a good man. It might not mean much right now, but it's true."

Declan didn't respond, too overcome to speak. He nodded twice and went to his room, but he didn't sit down and think. He started packing. Gathering up clothes and rolling them into a ball, he thought about where he'd go from here. When he came out of his room, Liam was nowhere to be found. Declan got Leo's food and bed, shoving it into his duffel, and then pulled the cat carrier from the hall closet.

Leo came around the corner from the kitchen, but when he saw the carrier, he froze.

"Hey, buddy. I know you hate this thing, but I'll give you some cheese."

Leo's ears perked up at the mention of cheese and he followed Declan and the carrier back into the kitchen. Declan opened the fridge and pulled out some string cheese, and when he opened the wrapper, Leo stood up on his hind legs and put his front paws on Declan's leg, meowing enthusiastically.

Declan unzipped the carrier and set it on the floor before tossing a piece of cheese inside. Leo hesitated, even tried reaching in to bring the cheese hunk toward him, but Declan pushed him all the way in with a hand on his butt. He zipped up the door again and waved the cheese at Leo. "I'll give you more when we get to where we're going."

It took him another ten minutes to load up the car with the rest of Leo's things and Declan's toiletries, but when they finally pulled out of the drive, he looked around the town, unsure what to do. He didn't want to go to Clark and ask to crash at his place because Clark had a family. His only option was to use the old cot his dad kept at the store for the nights he'd stayed late counting inventory.

His phone rang next to him, and he checked the caller ID. His mom.

Declan let it go to voicemail. Not because he didn't want to talk to her but because he needed to think about what to say. How do you make up for alienating one parent for the sake of another, only to realize you backed the wrong horse?

Declan parked his truck and started carrying in the litter box and bed first, stopping when he saw a notice on his front door.

ALL VEHICLES MUST BE OFF THE STREET NO LATER THAN FIVE PM FRIDAY DECEMBER 13TH FOR THE PARADE OF LIGHTS. VEHICLES LEFT IN THE AREA WILL BE TOWED.

THANK YOU FOR YOUR CONSIDERATION,

MISTLETOE CITY COUNCIL

He left the paper up for customers, but tomorrow he'd move his truck to the back.

When everything was inside and situated, Declan locked his truck and carried Leo through the front door and back to the studio. He shut the door behind them and unzipped the carrier. Leo bounded out of the carrier, curiously looking around the concrete room.

"I know it's not home, but it will do until I figure out our next move." Declan unfolded the cot and rolled his sleeping bag out on the surface. When he laid down on top with his head on the pillows, his back protested the hard spring surface beneath.

Leo jumped onto his chest and kneaded his stomach, turning his rear end toward Declan's face.

"Dude, I've told you how rude it is to put your butt in my face," Declan said, picking the cat's back end up and swinging him around until he was looking at Leo's half-closed eyes. "See? Not so bad, right?"

Leo settled in and Declan closed his eyes, his thoughts racing over the events of the day and how he was going to make amends with not just his mom but Holly too.

His mind flashed back to his mom sitting on the side of his bed, singing "Tomorrow" as she stroked his hair back after a rough day at school, telling him that everything would look brighter in the morning.

He really hoped she was right.

CHAPTER 19

FRIDAY MORNING, THERE WAS A persistent knocking at Holly's front door and when she opened it with a drowsy glower, Delilah stood on her front step, doing a little dance in her hot pink coat and cat-eared beanie.

"I finished my article!"

"Good for you. Did you have to bang on my door at the butt crack of dawn to tell me?"

"Wow, someone's cranky. Are you going to let me in for coffee or shall I freeze to death out here?"

"While freezing would get me out of a murder rap, I kind of want the satisfaction of strangling you."

"Hey, I'm not the only early riser. I saw Declan Gallagher setting up a ladder on the side of your house."

Holly was suddenly wide awake and grabbed Delilah by the front of her coat, dragging her inside. "Get in here before he sees me."

"Why do you care if he...wait." Delilah covered her mouth with a pink gloved hand. "Do you like him?"

"I may have undetermined feelings for him, but I don't want

him to see me braless with my hair standing on end!" Holly ran to the sliding glass door in the kitchen and shut the blinds inside in case he decided to come around the back.

"So what happened between last week when we were getting glitter bombed to now with him decorating your house? I didn't even know he did that kind of work. I thought he was all 'Grrr, I hate Christmas. You ho ho hoes suck.'"

"He was, I mean, still is, but it's almost like we're dogs."

"Dogs?" Delilah repeated slowly.

"I know it sounds weird, but at first we were circling and snapping at each other. Then something shifted and we were warily curious. Then we started sniffing each other and feeling each other out—"

"Whoa, wait, you guys did butt stuff?" Delilah shrieked and Holly slapped her hand over her friend's mouth.

"No, now will you keep your voice down? It's a metaphor! You're a writer, don't you know what that is?"

Delilah grabbed her hand and pulled it off her mouth. "First, I am not the one comparing myself to a dog, and second, I haven't had any grown-up brain juice yet."

"Let me get through this and then I'll make you coffee. Where was I?"

"You were feeling each other up."

Holly rolled her eyes. "Then he's asking if we can try to get along and I'm telling him I want to take it a step further and then suddenly as he's walking out the door last night he kisses me."

"Oh, was it good?"

"I think so, but it was so brief, like a kiss and run, that I need a repeat to be sure." Holly went around the counter to start the coffee. "But then he was talking about his dad selling the hardware store and leaving town before it happened."

"That's perfect for you though, 'cause you don't get attached."

"Yeah, I thought the same thing."

"You're not thinking that way now?"

Holly sighed, snapping the lid down on the coffee maker. "I don't know what I'm feeling, except being around Declan makes me feel charged, like a thousand volts of electricity racing through me, and I love that sensation."

"Heck, I like the sensation and I'm living it vicariously through you. So what are you going to do about it?"

"Drink coffee. Get ready for work. Leave."

"Uh-uh. You're going to shower while I finish this, put on something to make that man go *damn*, and I'll take my caffeine to go so you can get your round two."

"Delilah, he's trying to get my display up. I don't want to distract him, but—oh! That reminds me. I think Mr. James next door has been sabotaging me!"

"Whaaaat? Why do you think that?"

"I was the last one on the circle list to have their display set up and everyone on the crew suddenly came down with a mysterious illness they won't get over in time to put up my decorations. Every other company is booked solid. And someone got into my shed and messed up the order of my display."

"Babe, you know I love and support you, but that sounds paranoid."

"I thought the same thing, but when I brought up that I'd

installed cameras and a security system, Mr. James got super squirrely."

"It actually wouldn't be a bad idea to put in a security system. You've got expensive stuff in the front yard anyone could make off with while you sleep."

"I ordered one last night. Let's just hope the holidays don't delay the shipment." Holly set the cup of coffee down in front of Delilah with a smile. "Now, I'm thinking I might take you up on your offer and get cleaned up."

"Yeah baby, and then you can get dirty again. Ha!" Delilah laughed when Holly nudged her shoulder as she passed. "Bestie abuse!"

Holly found herself moving at lightning speed to get dressed and ready, coming back into the kitchen to find a note from Delilah and a cup of coffee just the color she liked it.

Sniff that booty, girl! Love you!

Shaking her head, Holly warmed up her coffee, planning in her head what she wanted to say. She didn't have any trouble with men, but Declan was a flight risk and she didn't want him bailing before he explained what that kiss meant.

Or did it again.

Holly grabbed her coffee from the microwave and stepped outside. There was no sign of Declan, but she saw scenes one and two were set up on the ground. She followed the walkway down to the other side of her garage where a ladder leaned against the house and she spotted Declan on the roof bent over, his jean-clad butt in the air.

Nice butt.

"Morning," she called.

Declan stood up and took a step back to look over the edge of the roof at her, his expression unreadable. "Good morning."

"Want some coffee?"

"I grabbed some at the café, so I'm good. Thanks."

"Sure. How long before you come down?"

"I'm anchoring these down right now, so five minutes?"

"Okay, I'll come help you," she said, setting her coffee down on the ground.

"You don't have to do that," he protested, but she was almost to the top before he finished. Holly took the hand he held out to her and stepped onto the roof with a grin, careful not to crush the strings of white lights that looked like fallen snow when they were lit up in the dark.

"Whew, I forget how pretty the view of town is from up here."

"It is a good view, but you could have waited on the porch."

"Why, when I could be up here helping you?" Holly glanced around at the bare gables above them, hating to ask but looking for honesty. "Are you sure you're going to get this done?"

"I hope so, but you've got a lot of lights. I can see why the guy who usually does this didn't want to take the job without a full crew."

Holly's heart sank. "I appreciate you trying at least."

"The day ain't over yet." Declan nodded to the wooden chimney cut out with the Grinch popping out the top. "You hold onto it while I make sure it's secure enough to stand on its own."

"I can do that," Holly said, lifting the display into place, watching the top of Declan's head as he squatted down.

"I'm sorry about last night," he said abruptly without looking up from what he was doing.

Holly almost let go of the wooden piece, thrown by his apology. "What exactly are you sorry for?"

"Kissing you. It was inappropriate and I hope you won't tell Sam. It was a momentary lapse that won't happen again."

Tell Sam? Momentary lapse?

Declan stood up, waving a hand. "Go ahead and let go. Let's see if I need to tighten it." Holly did what he asked and the object didn't budge. "Perfect."

"What did you mean by 'don't tell Sam'?"

Declan rotated her way, his gaze shifting briefly over her shoulder before returning to meet hers. "Aren't you two dating?"

Holly smothered a laugh. "No, we're just friends. Although I don't know how I feel about you kissing me when you thought I was dating Sam. Oh God!" Holly covered her mouth. "Did you think I was with Sam when I suggested we work stuff out of our system?"

"Yeah, I did," he said, sheepishly.

"Wow, you thought I was a cheating hussy and you still kissed me." She tsked. "What does that say about Declan Gallagher?"

"It was just a small peck. Barely worth mentioning."

That stung. "Every kiss means something. It doesn't have to be anything more than "Hey, your lips are pretty" or "I want to taste your lip gloss," but you make a conscious decision to kiss someone. It's not like in the movies where suddenly you're kissing out of the blue. Thoughts and feelings led up to it and if you were just going to sweep it under the rug and forget it ever happened, why did you do it?"

He hesitated for a second before his hand came up, brushing along her cheek. "You're right. It wasn't random. I wanted to kiss you because I heard you defending me to Mr. James, even when I've been an asshole to you more times than I can count. I didn't have any coffee or chocolates, and I guess I could have just given you a hug, but—" Declan cleared his throat, his gaze shifting away from hers. "I wanted to do more. We were having fun and then you took up for me, even though you don't know the whole story."

"What do you mean? With Theodore James?"

"Yeah, the guy hates my guts for something I did in high school."

"What did you do?"

"He used to give me a hard time. Even tried suspending me for calling him a dick when I got sick of him riding me, but my mom came in and talked to the principal, and they transferred me to a different teacher, excusing me from PE." Declan smiled sheepishly, motioning for them to sit and Holly dropped next to him on the roof, hanging on his every word as he continued, "The seniors on the football team wanted to pull off an epic end of the year prank and I suggested we find a wrecked version of Mr. James's car and set it up in the front of the school as if it ran into the wall."

"Oh my God, I remember that! Everyone thought it was real until they got close and realized it was a fake hole."

"We got the idea from a news article we'd seen about a senior prank in Wisconsin and it took us over a month to plan. We had keys made to his car and took it in the middle of the night before the last day of school, parking it in the auto shop bay. He had to get a ride to school, and he thought we'd really driven his car into the side of the school building. No one 'fessed up, but he came right out and said he knew I'd been a part of it. We cleaned everything up that night, so no one else was upset about it, they were actually impressed. But he's never been a fan of mine."

Holly shook her head. "That's crazy, but honestly, I think he's like that with anyone who doesn't agree with his way of doing things. He's the head of our homeowners association and a few years ago some of our neighborhood cats went missing. Turned out he was baiting and trapping them just to dump them in the woods. When the neighbors called him out on it, he told them it was in the by-laws that animals need to remain on your property or they could be deemed a nuisance and trapped. Several of the cat owners called the sheriff's department and the trap went away, but he gives them a really hard time."

"He's an asshole. If he trapped my cat, I'd do more than call the cops."

Holly hesitated, unsure if telling Declan of her suspicion, especially when he already disliked Theodore, would be a good idea. "I think he's messing with me."

"How do you mean?"

"I was going to tell you last night before you interrupted me with that kiss, but the way he keeps popping up and some of the things he's said to me got me thinking. He wasn't happy that I won the best display last year, something he's been first at for years. Then the week the display is supposed to go up, everyone else's houses are done but mine and the crew gets sick. Followed by every other crew being too busy and then him showing up last night to tell me I shouldn't use you? He's way too up in my business for my liking."

"It seems like a lot of trouble over a contest."

"You suggested someone must have got into my shed," she pointed out. "And he freaked when I told him I'd had cameras installed. I'm telling you, I'm like Velma. I sense a villain."

Declan took a lock of her hair, sliding it between his fingers. "Funny, I pictured you as more of a Daphne."

"I'm no one's victim."

"Fair enough. I'll keep my eye out if Mr. J comes around."

"Thank you."

"Just so we're clear—" Declan leaned over and whispered, "I'm glad you aren't dating Sam."

"Why?"

"Because at least I didn't sneak attack kiss a woman with a boyfriend."

Holly shared his smile. "Sneak attack kiss is a new one for me."

"You know what I mean. I didn't exactly give you time to say no."

"Or give me a chance to say yes before you were running out the door."

Declan stilled. "You wanted me to kiss you?"

"I've toyed with the idea a time or two before you did and I haven't been able to think about much else since."

"Really?"

Holly shrugged. "It's like getting a taste of artisanal chocolate. You expect it to be funky because they add weird stuff in, but then you take a small bite and suddenly you're craving the rest."

Declan chuckled softly. "You want to kiss me again because I have weirdness in me and you crave it?"

"That was a literal take, but yes."

"Yes?"

Holly leaned in until she pressed against the side of his arm, her mouth brushing the shell of his ear. "I want to kiss you again."

Declan's hand came up, cradling the side of her face, and he turned her until their lips were aligned. "I want to kiss you, too."

Holly closed her eyes when Declan's lips covered hers, the soft glide of his tongue creating frissons of heat throughout her body. That brief meeting of mouths the night before had left her dazed, but this deeper exploration brought out a hunger in her and Holly's hands came up to tangle in Declan's hair, drawing him closer.

When they finally came up for air, Declan chuckled. "I'd say we take this show to a lower elevation, but if I don't let you go now, your display isn't getting done."

Holly almost told him she didn't care, but that would be a lie. The last thing she wanted to do was disappoint the people who came from all over Idaho, some even from out of state, to see their neighborhood displays.

"All right, but I need to collect further data from you later. Maybe tomorrow after work you could come over for dinner?"

Declan kissed her again, pulling back with a grin. "Count me in."

CHAPTER 20

DECLAN GLANCED FROM HOLLY'S HOUSE to the pile of scenes, lights, and other items that made up the display on her front lawn. He'd played down the severity of the situation to Holly, but the truth was Declan was in way over his head and needed help.

Pulling his phone out of his pocket, he got ready to dial Clark when a familiar voice called, "It's a lot, isn't it?"

Declan turned towards Mr. James's raspy voice, his jaw clenching at the grinning old man.

"Just planning my next step."

"I told her not to throw her money around and go overboard, but young people like her think they know everything."

Declan looked over at the Peanut Gallery display Mr. James had at his place, with a large blow-up Snoopy doghouse and every square inch of the house covered in Christmas lights.

"Yeah, I can see you used common sense and moderation," Declan deadpanned.

"What was that?"

"I'm pointing out that Holly's display isn't any more elaborate than yours. She's just had a streak of bad luck that's put her behind." Declan crossed his arms over his chest. "Know anything about that?"

"Are you accusing me of sabotage, Declan? You, after what you pulled?"

"Oh come on, man, it was a practical joke that four other guys in high school were in on, but because you had an issue with me, you held a grudge. Your car was fine. The school was fine. Just let it go."

"You got away with it because you're an entitled little shit, just like the rest of your generation, including that spoiled brat next door. Flaunting money she didn't have to work for, just shaking her—"

Declan's entire frame went rigid. "You want to walk away before you finish that sentence. Now."

Mr. James's eyes widened. "Are you threatening me?"

"Physically? No, sir, but you're pissing me off and I don't think you realize I'm not an eighteen-year-old kid under your authority anymore. I know my way around power tools and how to cover my tracks, so if I find out you're giving Holly any more grief, I'm going to pop Snoopy's abode when you least expect it. Are we clear?"

"If you touch my house, Declan, I'll have the cops at your door."

"From what I hear, there are quite a few people in this town who think you have it coming. Point the finger at me? I'll drop ten more names who can't tolerate your attitude. Do us both a favor and leave Holly alone."

Declan walked away before he said something he'd really regret. There was no way he'd hurt the old jackass, but Holly wasn't a spoiled brat. She was sweet and sensitive and funny. Beautiful.

And he'd be damned if that asshole was going to beat her in this lights competition because Mr. James was a sore loser.

Declan stepped onto the porch, where a wicker chair and ottoman set were positioned parallel to the wall of the house, with red cushions and festive outdoor throw pillows covering most of the dark, woven wood. He sat down, watching Mr. James pull out of his driveway and take off. Declan took a deep breath before he tapped in Clark's number and hit the call button, listening to the high-pitched ring until Clark answered.

"Hello, Declan. What's going on?"

"Hey, I need your help. Holly's display is too big for me to handle on my own and I've got to have this up and ready to go by sunset. I know you're swamped with the farm during the holidays, but I need bodies. Lots of them. I wouldn't ask if it wasn't for your family."

"I'll tell Merry, and she can cover for me. It's slow today, so they should be good. Let me make some calls and I'll see you in twenty."

Declan was back on the roof twenty minutes later when a parade of cars pulled into the circle, parking along the street. Clark got out with his sunglasses on, a wide smile on his face. "You said a little help, right?"

"That will do."

"Oh, you ain't seen nothing yet. I guess there's a phone tree in this town and Holly's helped out a lot of people, so about two dozen favors were called in."

Declan shook his head, disbelief and wonder racing through

him as he climbed down off the roof. Nick and Pike got out of one car, greeting Declan with handshakes.

"Anthony will be by after two. He had to work," Nick said.

"And you two didn't?"

Nick shrugged. "I make my own hours, and besides, if my sisters need me, I'm there."

Pike yawned. "And I had nothing else going on."

Between Declan and Clark, they were able to organize everyone into groups to work on specific functions. They had about ten people running lights along the roof and sides of the house and the rest were split up into scenes, securing everything down.

Within a few hours, the display was finally coming together. Just in time for Mr. James to get home.

He rubber-necked the entire way up his driveway until he disappeared into the garage, only to come charging out of the house a few minutes later, waving a packet in the air.

"All of these cars are illegally parked and need to be removed!"

Declan rolled his eyes from his position at the edge of the lawn, while Nick smiled and waved at Mr. James, rushing over to meet the irate neighbor.

"Nick will calm him down," Clark said quietly. "The man has a gift. Everyone likes him."

When the packet waving didn't stop, Declan climbed to his feet and crossed the lawn to stand next to Nick, listening to Holly's brother's calm, cajoling tone.

"I get that it's against the HOA code of conduct, but we're going to be out of here in an hour or two tops, and we're not blocking any driveways. You can absolutely call the cops, but they're going to see we're doing a job, helping out a Mistletoe citizen who needs it, and keep rolling. If you want, you can grab some gloves and give us a hand. You know, be neighborly."

Mr. James clenched the packet in his hands until it ripped, and he stormed back into his house, slamming the door.

Nick shook his head, mouth pressed in a grim line. "No matter what my sister likes to call you, *that's* a fucking Scrooge."

Declan laughed, feeling a weight lift off his shoulders. As the morning rolled into afternoon, they tested animatronics, lights, and Declan got a clue what people meant when they talked about small towns coming together as a community. There were certain people in this world that could command this kind of loyalty and affection and Holly was one of them.

At half past four, most of the cars had trickled out of the circle, needing to leave to get ready for the Parade of Lights downtown, the annual celebration where local organizations and businesses created large floats covered completely in Christmas lights and drove them down a darkened Main Street. He'd thanked so many people his mouth was dry, and his whole body ached, even his eyeballs from staring at too many Christmas lights.

"Hey, Declan, let's go get some drinks and food!" Pike called, closing the lid on one of the totes and picking it up. "You're buying though."

"I'm down, but I want to stick around and see Holly's reaction." *And maybe snag another kiss or two.*

"All right, we'll meet you after the Parade of Lights?" Clark asked.

"When's that end?"

"Sevenish," Nick said. "We all work on my parents' float, so it might be a little after."

"I'll probably eat before it ends, but I'll meet you guys for a beer or two."

"Awesome. See you later," Nick said, walking around the car to the driver's side.

Clark didn't make a move to leave and Declan studied his friend. "What?"

"I'm just wondering something…"

"Spit it out."

"Was today really about the money? Or about making Holly happy?"

Declan didn't answer right away, mulling that over. "Twenty-eighty split."

Clark slapped him on the back with a laugh. "I knew the two of you would work it out. You should ride over with Holly to the parade. We can always use another set of hands."

"Thanks, but I'll pass. I've got to get back to the store and feed my cat."

"You keep a cat at the hardware store?"

"I meant at home," Declan said in a rush, hoping Clark would believe him when he added, "Sorry, I guess even my brain is worn out."

"Oh, I know all about those days. I'll text you when we leave the parade."

"Looking forward to it."

When Clark rounded the corner out of the neighborhood, Declan took a picture of the house and sent it to Holly's number.

What do you think? Acceptable?

A few moments passed before she shot back. **Omg it's gorgeous! I can't wait to see it in person. Thank you! I can't believe you finished.**

I had a lot of help.
Well, as much as you hate Christmas, you turned out to be Santa Claus with all his little helpers! Let me know what your favorite dinner is for tomorrow night!

Declan grinned and settled onto the couch, waiting until the sun went down. As much as he wanted to get back to the store and clean up before meeting the guys, he was determined to make sure the lights came on without a hitch.

Holly sent him a kiss, heart eyes, and dancing girl emojis and Declan laughed aloud. Holly's excitement was infectious and seeing how everything came together so well filled him with a sense of pride he hadn't expected from a bunch of Christmas decorations.

Was he growing up? Was it finding out about his parents' deception? Or was it being around Holly that had him opening his eyes to the world in a different way?

Declan couldn't say for sure, but as of right now he didn't hate the holidays quite so much.

CHAPTER 21

HOLLY CHECKED THE CLOCK AGAIN, wishing she could close up shop early today. With the Parade of Lights kicking off in a few hours, Main Street was dead anyway, and she was ready to be home.

She pulled up the pictures Declan sent her, smiling at what a beautiful job he'd done. Sure, he'd admitted needing help, but the fact that he figured out how to get it done with all the hiccups? He absolutely deserved what she was paying him.

Are you still at my house?

His response was almost immediate and included a picture of his legs and feet propped up on her porch chair ottoman with a view of her front yard beyond. Yep. I want to see your face when you get here.

She smiled so hard her face hurt. I'll leave here soon.

He included a thumbs up emoji and Holly wasn't sure if she should be disappointed there was no funny, flirty message attached or relieved he wasn't making a big deal about their intense, delicious kiss this morning.

Since her longest relationships had only lasted a few months, she wasn't expecting things with Declan to develop into anything deeper than attraction, possibly affection, but Holly didn't want there to be any resentment when they parted ways, considering they'd had enough of that the first two years of their acquaintance. What she was hoping for was a hot, down and dirty, spicy fling, and once they got the sexual tension banged out of them, they could move on with a new understanding of each other.

Still, the fact that he kept so much of himself close to the breast bothered her. Holly understood boundaries were healthy and important, but how did he expect to get close to people if he didn't even let them see the best parts? The sensitive, vulnerable parts?

The door opened and Santa called out *"ho, ho, ho"* startling the older dark-haired woman walking through it. She covered her chest with a laugh and said, "Oh my. That was better than a cup of coffee to wake you up."

Holly grinned. "Sorry it scared you. I've been reassessing my use of it, especially since people don't expect it and nearly jump out of their skin."

"I wouldn't change a thing. I think life should be full of surprises." The closer she got, the more familiar she seemed, but Holly couldn't put her finger on how she knew her. "Your shop is adorable. I haven't been back to town for years, so this is my first time in."

"Oh, well, welcome back to Mistletoe," Holly said, coming around the counter. "I'm Holly Winters, the owner. If you need any help finding something, let me know."

"Thank you. You're the YouTube star, aren't you?"

Holly laughed, cheeks warming after all these years anytime she was recognized. "Yes, the Adventure Elf, although I haven't been very adventurous lately."

"I've seen a few of your videos friends sent me. You definitely have a zest for life."

"Or a death wish, according to my older sister."

"Nonsense. I don't think anything you've done is too zany and you should experience as much as you can before you have children if that is in the cards for you. Playing catch up in your late fifties is brutal on your body. I tried parasailing in Florida and I needed four pain pills and an ice pack just to get out of bed the next day."

"Oh, I loved parasailing in Hawaii, but I've seen too many videos of parasailers looking down in Florida and seeing hundreds of sharks below. No, thank you."

"I thought I'd feel the same, but then I did a shark swim in the Bahamas after snorkeling and it's such a powerful feeling." She picked up one of the ornaments off the closest Christmas tree, a wreath made out of tools, and handed it to Holly. "I'll take this one for sure."

"Fantastic, I'll wrap it up." Holly pulled out the gift wrap drawer and took the tag off the ornament before safely surrounding it in a layer of tissue. "What are your plans while you're in town?"

"Mostly reconnecting with my family and old friends. I was going to stop in and talk to my son today, but he wasn't at the store."

Holly stilled in the middle of selecting a red-and-white striped gift bag, puzzle pieces clicking into place. "Who's your son?"

"Declan Gallagher."

Eager curiosity rushed through her like a shot of liquor, and she set the bag on the counter with a smile. "I thought you looked familiar. I've seen your picture." Holly's mind raced as she studied Declan's mom, wondering if Declan knew she was there or if this was supposed to be one of those awkward surprise visits they show in comedies that make people with social anxiety disorder uncomfortable. "Does he know you're in town?"

"He knows. Not sure if he approves, but that's just the way of things. Are you friends with my son?"

"Kind of. Depends on the day. Right now, he's at my place setting up Christmas lights."

"I saw the sign he left on the shop door about being out on a handyman job today." She held out her hand. "I forgot to officially introduce myself. Diana Thacker, formerly Gallagher."

"It's good to meet you."

"You've had him stringing Christmas lights all day?"

"Yes, I'm a harsh task mistress. Poor guy got stuck doing my display over on Evergreen Circle, so it's a little more than Christmas lights."

"Oh, I used to love going through there and seeing the different displays every year. We bought a house one street over, so I could at least see some of them from afar. You must be doing well to buy a house in that neighborhood."

"I do well enough, but I got lucky it even became available."

"I always wanted to live there, but my husband isn't exactly Mr. Christmas. Sorry, ex-husband." She picked up another ornament, a bemused smile on her lips. "We've been divorced for ten years but he still feels like mine, although I didn't think that way when we signed the papers. Time and distance really do heal, I suppose." Diana returned the ornament to the tree and turned to Holly. "Are you married? I don't see a ring, but a lot of women don't wear them anymore."

"No, I'm not married."

"I hate to tell you, but being married is a lot of work. On yourself and keeping a connection with your partner. It's easy to fall in love, but hard to maintain that love through life." Diana laughed. "I guess that's not entirely true. Your parents are still married, right?"

"Yes, over thirty years."

"If I ever decide to tie the knot again, I'll have to ask your mother's secret."

"I'm sure she'll tell you. My mother loves to dole out advice like its lollipops."

"I hope you take some of it. There are so many things I'd love to tell Declan, but I doubt he would hear them." Diana plucked a delicate ornament with five paint brushes crossed into a star shape, with trails of paint in various shades of green swirling along the outsides and up the middle to create the idea of a tree. "This reminds me of Declan."

"Except for the Christmas tree part." His mother met her gaze and Holly shrugged. "Declan isn't big on the holidays."

"Yes, I know. It breaks my heart because he used to always be in the kitchen with me, helping with the holiday treat containers we'd make for our neighbors and friends. His favorite song was 'Run Run Rudolph' and he used to slide around the kitchen in his socks trying to run as fast as he could."

"It is hard to imagine Declan doing any of that. I call him an old soul."

"Well, yes, he's always been that way. Serious. Creative. The football team helped him branch out a little socially, but he didn't really enjoy the sport."

"Declan's not a sports guy?" Holly asked, soaking up every piece of information.

"Oh no. He'd rather be in his art studio with a brush in his hand than outside playing."

"He painted me a landscape of my parents' tree farm. It's hanging up on my wall at home. Do you want to see it now? Declan might still be there and I'm dying to close up shop and check out my display in person."

"That would be lovely, but I don't want to ambush Declan. Our relationship is...complicated."

Holly resisted the urge to ask her anything else. Holly already felt like she was pumping her for information. "Maybe another time while you're in town. Are you going to the Parade of Lights tonight?"

"No. Liam, Declan's dad, and I have reservations at the Lodge tonight for dinner, and he's rented one of their rooms. I haven't been since our ten-year anniversary years ago, but I'm looking forward to it."

"We went a few times for my mom's birthday and it was delicious. I hope you have a wonderful time."

"I'm sure I will." She handed Holly the other ornament carefully. "I think just the two ornaments for now. I'll be back for a longer look sometime when you're not trying to get home."

"It's no trouble. I enjoyed talking to you."

"Same, dear."

Holly finished ringing her up and wrapped the other ornament, putting this one in a brown gift bag with pine trees on the side. She held out both bags to her and said, "Merry Christmas, Diana. Have a great dinner."

"Thank you, enjoy the parade."

Once Diana was out the door, Holly locked it and closed up the register, rushing through her nightly duties. The sun was slowly setting below the trees, and Holly planned to beat the darkness home. She needed to call Merry and see if she could get a ride back to the parade, because once she got home she wasn't getting her car out of there again before ten.

Holly went out the back of the shop and set the alarm, putting in her code on the keypad, securing the back door. She reached her driver's side and tapped in a message to Declan.

OMW

Declan gave her another thumbs up, and she scowled at the screen. The guy really had one emoji move.

Holly passed a few cars on her short drive from the shop to her house, but when the town had large events like this, most people used all-terrain vehicles to get close and walked the rest of the way. It saved space trying to find parking.

Holly dialed Merry, listening to the phone ring and on the third, an out of breath Merry answered, "Hello!"

"Hey, what are you doing? You're huffing and puffing over there like you ran a mile."

"I'm getting the last-minute touches on the float before we haul it into town."

"Can you pick me up on the way? I can't get out of here once the people start showing up."

"Yeah, sure. You know Nick and Clark are bailing, right?"

"No, what are you talking about?"

"They're going to help us get everything ready and then they're going out for drinks with *the boys...*" Merry dragged out the last two words with a heavy dose of sarcasm. "Said they worked hard on your display, even took on your angry next-door neighbor, and deserve to blow off some steam. So Mom and Dad are Santa and Mrs. Claus and we are their elves."

"I expect this kind of behavior from Nick, but Clark?" Holly clucked her tongue. "So disappointed."

"Yeah, I told him he better not get snookered with Nick and need a ride home 'cause I'll be sleeping."

Holly laughed. "What we should do is crash their boys' night and get our own drink on. We work hard, too!"

"Hell yeah we do!"

Holly took the left into her neighborhood, smiling when she saw Declan's truck parked in front of her house, then slowly turned into the drive. "All right, come get me and we'll make a plan. I just pulled into my house and want to take it in."

"Have fun! Bye."

Holly stopped her car at the bottom of the driveway, the wide grin on her face straining the muscles. It was gorgeous. The garage door was wrapped with a large piece of heavy plastic that was made to look like the front of Dr. Seuss's Whoville homes, with drapes of white lights hanging on either side. A crossroads sign that read Mount Crumpet and Whoville was placed at the corner of her lawn, and she saw the large Mount Crumpet looming over her front porch with the Grinch leaning over, hating the Whos. Various scenes of the story were scattered along the lawn, and on the other side of the driveway the Grinch was stealing a bright strand of Christmas lights.

It was better than she could have imagined.

Holly hit the garage button and pulled inside, closing it behind her. She went through the house and back around to the front porch, where she found Declan grinning in her oversized chair.

"So, what do you think?"

Overcome with happiness, Holly plopped down next to him, snuggling against him. "It's amazing. Thank you."

Besides the flare of surprise in his eyes for a split-second, he didn't hesitate to move his arm around her shoulders and pull her in close. "Like I said, I had a lot of help." Declan chuckled. "I've heard the phrase 'It takes a village,' but the minute your name was dropped, thirty people showed up here ready to roll up their sleeves and dive in. I couldn't believe it."

"Did you write down their names? I want to send them a thank-you card."

"People still do that?"

"My family does. My mom had us sit down after every birthday and write thank-you cards to everyone who came." Holly tilted her head against his chest and looked up at him. "By the way, your mom was looking for you."

Declan stiffened against her. "When?"

"Before I closed the shop. She came in and bought a few things. Mentioned she'd stopped by next door to see her son, and we got to talking—"

"About me?"

"A little bit, but other things too." She slid her hand up his chest, pushing up until she could look into his eyes. "Declan, whatever you're thinking, I wasn't trying to be sneaky or nose into your business."

"It's not you." He sighed, removing his arm from around her to sit up.

The pain in those three words tugged at her heartstrings, and she slipped her arms around his shoulders from behind. "I'm sorry."

"For what?"

"That you don't get along with your mom."

He didn't respond for several moments, the silence stretching like a blanket over the porch, until finally he whispered, "It's my fault."

"What is?"

"I blamed her for the divorce and alienated her because of it. I should have stayed out of the whole thing, but I thought I knew what happened. Turns out I didn't know a damn thing and I dug my own ditch with an assumption and I don't know how to climb out of it."

"You sure do love your metaphors," Holly murmured, pressing a kiss to the back of his right shoulder. "I don't know what's going on with you and your parents, but from what I can see, whatever you've done your mom still wants to have a relationship with you. If it were me, I'd swallow my pride and make amends."

"I'm working on it." Declan shrugged off her embrace, and while Holly's own pride was stung by that small rejection, he got up off the chair, straightening his jacket with a grim expression. "I better get out of your hair so you can get ready for the blinding eyesore parade."

Holly's eyes narrowed. "We're back to that now?"

"What do you mean? This is me, Holly. No ribbons or bows or holiday cheer. Your house was a job. It doesn't change my feelings about this town or the season. No matter what my mother may have told you, I'm never going to be into all this crap."

"And me? Are you into me, or was that kiss this morning nothing?"

Declan shrugged. "That kiss was great, but I've had all day to play over the scenarios in my head. What's the point of getting involved? I'm trying to get out of here, and you're happy in your fairy tale existence where you have an amazing, loving family and a town full of adoring citizens who drop everything to help some of their neighbors."

"What is wrong with that? What is wrong with wanting to live somewhere like Mistletoe, where we care about each other?"

"Don't fool yourself, Holly. They care about *some* people. Not everyone. This place has always been a popularity contest and you're one of the golden few. You can't tell me all those people showed up wanting nothing in return."

"Maybe not, but if I'm popular, Declan, it's because I participate in this community. I'm jumping in when the local theater troop needs an understudy, or I'm organizing a dinner chain for a new mother or grieving family. I know who my neighbors are, Declan. Do you? You're so angry at everyone around you, but did you ever stop to think that being an outsider is on you because you never took the time to open up and let people see you?"

"People around here don't want to see anyone who doesn't fit into a mold. I'm a big guy. I should play sports. I hated sports and that made me a reject to people like Mr. James and even my own father to some degree. Because I preferred art to getting knocked around on a football field."

"That's two people, a far cry from the whole town, but that isn't even the root of the issue. You're icy hot. I know you want to leave town and I'm not asking for anything more than that we stop fighting and have some fun, but trying to figure out who you are under all that grumbling hostility is exhausting and even after that mind-blowing kiss I'm not sure it's worth the effort to find out."

Holly's chest rose and fell rapidly with the force of her passionate monologue, but Declan's expression hadn't changed besides a tightening around his mouth. With a heavy, shaking breath, Holly got up from the chair. "Let me get your check."

She went inside, racking her brain for a reason why Declan's aloofness bothered her, especially since she wanted to have her way with him and be done. There was no long-term plan for forever, so why did it matter?

When Holly returned to the porch, Declan was gone. She shot him a text.

> I guess you didn't want to wait for your check. I'll
> drop it by the store Monday.

A single thumbs up emoji and nothing more.

CHAPTER 22

DECLAN SAT FACING THE BAR, peeling the label off his beer bottle and scowling off into space. Holly's explosion earlier was heavy on his mind. It was better with her back to being angry with him. Less complicated that way. After their kiss and the way the townspeople had come together to help her, he'd started feeling... something warm and close to joyous, no matter that he'd said the contrary to Holly, and he'd had to shut it down. If he started thinking there was a place for him here in Mistletoe, he'd only be disappointed when it didn't work out.

Keeping Holly at a distance was best for both of them. She'd drop off the check, he'd avoid her, and then maybe come January he'd be leaving even if his dad didn't decide to sell the store. And if his mom stayed with his dad, Declan would be comfortable making a move to Washington or even Colorado, something within a day's drive that gave him better opportunities. The two of them were going to have to clear the air eventually, and he'd figure out a way to forgive Liam if only to help work through his own guilt. Coming back to Mistletoe for visits here and there, he doubted he'd even pass Holly on the street.

Of course, he couldn't very well ignore her during Clark's and Merry's wedding, but he'd do his best to keep their interactions to a minimum. Unless she decided to be dramatic about their brief interlude—

"Whew, it's a good thing we aren't trying to attract girls 'cause Declan's expression is downright murderous. They'd take one look and avoid super-sized Bundy like the plague."

Declan turned his attention to Pike, who was sipping on a white blended drink with red stripes of syrup along the glass and drizzled down the peak of whipped cream on top.

"Sorry, I was thinking. Not about murder."

"Relieved to hear it, but what about?" Pike took a long drink from his straw and swallowed, tapping his fingers on the table. "Taxes? DMV fees? Doctors asking you to turn your head and cough? That's the look I reserve for those very uncomfortable, irritating situations I have to do but don't want to do."

"It's nothing like that, man," Declan said.

Anthony leaned back in his chair, fingers interwoven over his stomach. "It's obviously a woman."

"Holly?" Clark asked, a smug smile stretching across his face.

Nick groaned mid-drink of beer, setting the bottle onto the table with a thump. "Fuck me. Not my sister. Can't I get through one year without someone falling in love with one of them?"

"Nobody else better be admitting feelings for Merry," Clark growled, shooting Anthony and Pike a dark look.

"Not me," Anthony and Pike said in unison, before all sets of eyes turned back to Declan.

"I'm not in love with Holly!" Declan said, and Nick's frown deepened.

"Why not? What's wrong with her?"

"Nothing's wrong with her," Declan said.

"She's too opinionated," Pike offered.

Anthony snorted. "Just because you want women to adore you and never question your judgment doesn't mean every man feels that way. I like a woman who challenges me on all levels, but I do think she's a little short for the over-sixers like us, Dec." He patted Pike's shoulder roughly. "Something you wouldn't understand, Short-Red."

"Fuck you, and you're under six-foot."

"I'm six-foot-one!"

"In work boots, maybe!"

"Geez, do they always squabble like this?" Declan asked.

"Like an old married couple," Nick said.

"I think Holly's a wonderful woman," Clark said, before adding, "She is a wee bit frightening when she's angry."

"Though she be little, she be fierce," Pike said in a British accent.

"Can you stop talking about my sister's qualities like she's up for auction?" Nick asked.

"I second that," Declan blurted, surprising everyone at the table including himself.

"Seems you and I were right, Tony," Clark said, that irritating smirk still in place. "Declan's got woman troubles."

Declan didn't want to tell one of his only friends to go to hell, but he was tempted. Very tempted.

"You should ask our advice," Pike said, finishing off his drink with a loud slurp of the straw against the bottom of the empty glass. "We helped Clark save his relationship with Merry."

Clark glared. "I think that's an overstatement."

"Nope, it was all us. If they made your love story into some rom com movie, we—" Pike circled the table with his finger. "—would be the special appearances by big name celebrities like Ryan Reynolds and Chris Evans who give sage advice to the hero."

"I picture you as more of a Seth Green," Anthony quipped and Pike's ears turned crimson.

"Just because we both have red hair doesn't mean we look alike!" Pike snapped. "The point is we are here for you. Even if it's to get you something harder than that beer." Pike stood up with his glass in hand and bowed with a flourish. "I will return with libations, my good fellow!"

"What the hell is this new pirate thing he's doing?" Clark asked.

"He's practicing being British before we hit Vegas for New Year's. He thinks he'll get more women with an accent."

"That's stupid," Nick muttered.

Anthony shrugged. "It's Pike. I let him shine and act the fool, which makes me look better."

"Sound strategy," Declan said, watching Pike load a tray with various drinks onto it. "I hope he's not getting anything for me, because I have to drive."

Clark clapped him on the back several times. "I'm pretty sure they're all for you. This group got me hammered to the point where I was seeing triple once. Avoid any holiday drinks with whiskey, that's all I'm going to say."

Pike returned and set the tray on the table, placing a green shot in front of Anthony. "A Merry Elfin Christmas for my good pal Tony." A glass of something red with white and green sprinkles went to Clark. "Santa's Sack."

"I don't need anything," Declan said, but Pike ignored him, setting a shot glass of red liquid and a tall glass of frothy white in front of him with whipped cream and a green Christmas tree cookie sticking out the side. "A Clatter Shot for Declan with a Dashing through the Snow chaser. That's the big one."

"Nothing for me?" Nick asked.

"Hell no, you're driving us home." Pike settled back into his chair with a martini glass drink that looked like peppermint candy.

"Why don't I drive us home and Nick can drink?" Declan tried to move the drinks in front of Nick, but he held out his hand, shaking his head.

"Sorry, pal, I'm the chosen one, which means you must drink."

Declan picked up the shot and sniffed it, the spicy blast of cinnamon making his eyes water. He'd never been one to party in high school, and when he did go out for a drink with friends in college, it was usually a bottle of wine or beers, nothing harder than that.

He looked around the table at these men who had come out to help him today, not just because it was for Holly but because they considered Declan a friend. The friends he'd met in college wouldn't even help him move when he'd asked, but these guys barely knew him and were buying him drinks, offering to listen to his problems.

Damn it, he didn't want this. After two years of being stuck in this town again, he did not want to start liking it here.

Which had been part of the reason he'd run out on Holly earlier. The way she'd snuggled into him like it was the most natural motion in the world filled him with a sense of comfort and security. Having his arm around Holly felt like his happy place, and he couldn't let himself think that way.

Declan picked up the shot, holding it aloft. "To friends who come when you call and aren't afraid to climb ladders."

"Which is a good thing, considering your luck with them," Clark quipped, earning a glare from Declan before they tipped their drinks back. Declan's shot went down his throat in a burning rush, settling in his stomach and every part of him felt the glow from the heat.

"At least I have a hard-enough head to take it," Declan said with a grin.

"Is that hard head the reason you're having a rough time with Holly?" Tony asked.

"I didn't say it was Holly I was thinking about."

"So there's someone else twisting you up, then?" Pike said, pushing the other drink towards Declan. "Give this one a try, it will take that rasp out of your voice."

Declan took a sip, his throat cooling immediately, and he smiled at the sweet coconut flavor of the drink. "Delicious. There's no one else. I mean, there's no Holly or anyone. I may be leaving Mistletoe so it doesn't make sense to get involved with anyone."

"If you did, Holly would be the one," Tony said. "She doesn't do relationships."

"Then again, neither did Noel until Nick got his hooks into her," Pike said.

"You're walking on thin ice tonight, Pike," Nick said.

"Hey, I'm not saying it's a bad thing. The two of you are meant to be. It's just taking you a little longer to convince your woman to tie the knot than it did Clark."

Clark sat forward, obviously trying to keep the peace. "I think that everyone comes with their own baggage and couples take the next step when they are meant to."

Nick glared at Pike. "I'd marry Noel in a second, but she's still not convinced marriage is in the cards for her, although she's talked about kids a couple of times. I figure we've got time and if we never take those steps, I'll be an amazing uncle to Jace and any other rugrats you guys have."

"Thanks, man," Clark said gruffly. "That means a lot."

Declan knew enough about Clark that his parents were pretty much out of his life, and his brother, Sam, and son, Jace, were the only people he'd cared about before Clark took the job at the Winters Christmas Tree Farm. He'd formed his own family and for whatever reason he'd included Declan in it.

"Hey Declan, what did you mean about leaving? I thought you were running the hardware store now?" Anthony asked.

"My dad's talking about selling it. Since he's retired and it's not really what I want to be doing."

"Seriously? That's a great building." Pike shot Tony a look before he continued, "What is it you want to do? If it's not running the hardware store."

"I want my own art gallery one day, but I don't think I'll be able to do that in a town like Mistletoe. Maybe teach."

"Are you trying to say we aren't cultured?" Tony asked.

"I think he is." Pike set his drink down and cracked the knuckles on each hand, his expression blank. "He's calling us a bunch of uncouth rednecks."

Declan's eyes widened, and he stammered, "No, I mean—I just don't think arts are as appreciated as other things—" Declan realized the men at the table were holding back their laughter and glared. "You guys are a bunch of assholes."

Nick smirked. "Maybe so, but we are hilarious a-holes."

"I don't know why you think Idaho doesn't appreciate artists. Sun Valley and Boise have a ton of art galleries."

Declan threw his hands in the air. "You're right, Clark. Idaho has some great areas for art, but I don't think Mistletoe is one of them."

"Make it one," Tony said, echoing what Holly had told Declan last night, and when the entire table turned his way he elaborated. "I'm saying that we get a lot of tourists rolling through. Having a gallery featuring local area artists wouldn't be a bad thing."

"Maybe," Declan said, sucking down half his coconut drink before wincing as a brain freeze seized his forehead. He closed his eyes, fighting the sharp explosion.

"Hey, look who's here," Pike said cheerfully.

Declan opened his eyes and followed the others' gazes toward Holly, Merry, and a few of their friends standing just inside the door. While Merry headed straight for their table, Holly and the others hung around to talk to Sam, who seemed to have come in behind them. Holly laughed at something Sam said, leaning into the older man and giving him a lingering hug.

Declan's grip around his glass tightened as he watched Sam

run his hands over Holly's back, traveling dangerously low and setting Declan's teeth on edge. Telling himself that getting involved with Holly was disastrous didn't stop him from wanting to charge across the bar and drag her away from Sam's wandering hands like a Neanderthal.

God, he really needed to get his head on straight. This emotional roller coaster was giving *him* whiplash.

Pike stood up and Tony asked, "Where you going?"

"To get another round. I think Declan's going to need it."

Declan tossed back the remainder of the cold mixed drink and nodded. "You might be right."

CHAPTER 23

IT TOOK EVERYTHING IN HOLLY'S power not to turn to see if Declan was really watching her or if that tingle on the back of her neck was just her imagination. Merry and Delilah had rushed over to the table full of men the minute they walked in, but Tara and Sally hung back with Holly, drooling over Sam. Holly would have left them to do so, but she wasn't quite ready to face Declan yet and sitting at the bar alone seemed a little sad and pathetic.

"Not drinking tonight, Holly?" Ricki Takini said, refilling her soda without being asked. The beautiful bartender's long black hair was shaved on one side, with the remainder falling in loose waves around her bare right shoulder.

"Yeah, I'm in one of those moods that mixed with alcohol may be a dangerous combo."

"I don't know, I've benefited from some of your dangerous drinking experiences," Ricki teased with a wink.

Holly's cheeks warmed as she laughed. Though she'd dated a few women during college, she'd never gone further than a kiss before Ricki. Holly had newly returned to town and been looking for passion and fun. They'd hooked up for a few months, but while Holly hoped to find someone someday to share her life with, Ricki liked relationship fluidity and didn't believe in monogamy. They'd parted ways on friendly terms and hadn't crossed the line since.

"Unfortunately, it's the kind of dangerous that might have me committing a felony."

"Ouch. Who's the unlucky recipient?"

"If I had to warrant a guess, my money's on Declan Gallagher," Sam said, placing his elbows on the bar counter top beside Holly. "Do I win?"

"You do."

Ricki cocked her head to the side, her hair falling farther down her arm. "Why Declan?"

"He is a frustrating, loathsome jerk."

"She keeps saying things like that, but every time with a little less conviction," Sam said, holding his fingers up an inch apart and making Ricki laugh.

"Ah, so you think she's thawing towards Declan and that's why she's in a mood tonight?"

"Ding ding."

Holly shoved Sam with her shoulder. "*She* is right here and is not thawing, melting, or softening towards that grouchy man."

"All those words mean the same thing, sweetie," Ricki said, dropping a cherry in Holly's newly refilled soda.

"I know, I was just making a point. I don't feel anything for Declan Gallagher."

Except confusion, frustration, and lust, she thought, but no way was she admitting that out loud. Sam would have a field day.

"Sam, come dance with me," Sally begged from his other side, yanking him off the stool.

"Ooof, easy there! I'll come willingly, but you got to be gentle with me. I'm delicate."

When Sam reached the dance floor with Sally, Ricki snorted. "About as delicate as a rock and nearly as dumb."

Holly raised an eyebrow, smirking. "Well, well. Was that a note of jealousy in your voice?"

"Absolutely," Ricki admitted, and Holly's jaw dropped.

"You and Sam...?"

"A couple of times. Fantastic lay, but likes to cuddle and you know me."

Holly giggled. "I think you cuddled with me."

"You were too sweet to say no to."

"Then why the jealousy with Sam? If he's so annoying."

"Because I'm itching for a good time and the man is that and then some."

Holly took a sip of her drink. "If it helps, I don't think he has an ounce of interest in Sally."

"Hmm, probably not. Sam likes the chase." Ricki glanced over Holly's shoulder with a grin. "Speaking of interest, you sure about the whole loathing Declan thing?"

"Absolutely. Why do you ask?"

"'Cause he hasn't taken his eyes off you since you walked into the bar."

Holly sucked in a breath, instantly regretting the involuntary action when Ricki's eyes sparkled.

"Such a little liar, Holly Winters."

"Fine. There's still a speck of interest he hasn't crushed."

"Then why are you over here pouting instead of making him nuts?"

"I'm working up to it. I told him off earlier and it still seems like he got the upper hand."

"Oh, so this is a power play."

"You're kind of annoying, has anyone told you that?" Holly grumbled.

"Never. Now stop your stalling and handle business. I've got drinks to pour."

"Have a good night, Ricki," Holly called, picking up her soda and sliding off the bar stool. She glanced around the bar, searching for anyone else to sit with, but Merry waved her hand in the air. If Holly walked away now, it would cause more speculation about why.

Weaving her way through the tables, she pulled up a chair next to her sister, which happened to be situated right across from Declan.

"Hiya, Holly," Tony called with a smirk. "How was the parade?"

"It was fine. Got to dress up in a costume and throw candy at kids." She shifted her scowl from her brother to Clark. "While you two were here getting lit."

"Not me," Nick said, holding up his half finished beer. "I'm the DD. Pike's been plying Declan, Clark, and Tony with drinks though. What's that you're working on, Dec?"

Holly quirked a brow and met Declan's eyes for the first time. "Yeah, *Dec*, whatcha got in the glass?"

Declan tipped back a shot of something green with red sugar on the rim instead of responding.

"Pretty sure that one is an Elf's Sugar Stick," Pike said.

Holly didn't look away from Declan. "I pictured you more as a bourbon type of guy."

"I wouldn't want to waste Pike's money."

"Sweet of you," she said sarcastically.

"Whoa, what's all this tension," Pike said, doing an exaggerated tremble. "Do you two need to take this outside?"

"Nah, we're good." Declan got up from the table with a twirl of his finger. "I've got the next round."

"Yeah, that's my boy," Pike cheered, his mirth dying down when he caught Holly's stare. "What?"

"You know what."

Pike held his hands in the air. "Hey, you're the one putting it out there. I can't help picking up on your pissed-off vibes."

Holly leaned back in her chair with a huff, her attention on the tall, lithe brunette sidling up to Declan at the bar. She put her hand on Declan's arm, motioning to the dance floor. At first he shook his head with a small smile, but she seemed to be pleading with him.

"He doesn't want to dance," Holly muttered to herself, realizing too late she was halfway out of her seat. Merry watched her with wide eyes as she lowered herself back down in time to watch the brunette win out, holding Declan's hand as he followed her onto the dance floor.

"Holy cow, you're jealous," Merry whispered.

"I am not. Jealousy is a symptom of insecurity and I am not that."

"Or that you're into someone who is currently with another person," Merry said.

"He's not with her. They're dancing. I've danced with Pike and it doesn't mean I want to jump his bones."

Pike stroked his beard, studying Declan's partner. "I think they look good together."

"She's a good height for him," Tony agreed.

"What does that mean, Anthony? Someone shorter can't be with anyone taller? That's height discrimination."

His jaw dropped before he recovered. "I made a comment about how two people look together. I'm not discriminating."

"You did say Holly was too short for Declan earlier, though," Pike threw in, grinning wickedly.

"What?" Holly snapped.

Tony scowled at Pike.

"Why were you discussing me and Declan at all?"

"They were trying to figure out why he was moping. Thought it might have something to do with you," Nick offered.

"Just them?" Holly asked.

"Of course. You're my sister. I mind my own business."

Clark started coughing, which sounded suspiciously like suppressed laughter, and Holly turned her attention to her future brother-in-law. "You got something to say, Clark?"

"Nope," he wheezed. "In fact, I think it's time for another drink, right, boys?"

All the men stood up in unison and Holly hollered after them, "You're all a bunch of sissies!"

Merry laughed next to her. "I always wondered how you were able to intimidate grown men. Tell me your secret, sister."

"It's the hair. They automatically assume I've got attitude and a bad temper."

"Oh, not you. Sweet wholesome Holly Winters?"

"Shut it, sister dear."

Holly watched Declan, but he didn't get reeled in for another dance, instead heading back to the bar to join the rest of the guys. A rush of relief swirled through her as the gorgeous woman moved on to a man at the edge of the dance floor.

"That's a rather satisfied smile," Merry said.

Holly stopped smiling, setting her face into a blank mask. "Don't know what you mean."

"Holly, if you like Declan, why don't you stop playing games and go for it?"

"He's the one playing games. One minute he's kissing me and the next I'm nothing that he wants and we should just quit now."

"Ah, that sounds familiar."

"What do you mean?"

"Clark didn't want to get involved with me for similar reasons. What about the farm? Jace? We had a lot riding on whether or not we'd work out."

"The difference is I don't want a relationship with Declan. I just—"

"What?"

I wish I could stop thinking about him.

"I think I'll stop having this attraction to Declan if I can get him out of my system, but he keeps taking a step back every time I think we're headed somewhere good."

"Maybe Declan pulls away because he wants more and is afraid to take that step and lose you?"

Holly scoffed. "Please, the man wants to leave Mistletoe in his rear view. I think he doesn't enjoy feeling vulnerable and I like to know things about the people I go to bed with."

"Really? What things? Is there a list of questions you ask before you do the deed?"

"Mock me if you will, but while I joke about hating sex and one-night stands, I don't go to bed with people unless I genuinely like them."

"And you don't like Declan?"

"I didn't for a long time, but the last few weeks I've seen flashes of this man I *could* like. But then he's back to behaving like a pessimistic bastard and I just think maybe it's not worth it. I'll just buzz my lust for Declan into oblivion."

"Buzz your—oh!" Merry covered her face with a laugh. "You are such a turd."

"It's part of the little sister handbook. Gotta keep you on your toes."

All of the men came back to the table, with Tara, Sally, and Sam in tow. Sam took the seat next to Holly and before he was fully settled, Sally plopped down on his lap. Holly noticed Pike's face tighten before he turned his attention to Delilah, who was talking with her hands animatedly. Holly knew Pike and Sally had dated for almost six months. It couldn't be easy watching someone you cared about hanging all over someone else.

"Hey Sally, can I borrow your seatmate for a minute? I love this song."

Sam shot her a look of gratitude and started to dislodge Sally, but the other woman gave Holly a dark expression. "Really, Holly? A table full of men and you have to take Sam?"

It took Holly a second too late to realize how the move must have looked, and she stammered, "We're just good friends and I know he can dance so—"

"I can dance," a quiet voice spoke up from across the table.

Holly turned toward Declan, blinking her wide eyes. "What?"

"I said, I can dance." He shrugged. "Why not dance with me?"

Holly could think of a half dozen reasons, including his lackluster emoji choices, but rather than play out the dramatic little scene with Sally, she cleared her throat.

"Sure. Why not?"

CHAPTER 24

DECLAN STEPPED AWAY FROM THE table, his heart pounding as Holly rounded the people seated to get to him. He could have blamed the alcohol, but that wasn't why he'd awkwardly asked Holly to dance. He didn't like that Sam was her first choice, the guy she could count on, because Declan wanted to be that. He'd been an idiot on more than one occasion, but with the warm glow of a buzz lighting up his body, too many truths were popping into his head.

When Holly reached his side, Declan took her hand and drew her through the remaining tables to the dance floor. The upbeat country melody pumping through the speakers matched the thump of his heart as he wrapped an arm around her waist and took her hand in his. He led her around the dance floor in silence, searching for something to say.

"Thanks for the save," she whispered, loud enough to be heard as they passed the speakers. "I really stepped in it with Sally. I'm sure she thinks I'm interested in Sam, and I didn't mean to make it seem that way."

Declan cleared his throat. "I saw the look he gave you. He's not interested in her."

"He's not interested in me either. If anything, he was probably looking for an out without hurting her feelings."

"I'd rather someone was honest and shot me down up front. I wouldn't want to think there was hope for something and have the other person admit later they were trying to be kind."

Silence stretched between them and Declan wondered what she was thinking. When the song was almost over, Declan asked, "Do you really love this song? Or were you trying to escape the table because I came back to it?"

Holly jerked back, glaring up at him. "I'm not scared of you, Declan."

He chuckled quietly. "I know that. I'm asking if you're avoiding me."

"Seems like you're the one who was avoiding me, driving off before I could pay you."

"Maybe. Or I knew deep down I'd been a dick and didn't want to accept that check until I figured out how to apologize."

The edges of Holly's dark eyes softened. "Is that what you're doing? Apologizing?"

"No, I'm just giving you a what-if scenario." Holly stomped on his foot, and he winced, tightening his hold on her waist. "Bad joke. I'm sorry I keep sending mixed signals."

"And?"

"And what?"

"What does this apology mean? Are you going to stop with all the 'come here' and 'go away' or are you apologizing because you want the check and nothing more?"

The song ended, but instead of leading her back to the table,

Declan placed his hand behind her back and walked her through the throngs of people who'd been spilling into the bar since the parade ended. They walked out the back door to the patio area, the cold air hitting his face like a slap. He felt something chilly brush his cheek soft as an angel's wing and realized it was snowing.

Shrugging out of his jacket, he placed it around her shoulders and watched as she slipped her arms into the sleeves, the brown canvas outerwear swallowing her up.

"Thanks, but what are we doing out here, Declan?"

His gaze swept over the mostly empty area except for a couple smoking in the corner. He ran his hand over the stubble that had popped up across his cheeks and chin in the last week since he shaved, searching for the right thing to say.

The problem with words was every time he tried, it all came out wrong.

He took her hand, swinging them both around the corner and out of sight from anyone coming out that back door.

"Declan—"

Transferring his hand to cradle her face, he ran a thumb over her cheek. "I want you."

Holly's breath came out in a single word. "But?"

"No buts. I want you. I want to kiss you." His hands dropped to her waist and he pressed into her until Holly's back hit the wall. "To feel your body against mine."

"No more stop and go?" she asked, even as her hand slipped up to hang onto his shoulder.

"Not until we're both satisfied."

Holly's full lips curved into a smile in the dim light. "That might take a while."

"I bet I'll prove you wrong." Declan dipped his head before she could make a comeback and captured her lips, gripping her hips in both his hands as he kissed her. She tasted of soda pop and Holly, so sweet he caught himself nipping at her plump bottom lip. He lifted her up until they were eye level before pinning her lower body with his, and Holly didn't hesitate to wrap both her legs and arms around him.

It had been years since he'd kissed a woman, but not a single memory compared to Holly's eager mouth meeting his, her tongue fencing with his while her fingers ran through his hair, nails lightly scraping against his scalp and drawing a deep moan from him.

While he might be this side of buzzed, his inhibitions weren't entirely gone. Declan knew people liked to use the loop-around gravel drive.

"Holly," he murmured against her lips. "We need to go back inside."

"I thought we weren't going to play red light green light anymore," she countered, arching her lower body against his already aching cock as his fingers dug into her hips.

"I'm not, I swear. You have no idea how badly I want to make you come against the side of this building." He moved back enough so he could meet her dazed, heavy-lidded eyes and said, "But I also don't want our first time together interrupted when someone comes out here looking for you."

"Argh, fine." She gave him a hard-fast kiss before pushing him back, and he dropped her clumsily back onto her feet. "Let's tell everyone good-bye and go back to my place."

"Hang on a second." He took two steps after her, reaching for her arm. "I don't...I don't want anyone to know about us."

Holly stilled, spinning around to face him. "Why not?"

"I'm sort of friends with your brother. I don't think he'd like me and you—I just don't want to complicate this with other people."

Holly cocked her head to the side, and for a second he thought she was going to deck him. Instead she nodded slowly. "Fine. I can keep a secret."

"Thank you."

"Do you have your keys and phone on you?" she asked, holding her hand out.

"Yeah."

"Give them to me. I'll text Clark to tell Merry I'm taking you home because you drank too much and can't drive. With any luck, they won't jump to any conclusions considering you were drinking those sweet cocktails sure to make any man sick."

"Not women?" he asked, fishing through his pockets and handing her his keys.

"Pshaw, not me." Holly flashed him a sunny smile as she took them. "I can handle anything you throw at me. I just didn't want to drink when I was pissed off. Never a good combo."

"I guess that's my fault."

Holly leaned up on her tiptoes, and he dipped down to reach her lips. "I'm willing to forgive and forget. First we gotta get out of here."

"How are you going to explain getting from my place to yours if you drive me home?"

"I'll walk from your house. My sister will balk, but I'll tell her to mind her own business."

"You can't walk home from my place."

"Declan—"

"No, I mean, I'm sure you're capable, but I'm not staying with my dad. I've been sleeping at the store."

Holly stared up at him. "Why?"

"I told you, things with my parents are—" *Hiccup.* "—complicated."

"You've been sleeping at the store?"

"In the back room. There's a cot, and I set up all Leo's stuff."

"Leo...your cat? You and your cat are living in the hardware store?"

"Yeah. It's not so bad, except the cot hurts my back and there's not enough room for the two of us..."

"That's fine. I said I wanted to take you back to my place anyway." Holly reached for his hand, leading him around the building to the parking lot.

"Truck's parked over there," he said, pointing to their right, his thumb stroking along the soft skin of Holly's hand. Her palm fitted against his tickled, something he wasn't used to since hand holding wasn't a common practice for him.

They reached the driver's side door and Holly unlocked the truck with the fob. Declan grabbed the door for her, pulling it open.

"Geez, did you have to get it lifted?" Holly grumbled, reaching for the handle in the door.

"Need a boost?" Declan teased.

Holly glanced over her shoulder, one foot on the step. "You just want to touch my butt."

"Yes, please."

Holly laughed and launched herself into the cab, much to Declan's disappointment. "You getting in or staying here?" Holly shut the door before he could respond, and he rounded the front of his truck, surprised by how much his buzz intensified with every step. He'd had three drinks, right? Or was it four?

When he got into the truck and fastened his seat belt, he caught Holly watching him. "What?"

"You don't drink much, do you?"

"Why do you say that?" he asked.

"I noticed you're weaving a bit."

Declan chuckled. "Yeah, I don't, especially not hard liquor. My mom called me a late bloomer because while my teammates were partying every weekend, I was painting."

"What about girlfriends?"

"Wasn't really interested."

"Nobody you fancied, huh?"

"All vapid."

"Ouch," Holly said, starting the truck. "I'm going to let that one slide because you've mixed your alcohols and are not in the right head space now."

Declan rolled his head against the back of the seat, smiling. "You're pretty."

"Thank you. Now, what do you say we pick up your cat and you both stay with me tonight."

"What? That's crazy. He'll be fine for a few more hours if you want to go to your place for a bit, but we can't both stay with you."

"Why not?" she asked, backing the truck up with a spin of the wheel. "I've got extra rooms and I've got everything we need to prevent a hangover at my place. Besides, if you're worried about someone finding out, I promise to be discreet sneaking you inside."

"Your neighbors are going to see my truck."

"Not inside my garage." Holly reached over and patted his leg. "Why don't you just relax. I promise everything will be fine."

Declan woke up with a god-awful taste in his mouth and a steady hum in his ear. He blinked his eyes slowly, staring up into Leo's triangular face as he made biscuits on the pillow next to Declan's head. On the wall behind Leo's head was a painting of two children building a snowman and Declan's gaze scanned the room, trying to place the unfamiliar surroundings.

"Where are we?" The sound of his voice was raw and when he rolled over, Declan noticed a bottle of water on the nightstand next to him. He opened it, guzzling the contents down without taking a breath, before swinging his legs over the side of the bed. He'd gone to bed fully clothed except for his shoes, which were peeking out from under the bed. Declan noticed Leo's litter box and carrier were in the corner of the room as he headed for the door and on top of the dresser was his duffel bag.

Declan opened the door and once he stumbled out into the hallway, he recognized the dining room with no table and several ring lights propped against the wall. He saw the back of Holly's head outside on the back porch, sitting on her patio, where she was sitting on a lounge chair and watching the snow fall. He backed down the hallway slowly and grabbed his toothbrush from the side pocket of his duffel bag, wanting to give his mouth a good scrubbing before he knocked her down with the stench of his breath. Declan remembered the dancing, the kissing, and bits and pieces of the drive home, but how the hell had he wound up here?

Declan tossed his toothbrush and toothpaste back into his bag and grabbed a sweatshirt, pulling it over his head before he padded to the back door and opened it with a squeaky slide.

"Good morning," he said gruffly.

Holly turned her head so she was gazing up at him, a wide smile on her face. "Good morning. How are you feeling?"

"Like I got kicked in the head by a mule."

"I'll get you some meds when you're ready. I would have given them to you before you fell asleep, but I could barely wake you up enough to herd you into the spare room, let alone get you to drink or eat anything. You want some breakfast?"

Declan's stomach gurgled in protest. "I'm not sure if I'm ready for that."

Holly got up from the chair and took his hand. "Let's get you back in bed, then. You can take the meds and get some more sleep. When you feel up to it, there is bread in the cabinet next to the sink."

"Holly," Declan said, holding his ground. "Why did you bring me here?"

"What do you mean? You don't remember? You kissed my socks off and I said I was going to bring you home with me, but by the time I got Leo out to the truck you were nodding off. I figured the sugary drinks and the alcohol were making you sleepy, so I got you home, tucked you in, got Leo settled, and read for a while before I went to bed."

"You could have just dropped me at the store."

"No, I couldn't."

"Why not?"

"Because I wasn't going to leave you drunk and alone, sleeping on a cot. At least here I could keep an eye on you."

"You didn't have to do that."

"Come on, Declan. Only a total jerk would have dumped you at that store. I've got plenty of rooms not being used and I got to love on Leo, so for me it's a win-win." Holly wrapped her arms around his waist and gave him a gentle squeeze. "Well, kind of. There was big talk from you about being able to satisfy me in one round, but it's not my style to take advantage of inebriated men."

"I'll take some pain meds and get out of your hair," Declan said.

"Good gravy, you are stubborn," Holly said, keeping one arm around his waist as she led him back to the spare bedroom. "Listen, I'm going to get you something for the headache and I want you to take it and lie down and please do not leave until I get home from my parents' Sunday brunch. Promise?"

"Holly, honestly, I'm fine—"

"Will you just let me look after you, Declan? I know it's hard to let anyone see you vulnerable, but I want to talk about where we go from here when I get back. Unless you didn't mean anything you said last night—"

"I meant it," he said firmly.

Holly beamed. "Perfect. You rest, we'll talk, and then you can go where you want, whether it's home, back to the store, or the Bahamas."

Declan nodded, sitting down on the bed. "All right."

"Good. I'll be back in a few."

Declan looked over at Leo, who had made himself completely at home on top of the pillow he'd been kneading a few moments before.

"I guess she didn't have to tell you twice, huh?"

Holly came back into the room with another bottle of water and a pill container. "Take three of these. I'll be back in a few hours."

"Holly?"

She stopped in the doorway, leaning back in with a grin. "Yeah?"

"Thanks for taking care of me. It...doesn't happen often."

"I kind of figured that." Holly crossed back to him and gave him a brief peck on the mouth before pointing her finger at him with a mock stern expression. "Rest and replenish, and if I come back to find you gone, I will hunt you down like a dog."

Declan smiled, the warmth of her lips lingering on his. "We wouldn't want that."

CHAPTER 25

HOLLY CAREFULLY PLACED A *THANK You for Attending Our Wedding* sticker on the top of the round candle lid and set it to the side with the rest of the favors the Winters family was putting together. They'd finished brunch and Holly, Merry, Noel, and Victoria sat around the table with mimosas, working on the favors while Chris, Clark, and Nick had gone out to the flocking tent to get ready for the farm to open.

"How many more of these do we have?" Noel asked.

Merry set another round candle tin in the done pile. "Twenty-two. Total of sixty-seven."

"And then they have to go in the little boxes with a tissue," Victoria said, holding up a silver square before scrunching it into a small white box with a shiny black ribbon around the outside.

Holly set aside another candle. "It shouldn't take us long at the rate we're going, and except for the bachelorette party and any last-minute details, this should be the last wedding prep we need to do."

"I still can't believe you're going to miss the Christmas concert this year," Victoria grumbled.

"Oh, come on, Mom," Merry said, slipping the top of her favor box closed. "It's going to be wonderful with all the band and choir kids performing from Mistletoe's school district. I bet the turnout will be even better too because people are showing up to watch their children perform."

"I know, but I enjoy watching *my* children perform."

Holly grinned at Merry's eye roll. Merry, Nick, Noel, and Holly had been the headlining musical entertainment for two years, but when scheduling made sense to celebrate Merry's bachelorette party this weekend, they'd let the committee know they wouldn't be available.

"Let other people enjoy the spotlight, Mom," Holly teased.

"I do!" Victoria said, glaring at Holly. "I'm just incredibly proud of my children."

"We know," Merry said.

"You are still planning on staying close for the party? Not gallivanting off to Vegas to take in a Thunder Down Under show, are you?" Victoria asked, simultaneously fascinating and horrifying Holly.

"Do I want to know how you learned about that particular show?" Merry asked.

"Your mother has been on a girl's trip before, you know."

"I definitely don't want to hear about it," Holly said, shaking her head.

"No, you probably don't," Victoria countered with a wicked grin.

Noel chuckled. "We're staying local, Victoria, and there will be no strippers."

"They won't tell me what we're doing, so I can't give any details," Merry grumbled, shooting Holly a dirty look.

"Oh, stop giving me a death stare. You're going to love this, I promise."

"It's strange to have an odd number of party favors, isn't it?" Noel asked, and Holly wasn't sure if it was a purposeful change of subject but she appreciated it.

"We have a lot of single friends who did not RSVP for a plus one. Between that and people traveling for the holidays, we didn't end up with a full guest list, but I'm honestly okay with it. We wanted it to be cozy and intimate, but someone went a little crazy with the invites," Merry said, jerking her thumb in Victoria's direction.

Her mother closed the lid on her favor box with a sniff. "It was a few more family members and friends we've known since before you were born, nothing major. I just didn't want to hurt anyone's feelings."

"Then why not invite the entire town, Mom?" Holly teased.

"That's extreme and you know it. I added about twenty to the guest list, which made it just under one hundred people. The only way any of you are getting more than that is if it's a potluck. I've seen the way the citizens of Mistletoe eat during the free pancake breakfast at the fire station."

"When Nick and I do take that step, I'd like to keep it small," Noel said.

Holly and Merry shared identical surprised expressions. Noel didn't talk about marriage because she'd told everyone in her life on multiple occasions that she had no plans to walk down the aisle.

Instead of making a big deal about it, Holly snorted. "Yeah right."

"You're marrying our brother, the golden child," Merry added, obviously following Holly's lead of keeping her cool. "I bet Mom breaks her one hundred guest rule for the two of you."

"Excuse me," Victoria snapped, pointing at each of them. "I love all of my children equally and show no favoritism." Their mom took a sip of her mimosa and set it down. "When you do decide to marry my son, I will listen to all of your preferences."

"And completely disregard them," Holly joked.

"Young lady, you're awfully cheeky this morning," Victoria said.

Merry smirked. "Yeah, Holly, what's got you in such a good mood?"

"Or should we say who," Noel joined in, earning a dark look from Holly. The last thing she needed was her mother getting curious, or worse yet, excited, thinking that Holly might finally be getting serious about someone.

"What's going on?" Victoria's gaze swung around the table, inquisition evident in her eyes. "Does Holly have a boyfriend I don't know about?"

"No, I do not."

"But she left the bar early to make sure Declan Gallagher got home safe," Noel said.

"Wait, Declan?" Victoria turned toward Holly, her brows knitted in obvious confusion. "I thought you didn't like him."

"I don't," she said, ignoring Merry's scoff. "Regardless of my feelings for him, he was drunk and I was sober. His house is one street over, so it made sense for me to drive him there and walk to my house." There was no way Holly would tell them Declan stayed the night or there would be many conclusions drawn.

And she didn't want unnecessary speculations until she'd reaped the benefit of the actions.

"Wait, you walked at night?" Victoria frowned. "That's not safe, honey."

"No one is going to try to take me on, Mom."

"Still, you are a young woman and we do get bears in town occasionally. I'm sure Declan could have slept it off in his vehicle."

But I prefer him sleeping it off in my spare bedroom.

"Probably, but you taught me to be kind to my fellow human-oids." Holly tossed her hands in the air when her mom looked like she was about to argue some more. "It's a moot point! He's fine, I'm fine, we're all fine."

"Sounds like she doesn't want to talk about Declan with us," Merry said.

Under normal circumstances, Holly would be happy to discuss all the latest developments with her sister, Noel, and her mom, but Declan's request that they keep anything that happened between the two of them weighed on her mind. Keeping things casual was one thing, but a secret hook-up? She was a grown woman and if anyone had something to say about her love life, they could shove it up their wazoo. But she knew Declan well enough that it made sense he wouldn't want their personal business getting around town. He liked to keep his private life that way, and if Holly wanted to take the next step with him she'd need to honor that confidence.

As if sensing her emotional anxiety, Merry's Great Pyrenees, Daisy Mae, got up from the floor and ambled over to Holly, shoving her face in Holly's lap. Holly stroked the white dog's soft fur with a smile. "Aw, sweetheart, you feeling left out of the conversation? You wanna talk boys too?"

Suddenly, her parents' bloodhound, Butch, was pushing his nose in front of Daisy's, which started a wrestling match for the two of them.

"Butch!" Victoria hollered, standing up from her seat. "You two need to go outside and do that. There are too many break-ables in this house for roughhousing."

"It's funny, she used to say the same thing to us," Merry said, laughing.

"Merry, stop snickering and take these two out the laundry room door. I need to use the bathroom."

Merry called the dogs, who scurried after her out of the room and Victoria trailed behind them out of sight.

Holly finished the last of her mimosa and stood up. "I'm going to get a refill."

"Me too," Noel said. "I am not working tonight and I've earned a second glass."

Holly set down her empty glass on the island and said, "Same here. Put yours down and I'll fill them both up." She poured a quarter flute of champagne and filled the rest with orange juice.

"Thank you." Noel picked up her glass and tapped it to Holly's rim. "To the future, no matter what it brings."

"That's a weird toast," Holly said, taking a sip of her drink.

Noel shrugged. "Didn't you know I was weird?"

"You're right. Makes total sense."

Noel held her champagne flute stem between her fingers, watching Holly thoughtfully. "If it's any consolation, Declan seems like an okay guy. Quiet, but in a tortured Heathcliff kind of way."

"While I appreciate your opinion, it's unnecessary. There's nothing going on with Declan and me."

"Really? Because I'm the queen of *there's nothing going on* and when he offered himself up as your dance partner last night, I thought you two were going to light the place on fire with the sparks flying."

Holly heard her sister and mother coming down the hallway and whispered through gritted teeth, "Stop talking about sparks and dancing, all right?"

Noel dragged her fingers across her lips and locked them with an invisible key. "Whatever you say."

They all sat back down again and the subject jumped to the wedding and Christmas, while Holly's mind strayed to Declan. It was crazy for him to be staying at the store, and although she hadn't had a chance to broach the topic with him last night or this morning, she could only assume it had to do with his mom being in town. But why wouldn't he get a hotel room or find an apartment?

Holly half expected Declan to be out of her house before she got home, and the idea that he'd take off to stay in that cold back room instead of in her comfortable guest room bothered her.

Holly stood up suddenly, startling the other women at the table. "I need to make a phone call. Be right back."

"Who are you calling?" her mother asked.

"Delilah. We are supposed to have dinner later," Holly lied, grabbing her coat from the hook and stepping outside onto the front porch, closing the door with a snap behind her.

She scrolled through her texts and clicked on Declan's name, pressing the phone icon at the top of the screen. Holly put it to her ear, waiting for it to ring once. Twice.

"Hello?" a deep voice answered groggily.

"Hey, you still at my house?"

"Yeah, I hope that's okay. I've been sleeping."

"It's grea—I mean, yes, you're good. I just want to make sure you don't take off before we have a chance to talk."

"'Bout what?" he asked, sounding muffled.

"It's not important."

"If it wasn't important, you wouldn't have called to make sure I don't leave."

"I want to talk about your current living situation."

"What about it?" he asked.

"I don't think you should live long-term in the back of the store. First off, there's no shower, so you'll either be going back to your dad's or going without, and nobody likes man stank."

A hoarse guffaw erupted, but she couldn't tell if he was really laughing or choking.

"And here I'd always thought women like manly men who rubbed dirt in their wounds and never cried."

"Common misconception. We actually prefer guys with good hygiene who can articulate their emotions."

"No wonder I'm single," he joked.

Holly smiled. "I was just thinking that if you aren't ready to go home to your dad's, you could stay with me. Until you figure out whether you're going to stick around or not. You'd have your own room and bathroom, so you won't smell."

"I can't do that."

"Why not? I'm offering."

"I've got Leo—"

"Who I already adore and may not let you leave with him anyway, so why not postpone that fight?"

Declan chuckled. "Plus it would complicate…things."

"Things like…?"

"You and me. The whole town's going to assume we're sleeping together if I'm living under your roof."

Holly leaned onto the railing, staring out across the front yard. "Honestly, I'm not one to care too much what other people think I'm doing or with whom, but if it makes you feel better I will not take advantage of you as long as you're my tenant."

"Oh, so I'd be your tenant, huh? And how much rent will you be charging me?"

"That's something we can negotiate, depending on how long you stay. Oh, by the way, your check is on the kitchen counter for services rendered."

"I hope it wasn't for the full three thousand because I hardly did anything."

"I'm not going to debate this with you because I don't have a lot of time before my family comes looking for me. Would you like to use my guest room, all business, no benefits?"

Several moments ticked by before he said, "Pending further negotiations, I think I would."

"Perfect. I'll be home later this afternoon."

"I'll cook dinner."

Holly's jaw dropped. "Is your cooking edible?"

"I do all right."

"Then we might want to hold off on negotiations until after I've tried your food."

"Deal. I'll see you tonight, then."

Holly ended the call and turned to find Merry leaning against the front door, smirking.

"Busted."

CHAPTER 26

DECLAN WENT OVER THE LIST on his phone one more time as he stood in front of the dairy case, leaning his forearms onto the cart handle for support. His cart had a bag of dry cat food, litter, and various food items he needed for the dish he planned to prepare tonight. He wasn't sure how he'd ended up staying with Holly Winters of all people, but he couldn't deny the hum of excitement coursing through him as he imagined her reaction when she came home tonight.

"Declan?"

Declan stiffened, recognizing his mom's voice before he turned her way. She stood behind a grocery cart, wearing a red sweater and black slacks, her dark hair piled up on top of her head in a bun.

"I've been trying to catch you at the store. Did your friend Holly tell you?"

Declan swallowed, glancing around the store but there was no one around to overhear. "She mentioned you stopped by."

"I see. I thought after talking to your father we might have a chance to clear the air."

Declan met her gaze from across the cart. "What else is

there to say? He lied and I punished you because I believed you were selfish and cruel. How can we overcome ten years of bullshit?"

"By talking about it?"

"If you really wanted to talk, then why didn't you tell me what he did years ago?"

She sighed. "I didn't tell you because it had nothing to do with you. There are only two people in a marriage, and children, even grown ones, shouldn't be a part of that."

He shook his head. "You stayed because of me."

"That's partly true. I've loved your father since I was fifteen, and even though we drifted apart through the years we always found our way back to each other. I needed space to heal and forgive him, but your dad didn't understand that. He does now."

Declan snorted. "Don't delude yourself, Mom. He hasn't changed. He only told me about what he did because you came back. I don't think I can get over that."

His mom shrugged. "That's up to you and what you can live with. I didn't want bitterness and anger to consume me, so I chose to explore myself away from Mistletoe, to figure out who I wanted to be. You have to do the same and take responsibility for your own feelings."

"How do we get past the things I've said? How do I fix this?"

"Make up for lost time?" she said, coming around the front of the cart and reaching for his hand. He let her hang onto it for several seconds before he pulled away. "Declan, all of this happened a long time ago. Why don't you come back home and we can all talk together tonight?"

Declan shook his head. "I don't get how you can want to be with him. He wasn't honest and painted you as the villain."

"Like I've said several times, that's between me and him. As for you and me, how about I run the store through the holidays? Give you a break."

"You don't know how," he said.

"Your father will help me."

"He hasn't been there in months."

"We'll figure it out." She squeezed his shoulder. "Do what you need to do, but you can't blame your father for everything wrong in your life, just like I couldn't. I am responsible for my actions, and maybe if I had just left when it happened, things would have been better for all of us. I can't answer and can only say I made what I thought was the best decision at the time."

"For the record, I don't think any kid wants their parents to stay together if they're miserable." Declan shoved his hands in his pockets, adding, "How has he been?"

"Your father is doing well. We've been running around like a couple of kids, reacquainting ourselves with each other. He misses you, though."

Declan didn't respond to that, although he did miss Liam. "He can't be alone for long, you know that, right? It's early stages still, but sometimes he forgets to shut off the oven or the burner."

"Kim's with him now. Lovely woman." Before he had a chance to react, his mother gave him a hard, fast hug and pulled away. "You take all the time you need. Maybe this will give you a chance to figure out who you are and what you want. Just don't push me away anymore. I'm here to stay."

"Are you? Even knowing that in a few years he won't be himself anymore?"

"I'd rather have the few years building something better than what we had than regret not being with him. Nobody is perfect and lord knows love is a hard thing to hold onto, but I've managed to find it again and I plan on hanging around until one of us takes our last breath."

Declan didn't ask her again how she could forgive him. If she hadn't fully answered him yet, he didn't expect her to answer now. He'd never been in love with anyone and didn't think even love could let him forgive someone for cheating.

"Are you ready to check out?" he asked.

"I have a few more things to buy, but I'm going to text you every day. Are you still sleeping in the back of the store?"

"How did you know?"

"I saw your truck outside it the other night."

"No, I'm staying with a friend."

"Male or female friend?"

Declan's cheeks warmed. "Not that it matters, but a female friend."

"Is it Holly Winters?"

"Why would you ask that?"

His mom smiled softly. "Because I can tell she cares for you. She seems like a sweet girl."

Declan laughed. "Sometimes she can be, and then she'll be scraping across my last nerve."

"Ah, that's how all great loves start."

"Mom, I'm not in love with Holly."

"Maybe not yet, but I bet if you weren't so closed off from everyone you'd see that you *could* be."

"On that note, I better get these things home and feed Leo."

"Ah, avoidance. Classic Gallagher move." She lightened the rebuke by patting his cheek. "Don't stay away too long, you hear? Like you said, he doesn't have much time."

His mother dropped her hand and went around to take her cart handle with a smile. "I'm making Christmas Eve dinner if you and Holly would like to join us."

Declan returned her smile. "Shepherd's pie?"

"It wouldn't be Christmas Eve without it."

"I'll see if I can make it."

"You do that. In the meantime, think about what I've said."

"I will. Thanks, Mom."

"I love you, Declan." She didn't wait for him to say it back, but turned her cart down the first aisle and disappeared out of sight.

I love you, too.

Declan made it up front and through the checkout without losing it, fighting back the sting in his eyes. The sun setting had cast a warm glow over the quiet Sunday afternoon as he pulled out of the parking lot and headed left towards Holly's. He expected she'd probably beat him there, and when he pulled into the driveway the garage door was up, revealing her car inside. Declan pulled in beside hers and after gathering up the bags of groceries from his back seat, he pressed the button to close the garage door as he went through the utility door and into the house.

"Hello," he called.

"Hi!" Her voice echoed from across the house. "I'd get up to help you carry stuff, but I'm being pinned down by an adorable dude with whiskers."

"It's not Santa, is it? 'Cause I don't really need those nightmares," he said, grinning when he heard her burst of laughter. When he rounded the corner into the kitchen, he didn't see her, and set the groceries down on the counter to head down the hallway. She was stretched out across the love seat in the living room, with Leo perched on her chest making biscuits.

"I see how it is. I'm gone for a few hours and you replace me with her?" Declan said. Leo gave him heavy-lidded eyes before turning back to Holly, bumping her chin with his head.

"Why do you say *her* like that, as if you can't believe it? I'm awesome!"

"But that's my cat. I saved him from certain death, and even though I'm standing here he isn't leaping into my arms to pay me the proper respect."

Holly clucked her tongue, rubbing Leo's ears. "Do you hear all that belly-aching? So dramatic!"

"I'll show you dramatic," Declan growled playfully, picking Leo up and tossing him over his shoulder.

"Hey! Thief! I was getting kitty love!" She jumped up from the love seat, chasing him down the hallway as he carried Leo into the dining room.

"Not anymore. This is my cat and there will be no trying to steal him away from me."

Suddenly, something hard and sharp hit his butt with a burning *whack*. He turned around, staring down at her hunched, laughing form. "Did you just smack my ass?"

"Absolutely, and I'll do it again if you don't give up the kitty."
She held up her hand, eyes narrowed, and Declan snorted.

"I thought we agreed no benefits?" he asked, slowly bending
down to drop Leo on the floor.

"I wouldn't consider that a benefit."

"Not into spanking, huh? That's okay…turnabout is fair play."

Holly's eyes widened and her hands went behind her, as if covering her posterior would save her if he really wanted to smack her butt.

"Not now, but soon. You'll be distracted and I'll come in like
a ninja and get my revenge." Declan walked away from her and
washed his hands. "Right now, I have a meal to prepare."

"Then why did you take Leo?"

"Because you're going to help."

"Oh, no! I told you, I'm a terrible cook. I can bake cookies if
they're cut and drop, but if you let me in that kitchen with you, it's
not my fault when we burn down the house."

Declan chuckled. "I'll take my chances."

"Can I make a small request?"

"Maybe," he said, drawing the word out.

"Can I record this? Not you, but me trying to cook and you giving
me directions. You can be completely off camera, but I haven't done a
single new thing for my channel and I think this could be at the very
least entertaining." Holly sighed. "I'm struggling to find a new direction for my social media and I'm pretty much grasping at straws."

Declan didn't respond right away, unloading the groceries and
putting away what he wouldn't use while he considered. Finally,
he nodded. "All right, set it up, but only you. I don't want even
my elbow on camera."

"I got it."

While he prepped his area, Declan kept stealing glances at Holly while she carried over first one ring light and then the other, adjusting them. When she flipped on the bright white lights, he waved a slice of cheese at her. "Perfect. I needed more light."

"Yes, because it's all about you."

"Hey, I will revoke your social media pass into my kitchen."

"Wait a second, your kitchen?"

Declan turned around like he was searching the room. "Do you see anyone else in here offering to make you dinner?"

"I apologize. As you were."

"All right, I need a casserole pan and a pot."

"In the cupboard next to the oven," she said, snapping her phone into the holder attached to her ring light.

"I thought your thing was an elf that does stunts."

"It was, but I'm trying to find a different niche. I can't jump off rocks and do back flips out of planes forever."

"Back flips out of…" Declan shook his head, retrieving the pot and pan. "You're out of your mind."

"Hey, don't be a closed-minded jerk. The guys from Jackass were doing wild and wacky stunts long before I ever picked up a camera."

"Who?" he asked.

Holly rubbed her temples as if he was giving her a headache. "MTV. Reality stunt show. Pop culture."

He didn't say anything, and she pulled out her phone, tapping away at the screen. She pressed play on a trailer of a bunch of guys launching themselves in a shopping cart down a hill and Declan snorted. "Yeah, I'm sure they were geniuses."

"What are you trying to say?" she asked, crossing her arms over her chest, her phone still in her hand.

Well, this went south fast.

"I'm sorry. I just meant why would you risk your life doing crazy things like that?"

"Fame? Money? The thrill of it all?"

"I think I'll stay boring and broke."

Holly laughed. "To each their own, but I'm done with that stuff anyway. Gotta keep things fresh."

"Have you ever thought about giving up the social media stuff?"

"A time or two maybe, but as exhausting as it can be, I love it. I like being recognized and making people laugh. I'm sure there's a psychologist somewhere who would love to analyze me, but what's wrong with being honest? Actresses and performers do what they do because they love the spotlight and so do I."

Declan thought about everything he'd done throughout his life to avoid being the center of attention.

"It's like your art," Holly blurted, surprising him.

"What?"

"You love showing your work off. You're good and you know it, so even though you hang back as you create, when you finish? You can't wait for others to see what you've done."

"That's what you think, huh?"

Holly came up alongside him and bumped him with her hip, knocking him to the side. "Yeah, I do."

"You'd be right. When I think I've done good, I want to share it. Like the cooking process."

"Wait, let me turn on the camera," she said, skidding to the other side of him. Holly picked up a small remote from the other side of the counter and pressed a button. "There. Now we can start."

Before he could respond, Holly beamed at the camera and started talking. "Hi guys. Tonight, I'm trying something a little different. Those people who know me in real life realized a long time ago I have no culinary talents, but a friend of mine thinks he can change that, so he's going to be off camera giving me a cooking lesson while I try not to mess this up. Are we ready?"

Holly twisted her body so part of her faced him, and she grinned. "You're up, Teach."

Declan glanced at the camera and took a deep breath.

What have I gotten myself into?

CHAPTER 27

HOLLY STARED DOWN AT THE pan of Chicken Cordon Bleu, frowning. "I'm pretty sure I messed something up."

Declan chuckled, studying his two stuffed breasts on the left versus the ones she made on the right. While everything was spread and placed in neat layers inside his chicken, Holly's looked like she'd shoved the contents in with her fingers and the results resembled—

"Oh God," Holly gasped, clasping her hand over her mouth. "I just realized that they look like vajayjays!"

Declan attempted to smother his laughter, but it didn't work. "Your presentation needs work, but I guarantee you it will be delicious."

"No, but like, what was I thinking?" she asked, picking up the pan and showing it first to him and then turning it towards the camera. "I swear this was not on purpose."

"It will be fine once it's cooked." He took the pan from her and slipped it into the open oven. "Now we wait thirty-five minutes, and while that's baking we work on the sides."

Holly groaned. "This is how I feel after grocery shopping,

usually right before I call and order a pizza or a pick-up from Lord of the Fries."

"Not after you try my cheesy garlic mashed potatoes, and asparagus in lemon sauce. You'll never order take-out when you can make everything better at home."

"Ah, so does that mean we're done with the cooking lesson and you're going to do the rest while I watch?" she asked, shooting him a wink before she tried to escape around the counter.

Declan caught her by the back of her shirt, careful to stay out of what he hoped was the camera frame, and reeled her back. "Not so fast. You've got potatoes to peel."

"Ugh!"

"Don't give me that. Haven't you heard the story of *The Little Red Hen*?"

"A long time ago. My mom used to read me nursery rhymes and old fables like that."

"The moral of Little Red is if you're lazy and don't help, then you don't get to reap the benefits of someone else's hard work." He tossed her one of the potatoes he'd just scrubbed and pointed to the cutting board. "Your instrument is there. I want each of those potatoes peeled in less than twenty seconds or you're not getting dessert."

"You're timing me now?"

"Go!"

Holly started scraping away, losing her grip on the potato once and barely catching it in time to finish removing the last few strips, shaking with laughter. She set it in the colander and held her hands up for the next one. Declan tossed it to her and started counting.

"Come on, these take fifteen minutes to boil and we've still got to cube them up. Mush mush mush!"

"I'm going to take you zip-lining for this," she threatened, tossing her second potato into the colander.

"Last one," he said, launching the potato under his leg and up into an arc. Holly was laughing too hard to catch it and Declan wagged his finger at her. "And I don't think zip-lining in the dead of winter sounds safe."

"No, we'd wait until spring." Holly realized how presumptuous she sounded and cleared her throat. "If you're still in town, I mean."

Declan's expression softened for a split-second before he said, "Five seconds."

She got the potato finished after he made a buzzer sound with his mouth. "Oh, too bad."

"I don't like this game," she grumbled.

"Bonus round! Carefully cut the potatoes into quarters and put them into the pot of water." Declan handed her the knife, handle first.

Holly grabbed a potato from the colander and put the potato on the board then cried, "Hiya!" slamming the knife down into the potato. Holly grinned at Declan. "Like that?"

"Sure, if you want to end up losing a body part."

"Maybe I need you to show me," she teased, holding the knife out handle first.

Declan pursed his lips. "I'm not getting in front of that camera, Holly."

"You don't have to." She slid the cutting board to him with a grin. "Let's see what you got."

Declan grabbed the potato and flipped it flat side down, putting his fingers on either side as he slid the knife through the middle. "Hold the potato, cut away from you, and take it easy. Don't butcher the potato like it's a piece of meat." He picked up another potato from the colander and set it and the knife on the cutting board, sliding it back to her. "Try again."

Holly smirked as she followed his instructions to the letter and his eyes narrowed.

"You played me," he growled.

"I was just seeing if I could get you to come up behind me and show me how to cut a potato."

"Why?"

"Because I've always wanted a hot man to try that move, but I was born after it lost popularity."

Declan shook his head, setting the last potato down on her cutting board. "You are a trip."

"Why? Because I think you're hot?"

Declan rubbed his face where his beard had been slowly returning and turned her way, leaning a hip against the counter. "But you don't like facial hair."

She reached up and gave his short beard a gentle tug. "It's like you."

"What does that mean?"

"It's growing on me," she said softly.

Her words struck Declan like a lightning bolt, and he reached up to cup the back of her neck. "Funny, I could say the same thing about you."

Out of the corner of his eye, Declan saw the cell phone and

remembered her camera was still running. Even if that video wasn't recording, they'd agreed not to cross the line.

Then why was he tempted to obliterate the line and kiss her anyway?

He dropped his hand slowly, his fingertips trailing across her skin and then falling from her shoulder. It wasn't a good idea until they'd figured out how this living situation was going to work.

"Let me rinse these, and we can move on to the asparagus portion of the meal."

Holly frowned before heading around to mess with her phone. Declan thought she was turning it off, but then she moved the entire ring light to the other side of the oven.

"Need a better angle?" he asked.

"I guess you could say that." Holly removed the cutting board and knife and hopped up onto the counter, crooking her finger at him.

He leaned against the opposite counter, arms crossed over his chest. He wasn't worried about being on camera because he trusted Holly to respect his wishes and delete it.

"What do you want?"

"Seven minutes in heaven?"

"I thought we weren't going to do this."

Holly shrugged. "I figured what's the harm in kissing? People are going to talk regardless once they find out you're living here."

"You're probably right."

"Then why not enjoy ourselves and forget the rest of the world for a while."

Declan chuckled. "The asparagus takes ten minutes, plus I have to make the sauce."

"And the potatoes take fifteen to twenty, correct?" Holly reached down to the bottom of her green sweater and pulled it over her head, tossing it across the room. She sat there in the tiniest tank top he'd ever seen, showing off more skin than covering it, and his mouth went completely dry. She crooked her little finger again and Declan dropped his arms and crossed the room, placing his hands on the counter on either side of her thighs.

"We've got at least seven minutes," she murmured, "but only if you stop talking."

"I don't know what you have in mind, but I guarantee what I want to do to you is going to take longer than that."

Holly wrapped her arms around his neck, and he let her pull him in close. "Let's see who's right."

Declan didn't have a chance to respond before her lips covered his. He didn't think about how they shouldn't be doing this, that he should step back and keep things professional until he'd decided his next move. But kissing Holly was too sweet, her hands gliding over his shoulders and arms leaving trails of heat in their wake.

He stepped into her, deepening the kiss, his body flush against hers. Declan's hands came up to tangle in her hair, and her palms gripped his waist, drawing him even closer to her body.

The sound of a trilling alarm broke the moment and Declan looked toward the oven. "There's still fifteen minutes left on the oven timer."

"It's my phone," Holly said breathlessly. "I set an alarm to go off in seven minutes." She gave him a hard, fast kiss before pushing him back so she could jump down. "I warned you we were going to run out of time if you didn't stop talking. Now, I believe we have just enough time to finish dinner."

"And what about after dinner?" Declan asked, shaking with laughter. "Are you going to give me another limited time slot?"

"Depends."

"On what?"

"Do I get dessert?"

You are *dessert, Elf,* he thought. "I'll give you one bite for every kiss."

Holly shot him a sexy smile. "Now that sounds like fun."

Declan's phone buzzed in his pocket, and he glanced at the screen, seeing a group chat text message.

> Five days until the bachelor party! Who's ready to
> partay?

Declan didn't recognize the number, but the next message he knew was from Nick because he had it saved in his phone.

> I'm ready! Just leave the tattoo gun at home. I don't
> need to wake up with something embarrassing per-
> manently left on my body.

Declan stuffed the phone back into his jeans pocket. "All right, time for the green portion of our meal." His phone buzzed in his pocket again as he dropped the clean stalks into a frying pan and added a touch of the olive oil he'd bought. "We can work on the sauce while these cook."

His phone went off a couple dozen more times and Holly glanced down toward the pocket of his jeans. "You sure are popular."

"A group text for the bachelor party."

"Ah, fun. You ready for wild shenanigans?"

Declan looked at her with what he hoped was exasperation. "Do I really look like the guy who goes wild? Grab me a bowl, will you?"

Holly grabbed one from the cupboard next to the sink and sidled up beside him, setting it on the counter. "I don't know. A month ago, I'd have said you wouldn't know what fun was if someone slapped you in the face with it."

"And now?"

"You can be fun sometimes."

"I appreciate that small concession." Declan pushed some of her hair to the side and kissed her neck. "Go ahead and measure out half a cup of lemon juice." Declan's hands rested on the curves of her hips, standing behind her as he whispered instructions in her ear. When all the ingredients were in the bowl, he handed her a whisk he'd found in the drawer earlier, and he pushed his hard, aching cock into the swell of her ass. "Now, you're going to want to mix all the ingredients in sure, circular strokes. Like this." Using his hands on her hips, he swirled her body along with his in slow, rolling circles until her breathing was coming fast and hard. "Think you got it?"

"For now, but I might need another demonstration after dinner."

Declan chuckled against her skin. "I'm here to help."

CHAPTER 28

HOLLY SAT BACK IN HER chair, rubbing her stomach happily. "Oh my God, you need to start a restaurant. That was wonderful."

"You helped."

Holly snorted. "And yet neither one of us went for the chicken I prepared."

"I'm going to," Declan said, putting a second breast on his plate. "I was just being polite and waiting until you were done."

Holly leaned forward, watching him cut into the chicken. "You know, from this angle, with the cheese oozing like this, it kinda looks like—"

"Elf," Declan growled, cutting her off, and Holly's cheeks warmed at the nickname. She'd hated being teased for years about her elf persona, but the way Declan said it, a warm, low rumble filled with affection, created a glow in her soul.

"It's been a while since you called me that," she murmured.

"Whoops. I forgot you hate it."

"Not when you do it like that."

Declan met her gaze, setting his fork down on his plate. "You know what you're doing to me, don't you?"

"Sorry," she said with a smile, picking up her plate and utensils. "I'll behave."

Declan snorted. "I'll believe that when I see it."

Holly tugged his ear as she passed on her way to the sink, rinsing the dishes and loading them into the dishwasher.

"I can help you with that when I finish," Declan called.

"No, it's okay. You did the grocery shopping and most of the prep and cooking. I've got this. But I need my mood music." She called out to her home device to play *Six: the Musical*. The first song started and Declan came up beside her, his face scrunched in confusion.

"What the heck is this?"

"Divorced. Beheaded. Died." Holly turned her head to the side and hung her tongue out of the side of her mouth while simultaneously rolling her eyes up. With a laugh she explained, "It's a musical about the wives of Henry the Eighth. I play it every time I clean."

"Interesting choice." Declan squeezed closer, rinsing off his plate and utensils.

"I told you I would do that," she said.

"You did most of it."

Holly let it go and turned to gather up the rest of the dishes, spotting Leo up on the table helping himself to the last piece of Chicken Cordon Bleu. "Looks like Leo was hungry."

Declan turned and let out an angry *pssst*. "Leo! Get down from there!"

The cat looked up, licked his lips, and hopped down with a lazy drop onto the chair as Holly approached, picking up the side dish pans. "You should have let him have it at this point. He licked it so it's technically his."

"He knows better," Declan said.

"I see no evidence of that," she said, scraping the small amount of food left into the trash. "Pretty sure he likes to rule the roost."

"Nope, he's just testing boundaries because we're in a new place. I'm the boss."

Holly set the dishes in the sink and turned on the water, teasing, "Don't worry. If you say it enough times, I'm sure it will come true."

"Wow, such a smart-ass."

She was in mid-scrub when a hard smack landed across her butt, and she spun his way, the dish brush in her hand and brandished like a weapon. "Really?"

"Hey, I told you it would happen when you least expect it."

Holly dropped the brush into the sink and rubbed her abused posterior with a wet hand. "Just for that, you can finish the dishes."

Declan took her hand, stopping her from walking out of the kitchen. "Or we can let these soak a bit and sit down. Talk."

"What do we need to talk about?"

"Me staying here, for starters. I don't feel right about it unless I'm paying for my room."

"I don't need your money, Declan."

"Doesn't matter, I'm not living here rent-free."

"Fine." She leaned back against the counter and faced him. "Would four hundred for the room suffice, and we'll split the utilities?"

"Seems a little low for a one-bedroom apartment, which is essentially what I'm renting."

"What if you cook three nights a week?"

"Five meals of my choosing sounds acceptable to me."

"Glad that's settled," she said. "What else?"

"I know I said no benefits…"

"I remember."

"But I can't stop wanting you."

Holly's heartbeat sped up. "What do you suggest, then?"

"We keep our arrangement and us separate. You said that a relationship with me didn't interest you."

"And I meant it," she said.

"Good, because if my dad sells the store and my mom stays with him, I'll probably leave Mistletoe. The last thing I want to do is hurt you when I do."

"Then we're in agreement. Roommates for as long as you're in town, and the benefits are available until one or both of us is ready to move on. No hard feelings."

"Yes."

"Do we need to write up some kind of agreement?"

"I think verbal is enough," Declan said.

Holly pushed off the counter and grabbed him by the front of the shirt with both hands. "Then if you're ready and willing, I'd like to get started on those benefits."

Declan bent over, his big hands covering her butt, and lifted her up, holding her against him. Holly locked her legs around his waist, resting her hands on his shoulders when he headed out of the kitchen.

"Your room or mine?" he asked.

"My bed is bigger," she murmured, bending over to kiss him.

"Holly," he mumbled against her mouth. "I can't see where I'm going when you do that."

Holly laughed, retreating until he walked through her bedroom door. She'd left the bedside lamp on earlier and the yellow glow from under the floral shade cast shadows on the wall as he set her on the bed. Her legs fell away from him as she scooted back, watching him hungrily while his fingers worked the buttons of his flannel shirt. He slipped the shirt off one shoulder, revealing sculpted pecs, flexing biceps, and a glimpse at lovely defined abs. Holly regretted that she lacked Declan's artistic abilities. He would have made a beautiful painting.

When Declan discarded the shirt across the back of her corner chair, Holly took the opportunity to tug her camisole over her head. Clad only in her bra and joggers, she searched his face. Declan's eyes drifted over her and everywhere his gaze touched left a trail of heat on her skin. She'd never had a man look at her like he wanted to consume her, to taste every last bit of her, and anticipation throbbed between her legs.

Holly reached for the waist of her joggers and pushed them down her legs at the same time he unbuckled his belt. She crawled across the bed and reached for the top of his pants, kneeling on the end of the mattress to get a better angle. Declan's hand slipped around the back of her neck and his mouth crashed down on hers hungrily, licking and stroking her tongue as she blindly fought with the button of his jeans.

Discarding clothes was never quite as easy as the movies

portrayed it, and Declan's hands joined hers, helping her shove his jeans down his hips. She broke the kiss to finish the job and saw the waistband of his boxer briefs caught on the hard length of his cock, outlining the shape, and Holly licked her lips with anticipation.

"I love the way you're watching me," he said, stretching his waistband as he bent over to finish removing his clothes.

"You're definitely fun to look at," she murmured, reaching behind to unhook her bra and managed to slide it down her arms in time for Declan to pick her up and toss her gently back onto the bed.

"So are you," he murmured.

His mouth grazed her neck first, kissing his way down and along her collarbone, and she arched into his mouth. Holly wasn't the type to lie back and enjoy. An eager participant, her hands stretched, touching him everywhere, but she couldn't reach the one part of him she was dying to explore.

Declan took her left nipple into his mouth, tugging on it with a gentle suck, and Holly closed her eyes, hands threading through his hair, squeezing her legs together against the aching drum deep in her pussy.

Holly didn't go slow. She hit top speed in every aspect of her life, but no amount of urging detoured Declan from the steady, thorough exploration of her body. When his head dipped between her legs and she let out a breathless whimper, he looked at her, up the length of her body, and the intensity in those green eyes didn't match the small smile.

"Remember what I said? I'm the boss."

His words barely registered before his mouth was back, insistent and commanding, every flick of his tongue making her legs tremble. Oral sex was a crap shoot depending on the giver, but holy mother of sex, Declan was a master of the craft.

The orgasm came on like an earthquake, sudden and intense, vibrating from her core and outwards, spreading through her limbs, chest, and up her throat until she cried out her release loudly, calling his name with her hands gripped in her sheets. He continued to lick her, stroke her, bringing her back down in that patient, soft style, and she hummed as the tension in her body eased, leaving her a puddle of satiated mush.

Declan rolled onto his side next to her, slipping an arm under her body and pulling her against his. He pressed his lips to her forehead, his other hand resting on the curve of her hip. Holly turned in his arms, hooking her leg over his thigh and reaching between them.

"I don't have a condom."

Holly sat up and leaned across him, reaching for the drawer in her nightstand. He moved with her, rolling onto his back while she retrieved the condom and hovered over him, adjusting her legs to straddle his body.

"I gotcha covered," she said with a smile, dropping a kiss onto the center of his chest. She didn't give it to him, but made her way down his stomach, scooting along the length of his legs as she returned the favor he'd given her with gusto. Licking along his length and sucking him down, listening to him groan and gasp with every new stroke or caress of her hands and tongue. He was vocal about what felt good and Holly loved it, the sound of his happiness like the sweetest melody and she couldn't get enough.

When Holly ripped the condom open, he tried to take it from her, but she avoided him with a smirk.

"I'm the boss now."

Declan laughed deeply, leaning back on his elbows, his gaze trained on her, and she gazed back, even as she rolled the condom over his head and followed it with her mouth. Declan's eyes widened before they closed completely. "Fuck, Holly. You're incredible."

She released him and climbed up the line of his body until the head of his cock rested against her center. "I'd agree with that assessment."

"Always gotta have something smart to say," he murmured, giving her a light smack on her butt, and she gasped, his length sliding into her.

"I think I've created a monster."

"What do you mean?"

Holly rocked over him, watching his eyelids lower the deeper he went. "I think you like spanking me."

Declan smirked. "It's been a fantasy of mine for two years."

Holly laughed. "What?"

"I'm kidding. That wasn't what I thought about." Declan's hands gripped her hips and without warning brought her down hard. "This is." She cried out with pleasure as he stretched her inside, rolling her hips when he lifted her and brought her down again, finding the rhythm her body longed for.

"Every time you'd step into me with those dark, sexy eyes and that smart mouth running circles around me," he said, meeting her motions in swift, even strokes, "all I could think about was how much I wanted to take you behind that counter in your shop and fuck the anger out of both of us."

Holly moaned, unable to find a coherent reply as he drilled her, controlling the depth, the pace, picking up speed until she could only angle her body just right, the glide of him inside her hitting that spot again and again until—

"God, Declan, yes," she hollered, coming with a hard shudder that wracked her body, her arms trembling as they held her above him, watching his face tighten.

"Holly." The way he said it, like her name was a prayer, as if he was begging for salvation as he pumped into her, his body shaking under hers, fingers digging into her muscles but she didn't care. Being with Declan, falling onto his chest in the aftermath of their lovemaking, and the sensation of his big, callused hands trailing along the skin of her back, her ass, and thighs and back up, made her feel cherished. Cared for. While some men would have already pushed her off, Declan didn't seem in a hurry to let her go, and she liked that.

Maybe a little too much.

The thought had Holly lifting up and sliding off Declan. "I'm going to get cleaned up."

Declan sat up, catching her hand before she could retreat. "Wait." He stalled her escape, his green eyes locked on hers. "There's one more thing we didn't discuss."

"What?"

"After the benefits. Do I stay? Or should I go back to my room?"

Holly searched his face for any signal as to the answer he

wanted and finally said, "Sleeping together has certain implications. If we're trying to keep things from getting complicated…"

"Then I should go back to my room. I got it." Declan climbed to his feet and cupped her face in his hands. "Good night, Holly."

Regret twisted her stomach in knots. A soft brush of his lips, and he released her to gather his clothes. Holly didn't wait for him to finish before escaping into her bathroom, closing the door behind her.

If you wanted him to stay, why didn't you say so?

Holly's fingers brushed her swollen lips, the taste of Declan still lingering, and she didn't have a good answer.

CHAPTER 29

SLEEP ELUDED DECLAN, AND HE spent several hours staring up at the ceiling, with Leo pacing back and forth across his stomach as though he could feel Declan's discontent. The last time he'd had sex was with his now ex-girlfriend before he'd moved back to Mistletoe, and before that, spending the night after being intimate had never been a question with the girls he dated because they always wanted more, usually more than he was emotionally ready to give. Things between Holly and him were complicated, which was why he'd asked her what she wanted. He hated that he'd been more than a little disappointed by her answer, but she'd said repeatedly that she wasn't the relationship type.

Declan had thought the same way about himself, but now he wasn't sure. Sex was good, but with Holly he'd wanted it to be better. He'd enjoyed watching her come apart, relished the way she called his name when she came, and he wanted it to happen again. He wanted to enjoy what they had and not worry about what the other one was thinking, but that's exactly what he'd been doing for hours.

Declan set Leo off to the side and got out of bed, wearing only a pair of loose sweats. He opened the door and padded out to the kitchen for a glass of water. Maybe he'd grab one of the containers of stackable chips he'd bought earlier, too, and after a midnight snack be able to fall asleep.

Leo trotted after him, stopping off at his food dish by the back door and crunching away at his dry kibble. Declan grabbed a glass from the cupboard and filled it with ice, wincing at the loud clang of it against the glass.

"Couldn't sleep?" Holly's soft voice asked behind him.

Declan turned to find her in a long t-shirt night dress with a bear on the front, her hair thrown up in a messy bun.

"Not a bit."

"Me neither. I was listening to an audio book."

"Which one?" he asked.

Holly leaned across the counter on her forearms. "A romantic suspense about a stalker and the woman he's after. Sounded good, but then I got really creeped out."

"That's all that's keeping you up?" Declan opened the cupboard to grab the chips, realizing he sounded testy without meaning to. "A book?"

Holly sighed. "No. I feel…like a jerk about earlier."

"Earlier when?"

Holly shot him a sour look. "Don't be cute. About saying you should go back to your room after we…finished. I lay there thinking about how I'd feel if a man said that to me and I instantly regretted it, but I didn't want to come in there and wake you up to tell you that."

"Well, I wasn't asleep, but if you didn't want me to stay, Holly, then you don't have to apologize for your feelings," he said.

"That's the thing. With all our talk about benefits and you leaving Mistletoe, I thought that you wanted to go. And then I saw your face and I..." She trailed off, shrugging. "I figured I must have imagined your expression when you walked out that door."

"What did you think you saw?"

"Disappointment? I thought for a second you might have been unhappy about not staying with me, but you didn't say anything, you just left. Then I heard you out here and figured if neither of us could sleep, maybe that meant something."

"That we're insomniacs who think too much?" he joked.

"Or that we didn't want to be alone?"

Declan didn't want to tell her that it was more than that. The second he held Holly, it was like something clicked inside him. Being with her, touching her, sinking into her body brought on a sense of belonging and satisfaction he'd never experienced. He'd spent so much time keeping her at arm's length that now he didn't like having the counter between them, let alone a bedroom wall.

But Holly wasn't thinking that way, and if he came on too strong it might send her into a panic.

"Could be that," he said.

"Then I suggest," she said, coming around the counter and taking a soda from inside the fridge before snagging the chips from his hand, "that we amend the rules. We'll be honest about how we're feeling, even if the other might not be on the same page. That way there's no more confusion, and if we want to expand the menu of what benefits means for us, we can."

"I'm good with that. Why you stealing my chips, though?"

"Because if you want these," she said, waving them in the

air as she backed toward the hallway, "you're going to have to follow me."

Declan almost told her she didn't need the chips to lure him into her room, but he just grinned, trailing behind her. He left the door open and when she climbed up on the right side of the bed, he took the left happily, since it was what he slept on at home.

Thinking of home made him worry about his dad and how he was doing, despite what his mom said. Declan knew when something changed with Liam, if there was a shift in mood or behavior. Even if his dad sold the store, how could Declan consider leaving the town, let alone the state? If something happened to Liam and Declan couldn't get here fast enough, he'd have to add that to the stack of regrets that kept piling up.

"Hey, where did you go?" Holly asked, popping the top on the chips and holding it out to him.

That little voice in his head screamed not to tell her, that he needed to keep boundaries. To protect his privacy.

"We said we'd be honest with each other," she prodded. "Judgment-free zone, if that's what concerns you."

"It's not." Declan took a deep breath and admitted, "My dad doesn't want anyone to know—he's got Alzheimer's."

Holly stopped chewing, her eyes heavy with sympathy as she took a drink of her soda and swallowed. "I am so sorry."

"Yeah, that's one of the reasons I haven't told anyone. That and my dad asked me not to. I don't want everyone finding out and feeling sorry for us. You live long enough and some illness is bound to take you down."

"That's a...pragmatic way to look at it."

"Pessimistic and shitty, you mean." Declan reached for a chip, holding it in his hand with no desire to eat it anymore. "It's something my dad says."

"If he's sick, why did you leave the house?"

"Because I found out he lied to me for years."

"About what?" she asked.

Declan knew he'd opened the door and there was no use turning back now. "When my mom left, my dad was so angry. I figured that whatever happened, she didn't appreciate him and all he'd done. I shut her out and took his side." Declan ate the chip, leaning back against the pillow as he continued, "Christmas was her favorite holiday and everything was a reminder of what we lost. When he was first diagnosed after his fall, I stayed in town and took over the store, thinking that my entire life, all my dreams, were gone."

"No wonder you were such an angry man," she murmured.

"Maybe. Now that my mom's back, she's been having sleepovers with him and saying she's moving back for good. I thought if he sold the store, and she was here, I could get back to my life, but the thing is…"

He trailed off, putting everything together in his mind before he finished, but Holly poked him in the knee impatiently. "The thing is?"

Declan chuckled. "Can't a guy collect his thoughts?" Without waiting for an answer, he continued, "My life isn't mine anymore. I moved back two years ago, thinking that the world was against me, bringing me back here, but the truth is I like being a handyman. I like going to my studio to paint without someone constantly comparing it to another artist. I like being nearby in case my dad needs me, and I've finally made a group of friends I wasn't expecting."

"Please do not tell me you decided to stay because of my brother, Pike, and Tony, because that's just depressing."

Declan chuckled. "And Clark. You can make fun of me all you want, but they are good guys. They kind of blindsided me and by the time I realized that they made being here better, that they were the most supportive friends I'd ever had, it hit me like a bat to the chest: I didn't want to leave them."

"I'm still wrapping my head around the fact that Clark, Nick, and the goon squad are the reason you're considering not leaving."

"I don't know if I'm really going to stay. I was ready to take off and move on a few weeks ago, but the longer I live here, the more I ask myself what's waiting for me out there that's so great? I may find it ridiculous sometimes, but in Mistletoe I have friends. Work. My studio."

"You're saying maybe living the small-town life isn't so bad?"

Declan smiled. "I've discovered a few perks and had to reevaluate my opinion."

"What would you do if you stayed? You talked about running a gallery or becoming an art professor. Not exactly jobs you'll find here. And I get you like being a handyman, but what about your art? Are you just going to keep painting and stacking them against the wall?"

He cocked his head to the side, studying her. "You looked through my canvases?"

Holly blushed. "When I was grabbing Leo. You were sleeping in the truck and I—Declan, they are gorgeous. You should really look into having them displayed."

He shrugged. "It's not about that. I love painting, and showing people my work is great, but I want to inspire others to tap into their artistic sides."

"What about opening your own gallery here? If your dad is planning on closing the store anyway, why not buy his building and you can do exactly what you want. You could even hold art classes for locals and tourists."

"And fill it with all of my paintings?"

"You think that this area doesn't have local artists, but we do! I'm telling you, build it and they will come."

Declan frowned. "That's from a movie, isn't it?"

"Really? You skipped *Peter Pan* but know *Field of Dreams*?"

"My dad loves sports and action flicks, what can I say?"

"Back on track, if you want to stay here, and your dad agrees, I think you can do it. If you need another reason to stay, that is."

Declan didn't say it out loud, but Holly may have played a role in his revision of his opinion on Mistletoe and why he wanted to stick around. She was amazing, different from anyone he'd ever known, and he needed to figure her out. He'd been rolling through life like a train, never getting off the tracks, and boom, along came Holly and her smart-ass, take no crap attitude and she'd derailed everything Declan thought he wanted.

"I'd have to run the finances and follow up on artists and interest."

"Let me know if I can help." Holly handed him his chip container and hopped off the bed. "I'm going to brush my teeth again and grab a water. Don't go anywhere."

Declan had a few more chips while she was gone and returned

the chips to the cupboard before brushing his own teeth in the guest bathroom. When he returned to her room, the light was off and she was already in bed, with her back to him. He climbed in beside her and before he'd even settled in, Holly was backing her butt up into his crotch.

"Are you hinting at something or what?" he asked, smiling as he slipped his arm around her waist.

"Yeah." She glanced over her shoulder, and he caught the flash of her grin with the light streaming in from the window. "I want to be the little spoon."

Declan chuckled, his hand splaying over her stomach as he pulled her back into his body, his mouth caressing the exposed line of her neck. "Are you tired?"

Her response was to roll her ass back against him, while taking his hand on her stomach and sliding it farther down her body. "Not at all."

His hand dropped beneath her night dress and lifted it up, his fingers trailing around her bare skin until he reached the curve of her hip, noticing she'd neglected to put her underwear back on. Gripping the inside of her thigh, he rolled her back against him, spreading her leg and hooking it over his thigh.

When his fingers glided along her seam, he listened to her intake of breath. Felt the first shiver when he found her clit, rubbing it between his fingers. Every exploration of what brought Holly joy filled him with a sense of pride and satisfaction.

"Declan," she whispered, her hand coming around to cradle the back of his head as she turned her face, reaching for his lips with hers. Declan met her kiss as Holly's body jerked and trembled.

He continued his onslaught until she'd fallen back against him limply, a soft sigh escaping her lips as their kiss broke.

"Wanna go for round two?" Holly murmured, releasing a small yawn.

Declan kissed her nose with a laugh, rolling her towards him until her head rested on his chest. "I appreciate your enthusiasm, but I'm good."

"Just don't wake me up for smexy time, or I may kill you in an exhausted rage."

Declan smiled, pulling her tighter against him. "I'm not much of a morning person either."

"Look at that. Something in common."

"Good night, Elf."

He held Holly as her breathing deepened, feeling a sense of a sense of contentment—no, it was stronger than that than that. It was as warm as a shot of whiskey rolling down his throat and spreading through his body, and made him dread when the alarm would go off in a few hours and she'd leave for work. For the first time in many years, he understood the happiness being with another person could bring.

If he'd known falling asleep with Holly Winters would be the best part of his day, he would have stopped fighting with her two years ago.

CHAPTER 30

TUESDAY MORNING, DECLAN SNUCK OUT of bed and pulled on a pair of boxer briefs, leaving Holly sleeping soundly on her stomach with the blanket pulled up over her naked form. Leo was curled up on the pillow next to her head, the top of the cat's face lost in her wild red hair. When she'd arrived home from work last night, Declan had dinner ready, but after they finished the meal she'd gone to the fridge and held up a bottle of chocolate sauce and a can of whipped cream.

"I'm ready for dessert."

He'd protested, telling her the movies made that kind of thing look sexier than it was.

"Have you tried it?" she asked.

"No."

"Neither have I, so how about you get your butt back to the bedroom and we'll experiment. If one of us hates it, at least we'll know."

The movies were partially right. Being turned into a human sundae was messy but fun. Especially getting cleaned up in the shower together, another first for Declan. He'd never been the adventurous type but something about Holly made him want to try anything and everything she asked him to.

Declan grabbed the gallon ziplock bag from the cupboard that contained the pancake mix he'd made from scratch the day before, plus the vanilla, chocolate chips, and eggs from the fridge. He'd planned to make Holly his grandmother's pancakes for her birthday with the chocolate chips as a twist. He'd bought bananas as well to slice and what was left of the whipped cream as a topping. Declan quietly bustled around the kitchen, starting a cup of coffee before he poured the dry ingredients into a bowl. The last time he'd made these pancakes was with his mom the morning of his high school graduation, and he didn't take the time to write down what went into them but he'd asked Diana over lunch yesterday if she could send him the recipe and she'd happily done so, with a healthy dose of guilt added for not talking to his father yet. He'd firmly told her to stay out of it, but he didn't think she'd listened.

He pulled a pan out of the cupboard and set it on the stove, twisting the temperature knob to medium. While that warmed up he finished mixing his batter together, and a niggling of doubt poked at the back of his mind, wondering if this was too much for two people who were keeping things light.

Declan heard a door opening and closing, but the additional jingle to it sounded like the bells on Holly's wreath.

Which meant someone was coming in the front, and he was standing in the middle of Holly's kitchen in his underwear.

Delilah rounded the corner from the hallway into the dining room and the moment she saw him, she yelped. "Oh!" She turned her back to Declan, calling over her shoulder, "Why are you in my best friend's kitchen?"

"Making Holly a birthday breakfast."

"*Naked?*" Delilah squeaked.

"No, I'm wearing boxer briefs!"

Delilah turned, peeking around the corner as if to suss out if he was telling the truth. "Thank goodness for that. I brought her a birthday mocha and wanted to surprise her!"

"Do you always just let yourself into her place?" Declan asked.

"Not usually, but she doesn't mind when I use the spare key—Why am I explaining this to you?" Delilah pointed to her chest. "Me, best friend. You, booty call!" she finished, swinging that finger his way.

"What is going on out here?" Holly called, a raspy edge to her voice as she stumbled out of her room.

Declan watched Delilah hold up the cups of coffee she carried in each hand. "Happy birthday, Bestie! I got you a mocha, but apparently Declan already gave you a little birthday delight by the looks of things."

Mortified, he scraped a hand over his face, glaring at the back of Delilah's head. The woman had no tact whatsoever. Holly looked past Delilah, and catching Declan's gaze her eyes widened and Declan would have laughed if he wasn't incredibly uncomfortable.

"De, why don't we go out onto the front porch to drink these and let Declan put some clothes on."

"I know you can't see over the counter, but I'm wearing boxer briefs. I'm not naked!"

"Close enough," Delilah said. "Those boxers leave little to the imagination and girl, I gotta say—"

"Ahem!" Holly interrupted, taking a coffee cup from her. "Get out there and stop making Declan uncomfortable, you pervert! Wait, no, you should apologize."

"I should?" Delilah asked, and Declan could see by her profile that one eyebrow was cocked.

"Yes! While I do not care if you let yourself into my place, you do not have the right to ogle him like a lecherous fiend. I wouldn't let anyone treat you that way if the tables were turned."

"When I stay over, I don't walk around in my skivvies, but fine." Delilah turned all the way around to address him. "I apologize for being skeezy and making you uncomfortable."

Declan nodded. "I appreciate that, but it was more being caught off guard than truly offended."

"See, not offended!"

Holly took Delilah by the arm and started dragging her out of the room. "I can't believe you just walked in."

"Hey, you told me he was crashing with you, not that you were bumping uglies," Delilah said, her voice carrying down the hallway.

"Ugh, I hate that turn of phrase."

"Besides, who knew what he had going on under that shirt? I couldn't help staring because that man's chest is vavavoom, and he should take it as a compliment."

"No, he should not and that is sexist to say!" The front door opened with a loud whine and a jingle. "I'm going to smother you in the snow until you get your head right."

Declan shook his head, trying to hold back the laughter bubbling up in his throat. He didn't care if Delilah thought he was attractive, but he was a little concerned she'd mentioned discovering him half naked cooking and people would draw their own conclusions.

What does it matter at this point? Might as well accept the inevitable that being with Holly even casually is going to draw attention.

Declan went to his room and grabbed a pair of jeans and a t-shirt, dressing swiftly. When he got back, he dropped a hefty spoonful of butter in the pan and went back to stirring his ingredients.

The front door opened and closed again, and he heard the soft fall of Holly's feet before she came around the corner, a sheepish smile on her face before setting the to-go coffee cup in her hand on the counter.

"I'm so sorry about that. I should have mentioned she sometimes stops by to have coffee with me, but she usually knocks. I hadn't told her about our recent development."

"It's fine, she didn't have to go."

"Actually, she has a substitute job so she did. Hey!" Holly took a drink from her cup before she continued. "Being a substitute is a great way to get in with the school district. If you're interested, we could have D over for dinner one night and you could pick her brain."

"I'll think about that," he said, crossing the kitchen to kiss her forehead. "It was nice of her to deliver you coffee for your birthday."

"Delilah and I share a common obsession with wake-up juice and always buy each other a drink to celebrate our birthdays. Iced for her in July, hot for me." Holly wrapped her arms around his waist, squeezing him to her. "However, the cat is really out of the bag about us. Merry and Noel know and now Delilah knows, and although they won't say anything, I think our favorite neighbor is getting suspicious."

Declan held her loosely against him, cocking his head to the side. "I'm trying to get right with some people knowing my business, so don't worry about me." He kissed her forehead. "Although I hope she doesn't mention seeing me in my underwear to your sister."

"Ninety-five percent chance you're safe, unless alcohol is involved and then all bets are off."

"Well, at least I'm fairly certain she'll have good things to say, based on your conversation on her way out."

Holly shook her head. "I was hoping you wouldn't hear that, but sound carries. Delilah is boisterous, but she's a kind, loyal, amazing friend."

"You don't have to tell me that. I know you wouldn't suffer anyone in your inner circle who was a jerk." Declan chuckled. "Present company excluded."

"I don't think you're a jerk...anymore," she amended with a smirk.

Declan patted her hip. "Wow, high praise. Just wait until you get a mouthful of these pancakes."

"I do love breakfast foods, especially the sweet stuff."

"Speaking of sweet stuff," he said, leaning down to kiss her.

But before his lips touched hers, Holly burst out laughing. He reared back, frowning. "What's so funny?"

"That was insanely corny."

Declan pursed his mouth, hiding his amusement. "Damn, I was going for nice guy, maybe even a little flirtatious. Forgive me, I'm new at this whole thing."

"What whole thing? You've had girlfriends in the past, right?" Declan jerked in surprise and her eyes widened. "I didn't mean I was your girlfriend. I should have said you've dated girls. Or—crap. Don't mind me, always sticking my foot in my mouth."

"I've dated women, but we've never been…playful. I'm usually a serious guy—"

"You, really?" Holly said sarcastically. "I would have pegged you for class clown in high school."

"Back to what I was saying, Elf," he said, pinching her butt cheek. "I'm new to the flirty, fun stuff. Most of the women I've dated were practical, we had things in common, and I was comfortable with them."

"Bored, right? Isn't that the word you're looking for?"

Declan didn't want to admit that out loud and instead asked, "What about you? No overly sweet, corny guys in your past, huh?"

"One or two, but they didn't last long. I think your butter is burning."

Her words registered at the same time the charred scent hit his nostrils, and he released her to remove the pan from the stove and rinse it out. "Shit."

"At least you didn't waste any batter."

Declan put the pan back on the stove and gave her a mock

glare. "I'm going to have to kick you out while I'm cooking. You're too distracting."

"Why, thank you," Holly said, stretching onto her tiptoes. "See, that's the perfect mix of spice I've come to expect from you."

Declan gave her the kiss she silently asked for, lifting her up off her feet.

Until the doorbell rang.

He dropped her back to the ground with a laugh. "You're popular this morning."

"Hey, it's still my birthday," Holly said, stepping backwards away from him and disappearing down the hallway. Declan heard Holly talking to someone at the door, the musical lilt of her laughter echoing through the house and a deep voice responding.

Declan poured a small amount of batter into the pan. When another peal of laughter rang out, a spike of jealousy impaled him. Against his better judgment, he walked over to the edge of the hallway, listening to Holly and the man talk.

"I'm not sharing a room with you to protect you from Sally, Sam," Holly said firmly and Declan stiffened. "Besides, I've already got the rooms assigned."

"I can't have my own room," Sam pleaded. "If I'm alone, I know three shots into the party I'll try to crawl into bed and find her between my sheets waiting for me."

"I'm supposed to be the dramatic one between the two of us, but after the other night at Brews and Chews, I don't want to get in the middle of this. You need to be honest with her."

"I told her I wasn't interested."

"Then what's the problem?" she asked.

"It's almost as if she thinks I'll change my mind. But if I'm hanging with the beautiful, kind, funny Holly Winters—"

"Flattery will not work."

Sam sighed. "Fine. Then you take the single and put me with another dude."

"The only other guy with a double is Declan."

"So?" Sam said.

"I don't know how he'd feel bunking with you. He likes his space."

"I'll give him all the space he wants."

"You know, being irresistible to women isn't usually a problem for men."

"You're telling me you've never had unwanted attention from someone who wouldn't take no for an answer?"

"Point taken."

Declan waited, listening to the drawn out pause before Holly said, "All right, I'll talk to him and if he's okay with it, I'll put Delilah and me in our own separate rooms."

"This is why you're my favorite person."

"For the moment," Holly amended and laughed.

There was a loud groan and Declan couldn't resist peeking around the corner to find Holly leaning out her front door, male arms around her waist hugging her. When she stepped back, Declan did too.

"By the way, you didn't ask anyone else's opinion on who they wanted to bunk with. What makes Declan special?"

"I didn't say he was special. Of everyone going to the bachelor/bachelorette party, only you and Declan are relatively new. Pike and Tony, Sally and Tara, Delilah and I—we've all been friends since we were young. With the couples rooming together, it made sense to put you in your own rooms. You told me your opinion. Why wouldn't I ask him if he minds?

"Whoa, easy, killer. It was just a question. I'm going to get out of here and go to bed because I've been up all night. Drink your coffee, enjoy your birthday, and let me know about the sleeping arrangements."

"I will. Thanks for the drop by and the card, Sam."

"Anytime, Hol. And I didn't mean to put you in a tight spot."

"We're good."

Declan strode back to the stove, dumping the burnt pancake he'd left too long in the trash beneath the sink. He poured some more batter into the pan and kept his back to her when she came into the room. Declan felt like a heel eavesdropping on her and Sam, but their easy, flirtatious relationship twisted like fencing wire inside him. He knew what it was, even though he'd only ever experienced it with Holly. Jealousy.

And he hated himself for it.

"That was Sam," she said, sniffing the air. "Is something burning?"

"I had the pan too hot and lost one."

"Oh." Holly came up alongside him, leaning against the counter. "So, spoiler alert, we're having a joint bachelor/ bachelorette party. We rented a big house on the lake and I had everyone assigned to a room, but turns out I need to switch some things around. Would you mind rooming with Sam? It's got two twin beds, so it's not like you'd have to share."

Declan didn't want to tell her no, but the truth was if he was going to room with anyone, he wanted it to be Holly. He couldn't tell her that though because they weren't a couple.

"Sure, sounds like fun," he lied.

Holly kissed his arm at the highest point she could reach while he flipped the pancake. "Whew, you saved me. I thought for a second I would have to share with Sam. Fair warning, he snores."

How do you know that?

He couldn't ask that out loud and risk sounding like a jealous boyfriend, so instead he let out a strained laugh and said, "I'll bring my headphones. Now, stop distracting me. These pancakes aren't going to make themselves."

CHAPTER 31

WITH A WEEK BEFORE CHRISTMAS, A Shop for All Seasons had been hopping all day with people shopping for stocking stuffers, ornaments to exchange at the annual office party, and items they didn't even know they needed. By the time the last person walked out the door and Holly locked it behind them, her feet throbbed with pain and her back ached when she moved.

"That was exhausting!" Erica groaned, falling to the floor in a heap. "Seriously, leave me here to die."

Holly laughed, stepping over her employee on her way to count the drawer. "Or you could go home and rest."

Erica lifted her head. "But this place is wrecked."

"And I'm too tired to deal with it tonight. I'm going to close shop and I'll come in early tomorrow to straighten up."

"Not that I'm complaining, but you've been wanting me to skate out of here early all week. You got a hottie waiting for you I don't know about?"

Holly kept her head down as she opened the till, hoping Erica couldn't see the blush she knew suffused her cheeks. While they weren't being super secretive about their relationship, she hadn't been advertising that she couldn't wait to beat Declan home and get cleaned up from the day before he walked through the door. It had been nice having Declan to talk to, to laugh with, and even bicker some, although that had all but disappeared since Sunday night. Still, she wasn't ready for her friends and family to really be a party to what was going on with Declan, especially since she hadn't fully decided for herself yet.

"Nope. I'm just ready to head home and soak in my bathtub."

"I'm just joking. Either way, I'm taking you up on leaving early. I am completely fubarred and ready to sleep." Erica got to her feet again and limped over to the counter. "You sure I can't do anything else before I leave?"

"Not a thing. See you in the A.M?"

"Yes, you will. Have a safe drive home, boss."

"You too!"

When the door closed behind Erica, Holly made sure it was locked once more and finished up her close. The last thing she did was put the money in the safe before heading back up front with her phone in hand, tapping her TikTok app to check the traction on her latest videos.

Monday afternoon, she'd posted the edited version of Declan's first cooking lesson and been surprised with the positive response to the video, if a little spun out by the comments.

> I'm dead! Vajajay chicken!
>
> The way he pulled you back into frame! Great arm!
>
> Omg, you're glowing! Who is that?
>
> He sounds so hot!
>
> We need a chef reveal!

The video went viral in a few hours, and Holly had followed it up with Declan talking her through tacos with Spanish rice and a cilantro aioli. She'd undercooked the rice and when she took a bite and it crunched in her mouth, Declan had laughed uproariously off-camera, and she'd launched a spoonful of it at him, then giggle-screamed and ran off-camera when he made like he'd give chase. A large arm came into view, crooking a finger at her, and Holly called him insensitive as she walked back into frame. He told her the lesson wasn't over and assured her he'd share his rice with her, and her female followers went wild.

Aw, the way he said he'd share! #couplegoals

Can we talk about his laugh? Cause whoa daddy!

Haven't even seen his face but girl, I'm jelly!

She'd tried making a video of her attempt to follow a recipe and surprise Declan with dinner, although she never called him by name, but she'd accidentally misread a step and set the fire alarm off. He'd come running into the kitchen hollering, and when the smoke cleared and he got a look at her ruined dinner, he'd pulled her into his arms with a smile, murmuring about how much he appreciated her trying.

Holly had shown him every video before she uploaded it to make sure he was comfortable, and he'd approved all of them, even the last one which showed his arms around her and Holly's face resting against his chest, everything from the neck up cut off by the angle of the camera.

She scrolled through new comments and follows, a smile curving her lips as she walked through the door and locked it behind her. More commenters praising her new content, including a DM from one of her followers @OKintheUSA which blew her away.

> Hey Holly! Longtime fan! I've always loved your content, but your new videos really hit different. You've been this spellbinding, courageous force, doing all the things I've never been brave enough or able to try, but the one thing I've always excelled at is cooking. And it's so great to see this side of you who struggles and tries but doesn't give up. Who laughs at herself and shows us what we already knew. You are perfectly imperfect and we love you for it. Seriously wonderful! I've attached one of my favorite recipes and I hope you'll give it a try!

Holly closed out of the app and shot Declan a text. Are you home or painting?

A few seconds passed before her phone beeped. Next door. Back door's open.

Holly walked around the hardware store and down the alley, using her phone as a flashlight, her heart hammering in the dark. Although she was an adult, she hated not being able to see and often slept with a lamp on. There was something creepy about the shadows and what lurked there and Holly picked up the pace, her imagination going wild.

When she finally made it through the backdoor, it opened wide, nearly knocking her back, and Declan's warm smile washed over her, along with a wave of relief.

"Hey, everything okay?"

"Yeah, it's just super creepy out there by myself."

He chuckled, closing the door behind her as she stepped inside, but stopped before he reached for her. "I probably shouldn't touch you. I've got paint on my hands and clothes."

"I don't care," she murmured, snuggling into him. "I need this."

He wrapped her in a hug with his arms around her shoulders. "Something in particular spook you?"

"No, just being alone outside with a flashlight and those eerie yellow streetlights from fifty years ago gave me a small case of the willies."

"So, no snakes or darkness rules out...cave spelunking?" he teased.

Holly pinched his side. "Don't be cute. Haven't you noticed I keep the lamp on in my room all the time?"

"Yeah, but you turn it off when you sleep."

"Only when you're there," she whispered. Holly didn't elaborate why Declan being in bed with her made her feel safe enough to let go of her security light, partially because she didn't want to scare him. Holly hadn't realized how lonely her life was until Declan and Leo moved in. She went from nights of takeout and watching TV or reading before bed, to sharing a meal with someone and spending that time before she eventually fell asleep learning about each other in and out of the bedroom. While before there were moments Declan would clam up when she asked him something personal, lately he'd answered every single one, which Holly knew was progress.

When Declan didn't respond to her admission, she needed to fill the silence and asked, "Guess what?"

"You sold all of your gnomes?"

"No, although Merry wasn't wrong about them being in

demand this year." Holly stepped back out of his embrace and pulled out her phone, tapping across the screen until it settled on her TikTok profile, and she turned the screen toward him. "Look at the views and read the comments. Everyone is loving the cooking videos." Declan took the phone, scrolling through. "I'm trying to decide what to change my channel name to."

"Why don't you give me the options while I finish up in here?" he said, handing her the phone. "Then we can go home and I can teach you how to make honey garlic pork chops."

"That sounds tasty." Holly trailed behind him into the room and took a seat in the corner, watching him step back behind the easel. "Did you see your dad at all?"

"No, it was just my mom when I got here. I guess he got tired, so she took him home around lunch."

"Do you think he's okay?" Holly asked, watching his shoulders stiffen as he picked up his brush.

"I'm sure he is. He'd have days like this, but he was usually home when it happened. Now, give me name options."

She tapped on her notes app and recited, "Holly the Culinary Disaster?"

Declan grunted. "Next."

"Wrecking Recipes with Holly?"

"It has promise, but what happens when you learn to cook and the name no longer applies?"

"I can change it every thirty days, but be honest, do you really think I'm going to be able to cook anything without screwing something up?"

"I do. It just might take a lot of lessons to get there." Holly flipped him the bird, fighting a smile when he waggled his eyebrows. "Later. We've got names to choose and I want to finish this section before we go home."

Holly's grin stretched across her lips when he called her house his home and it wasn't the first time she'd been spun out by this reaction. She'd never lived with anyone, and while their situation wasn't conventional, Holly didn't run screaming for the hills at the sight of Declan's toothbrush in the bathroom drawer. She knew that the first few weeks of any living situation was the honeymoon period and most people were on their best behavior, but Holly noticed Declan was a lot like her in the way he cleaned up after himself, especially while cooking. Throwing away trash as he went, and not leaving dishes in the sink, unless they got busy doing other things.

Holly knew she should steel herself for the day when Declan moved on. Whether it was getting his own place and staying in Mistletoe or leaving town, she couldn't keep him.

Even if for the first time in her life Holly wanted to.

"But I still think that if you want to make this your new niche, it has to be about more than you not being able to cook."

Holly realized Declan had been talking through her deep thoughts and nodded, pretending she'd been listening the entire time. "Right."

Declan cocked his head to the side. "That's all you have to say?"

"You could always do it with me. Everyone keeps asking about you."

Declan shook his head. "*You* built your following by being authentic and fun all by yourself. You keep that up even while going in a different direction and people will continue to be drawn to you."

"How do you know that?"

He dropped his brush into a mason jar of water and walked over to her chair, placing his hands on either side of her thighs on the seat. "Because it works for me."

Holly's heart pounded at the deep timbre of his voice, rumbling through her pleasantly. "My authenticity is what you like about me?"

"It's one of the things." His lips hovered over hers. "Then there's this smart mouth." He kissed her, barely brushing her lips with his. "Your eyes." Declan's mouth trailed along her neck. "Your skin."

"Hmmm, go on."

Declan chuckled, kneeling down on the floor in front of her. "The way you spoil my cat and think I don't notice."

Holly laughed. "Hey, it is not my fault he figured out where I hid the catnip."

"Or the new cat tree in the living room? The kitty tunnel in the dining room?"

"They had a holiday sale online." Holly ran her hand over his face, her fingertips playing with the soft hairs of his beard.

"Well, you talked about getting a cat, so when the two of us move out, you'll already have half the supplies you need," Declan said.

Holly's heart bottomed out, knowing he was only being honest, but in the four days Declan and Leo had been living with her, she'd found herself making plans without realizing what she was doing. The cat toys and furniture were a part of that, but she'd also been thinking about setting up one of the other rooms as a studio in case Declan's talk with his dad about the store didn't go well. It wasn't as if there was anything in that room and it wouldn't take much to get it set up for that.

Except you're supposed to be casual roommates, not a couple.

"You're right," Holly said, clearing her throat. "I'm going to keep thinking about the name." The sudden urge to curl into a ball and cry consumed her, and she started to get up. "I should get going. See you at home."

"You don't want to see what I'm working on?"

"I thought you didn't like to share before it was finished?"

"Hey," Declan said, taking her chin in his hand. "What's up? Are you not feeling this anymore?"

"No! I mean, I am. I'm just tired. It was a long day."

Declan's green eyes searched hers, then he released her and slid his hand to the back of her neck, massaging it. "Maybe we should put a hold on the pork chops and just order a pizza tonight?"

"That might not be a bad idea," Holly said, glancing down at the screen of her phone. "Considering we have fifteen minutes to get back to the house before people start showing up to see the displays."

"Well, shit. Maybe we should go out for dinner then."

"I don't know," Holly said, smirking. "Not exactly low profile. If people see us sharing a meal, they might get the wrong impression."

"Like we're out on a date?" he said teasingly. "Who'd ever think something crazy like that?"

Even though she knew he hadn't meant it rudely, the words

stung and Holly pushed her chair away from him so she could stand. "Actually, I should probably check on Delilah. She wasn't feeling well earlier." Which was true, but mostly Holly wanted to talk to someone about Declan and Delilah didn't have upcoming nuptials to worry about.

"Really? That sucks." Declan climbed to his feet and leaned over to give her a fast, hard kiss. "Give her my best, all right?"

"What are you going to do until the crowds die down? Go talk to your dad?"

Declan sighed. "You're pushing, Elf."

Holly threw up her hands. "I know, but I don't want you to regret not working things out sooner. I know his actions hurt and I'm not excusing them, but you love him, right?"

"Of course I do."

"Then tell him that. You can work on the forgiveness part slowly, but you need to tell him how you feel because tomorrow is not guaranteed."

"Very meme-ingfully put."

"Fine, make a joke," she grumbled.

Declan touched her arm, concern etched in the fine lines of his forehead. "Are we okay? Anything I said or did to piss you off?"

Holly shook her head. "We're good."

"Then how about we walk out the front together so you don't get the heebie jeebies again?"

"Sure, that would be great."

Holly watched Declan clean up, paying close attention when he stripped off his painting clothes and redressed, hungrily taking in the muscles of his back. As emotionally mixed up as she might be right now, seeing Declan shirtless could always get her motor running. The man was a beautiful thing.

When he caught her staring, he grinned. "See something you like?"

"Everything."

Declan crossed the room shirtless and lifted her against him, backing her against the door. "Why do I feel like we're fighting?"

"What? I haven't said a word."

"But there's tension. Am I imagining it, or is there something you're not telling me?"

Ninety-nine percent of her wanted to admit that she hated the thought of him not being in her life, but that one percent screamed it was too soon. That she sounded like a needy woman looking for a boyfriend when she swore up and down that was the last thing she wanted.

Holly relaxed against him, looping her arms around his neck. "Like I said, long day and I'm tired and sore. Makes for Bitchy Elf."

His hands slipped between her and the door, nimble fingers pressing into her lower back, and she moaned as his fingers rubbed in circles, kneading the muscles there and working his way down her butt and thighs. Holly's forehead dropped onto his shoulder, melting into him with a hum of pleasure.

"Any better?"

"So much," she murmured, lifting her head and finding his mouth with hers.

Declan deepened the kiss, and she lost herself in him, the way his body molded into hers and how his hands held her tight like he wanted to keep her and never let go.

Holly broke the kiss at the intense thought. "I should probably go."

"Or you could text Delilah to check on her, I'll talk to my dad tomorrow, and the two of us could find another way to pass the time."

Declan's mouth found that spot on the side of her neck that turned her to goo, and she caved, her fingers tangling in the back of his hair, giving the strands a little tug. His mouth came back to hers and the kiss wasn't gentle or playful but fierce and wild, breaking only to shed their clothes in swift, jerky motions. When Declan grabbed a condom from his wallet and sat in the chair, she watched him roll it over his hard cock, anticipation coursing through her like electricity.

Declan reached for her and Holly came without hesitation, straddling his lap and the chair, sinking onto his length as her sore feet and calf muscles protested their use. Declan's hands covered her hips, his fingers digging into her butt cheeks, and he took over, rolling her hips with his hands over her, maneuvering into her a little at a time. Declan's mouth covered her left nipple when she was fully seated, sending lightning bursts exploding behind her eyes as she closed them, all thoughts chased away as Holly forgot to breathe. Her fingers got lost in the soft strands of his hair as he loved her, the intensity of his thrusts increasing with the pressure of his mouth. Holly gasped when he switched to her other breast, falling into a sea of satisfaction as her orgasm crashed through her.

"Declan," she cried out, holding onto him as her body trembled against him, and all the while he continued to thrust again and again until suddenly he was shaking too. He clung to her, his mouth everywhere at once, and she opened her eyes when his lips found hers, moss-green orbs staring into hers. She'd always believed kissing with your eyes open was awkward, but at this moment, watching Declan's pleasure and being completely connected to him was breathtakingly beautiful, and she wanted to freeze this feeling. And that's when she knew.

Without a doubt, she was falling head over heels for Declan Gallagher.

CHAPTER 32

"YOU REALLY AREN'T GOING TO tell me what we're doing for *my* bachelorette party?" Merry asked, climbing onto the party bus with a laugh.

The converted school bus Holly rented had a stripper pole in the front, a bar in the back, and a long bench seat on either wall. A strobing disco light hung from the ceiling, flashing rainbow lights throughout. She'd arranged for the bus to pick everyone up at the Winters Christmas Tree Farm even though it was a few miles outside of town; at least the parking lot was big enough to accommodate everyone's cars until they returned tomorrow.

"I'm really not going to tell you what we're doing, but hopefully you'll love it." Holly stepped in after her sister, who was decked out in a simple black sweater and jeans with her blond curls loose around her shoulders. Holly had warned everyone to dress warm and comfortable, which had brought about questions of why they weren't barhopping, but Holly diverted their questions.

"I'm sure I will, but please tell me you didn't hire anyone to work that pole."

"On the other hand, I'm back here praying she did," Sally called from the seat closest to the bar.

"Amen!" Ryan cheered, the only man invited to their night of fun who wasn't a groomsman. Even though he wasn't an official member of the bridal party, he'd been a huge help with planning the wedding.

"That's because you two are as painfully single as everyone else here except for Merry and Noel," Tara piped in, wrapping her hand around the pole and twirling around. "Whew, this is going to be fun later."

Noel and Delilah sat on the bench across from Sally and Ryan, and Merry and Holly went to join them.

"Why did you rent this big old bus for just us?" Merry asked.

"You never know who we're going to meet on our travels."

Merry groaned. "I do not like the sound of that."

"Speak for yourself, Mer," Tara said, dropping down next to Merry. "Are they hot? Half-naked? Sweaty?"

"Ew, why would you want sweaty?" Merry shivered.

"Depends on what he was doing to get that way and how he smelled," Holly said.

"Mmm, sweaty Sam," Sally quipped. "I wouldn't kick that man out of my bed for eating crackers."

"Pretty sure Sam has a thing for Holly," Tara said loudly and Holly glared at her. "I'm just saying I've seen you guys together. He's always hugging on you and seeking you out."

Holly watched Sally's smile dim and wanted to kick Tara for being a loudmouth gossip.

"I've heard from more than one person that they have a secret relationship they don't want anyone to know about," Ryan offered, shooting her a sly smile. "Of course, if I had a hunk of extreme sexiness like that on my arm, I'd shout it to the mountaintops."

"Sam is a flirt. We are not secretly dating and he does not have a thing for me."

And even if he did, my interests are engaged elsewhere.

Declan had brought some of his supplies home yesterday, and she'd found him in her empty dining room with a large plastic sheet on the floor, finishing a beautiful scene of her backyard covered in snow and a few birds hopping around on the ground. It was pure talent, and she told him so, although he brushed her praise aside. That seemed to be Declan's way: Anytime she said anything kind, he'd change the subject. He liked to hide what a good guy he was and Holly had no idea why.

"I threatened Sam with bodily harm if he tries anything with Holly," Merry said.

Tara patted Merry's shoulder. "I don't think that would scare a man like Sam away, pumpkin."

A woman in a white t-shirt and black vest climbed onto the bus and headed straight back to the bar area, while a man in his fifties followed her wearing a silky black top and sporting a thick mustache. He stood in the center of the bus and in a great booming voice said, "Good evening, folks! Are you ready to have a good time?" They all whooped and hollered until he waved his hands to quiet down. "Excellent. I am Nathaniel, and that beautiful lady ready to make you something tasty to drink is my partner in crime, Mona. Unless you are procuring a beverage, please stay seated at all times while the bus is in motion, and if you must vomit, yank any of the orange cords and it will alert me to pull over. Emergency protocols are get the heck off either there, there, or back there. And away we go!"

"This is cool. I wonder what Sam planned for Clark and the guys," Merry mused.

"Do you really want to know?" Holly asked, shooting Sam a text.

"I don't need to know," Merry said. "I'm not worried about Clark. I just want everyone to have a good time."

"I'm going to grab us some drinks," Tara said, hopping to her feet right as the bus took off, and she ended up in Holly's lap. "Whoops."

"Steady on your feet now, Missy," Nathaniel called, looking in the rear view.

Tara pushed off and held onto the seat as she made her way to the bar, while Holly watched the streetlights zoom past.

Merry elbowed her in the side. "How are things going with Declan? Having fun playing house?"

"We aren't playing house. He needed a better place to stay than a cot in the back of the hardware store while he figures out what he wants to do next."

"But I thought you guys were having fun," Merry teased.

Holly hadn't told her sister much except that they were feeling things out, which wasn't far from the truth. So far, her mother hadn't started asking questions, but the longer Declan crashed with her the more likely news was going to be all over Mistletoe. And while she was enjoying having Declan all to herself and discovering a plethora of things she'd never suspected, crossing the line with him hadn't dimmed any of the attraction between them, at least not on her side. In fact, it had done the opposite for her. Holly enjoyed spending time with Declan, in bed and out, and had already been brewing a plan for this weekend that included the two of them sharing a room at the house she'd rented for the party.

"We are having fun, but I think…it's a bit more than that for me and I could use some advice."

"Uh oh. Lay it on me."

"I've never had a relationship, let alone been in love. How do you know if that's what you're feeling?"

"Well, infatuation can feel a lot like love at first, but your case is unique because you two started out not being able to stand each other. Do you want to be around him?"

"Pretty much all the time."

"Do you guys talk and do other things, or is it mostly bedroom stuff?"

"We do both. He's teaching me how to cook."

"Lord help him," Merry teased, earning a glare from Holly. "Sorry. Honestly, Holly, it sounds like you two are headed in the right direction, but I can't tell you if it's real or not. You have to decide that for yourself."

"Gee, that's helpful. What about the relationship thing? I told him I didn't want one and if I tell him I do now, he's going to run screaming for the hills."

"Why do you have to label it right now? Why don't you just go with the flow like you always do?"

"Because I don't want him to leave."

Merry pointed at her. "That's your answer then."

"Do I tell him or just wait?"

"I would be honest, because if he's really not feeling the same trajectory as you, hanging on will just hurt worse in the end."

"I was afraid you'd say that."

"Or you could disregard my advice like you do in every other aspect of your life and see it through your own way. The path to love is different for everyone."

Holly contemplated the truth of her sister's words as the bus took a right into the Brews and Chews parking lot just as Tara sat back down with two cups in her hands.

"These are for you," she said, handing them off to Merry and Holly.

"Where is yours?" Merry asked.

"Already drank mine. We're going to Brews?" Tara griped. "Man, I was really hoping for a road trip to Boise."

"It is seven o'clock on a Friday night," Sally replied, her tone heavy with exasperation. "By the time we got to Boise, we'd be too tired to party."

"I know, but a girl can dream."

"I voted for a weekend in Vegas, but I was shot down," Ryan complained, moving across the aisle to sit on the other side of Merry, laying his head on her shoulder.

Holly leaned out to look around Merry at Ryan. "It's all about the bride, Ryan, and Merry wanted to stay local."

He met Holly's gaze with a huff. "Please, she doesn't know what's good for her."

"Sitting right here!" Merry said, patting his knee.

Ryan chuckled. "I know, ruiner."

"Rude!"

Holly turned to Merry with a smile. "We're just picking something up. Don't be disappointed."

"I'm not, I swear." Merry reached between them and took her hand, squeezing it. "I can't wait to see what you have planned."

Nathaniel parked the bus at the edge of the parking lot and stood up, announcing, "All right, we've arrived at the rustic watering hole, Brews and Chews. Your prizes will be arriving shortly."

"Prizes?" Sally said, hopping up from the seat, with Tara right behind her, watching out the window.

The bachelor party walked across the parking lot, with Sam in the front talking animatedly to Clark who was grinning from ear to ear.

"Uh, Hol, we're not crashing the bachelor party, are we?" Merry asked.

"Nope, this was all planned. We're doing a combined activity for both."

Nathaniel opened the doors and the guys climbed inside, Clark making a beeline for Merry and giving her a kiss.

"Don't sit yet, gentlemen," Holly said, rising to her feet. "We have to pick partners first."

"What do you mean, partners?" Sally asked.

"I'm so glad you asked." Holly pulled a small pouch from her purse with a grin. "Inside this bag are scraps of paper with the names of everyone in the bachelor party written on them. You pull a name and that person will be your activity partner for the night. There will be no complaining or repicks or I will leave you here to find a ride home. Am I clear?"

"Yes," the group said collectively and Holly held it out to Merry.

"Bride first, and you get to pick a bonus team member since we have an odd number of people."

"She picks me, obviously," Ryan said.

"He's not wrong." Merry stuck her hand inside and rummaged about before pulling out a slip of paper and unfolding it. "Pike."

"Hey now, shouldn't bride and groom automatically be together?" Clark protested.

"Clark, don't make me kick you out of your own bachelor party," Holly threatened, snapping her fingers at her sister. "Go retrieve your buddies and have a seat."

Merry got up from her seat and kissed Clark before moving past him to grab Pike by his arm and hauling him to the back by Ryan.

"Who's next?" Holly asked, shaking the bag.

One by one the women stepped forward, drawing a name from the bag. Holly found herself sneaking glances at Declan, who sat next to Clark in a green hoodie and a gray ball cap on his head. Declan gave her a small smile, and even though it wasn't fair, she quietly wished she'd rigged this so they would for sure be partners.

Delilah pulled Anthony's name and Holly recognized the forced smile. She'd once told Holly Anthony's quieter countenance made her nervous because she hated lulls in a conversation, but hopefully spending a few hours together would bridge that awkwardness between them. Noel and Clark high-fived when they paired up, and Tara and Nick argued over who was in charge as Holly held the purse out to Sally, two names inside. Sally stared at Sam as she stuck her hand into the bag and withdrew a name.

"Declan," she read aloud, her tone heavy with disappointment.

Holly shared her frustration as she waved at a grinning Sam as he strode across the bus to give her a bear hug, picking Holly up off her feet.

"I guess that means it's you and me."

"I guess so."

"Wow, don't knock me over with your enthusiasm, Holly," Sam said, frowning.

"Sorry," she mumbled.

"Were you hoping for someone else?" he asked.

Holly's gaze strayed to Declan, whose hat brim shadowed his deep green eyes. Sally flopped between him and Tara, obviously displeased with her partner choice. If she hadn't made such a big deal about not switching partners, Holly would have put a smile on Sally's face, but she couldn't do that to Sam. He deserved to have fun tonight too and not stress over accidentally giving Sally mixed signals. She'd see Declan at the house, and they'd have fun later on when she got him alone.

"No, I wasn't hoping for anyone else. We're going to kick ass." Holly slipped her arm through Sam's and waved it to the crowded bus. "Should we tell them what's going down?"

"Yeah, what are we doing tonight," Tara asked.

"We're going to play a game of trivia first on the drive to the main event and make a stop along the way. And I just want to add that I'm on the hook for the cleaning deposit, so have a good time but be adults. Drink in moderation."

"Yeah, Fish," Noel said loudly, to which Pike flipped her the bird.

"And since tonight is all about Merry and Clark, they will be the focus of our trivia game." A few groans erupted, but Holly couldn't tell who did it so she ignored them and continued. "When Nathaniel delivers us to our pit stop, I will hand you a task list, which will be different from everyone else's on the bus. Your mission is to finish the tasks and be back within the time frame or you'll have to pull a dare card. Are we ready?" Everyone cheered and whooped. "Good, now give Nathaniel your full attention so we can seriously get this party started."

Holly sat down in the only empty space, next to Sally, who didn't say anything to her as Nathaniel went over his speech again about safety.

"I'm going to get a drink, do you want something?" Sam asked, standing over the two of them.

Holly shook her head. "No, I'm good."

"Sally?" She perked up when he said her name, and he waved his hand. "Want a drink?"

"Oh, I'll go with you!" Sally said, getting up from the bench, and Holly caught the pained expression on Sam's face before he headed toward the back without waiting, Sally trailing behind Sam, talking a mile a minute despite Nathaniel still speaking on not trashing his bus.

Declan leaned over, the brim of his ball cap brushing her hair. "You look nice."

Holly glanced down at her low-cut brown sweater and blue jeans, smiling. "Thank you. I like the cap. I haven't seen you in one since the summer."

Declan chuckled. "I only wear them when I need a haircut."

"I like your hair. Gives me something to hold onto when we—" Declan's eyes widened at her pause, and she continued, "kiss."

Declan grinned. "Such a tease."

"Well, you know that's not true."

He rested his mouth next to her ear. "You have no idea how badly I want to kiss you right now."

It was on the tip of her tongue to tell him to do it already, but she didn't want to challenge him. For the first time in her life, she wasn't in a hurry. The faster they went, the sooner their time together would be over, and Holly wasn't ready to stop yet.

Instead, she replied, "I can't wait to get you alone. I was so tempted to cheat and pull your name, but my integrity won."

"Sam seemed excited to partner with you."

There was something in Declan's voice that drew her attention, and she thought about what Ryan had said about her and Sam. Was Declan jealous? And if so, what did that mean for the two of them?

Before she could ask him, Nathaniel finished his safety speech and pointed at Sam, who was taking a drink from Mona the bartender.

"Sam back there is going to take over the party helm and run the trivia game while I get behind that wheel. So stop hitting on my woman, son, and do your job!"

"Hang on!" He downed the contents of the plastic cup and tossed it into the garbage can. "Now I'm ready."

Holly laughed, watching Sam take the seat next to her while Sally squeezed in on his other side instead of sitting with Declan. Holly thought that was rude to do to someone but wasn't going to tell Sally that.

Sam retrieved a piece of paper from his pocket and opened

it with a flourish, clearing his throat loudly. "Question number one: Where did Merry and Clark have their first kiss?" Sam's eyes traveled around the group, finally settling on Declan. "Declan?"

Declan stiffened next to her. "Yeah?"

"Care to take a guess where Clark and Merry shared their first kiss?"

Holly covered her mouth with her hand to hide her smile as Declan looked around for help, finally offering, "I don't know, man. That's kind of personal. Her porch?"

"Wrong. Holly? Do you want to take a stab at it?" Sam asked.

"Clark's house."

Sam arched one eyebrow. "Which room?"

"Wow, that specific, huh? His?"

"Bzzzt, wrong. Man, and just when I was thinking what a lucky guy I was to have you as a partner."

"You are." The dark, angry response erupted from Declan's stiff form and everyone on the bus turned his way, including Holly. Declan's face flushed, and he stammered, "I mean...you could have ended up with someone like me. I suck at trivia."

The people on the bus laughed and everyone went back to the game except Holly. He'd played it off well, but did he really mean that? Not that she wanted him to be truly possessive, but a little jealousy meant he cared, right? Deeper than if they were just roommates with benefits?

With a small smile, she discreetly brushed her hand against his, but it slipped away when he stood abruptly. "I'm going to get a drink."

Holly's gaze followed him to the back corner, wondering if

she'd read him wrong. Maybe he had just been making a joke about his trivia skills and didn't think anything at all about her being partners with Sam. She was projecting her feelings onto a man who wanted nothing more from her than what they had.

And if that was true, would it be enough for her?

CHAPTER 33

DECLAN WATCHED HOLLY HAND OUT envelopes in various colors to every partnership, seeming happy and not at all disturbed that he'd practically bitten Sam's head off. He hadn't meant to be harsh, but the comfortable way Sam treated Holly as if she was his girlfriend and not just a friend had rubbed him wrong for a while, especially now that they were...

What? Casual?

Declan knew he had no right to feel this way, but when he'd noticed the easy way Sam touched Holly's knee when he spoke to her during the drive, all the while Declan sat silently beside her, it took everything in him not to haul her closer to him so Sam would get the message that she was with someone.

Only it wouldn't be true. He couldn't claim that they were just roommates with benefits and then get mad when another man flirted or showed interest, but being honest about the way she made him feel could come with catastrophic results. Free-spirited Holly, the one who'd done some truly insane stunts on her YouTube, which he hadn't admitted to watching, was independent and didn't need anyone, especially

Declan, who couldn't make up his mind about what he wanted anymore except…

Her. He wanted Holly Winters with every fiber of his being, and he had no idea what to do about it.

The bus parked on the west end of town near the twenty-four-hour gas station, the Bear Claw biker bar, and a large expanse of woods, with the heart of downtown only a few streets over.

"All right, this is it!" Holly called, getting to her feet. "Remember, the color of the envelope you're holding is your team color and all of your clues will be in the same shade. You'll have one hour to complete the tasks and find the clues they are leading you to. No cutting corners. Every team has special transportation waiting for them, so no matter what it is, you have to do it! Everybody got me? Then let's go!"

Declan watched as a few of the teams approached Holly, probably with questions. Sally was over in the corner talking to Sam with animated gestures that made her look like an angry seagull flapping its wings. When she stormed away from him to join Tara and Nick, Sam crossed the bus and stopped alongside Declan.

"You all right, man?" Sam asked, slapping him on the back. "You seem quieter than usual."

Declan got to his feet with a nod. "I'm good, just taking it all in."

"You aren't pissed about me putting you on the spot, are you? I thought for sure Clark would have told you something."

"We don't get into personal things, but it's fine."

"You didn't tell him about shacking up with Holly?" Sam asked.

Declan's eyes narrowed. "We're not shacking up."

Sam's affable countenance dissolved into a hard expression. "Well, whatever you're doing, Holly is an amazing girl and like all the Winters family she's a good person. I don't want her taken advantage of."

"If you think Holly would let anyone, least of all me, mistreat her in any way, you don't know her. She's more than happy to tell me where to stick it when I piss her off."

"Just trying to figure you out. I thought you two didn't get along and suddenly she's helping you out, giving you a place to crash. You gotta know how that looks."

"I don't, actually."

"Holly's done well for herself and you're almost thirty and living with your father. Not a good look, man."

Declan's fists clenched at his sides. "I'm not after Holly for money. I pay to rent my room."

"It's all about perception and I just want you to be aware and know that the people in this town love Holly. No one will tolerate her being hurt."

Declan studied the other man's face, wondering if Holly was wrong about there being nothing more between her and Sam. Maybe not on her side, but Sam's underlying threat was unmistakable. *Hurt her and you'll deal with me.*

Declan waved a hand in Sally's direction. "Seems like you've got your own problems with women and don't need to take on mine."

Easygoing Sam looked like he wanted to rip Declan's head off. "I was honest with her about where we stood, and she didn't like what I had to say."

"What are you guys talking about?" Holly asked, coming up next to them, her gaze shifting from one to the other.

"Best man to groomsman stuff," Sam said.

"Really?" She turned her attention to Declan. "What kind of stuff?"

"We're pitching in to get Clark a gift from all of us and Sam was asking my opinion." Sam nodded in agreement, obviously on the same page about keeping this between the two of them.

"Oh, that's a great idea. I'll see if I can get the bridesmaids to do something for Merry." Holly took a step closer to him and seemed to realize Sam was watching them and stopped. "You going to try to have fun with this?"

"I'll participate, but fun?" he said, suppressing a smile when she released an exasperated sigh. "I'll pretend."

Holly grinned. "I guess that will have to do."

"Hey Declan, I've got our list," Sally said, coming up alongside him and slipping her arm through his, surprising him. She'd barely said two words to him since she'd pulled his name. "Should we get started?"

"Uh, sure." Declan looked at Holly, who was staring at their joined arms with narrowed eyes. "I'll see you back here."

"May the best team win," Sam said, smirking.

With a hard yank, Sally pulled Declan toward the exit.

Declan glanced back at Holly in time to watch Sam drop an arm around Holly's shoulders. "Ready to roll?"

Declan knew the other man was messing with him, and unfortunately it was working. The only satisfaction he got was Holly stepping away from his touch, her gaze following Declan off the bus.

He had to talk to her. They'd said honesty, and even if he had to sneak into her room after everyone went to bed, he needed to tell her that he had feelings for her. Deep, scary ones he hadn't thought he was capable of.

"Should we look at our clue first or walk and strategize at the same time?" Sally asked, once they'd stepped off the bus.

"This is your show. I'll follow your lead."

She opened the envelope and retrieved the slip of paper inside. "Your carriage awaits two blocks east on 11th in front of the gaming store. On the seat will be your first important task. Read the clues and move along. The clock is ticking, so don't be long."

Declan smiled. Of course there would be carriages involved. Holly would plan tonight with flair.

"I'm actually surprised that Holly didn't rig this whole thing to pick your name. You two are living together, right?" Sally asked.

Declan stiffened with surprise. "I'm renting a room from her."

"So it's not serious?"

Yes, it is!

"No, she's helping me out."

"Too bad. I've always liked Holly. I've been a little perturbed with her lately, but now I know none of what's been going on is her fault. Can you believe Sam asked her to run interference between us? Like I'm some emotionally disturbed woman who wouldn't take no for an answer."

Declan had no idea why she was telling him this, but it was obvious by the way she looked over at him that he was supposed to have some kind of reaction, so he simply made a non-committal "hmm."

"I mean, why can't men be honest? Is it really so hard to discuss your feelings? Like, you probably told Holly how you felt, right? That's why the two of you are able to keep things civil, even though you aren't together."

Declan did not want to talk about his relationship with Holly, but her words struck a chord. He wasn't being entirely honest, especially about his deepening affection for his hostess.

"I don't know what Holly and I have to do with what you're talking about but—"

"I'm simply making a point that men can behave like grown-ups sometimes. Sam said he wasn't interested in me, but he'd flirt like crazy and it was so confusing. I think he liked my attention and didn't want that to stop, so he gave mixed signals to keep me dangling after him."

Declan tuned Sally out as they kept pace on the sidewalk, and pulled out his phone to use as a flashlight. They made a right onto 11th, and Declan wished Holly hadn't put forth that rule about not changing partners. He didn't want to spend the whole night listening to Sally complaining about Sam. They stopped in front of Hot-Wired Gaming, but there was no carriage waiting. Declan looked up and down the street, but everyone else had dispersed to their own areas to complete whatever task they'd been assigned.

"Especially since Holly doesn't give Sam the time of day and it kills him."

That caught Declan's attention. "Sam's into Holly?"

"Of course, can't you tell? He plays it off like they're friends, but you have to be an idiot not to see the signs."

"What signs?"

"He's always touching her when they're near each other. Physical contact is a huge indicator of attraction." Sally huffed. "Honestly, he's hot, but it wasn't like I wanted a deep, meaningful relationship with him. It's hard to find a man who has his life together, knows what he's doing in the bedroom, and has a compatible personality and life goals that fit with yours. Sometimes you just need to scratch an itch, and when you get bored, you move on."

Sally's statement landed like a cold brick on his shoulders, weighing him down as he imagined that was exactly what he was to Holly. Someone to fill a void.

"What else makes you think he's into her?" Declan asked.

"The way he talks about her, you'd think she was a perfect goddess. You haven't noticed?"

Before he could answer, the clip-clop of hooves preceded a horse-drawn carriage coming around the corner at the same time Sam and Holly followed the way they came, heading toward them.

"Oh no," Sally murmured, gripping his arm. "I don't want him to think I care. Please play along."

"Huh?"

Sally addressed Holly, keeping her hands wrapped around Declan's arm. "What are you two doing here? I thought each team had their own scavenger hunt list."

"They do," Holly said, a pleasant smile pasted on her face. "We just happened to get the envelope that includes a carriage ride too."

"What a happy coincidence," Sally said sarcastically.

The carriage pulled to a halt in front of them and the driver stepped down and addressed them.

"Good evening, folks," the driver said, getting the door, holding it open for all of them. Sam climbed up first and held his hand down to help Holly and Sally inside, but the latter brushed his hand aside. Declan came in after Sally, noting Sam and Holly were already situated across from them, and slid into the open seat next to Sally. Sam shot him a little smirk Declan interpreted as triumphant and resisted the urge to knock the smug expression off his face.

The driver turned around, all smiles while passing back two envelopes. "Hang on tight, everyone."

Sally took the envelopes, handing Holly the yellow one and keeping the blue.

They opened up the envelopes at the same time, but Sally went first. "When the carriage stops, it's time to shine," Sally said, her words coming out in a singsong voice. "Head to the park where the trees intertwine. Ignore the bright glow of Santa's sleigh, what you need is buried in mountains of hay."

"The Live Nativity in the park?" Declan offered.

"That would be my guess." Sally turned to Holly. "Did you make these?"

"My parents did, so this is new to me too."

"What does yours say?" Declan asked.

"Bear with me as I try to explain the importance of these bags you must claim. The contents inside may be high in the sky, but together you can retrieve it if you know how to climb."

Holly covered her mouth with her hand. "That doesn't sound good."

The carriage driver called out "Whoa!" and the vehicle

stopped. To the left was Mistletoe town square and the city park. The driver turned around in his seat. "I'll wait right here for you."

"Thank you," Holly said, standing up. Declan preceded her out of the carriage. His feet hit the ground, and he helped Holly down by placing his hands on her waist and lifting her, his heart racing as she leaned into him with a smile. Declan lowered her to the ground, his body alive with awareness.

Sally jumped out of the carriage without waiting for help and started heading across the street, pausing when she'd crossed to the other side. "Declan, are you coming?"

Declan squeezed Holly's waist. "See you back here."

"Not if I see you first."

Declan jogged after Sally, keeping pace with her once he caught up.

"You don't have to worry about Sam, you know," Sally said out of the blue.

"What do you mean?"

"It's obvious Holly is completely into you. I don't know if you're serious about her, but in case you had doubts, I wouldn't stress."

"While I appreciate the assurances, I don't really want to discuss my love life with anyone."

"Wow, you really are a grouch," Sally said with a huff, stomping ahead of him.

"So I've been told."

CHAPTER 34

"YOU LIKE DECLAN, DON'T YOU?" Sam asked, keeping pace with Holly across the snow-covered park.

Holly's first reaction was to scoff and tell him he was crazy, but she was tired of hiding it, especially from herself.

"I do." Holly looked up at Sam, frowning. "Why do you ask?"

Sam nudged her shoulder with his. "As your secret boyfriend, I feel like I should get some say in who you spend time with."

"Secret boyfriend?"

"Oh yeah, you haven't heard that rumor? You and I are keeping it on the low until after the wedding and then we're going public."

"Interesting. And who started this rumor?"

"I'm not sure, but Sally asked if it was true, and she's not the first one."

"Declan thought the same thing."

"Really? And he didn't give you up? Brave man."

"Speaking of brave men, Sally didn't even look at you tonight. Did you finally come clean with her?"

"I did."

"It didn't go well, huh?"

"She didn't appreciate my honesty the way you thought she would."

"Sally is gorgeous, so I'm not sure why you *aren't* interested. Not to slut shame you, but you haven't exactly been particular about your sexual partners."

"Haven't you noticed I don't sleep with women in my inner circle because I don't need the complications? If I take Sally up on what she's offering, Merry will slit my throat for hurting her friend and you know me, Hol. I don't mean to be a dick, but I'm not the guy you marry. I'm the fun guy who screws your brains out before you meet the one."

"I don't think anyone is immune to the one, even you, but you're right. Getting involved with friends, even friends of a friend, isn't a good idea."

"Are you trying to talk yourself out of dating Declan?" he asked.

"No, I'm just agreeing it's a bad idea, but that doesn't mean I have to follow it."

"Just be careful. Us being an item isn't the only rumor I've heard."

Holly slowed her pace to a full stop and faced Sam. "What other rumors are circulating?"

"People think Declan's using you."

Holly snorted. "That's ridiculous."

"I hope so. He's always seemed like a stand-up guy, but people are wondering how the two of you went from not being able to stand each other to living together."

"People grow and change all the time. Besides, he rents his room and—you know what? I'm not even going to entertain this stupidity because Declan isn't some shady, selfish person. He came home to run the store because his dad…" Holly's voice trailed off as she realized she'd almost broken Declan's confidence. "All you need to know is that Declan is not using me, and furthermore I have a brother and an over-protective sister, Sam. I don't need you all up in my business too."

Sam threw his hands in the air with a laugh. "All right, I'm only concerned because I care about who dates my pretend girlfriend. From the way you're defending Declan's honor, I am going to go out on a limb and say he's a great guy." Sam cupped one side of her face and kissed her cheek softly. "Which is perfect because you deserve the best."

Holly gave Sam a hard hug. "That is the sweetest thing you've ever said to me."

"Please, I'm always sweet."

"Flirty sweet, but that was genuine concern for my happiness and I appreciate it."

"Speaking of happiness, we should find these bags or whatever we're looking for because I think the others are done and ready to move on."

Holly followed his gaze over her shoulder and spotted Declan and Sally heading toward them across the lawn.

"Based on your boy's expression, I'd come clean about my feelings sooner rather than later. He looks ready to kick my ass."

Holly grinned mischievously. "Maybe you could use a little ass-kicking."

"If that's how you're going to be, I fake break up with you," he said, pretending to wipe his hands.

"Good, 'cause you were a lousy fake boyfriend."

The others caught up to them near the line of trees which were lit up with Christmas lights, and Holly studied the limbs, looking for anything that resembled bags.

"What's taking you two so long?" Sally asked, carrying a small tote.

"We're talking instead of searching," Holly said, smiling at the two of them. "Wanna give us a hand in finding them? The big bear statue is right there, so we figured it's got to be in these two trees."

"I think that's cheating."

Declan's tone was cool and Holly's attention jerked to his face. His inscrutable expression gave nothing away, but the way his gaze seemed fixed on Sam, she thought maybe he'd gotten the wrong impression about them.

"I don't care about winning, but I'm pretty sure what's hanging in the tree is all the dry groceries we need for this weekend," Holly replied.

"I guess we better find them then," Declan grumbled.

Holly frowned. "What's wrong with you? I thought you were going to pretend to have fun."

"I am pretending. Joy, joy, fun, yay."

"You're a terrible actor."

"What's your problem, Declan?" Sam asked.

"You for starters."

Holly's jaw dropped as Sam took a step toward him. "That right?"

"Boys!" Sally yelled, clapping her hands. "No fighting. I'm officially calling a cease fire."

"You'd better get your boy, Holly, before I teach him a lesson in respect."

Declan bristled, but Holly and Sally stepped between them at the same time, Sally pushing Sam toward the opposite end of the tree. "Come on, Sam, let's look on this side, but don't get any ideas 'cause this ship has sailed, buddy."

Holly didn't hear Sam's response as they rounded the big pine and she was left alone with Declan.

"What is wrong with you?" she asked, planting her hands on her hips. "Are you grumpy because you hate this game or something else?"

"Who says I'm grumpy?" Declan asked, heading around the other side of the tree with Holly hot on his heels.

"That tone. The tub of sarcasm you just dumped all over me. The fact that you just about started a brawl in the middle of the park during your friend's bachelor party."

"I don't like that guy."

"But everyone likes Sam."

"Everyone being you?" Declan stopped and turned to face her, the lines in his face tight.

"Sam is just a friend."

"I didn't like seeing another man putting his hands all over you."

Holly's heart hammered at the raw jealousy in his voice. "It was just a kiss on the cheek."

"I don't care. I hated it. I wanted to lay Sam out flat. I used to think he was a good guy, but now all I see is that smug smirk as he puts his arm around you and thinks it's okay to do whatever he wants. On the bus, in the carriage—"

Holly grabbed his arms and shook him as best she could. "I don't want Sam!"

Declan stared down at her, his jaw clenched. "Fuck, I'm not this guy. I'm not this jealous, possessive guy. But I see you with him and it's just easy with you two. There's no baggage, he doesn't say the wrong thing or hurt your feelings the way I have."

"There's also no spark. What Sam and I have is fun and super-ficial. He's not the guy who makes me feel safe when I'm nervous or teases my bad mood away. Just you." Holly stepped closer, moving her hands to his chest. "I don't want anyone else."

Declan's hands came up and cradled her face. "What's that mean?"

"Hey!" Sam called.

They pulled back enough to see Sally and Sam coming around the wide pine's base.

"He did that on purpose," Declan grumbled and Holly patted Declan's chest.

"We'll pick this up later."

"The bags are on the other side, but they're too high for us," Sally said breathlessly as if she'd been running. "We need Declan."

Holly took a step to follow, surprised when Declan's hand slipped down and threaded his fingers with hers, his eyes on Sam, who grinned.

"So that's the way of it, huh?"

Holly pulled Declan along behind her, poking Sam in the stomach as they passed.

"What was that for?"

"Causing trouble."

"Trouble is my middle name," he quipped before holding his hand out to Declan. "No hard feelings, man. I just thought you two needed a little come to Jesus moment."

"What do you—you're telling me hanging all over Holly was just to get a rise outta me?"

"No, I mean, partly. I like hanging on Holly. She's soft and smells good—"

"Sam, shut up and stop making it worse," Holly growled, squeezing Declan's hand. "He's being a turd."

"All right, I am, and I'm sorry. Bygones?" he asked, his hand still extended between them.

Declan took it, and Holly noticed Sam's grin widen. "Now that we've settled this, let me show you our dilemma."

The four of them trekked to where three bags hug off the pine branches. Sam pointed to a spot right in front of the tree.

"You stand right here, I'll climb up onto your shoulders and get the bags."

"You'll do what now?" Declan asked.

Holly bit back a laugh, sharing an amused look with Sally.

"I already tried with Sally and Holly is shorter than her. It makes sense for us to combine our heights for maximum vertical advantage and since you're taller, you should be the base."

"Come on, Declan, take one for the team," Sally said, her camera phone out and aimed at them.

Declan took several beats to respond, shrugging out of his large coat and handing it to Holly. "This is ridiculous."

Declan went to the spot and knelt down on one knee. Holly watched Sam walk over and swing a leg over Declan's shoulder, hopping on one foot. When the two of them keeled over, Holly erupted with explosive laughter.

"Holly, be a dear," Sam called, climbing to his feet, "and get over here. I need you and Sally to hold us steady while I climb up."

"Sure, we can do that. Come on, Sally."

Each woman got on either side, helping Sam up and Declan to his feet. When they were fully erect, Holly pulled her phone from her pocket and once they got the first bag, called, "Smile!"

Holly snapped their picture and put her phone back in her pocket. "Great job, guys, but I think it would be easier to use that ladder propped against the standing bear to get the rest."

Declan shuffled with Sam still on his shoulders, following her line of sight. When he faced her, his eyes were narrowed and dark. "How long have you known that was there?"

"I spotted it after your first attempt, but this was a lot more fun to watch. Right, Sally?"

"Absolutely."

"Sam, slide off," Declan said and once Sam's feet were on the ground, Declan bent over, balling a lump of snow between his hands.

"Declan!" Holly screamed, also dropping to gather up a fistful of snow before she took off running. A snowball whizzed past her ear and when she spun around to let hers fly, Declan was almost on top of her. She caught him right on the cheek as his arms wrapped around her, lifting her off her feet.

"I can't believe you went along with that. Do you know how heavy Sam is?"

"Hey!" Sam said, tossing a snowball at the two of them.

"I can't wait to play this video when we get back to the bus," Sally said.

Declan dropped Holly to her feet and Sam took off toward Sally. Declan made a move to join him, but Holly jumped on his back. "Oh no you don't!"

Declan reached around, cupping her thighs and giving her a little jump further up before he jogged after Sam, who was chasing Sally around the tree.

"You guys, we don't have time for this!" Holly squealed, bouncing on Declan's back as he tried to intercept Sally.

"You had plenty of time to punk us though," Sam countered, getting Sally around the waist.

"Excuse me!" someone shouted from the sidewalk, and all of them looked up to find Merry, Pike, and Ryan standing on top of electric scooters watching them. "No one said anything about joining forces and combining groups!"

"Whoops! Didn't anyone tell you, Mer?" Holly said, pointing a thumb at herself. "I make the rules!"

"Cheaters never prosper, Holly!" Merry called as they zipped away in the direction of the bus.

"We'd better get this done and get back," Sally said, pushing Sam's hands away.

Holly slid off Declan's back, but to her surprise and delight, he took her hand in his again.

"I thought I'd give this a try, if you're okay with it," he said.

"I am. How does it feel?" she asked.

"Right."

CHAPTER 35

THE BUS PULLED UP TO the large lakeside home, the high arches lined with sparkling multi-colored Christmas lights and the front porch light illuminating a frosted wreath with a large red bow in the center of the door.

Holly sat next to Declan, her hand in his. When they'd returned to the bus, Declan noticed the curious eyes that followed them and it took everything in him to ignore the attention. No one had said anything, but he assumed that once Nick or Clark got him alone, there would be a number of questions needing answers.

"All right," Holly called, squeezing his hand before she dropped it and stood, addressing everyone on the bus. "Everyone has been assigned a room. The two suites on the main level are for the bride and groom and Nick and Noel."

"Whoa, why do they get the good rooms?" Pike called.

"Because I said so and I'm the boss. Now, the other two rooms on the main level are Pike and Tony and Sally and Tara. On the upper floor, first bedroom on the right is Sam and Declan, Ryan gets the second room, and Delilah will be in the third room. I will be in the attic. Any questions or concerns?" No one said a word and she clapped her hands. "Great. Gather your stuff, and because Sam, Sally, Declan, and I were disqualified, we will be the ones to unload all of the scavenger hunt items from the bus."

"What about your dare cards?" Merry called.

"Once we've got everything situated, we will fulfill our dares," Holly said grimly.

Declan fought a smile. His dare was to put as many Santa marshmallows in his mouth as he could fit, which wasn't so bad, but Holly's was to perform a rendition of "Santa Baby" in a very special outfit. He hadn't seen it yet, but Holly didn't seem pleased about it.

He climbed off the bus and went to the cargo area on the side, waiting until everyone gathered their bags. A hand landed on his shoulder, and he glanced over at Sam standing next to him.

"How's it going, Roomie? Still want to beat my ass?"

"Not at the moment, but you'll be the first to know if that changes."

Sam chuckled. "I did a public service and one day the two of you will thank me for it." Sam grabbed his bag and one of the gray totes, shooting Declan a wink. "See you in there, snuggle bug."

Declan grabbed his bag and the other gray tote, when Holly came up alongside him. She reached for a pink duffel, but Declan set his burden down and tossed it on top of the tote.

"What are you doing?" she said.

"Carrying your stuff into the house like a gentleman."

"You don't have to do that."

"I know, that's why I'm doing it."

"Hey," she called, chasing after him. When she got close enough, she lowered her voice. "Put your bag in my room."

"I thought I was rooming with Sam."

Holly arched a brow. "Do you want to room with Sam or me?"

"I mean, he did call me snuggle bug," he said, grinning playfully. "I kind of liked it."

"Up to you, but—" She picked up two of the sacks of food and said, "I packed with the specific idea of sneaking you into my room for a little holiday surprise. You have fun with Sam, though."

Declan laughed, following her into the house. The high ceilings and cedar walls made the space feel open and welcoming. A ten-foot Christmas tree in the corner of the family room was decorated in red and white balls, with a plaid star on top and matching ribbon looped through the branches.

"That tote goes by the fireplace, Declan," Clark said, pointing to the other wall. Once he dropped it off, Declan climbed the stairs, walking past three doors until he spotted another open door at the end and a staircase inside.

"Hey, where you going, pal?" Sam asked.

Declan held up Holly's duffel. "Dropping off our stuff."

"Our stuff? Hmmm."

Declan rolled his eyes and headed up the stairs, dropping the bags at the end of the bed, checking out the king-size bed and large window overlooking the moonlit lake. It was beautiful and romantic, something that had never struck him before.

He started climbing back down the stairs when he heard Sam let out a yelp of pain and stopped. "Damn it, Holly, that's my nipple!"

"Stop antagonizing Declan. He already thinks you have a thing for me."

"And now he's holding your hand and showing his cards. You're welcome."

"I don't need you trying to manipulate him into making moves he isn't ready for. I love you for looking out for me, but I'm a big girl and if I get my heart broken, I'll put it back together."

Declan sucked in a breath. Holly wanted more from him? She'd been worried about him breaking her heart, and he'd been stressing over the fact that he didn't want to leave Mistletoe for all the reasons he'd told her a week ago, but also because of her. Having Holly in his life had shown him how much he'd been missing by playing it safe, and he wanted to tell her that and so much more. That as long as he had breath in his lungs, he'd do everything in his power to keep every part of her safe, especially her heart.

"Declan, we're in charge—oh!" Holly stopped coming up the stairs when she spotted him, a black bag hanging over her arm. "Hi! So, we're making tonight's dinner and a fan sent me a recipe she wants me to try, but I could really use your direction. You feel up to it?"

"Yeah, let's do it."

"I'll meet you down there. I have to change into my dare outfit." She reached the step he was on, and they both turned to face each other so she could pass, but before she made it, Declan stopped her with one arm on the wall and the other came up to cup the back of her neck. She looked up at him with startled brown eyes, and he brushed his mouth over hers.

"What was that for?" she asked breathlessly.

"There's mistletoe."

When she looked up, her brow furrowed in confusion. "No, there's not."

"Huh, I could have sworn I saw some."

Holly laughed. "You don't have to make up an excuse to kiss me."

"In that case—" He pressed her into the wall and delivered a searing kiss, cradling the back of her head with both hands. When he finally pulled back, she blinked at him dreamily.

"What's gotten into you?"

"You, Elf." He released her slowly, kissing her nose. "Send me the recipe so I can get everything prepped."

He descended the stairs with a wide grin on his face and jogged down into the entryway, where Nick, Pike, and Clark gathered around the large kitchen island.

"Hey, there's our chubby bunny!" Pike said, shaking a bag of marshmallows at him. "Ready to get crazy?"

"Let's wait for Holly."

"Yeah, speaking of Holly," Nick said, popping the top on a beer. "I thought I said no falling in love with my sister."

Declan wasn't going to deny loving Holly, but he also wasn't going to admit it out loud to anyone but her.

"You told me not to be mean to her, too."

"I said that?"

"You did say that," Clark said.

"Well, shit." Nick opened another beer and handed it to him. "I guess if you're making my sister happy, I can't give you too hard a time."

"Why not?" Clark asked. "You threatened to throw me off a mountain."

"Threat is such a strong word," Pike chimed in. "It was a little friendly banter between bros. Besides, you're still alive and marrying his sister."

"True," Clark said with a grin. "I'm a lucky man. I've got an amazing woman who loves me and my son, an awesome brother-in-law, and good friends as a bonus."

Declan tapped the neck of his beer bottle to Clark's. "Cheers to that."

"What are we toasting?" Sam asked, coming down the stairs in a pair of joggers and a t-shirt.

"Clark marrying my sister."

Sam came up alongside Clark and slapped him on the back. "I'm happy for you, little brother. You got a good one."

The sound of a sliding glass door echoed in the room before Merry, Noel, Tara, and Sally came around the corner.

"This place has an indoor hot tub and heated swimming pool!" Noel said, slipping her arms around Nick's waist. "When we buy a house, can we get one?"

"You're going to have to help deliver a lot more babies for one like this."

Noel laughed. "I'll work on it."

"Where's Holly? I'm ready for my entertainment," Merry said, doing a little shimmy.

"She's getting changed," Declan said.

"Should we make all the other losers do their dares while we wait?" Pike asked.

Sally whacked him on the back of the head. "Who you calling a loser, dingleberry?"

"I meant loser like you lost, not—never mind."

Sam stepped away from the table and grinned, fingering the string of his joggers. "I'm ready for mine."

Without warning, Sam grabbed the edges of his pants and ripped them off, the snaps popping like fireworks. Declan didn't have enough time to register that Sam was buck naked under the pants and stripping off his shirt as he ran out the front door.

"We're going streaking," he yelled, disappearing outside and flying by the glass window.

Everyone in the living room cheered and laughed, even Declan, appreciating the fact that he hadn't drawn that dare card.

"All right, Sally, you're next," Tara said.

"Why me?"

"Because Declan is shoving a bunch of marshmallows into his mouth. Boring."

Sally sighed. "Fine. Come here, Pike."

"Why me?" he asked.

"Because you're the only one down here who isn't currently attached—wait, where's Anthony?"

"Fuck Tony," Pike said, reaching for Sally's arm and swinging her into his body. Everyone hollered and screamed when he dipped her back over his arm and kissed her, with one leg in the air and her hair falling to the floor. When he set her back on her feet, he picked up his beer with a grin.

Sally pushed her hair out of her face, her cheeks flushed. "Who's next?"

"Guess that's me," Declan said, grabbing the bag of marshmallows. He opened them up and packed one into the back of his cheek. Sam came back in wearing a towel and joined the group as they counted off each fluffy red Santa he shoved into his mouth until he was barely able to keep his lips closed.

Pike picked up his arm and lifted it into the air. "Damn, that's a big-mouth boy! Twenty-one makes Declan the chubby Santa champion!"

"Who's ready for this?" Holly hollered, drawing everyone's attention to the top of the stairs. She descended the steps, one foot in front of the other, a lot of bare leg showing as Declan's eyes traveled up her body until he got a good look at what she was wearing and sprayed marshmallows all over Nick and Clark.

"Declan!" Nick yelled, wiping slimy-looking red and white marshmallows off his cheek. "Nasty, man."

"I'm so glad I got that on camera." Tara laughed, holding her phone up.

Declan didn't bother to tell her to put it away and ran to the trash to spit the rest of the gunk out of his mouth. He grabbed a roll of paper towels from the counter and brought them over to his friends, scrubbing his own face with one of the sheets and then cleaning up the counter. "Sorry, I wasn't expecting *that*."

Holly circled around the group and struck a pose, showing off the oversized T-shirt printed with a hairy man body sporting a red Speedo under the beer belly and shiny red pasties over the photo's nipples. A sparkling red Santa hat perched jauntily on top of her head.

"Did I surprise you, Declan?" she asked, her voice shaking with laughter.

Declan turned around to face her, nodding his head. "A little bit."

She reached up with her thumb and wiped the edge of his mouth before belting into an off-key version of "Santa Baby." The group laughed, some of them covering their ears, and after a few verses Declan reached out and covered Holly's mouth with his hand to stop the torment.

"You have many talents, Elf, but singing is not one of them."

"Mmmm-mmmmm."

Declan removed his hand. "What?"

"How rude," she said, her eyes twinkling, and he was keenly aware of everyone watching them, knowing what his next move meant. Before she could look away, Declan lifted her up against his body and gave her a short, smacking kiss.

"All right, gang, that is our cue to leave the lovebirds alone," Sam said loudly.

Holly cleared her throat, her cheeks flushed. "Declan and I are making dinner, so you're either in your rooms or in the pool, but we're recording, so scoot."

Declan dropped her to the floor, tugging gently on the end of her hat. "You're going to wear this?"

"Yeah, what's wrong with it? I'm thinking of doing a little dance to 'I'm Too Sexy.'" Holly shook and shimmied over to the kitchen table where a short ring light had been left and carried it back to the island. Declan caught Nick's eye, and his friend threw his hands in the air.

"Hey, you kissed her, so she's yours. Have fun, kids. Make sure you don't let her do too much, 'cause I'm pretty hungry."

Holly grabbed a marshmallow from the bag and launched it at her brother. "You can fend for yourself, jerk!"

Once everyone else had cleared out, Declan leaned against the counter with a smile. "So, I didn't have time to prep because we were all doing our dares."

"That's okay, I wanted to show you myself." She waved him next to her, and he watched as she opened the app, bringing her profile closer to his face. "What do you think of my profile name?"

He read the bold username and wrapped his arms around her waist. "Perfectly Imperfect Holly?"

"Not calling me a failure, but leaves room for improvement."

Declan kissed the side of her neck and held her close. "I don't know. I think you're pretty perfect for me."

Holly turned in his arms to look at him, her eyes shining. "Declan..."

Footfalls on the stairs intruded on the moment and Declan watched Delilah and Tony coming down the stairs, appearing slightly disheveled.

"Hey, where is everyone?" Tony asked.

Holly cleared her throat. "Out by the pool. Where have you two been?"

"Exploring—" Delilah blurted at the same time Tony said, "Talking."

Delilah's cheeks turned red, and she hurried out of the room, Tony slowly trailing behind.

Declan released Holly's waist with a chuckle. "That was unexpected."

"You don't actually think..."

"You have doubts?" Declan asked. "Didn't you see them?"

"But she's totally into Pike."

Declan shrugged. "People are allowed to change their minds about the things they want." He stepped in to her, tucking a strand of hair behind her ear and praying no one else would come inside before he got this out. "For instance, I thought I wanted to get out of Mistletoe, and I especially never expected to find someone who made me lose my cool every time she walked in the room and like it, but here you are. Making me fall harder for you every minute we're together. And when I'm away from you, I can't wait to get back into your arms."

"Me too," she murmured, her voice breaking.

Declan cupped her face in his palms, wiping away trails of tears from her cheeks. "If you're all right with it, I'd like to have another sit-down when we get home and rework the rules of our arrangement."

"Like what?"

"First, I want to take you out on a real date New Year's Eve at the Lodge. We skipped a few steps with me moving into your place and I want to do this right."

"What else?"

He leaned over and kissed her. "We can figure it out later. Right now, I want to feed these people so I can get you alone."

"You know we have two more days with them, right?"

"We may have to leave early."

CHAPTER 36

DECLAN PARKED IN FRONT OF the hardware store on Monday morning and took a deep breath. He'd been mentally preparing for this moment since they'd returned home yesterday and negotiated the new rules of their relationship. One of Holly's requests included him reconnecting with his father. He knew it was time, but he couldn't figure out what he wanted to say, no matter how many times he played the possible conversations over in his mind.

Although Holly's request was the kick in the butt he needed, talking to his dad was ultimately his decision because with everything going on, all the changes to his plans and what he wanted for his future, Declan wanted both his parents to be a part of it.

Especially because he had a lot riding on his new dream.

Declan opened the door and stepped into the quiet entryway, his eyes locking with his father's immediately. His mom had her back to him, but his dad came around the edge of the counter, stopping a foot from him.

"Hello, Declan."

Declan's mom spun around, a wide smile on her face. "Declan! What a pleasant surprise."

"Hi, Mom," Declan said, shoving his hands into his pockets. "Hi, Dad. You look good."

"Thanks. I've been walking in the mornings with your mom. She's got some crazy idea about walking some mountain trail in California in the spring."

"You'll have fun!" Diana said, coming up alongside him. "You love the outdoors."

"I'll have fun because I'm with you." When his dad pulled her in with his arm around her shoulders and kissed the top of her head, it was reminiscent of happier times in his childhood and an emotional lump rose in Declan's throat.

"Mom, do you mind if Dad and I go into the back office to talk?"

"Not at all. I'll be here."

The two of them walked down the aisle of screwdrivers and wrenches without saying a word. When they stepped into the office, Declan closed the door behind him and they both took a seat, the silence stretching for several moments.

"I've missed you, son," his dad finally said.

"I've missed you, too." Declan put his hands on his knees, trying to come up with the best way to start. "I know what happened between you and Mom was none of my business, but it still affected me. I can't get those years back being angry with Mom, but that doesn't mean I need to waste time punishing you. It's done. Mistakes were made and if you and Mom are having another go at it, then there's no reason for me to keep you at a distance."

"I am so glad to hear you say that," his dad said, getting to his feet.

Declan held his hand up. "I do have a few more things to address."

"All right," his dad said, still standing.

"You said you'd been thinking about selling the store, but I need you to understand I won't run the hardware store anymore even if you decide to keep it. I know that it's been in our family for years and that you love this place, but I don't. I love art, and while that might not earn a living here, I make excellent money as a handyman. I'm able to plan my own schedule, which gives me time to paint and enjoy life. I hope you can understand that."

"I do. Your mother and I have already talked about this and we were going to bring it up with you, but I wasn't sure how you'd really feel after handling it for two years."

"I'm good with it," Declan said.

"That's settled then. I've already had buyers approach me, interested in the space."

"Wow, you've been talking about this with people?"

"No, I haven't. I thought it might have been you since it was a couple of friends of yours. Anthony and Pike?"

Declan sat back in his chair. "What do they want it for?"

"Some kind of adventure guide company. They brought in a business plan and had a loan approval for what I'm asking with cash down, but I didn't want to say yes until I spoke with you."

Declan thought about what Holly had said about opening a gallery in the space, but it would take him years to get everything together to launch it properly; meanwhile Pike and Anthony were prepped and ready to go after their dream. He didn't want to take that from them.

"I think that's amazing, Dad."

"There's something else. We were going to give you a third of the proceeds from the sale. That way if you want to move and start again somewhere else, you have a little something to give you a leg up."

"Thank you, but I'm not going anywhere. I'm staying in Mistletoe."

His dad ran a hand over his thinning hair with a sigh. "Well, that makes this next decision a little tricky. We were planning on selling the house, too."

"Really? The doctor said you need a familiar space—"

"Declan, my memory is going to go one way or the other. I haven't been out-of-state in over forty years and I'm ready. We're going to buy an RV and explore the US until I can't anymore."

Declan reached across the space and squeezed his dad's hand. "You should. And don't worry about the house. I'm renting a room and I'm happy where I'm at."

"You mom told me. She also mentioned you might come over for Christmas Eve dinner?"

"Yeah, I was going to bring Holly, if that's all right."

"That's great. I always liked her. A little high energy, but she reminds me of your mom in some ways."

Declan groaned. "Don't say that, please."

"Why not?"

"I don't want to think of the woman I'm in a relationship with having similar traits to my mom."

His dad chuckled. "Sorry."

The two of them embraced, and they walked out to the front,

where his mother was pretending to look busy but the minute she saw them, she grinned.

"Well, did you tell him?"

"Of course I did, what do you think I was doing back there?"

"Hey, don't get smart."

"I'm sorry, love," he said, kissing her cheek.

"When do you guys plan on leaving?" Declan asked.

"As soon as everything sells." His dad put his arm around his mom and Declan hadn't seen his face so relaxed in years. "I never considered myself the adventurous type, but I'm looking forward to this."

"Adventures can be life-changing, but they are better with someone you love," Diana said, kissing Liam.

"Um, okay, on that note, I'm going home to Holly. I'll see you Christmas Eve and if it's okay with you, I'll clean out my studio after the New Year."

"Sounds good. Looking forward to seeing you both."

Declan gave his mom a hug and his dad a friendly back slap before walking out, taking the left out of the store. It was nine-forty-five, so he knew the front door of Holly's shop would be locked. He knocked gently on the door pane, listening for her footsteps as she approached.

When it opened, Holly leaned against it, her gaze traveling over him playfully. "Hmmm, I like a man with soft hands."

"As opposed to someone who pounds on the wood with meat paws?"

Holly laughed, waving him inside and closing the door behind him. "Sometimes a pounder can be fun."

"I'm trying not to hear that," Erica called from across the shop.

"Put your earmuffs on then, 'cause I'm about to kiss my man," Holly said, throwing herself against him. "What did your dad say?"

"Wait, where's my kiss?"

She stretched as far as she could, and he leaned down, just out of reach until she grabbed the hairs of his chin and gave them a sharp tug.

"Hey, gentle."

"I will be when you give me what I want."

"So demanding," he murmured, giving her what she was asking for in the form of a long, slow kiss. "How's that?"

"Pretty good. B minus."

Declan swatted her butt. "Your brother's right. You can be a brat."

"You're about to earn yourself a one-way ticket to spare bedroom city," she said, lips twitching as she stepped away.

"Kicking me out already?"

"Not if you tell me what happened with your dad before I have to open the door and let people in."

He leaned against the opposite wall, folding his arms over his chest. "I told him I didn't want to run the store, and he let me know he was selling it."

"Did you ask him about the gallery?" Declan shook his head and Holly sighed. "Why not?"

"'Cause I don't want to go back to suits and ties and schmoozing. I'll figure out a way to get my art out there, but I'm going to spend the next year getting Gallagher's Handy Works off the ground—"

"I don't know about that name, babe."

Declan's chest squeezed at the pet name. "It's a work in progress. Like me. A lot of what I thought about my family and what I wanted for my life turned out to be wrong, and I want to take some time to figure out what my life is going to look like. And with my parents selling their house too, I was wondering how you'd feel about me renting from you indefinitely."

"Of course I want you. And Leo."

Declan frowned. "Sometimes I think you're using me for my damn cat."

"No, I want you both, but you do not have to pay—"

"Oh, I'm paying," Declan said, pushing off the wall. "You bought your house with your success, and I am so proud of you, but it is yours. Even if I convince you to spend the rest of your life with me in the future, that will stay yours. I never want anyone thinking I love you for anything other than who you are. My beautiful, kind, funny, adventurous, culinarily challenged Elf."

Holly took a step closer to him, her eyes shimmering. "Did you just tell me you love me?"

"I did."

"He also said you can't cook," Erica chimed in.

"Can I fire her?" Declan asked.

"She's the best employee I have."

"The only one, actually, but I'll let that slide because I'm just happy to see you two getting in touch with your actual feelings. If you'd like to take him in the back and finish this conversation, I can open the shop."

"Never mind, you need to give her a raise," Declan said,

picking Holly up and carrying her into the back. Holly slipped her arms around his neck and held on, until he closed the door behind him and let her slide down his body.

"Now, where were we?"

"You told me that you love me."

"And do you have anything to say in response?"

"Of course I love you. Couldn't you tell?"

"In case you haven't noticed, I need things spelled out for me."

"I-L-O-V-E-Y-O-U."

Declan cradled her face in his palms, shaking his head. "There's that wonderful, infuriatingly sexy smart mouth I love so much."

"You know my love language is affirmation, right? So I'm going to need to hear all that at least five times a day."

"Only five?" he teased, his lips grazing hers.

"Maybe seven, depending on my mood."

"I can do that." He kissed her again and pulled back reluctantly. "I'd better get out of here before you're swamped with customers."

Holly beat him to the door and locked it. "Not quite yet."

Declan laughed, catching Holly when she launched herself at him. "People are going to wonder where the boss is."

"I'll let them know I had pressing business to attend to. Like making out with my very large, extremely hot boyfriend because I can't help myself."

"Who could argue with that?"

Chapter 37

WITH THE DESIGNATED WEDDING DANCES out of the way, the reception was in full swing. While the older relatives sat at the tables scattered around the community center, young people and kids were tearing up the dance floor.

And Holly was right in the thick of them, her arms wrapped around Declan's neck.

"I still think it was rigged," he griped for what seemed like the hundredth time and Holly rolled her eyes.

"Babe, I got second place. Let it go."

"You cannot tell me their display was better than yours. It was just a bunch of cut-outs of their cat."

Holly's neighbors across the street had won best outdoor display with their large wooden depictions of their cat and family, which the judges found unique, but Declan hadn't gotten over it.

"It could have been worse. Theodore James could have won. And technically I got first prize for Mistletoe Hardware's window display and second prize for my shop. If you consider those wins, I kicked a lot of butt this year."

"You did, and I enjoyed watching that crotchety dick next door stomp back inside with nothing."

Holly caught the startled eye of the older woman dancing next to them and mouthed Sorry.

"Honestly, I feel bad for him," Holly said.

"You shouldn't. Some people are just awful and can't be changed."

Holly grinned up at him. "I'm glad that wasn't the case with you."

He returned her smile before leaning close, resting his mouth against her ear. "Have I fulfilled my dance quota for the evening yet or do you plan to torture me all night?"

"Please, do you really hate this so much?" she whispered back. "My body pressed up against yours, swaying to music. Knowing that later it's just you, me, and Leo curled up on the bed watching another episode of *Ice Road Truckers*."

"Now that's hot."

Declan turned his head and covered her mouth with his, a deep kiss that made Holly hum with delight.

Holly heard a throat clearing and broke the kiss with a laugh when she saw her dad and mom behind them, dancing a proper waltz.

"That's my baby, Declan," her dad warned.

Declan looked over his shoulder and shot her dad a sheepish expression. "Sorry, Chris, I tried to stop her, but she drags me down by my beard and tells me I'm irresistible."

"Maybe you should shave, then."

Holly smothered a laugh and her dad grinned, shooting her a

wink. When she'd brought Declan home on Christmas Day, her dad had caught her on the porch to ask her about their relationship. She'd given him the PG version of how things had turned around for them, and when she finished, he'd nodded and informed her that he'd always liked Declan, walked back into the house, and proceeded to show her new boyfriend no mercy. The razzing had been non-stop for days and even Nick and Clark had gotten in on it.

The funniest part was Declan, who hadn't been sure how to respond at first, firing back on all cylinders. She knew then that he was going to fit right in with her family.

"You're sure we have to stay for the entire reception?" Declan asked, nodding his head to the side exit. "I doubt Merry and Clark will even notice if we slip out."

"There is one last important event before they cut the cake and I can't miss it. I'm sorry, babe."

"I thought I'd give it one last shot, but I should have known I wouldn't be able to get Holly Winters to skip out on a party."

"Not while I've got boogying left in these dancing shoes," she said, doing a little shake.

"God help me."

Holly laughed, snuggling closer. Her grumpy, handsome artist slash handyman loved to put on a front, but she'd noticed him tapping his feet on the floor before she'd even asked him to dance.

The song ended and the DJ announced the bride would be tossing the bouquet. Holly leaned up to kiss Declan one more time and said, "You're not going to take off running if I catch the bouquet, are you?"

Declan chuckled. "I guess you'll have to grab it and see."

"Holly, come on!" Delilah said, grabbing her hand and dragging Holly along with her as they headed out to the middle of the dance floor.

Merry stood at the front of the crowd of young women eagerly vying for the flowers.

Merry made a big show of tossing the bouquet, but when she held onto it instead, the entire group started murmuring, parting as Merry made her way through the crowd, past the last bachelorette and to the people lining the edge of the dance floor, stopping in front of Nick.

"What are you doing?" he asked.

Merry handed off the bouquet to him and Holly joined her, spinning him around by the shoulders.

Down on one knee in her bridesmaid dress was Noel, an open ring box in her hand.

"Nick, your sister graciously allowed me to steal a few minutes from her day because I wanted to do this with the flourish and romance you deserve, surrounded by your family and friends. I know this has been a long time coming and I love you for your patience, understanding, and acceptance of me and all my baggage. Thank you for waiting." Tears streamed down her face as she pulled the ring out of the white cushion, her hands visibly shaking. "What do you say? Want to marry me?"

Without hesitation, Nick took Noel's hands and lifted her up, his mouth covering hers in a passionate kiss, drawing a loud cheer from the entire reception. Holly's eyes misted as Nick pulled back from his fiancée and shook his head, addressing his sisters. "I can't believe you two were in on this."

"Are you kidding?" Merry said. "I love watching these proposals on social media and was more than happy to be a part of yours today." Merry hugged Noel and Nick. "I love you both."

"We love you," Noel said, wiping her eyes with a laugh.

Holly went in for her hug and whispered to her brother, "I'm so happy for you."

"Thank you, baby sister."

"Thank you for giving me a big sister I don't want to kill every other hour," Holly said, hugging Noel.

Merry thumped her on the arm. "Rude."

Noel slipped the ring onto Nick's finger, and they were kissing again, the crowd converging on the newly engaged couple and pushing the two sisters to the edge of the action.

"It's funny, isn't it?" Merry sniffled.

"What's that?"

"We all found love the same time of year, in the most unexpected places. I think the holidays really are magical for the Winters family, don't you think?"

Holly's gaze sought out Declan, who was over by the bar talking to Pike and Tony, her heart squeezing when his green eyes caught hers.

"I think you might be right."

Clark burst in on their moment and announced it was time for the garter toss. Holly hugged her sister and made her way back to Declan, a wide smile on her face.

"I'm not going out there to catch the garter, if that's what you're grinning about."

Holly poked him in the stomach. "I'm grinning because we can go home now. If you still want."

"Oh, I want," he said, taking her hand in his.

Holly let him lead her out to his truck and help her inside, a little pinch of guilt hitting her when he joined her in the cab. "I probably should have said goodbye to everyone."

"You make your goodbye rounds, and you're practically flashing a sign at your parents that I want to leave early to defile their daughter."

"Why do you automatically think they'd assume it was you? Maybe defiling was my idea."

"I wouldn't be surprised," Declan said, pulling out of the parking lot and heading home. He reached across the console, and she opened her fingers to interlace with his.

When they pulled into the driveway, Declan stopped the truck without opening the garage door and Holly stared at the new addition to her display. The Whoville background had been removed from the flat surface and in its place was a sign, roped out in Christmas lights.

@DLovesArtandHolly

"Before you say anything, that symbol was a bitch to get right, so don't judge me on it."

"What does it mean?"

Declan removed his phone from the middle console of his truck and held it out to her. "Click on the TikTok app."

Holly scrolled through the screen until she found it and opened it, tapping on his profile icon in the lower right. What she saw stole her breath.

"Your screen name? You got on social media?"

"Technically, just my hands, but click on the top pinned video."

Holly did what he asked and 'Mistletoe' played in the background while Holly watched Declan's masculine hands sketch a couple at three times the speed, wrapped up in Christmas lights, gazing at each other while an orange tabby playfully batted at the end of the cord. When it finished, they looked a lot like Declan and Holly.

Holly's vision blurred, and she turned in the seat, unbuckling her seat belt with trembling hands. "I love it." She climbed across the console and into his lap. "I love you." She kissed his lips, his bearded chin, his cheek.

Declan cradled her cheeks, stopping her frenzied kisses and brushed her lips with his. "I love you, too. I didn't think I would ever feel this way about another person until an infuriatingly optimistic redhead walked into my family's store and shook up my life. Showed me what true happiness is and I'll be forever grateful for it." He smoothed her hair back with a laugh. "I definitely never thought I'd put my art out on social media and people would like it."

"If I thought it was a possibility to lure you online, I'd have told you they would. I'm so proud of you." Holly wrapped her arms around his neck and kissed him, hands roaming as their tongues danced.

Someone knocked on the glass hard, and they jerked apart to find Mr. James on the other side.

"Can you kindly take your public displays inside? It's indecent."

He turned and walked away, disappearing into his yard. Holly and Declan fell into each other's arms laughing.

"We might have to move," Holly said.

"No way. Next year, your display is going to be the best of the neighborhood."

"I thought you didn't care about the holidays or silly competitions?"

"I don't, but I love you, and that guy annoys me so much I'm willing to put aside my principles to kick his ass."

Holly giggled. "Should we take our indecent display inside?"

"Only because I want you naked and all to myself."

"I like the way you think."

ACKNOWLEDGMENTS

To my husband and kids. Thank you for letting me work in peace...for the most part.

For my agent, Sarah, who has my back. Thank you.

To Allison, my wonderful editor. Thank you for helping me bring Mistletoe to life.

Tina Klinesmith, my sister from another mister. Thank you for being there for me, always.

My darling Erica. Thanks for the laughs and the listening ear.

Special shout out to @bdylanhollis who is my favorite TikToker. Thank you for the three-ingredient peanut butter cookie recipe! It got me through some stressful times with this book.

And last but never least, to my wonderful readers! Thank you for going on this amazing ride with me!

ABOUT THE AUTHOR

Codi Hall is the Mistletoe pen name of Codi Gary, author of twenty-nine contemporary and paranormal romance titles. She loves writing about flawed characters finding their happily ever afters because everyone, even imperfect people, deserve an HEA. A Northern California native, she and her husband and their two children now live in Southern Idaho where she enjoys kayaking, unpredictable weather, and spending time with her family, including her array of adorable furbabies. When she isn't glued to her computer making characters smooch, you can find her posting sunsets and pet pics on Instagram, making incredibly cringy videos for TikTok, reading the next book on her never-ending TBR list, or knitting away while rewatching *Supernatural* for the thousandth time! Codi is represented by Sarah Younger at NYLA. To keep up with all Codi's hijinks, join her newsletter at codigarysbooks. com. You can also find her on Instagram @authorcodihallgary, on Twitter @AuthorCodiHall, on TikTok @authorcodihallorgary, and on Facebook as AuthorCodiHall.